Charades

Charades

Janette Turner Hospital

BANTAM

TORONTO · NEW YORK · LONDON · SYDNEY · AUCKLAND

CHARADES

A Bantam Book / March 1989

PRINTING HISTORY

University of Queensland Press (Australia) editon published 1988

Published in Canada by McClelland & Stewart

Grateful acknowledgment is made to reprint the following:
Excerpt on page 277 from *The Mind-Boggling Universe*
by Neil McAleer. Copyright © 1987 by Neil McAleer.
Reprinted by permission of Doubleday, a division of
Bantam Doubleday Dell Publishing Group, Inc.
"At North Farm" on page 275 from *A Wave* by
John Ashbery. Copyright © 1984 by John Ashbery.
Originally published in *The New Yorker*. Reprinted
by permission of Viking Penguin, Inc.
Excerpt on page ix from BORGES: A READER edited by Emir
Rodriguez Monegal and Alastair Reid. Copyright © 1981
by Jorge Luis Borges, Alastair Reid, Emir Rodriguez Monegal.
Reprinted by permission of the publisher, E.P. Dutton, a division
of NAL Penguin Inc.
Excerpt on page ix from I DIDN'T SAY GOODBYE by Claudine Vegh,
translated by Ros Schwartz. Copyright © 1979 by Editions
Gallimard under the title JE NE LUI AI PAS DIT AU REVOIR, English
translation copyright © 1984 by Caliban Books. Reprinted by
permission of the publisher, E.P. Dutton, a division of NAL Penguin Inc.
Excerpt on page 1 from SCIENCE AND THE COMMON UNDERSTANDING,
by J. Robert Oppenheimer. Copyright © 1954 by J. Robert Oppenheimer,
renewed © 1981 by Robert B. Meyner, executor for author
J. Robert Oppenheimer. Reprinted by permission of Simon & Schuster, Inc.
Excerpt on page ix from THE DROWNED AND THE SAVED, by Primo Levi.
Copyright © 1988 by Simon & Schuster. Reprinted by permission of
Summit Books, a division of Simon & Schuster, Inc.

BOOK DESIGN BY CLAIRE M. NAYLON

FRONTISPIECE WOOD ENGRAVING BY BETSY NAYLON

Library of Congress Cataloging-in-Publication Data

Hospital, Janette Turner, 1942–
Charades.

I. Title.
PR9199.3.H596C4   1989   813'.54   88-7675
ISBN 0-553-05346-9

*Bantam Books are published by Bantam Books, a division of Bantam Doubleday Dell
Publishing Group, Inc. Its trademark, consisting of the words "Bantam Books" and the
portrayal of a rooster, is Registered in U.S. Patent and Trademark Office and in other
countries. Marca Registrada. Bantam Books, 666 Fifth Avenue, New York, New York
10103.*

PRINTED IN THE UNITED STATES OF AMERICA

O   0 9 8 7 6 5 4 3 2 1

DEDICATION

For my father and mother,
who taught me that love is rich and redemptive
whatever costumes and guises it wears

ACKNOWLEDGMENTS

First and foremost, I acknowledge with gratitude the assistance of the Literary Arts Board of the Australia Council, whose support made the writing of this book possible.

I am also most grateful to Dr. Alan Guth, of the Physics Department at MIT, for his generosity: He gave me time, patience, and permission to quote from his article "The Inflationary Universe," co-authored with Dr. Paul J. Steinhardt. I hasten to add that other than the attribution of this article to Koenig, no correlation whatsoever exists between my fictional character and Dr. Guth. Furthermore, Drs. Guth and Steinhardt must be absolved from any misinterpretations I may have made of their theory on the origin of the universe.

Thanks are also due to my own students at MIT. They gave me fascinating insights into a mind-set quite different from my own, as well as into the mores of dorm life.

I found several books (*The Second Creation* by Robert P. Crease and Charles C. Mann; *The Tao of Physics* by Fritjof Capra; *The Mind-Boggling Universe* by Neil McAleer) particularly helpful for background material, and their influence will be apparent, but again, any misunderstanding or misinterpretation is entirely my responsibility.

Quotations from the journals of Captain James Cook, William Dampier, and from other documents of early Australian history were taken from *Sources of Australian History,* selected and edited by Professor Manning Clark.

I would like to pay tribute to Claudine Vegh's *I Didn't Say Goodbye: Interviews with Children of the Holocaust* (Dutton, 1984) which had an indelible effect on my imagination.

Though the Zundel trial in Toronto was an actual event, the characters in this novel who give testimony and otherwise participate in the trial are entirely fictitious.

INVOCATION

May the legends of the men of old be lessons to the people of our time, so that a man may see those things which befell others beside himself: then he will honour and consider carefully the words and adventures of past peoples, and will reprove himself.

—THE BOOK OF THE THOUSAND NIGHTS AND ONE NIGHT

To modify the past is not to modify a single fact; it is to annul the consequences of that fact, which tend to be infinite. In other words, it involves the creation of two universal histories.

—Jorge Luis Borges: The Other Death

I intend to examine here the memories of extreme experiences, of injuries suffered or inflicted. . . .
Once again it must be observed, mournfully, that the injury cannot be healed: it extends through time. . . .

—Primo Levi: The Drowned and the Saved

For my part, I have no illusions; what took place can happen again. We are only entitled to a respite, a reprieve between two . . .

—Testimony of André to Claudine Vegh,
in I Didn't Say Goodbye: Interviews with Children of
the Holocaust

Part I

Charade

If we ask, for instance, whether the position of the electron remains the same, we must say "no"; if we ask whether the electron's position changes with time, we must say "no"; if we ask whether the electron is at rest, we must say "no"; if we ask whether it is in motion, we must say "no."

—ROBERT OPPENHEIMER

Part I

1. *Charade*

The grand unified theories, Koenig writes, *are difficult to verify experimentally. Nevertheless, they illuminate our understanding of elementary-particle interactions so elegantly that many physicists find them extremely attractive.*

"What an extraordinary sentence," she says.

He is deeply startled and spins full circle, almost pitching his desk chair off its base and virtually colliding with her. "Good God!" he says. "How—?"

"So *elegantly.*" The girl brings her hands together in an odd gesture of wonder. A mass of hair, which is fair and unruly though tamed into a single thick braid, falls over one shoulder. Her eyes are a curious color, a kind of borderline blue, intense; or perhaps (it is the middle of the night, and the desk lamp casts odd shadows) a sort of sea-green.

"So *elegantly,*" she repeats, opening her hands, looking at them as if the words, mysterious and glittering, were cradled there. Her smile is speculative, dry, possibly mocking. "Elegance as scientific methodology?"

He blinks. From the corner of his eye, he notes with dismay a ketchup stain on his corduroy pants; also a protruding loop of undershirt. He is embarrassed. He clears his throat. "You shouldn't . . ." (What is the matter with his voice?) He coughs into his fist, frowns, clears his throat again. "You absolutely shouldn't be here."

And her eyes, contemplating both his trailing undershirt and the words in her palms, flash blue-green with surprise. "I shouldn't? Why? Where am I?"

"Building 6," he says inanely—though it is not his office, which is upstairs. This is the office of a younger colleague, an experimentalist, as must surely be obvious from the congestion of equipment. "The main computer," he adds. "My—ah—a colleague of mine . . ."

The girl's skin seems unnaturally translucent. Of course, the weird light from the monitors is responsible.

"A colleague?" she asks.

"An *experimentalist*." It is discreetly done, this indication of a drop in social scale. "His—ah—his office."

Behind her head a loop of polyester tubing snakes across the basement ceiling and throbs like a vein. The colon of MIT surrounds him. Heating ducts and eccentric plumbing and pipelines for argon gas tie themselves in intestinal knots.

"I'm looking for someone," she says.

Ah, he thinks. It is rumored that his colleague sometimes engages in non-academic activities late at night in this very room.

"Actually," the girl says, "to be more accurate, I'm looking for several people."

Her accent puzzles him. "Where do you . . . ? From where . . . ?"

"Harvard Square. I came by subway."

"No, I mean—"

"Are you Professor Koenig?"

"Yes, but—"

"They said you worked late. I'm Charade Ryan." She extends her right hand, quaintly formal, and he shakes it. Shock. Currents pass back and forth. He thinks of quarks and uneven fractional charges. "And the connecting link is Katherine Sussex," she says, quite cool and businesslike. "You remember Katherine?"

4

He stares at her blankly, the name meaning nothing at all.

"I see," she says. It seems a great deal has been revealed by this response. He has a sense of her jotting down data in a logbook somewhere. "Perhaps," she says carefully, "if I mention your former wife, Rachel, and the trial in Toronto?"

He is stunned. For a moment his vision blurs, his ears sing; he thinks he might faint, or be sick, or do something equally disgraceful. The room spins, the Toronto court is packed with the argon canisters, the computer monitors, the MIT bulletin board, the basement ducts, pipe elbows, plumbers' clasps, valves, silver insulation packing. Nothing can be counted on to stay in its proper place. He opens his eyes very wide, testing, and presses his fingers against the sockets. Warily, he focuses on his arms and legs in case they go into spasmodic behavior, in case his hands make a telephone call, in case his legs take him out to Logan Airport for another Boston–Toronto flight. He sinks back into the swivel chair and closes his eyes and forces himself to take deep and regular breaths. Inhale, count of ten, exhale.

When he shakes himself clear of shock and looks again, the girl has vanished.

Of course, he is certain he has invented her. Or that he has fallen asleep at the desk and Rachel, his ex-wife, has spooked another dream. Well, not Rachel really. His own guilt, he supposes, which comes in a thousand and one different guises and plays many games.

In the large tiered lecture hall of Building 6, Koenig draws chalkboard graphs of both the standard and the inflationary models of the origins of the universe. His field of scholarly inquiry is the first second after time began; specifically, that space between 10^{-30} and 10^{-35} of a second after the Big Bang itself, a crack large enough to swallow a life.

He is discussing energy densities and the "flatness problem" arising from the standard model—"First pointed out," he says, glancing back over his shoulder at the class, "in 1979 by Dicke and Peebles at Princeton." Two hundred students dutifully scribble this into notebooks. "And further elaborated," he says, but something in peripheral vision troubles him and he falters, turns back to the chalkboard and continues with his three-dimensional representation of two Higgs fields, falters again, the chalk poised like a wary sentry. "And further elaborated . . ." He casts about in his mind, bewildered, not yet quite alarmed, and mercifully words swim up to the rescue: ". . . further elaborated on page twenty-three of the offprint I handed out last week." The unease passes. He labels the false vacuum, the energy barrier, the true vacuum. The students make faithful transcriptions. In the shallow concavity of the false vacuum, he draws a ball and fills it in, scribbling, chalk dust powdering his fingers and thumb.

"This represents the universe," he says. He draws an arrow. "This is how the ball, the universe, would roll if the Higgs fields were pushed from their initial value of zero by thermal or quantum . . . or quantum . . ."

Something is unsettling him; he feels slightly asthmatic and dizzy.

"Thermal or quantum fluctuations," he says decisively, wrenching his concentration back on track. He draws another arrow.

The chalk breaks.

"Ah . . ." He turns to the tiered seats and holds on to the podium. "I believe I may have to . . ." The room is fogging before his eyes. "You can pick up copies of my article at the departmental office. I'm afraid that I . . ."

He sees her then, third-highest tier, near the middle. He could swear she has never been in his class before.

"I think," he says, a clammy hand to his forehead, "that I am not . . . I'll let you go early. Read the article for—"

A din of shoes, of books and bookbags being scraped up, swamps his voice. White noise prevails. He leans back against the chalkboard, lightheaded, and watches them file past. His colleague, the experimentalist, nods on the way out. (His colleague? What is his colleague doing sitting in on the introductory course?) Then the girl, who might have set her compass by Koenig, comes straight down the center aisle looking a bit like one of those long-legged birds—herons is it?—graceful but with a hint of precariousness as

she negotiates the steep tiers. He could almost say she staggers slightly, except that her body movements are far too delicate.

For a moment she pauses on the other side of the desk and looks at him across the lab sink and the high chrome curve of the faucet. There is nothing hostile or impertinent about her look, but she does not smile.

"Are you . . . ?" He fidgets with papers on the desk. "Are you registered or auditing? I don't seem to remember . . . ah, here it is." He has the computer printout and looks up. "What was your name again?"

"Charade Ryan."

"Shuh . . . ? Shuhrahd Ryan?" He frowns. "I can't seem to . . . How do you spell it?"

What is particularly unsettling is the quality of . . . of what? of *knowingness* in her smile.

"Ryan with an *R*," she says, the ironic tone so exquisitely muted as to seem like a compliment. Or an invitation?

"And Charade with a *C-h*. As in *Paris talks are a bloody charade, Prime Minister says*. My mother thought it was a French word."

"I see."

Prime Minister?

He runs his eye down the printout. "I still can't seem to—"

"I'm not an undergraduate," she says.

At the door, his colleague calls sharply: "Charade."

She nods and leaves.

She forgets to pick up her folder of lecture notes. Koenig hesitates, thinks of calling after her down the corridor, picks the folder up warily, shoves it into his briefcase. No doubt she will return for it. It is a standard red folder with the MIT crest on its cover. Also on the cover are her name, her dorm room, a phone number.

2. The First Night

"Any object looked at steadily . . ." Charade begins, her eyes fixed on something not in Koenig's apartment. He watches her, fascinated, as he rebuttons his shirt.

The sequence of events leading up to this moment is hazy.

He watches her. She could be eighteen or thirty; her body is slight and boyish, but her eyes seem old. She is certainly not beautiful, not at all the type he usually . . . Striking, perhaps, though he cannot quite pinpoint why. And there is some quality that tugs at him: the way she stands with her head slightly tilted; the way she crooks her knee and balances one bare foot against the other ankle.

Whatever has been absorbing her gaze releases her and she nods to herself. "Yes," she says. "Any object looked at steadily and intently for too long begins to disintegrate before the eyes, isn't that so? And Katherine—Katherine Sussex, whom you don't seem to remember—Katherine thinks that is the explanation. You know how it is: molecules float away from each other, they drift across the iris in little haloes of gold, atoms peel them-

selves off from the molecules, electrons go flaking away from the atoms. . . ."

What he listens to is less the words themselves than her exotic accent, the amazing shapes the sounds make in the air.

"Ah," she says, misreading his smile and turning defensive. "I see I haven't got that quite right." And he thinks of tracks made by muons and other particles in bubble chambers; he thinks of the lucent spirals and hairlines of light that they leave in their wake.

She perches, still naked, on the end of the bed and hugs her knees up under her chin. Is the action deliberate? he wonders. Deliberately wicked?

"I'm way off track, aren't I?" she asks. "I'm completely misinterpreting what you said about subatomic particles."

Then again, perhaps she is unaware of the effect she creates. He can think of nothing at all. His buttons and buttonholes are hopelessly mismatched, and she smiles a little to see the odd loops of shirtfront. He begins again, making an effort not to appear flustered, but forgets that he has already tucked his top into his pants and goes on pointlessly pushing at the fabric and hiking up his belt.

"I do get distracted in your lectures," she says. "Especially when you do things like that. I've sneaked into your big introductory class several times, you didn't notice, did you? Course 8.286, that is. 'The Early Universe.' And did you realize you do that in front of the class sometimes? Check that your belt is still there, I mean. And rake your fingers through that shock of hair that falls into your eyes . . . Yes, like that . . . I realize it's a nervous gesture, but it's very attractive."

"Ah . . ." he says, as she swings her legs over the side of the bed in a neat arc and crosses to his dresser. "Um—I'm not sure why I . . ." He watches her fiddle with his car keys, a set of cuff links, a silver hairbrush. "Um—nervous like this, I'm not usually . . ." Of course he knows perfectly well the reason why; it is because she mentioned Rachel in the middle of the night, when she appeared beside his desk in the computer room. At least, he thinks she mentioned Rachel. He is afraid to ask, in case he imagined it. He is afraid to ask, in case he did *not* imagine it. "I'm not usually like this," he says.

"So I hear."

He jerks the belt a notch too tight. "Indeed?"

"Yes." She leans against his dresser, arms folded, and studies him. "Energetic lover, very polished, very smooth: that's what they say. But a specialist in quick and tidy exits. Positively obsessive about it. A good fuck, a quick parting kiss, and then off with my lady's head. Well anyway, get her clothes back on her and shunt her out the door before the afterglow fades. That's what they say about you." She shrugs disarmingly. "Around the dorms, that is." She gestures with her hands to show how little this gossip affects her. "Anyway, I'm nervous too, which must be apparent. I'm sorry. I'll try to stop fidgeting with your things."

He waves this aside and pulls on his socks while she watches. Probably, she thinks, he does everything with this kind of intense concentration. Probably it is an article of faith with him that socks hug ankles with the exactness of a mathematical matrix. A vibration crosses the floor and he feels it through one socked foot and looks up.

"Apparently," he says stiffly, "this is very amusing."

What she is doing, actually, is biting one fist to keep a gust of laughter back. "I'm sorry. It's just ... Well, we do look bloody ridiculous, pardon my Australian."

"*Australian,*" he says. "I wondered where that accent—"

"You're not used to this, are you? You really are used to the quick fix." She adopts a mock documentary tone. "Questioned under oath, the famous physicist confessed that he did prefer a woman to make a discreet and unmessy exit as soon as possible, and furthermore he expected her to be decently uneasy when invited into his Cambridge apartment, the air of which is so thick with the symbolic presence of his recently departed wife and children." She takes a deep and rather dramatic sigh and reverts to her normal voice. "Actually it *is* ... There's this domestic and familial *humidity* everywhere, it's a bit hard to breathe, but I'm afraid you've lucked onto the essence of unorthodoxy in me, you can't really count on any of the usual things making me feel uneasy."

He is perfectly astonished by this little sermon and declaration of immunity. *Recently departed wife and children,* he thinks, stunned. He is astonished, too, by the speed at which she delivers pronouncements, and by the flashing ballet of her hands. It occurs to him that if they were tied behind her back, she might be unable to talk. It is as though she has suddenly been wound up tight, to full pitch, and let go. She cannot stop.

"Just the same," she says, "I will admit to a strong sense of the ludicrous, I admit I feel ridiculous—not uneasy, or indecent, just ridiculous—pacing around your living room naked while you sit there watching. Do you always dress so quickly afterwards? The pipe, yes, I'm used to that. It's the first thing all academics do afterwards, but a great many, you know, are quite content to sit there propped up on pillows, with maybe the sheet pulled partway up, puffing away contentedly and talking, sometimes for hours. What's really getting to me is that now you're even putting your tie back on, which I think has to be construed as the most pompous, the most heavy-handed . . . No?"

He is staring, puzzled, at his own hands knotting his tie. He still has a dazed sense of her voice hurtling on and on, but what startles him is the realization that the last thing he wants her to do is leave; the last thing he wants to find his hands doing is dropping heavy and involuntary hints.

"Still," she says. "If you could just toss me my shirt, I'd feel a little less . . . Thanks."

While she does up a button or two at her midriff (not bothering with any other item of clothing), he loosens his tie, removes it, and throws it onto the bed.

"How daring," she laughs. She curls up in his armchair and hooks her legs over one side. That maddening knowing little smile of hers flutters in his direction, then rests on the abandoned tie for several seconds, then turns inward again.

He waits.

"You know," she says at last, "I can't stop thinking about the implications of your lecture last week—Heisenberg's theory, wasn't it?—about uncertainty as the essence of science, about the *necessity* of uncertainty, about how we simply have to accept that electrons are always in only a partially defined state, that there is, in fact, no other way they *can* be. That's right, isn't it? Yes, I copied it down, because it seems to me to have a bearing on my life. Philosophically speaking, that is.

"And on yours too, right? All that energy pro and con, the things that did, that absolutely without question *did* happen; but which also, according to other people, *couldn't* have happened. I mean, you know, your former wife, Rachel, and the trial in Toronto."

Something alarming happens to Koenig's breathing, he takes quick little in-out in-out in-out breaths, counts to ten, inhales slowly (from the diaphragm), holds, exhales, wills his muscles to unclench.

She swings her legs across to the other arm of the chair.

"Katherine says either we're all slightly mad, we've all hallucinated our own pasts (which is a reasonably tenable theory, I think), or else there's a perfectly rational explanation if we could just put our fingers on it. Katherine thinks—I say 'Katherine' for reasons of formality, but in fact she's my aunt Kay. Well, strictly speaking, she's not *really* my aunt, but we do that in Australia, you see. I mean, I don't feel comfortable calling her just Kay. We're still rather shocked at the casual way American children do that, call their elders by first names—even for total strangers they've just met, right?" She leans toward him, eyebrows raised. "Did you realize we find that abrasive?"

He tries to concentrate on the question.

"Anyway, in Australia, we don't do that. Give kids free rein, I mean. Give them absolute social rights.

"Speaking of children"—she gestures toward the kitchen—"I saw the drawings on your fridge door. Second marriage obviously."

He is mildly startled, but makes a noncommittal sound.

"It's Joey, isn't it?—yes, he's signed his name—who drew that crayon rainbow over a number of green teddy bears. Was it you or your wife, by the way, who chose to display that particular drawing? Green teddy bears. It invites analysis, doesn't it? Joey's your more interesting artist, I think. Sara's drawings are too neat and proper; it's happening already, you see—it gets to girls awfully quickly, the desire to please the teacher, to do things right. You're going to have to watch that; it's a real killer. Though I myself was spared from the worst of all that by having a mother who was known as the Slut of the Tamborine Rainforest."

He considers how best to explain Joey and Sara and the presence of their drawings in his kitchen, but instead, slightly dazed, echoes: "Tamborine Rainforest?"

"Outside of Brisbane. You do know where Brisbane is?"

"Uh"—he gestures apologetically—"well, Australia. But I guess I'm a bit vague about the precise . . ."

She shakes her head. "That's another thing about Americans—you're so *parochial*. Your geographical ignorance is absolutely stunning."

"Well," he begins, "I suppose it's . . ." and trails into an uneasy silence that spreads and fills the space between bed and armchair and settles onto the girl. He cannot bring himself to ask what news she is bringing of Rachel, nor what the mysterious Katherine Sussex has to do with anything (though that name is beginning to evoke a pervasive and nonspecific dread).

The blues music of Cambridge traffic, muffled, rises into the room and holds them in some kind of spell. When it is fractured—a collision somewhere, quite close—they both jump, and Charade continues as though the track of her thought, briefly on hold, has been nudged back into sound.

"The consequence of having Bea for a mother," she says, "and having no father at all—although in another sense of course, I had scores of fathers, but I could take them or leave them, you see—the consequence was I escaped a lot of that caging, the bound-feet business, the stuff that happens to girls everywhere but especially in Australia. 'Charade,' my mum would say . . .

"By the way, you keep mispronouncing my name. It's Shuh-*rahd*. I hope you don't mind my pointing it out. It's because Americans mispronounce the word itself. The word *charade*, I mean. The proper way—well, the Brit way, which is much the same thing isn't it?—is the way I say my name."

Koenig is aware of a rising sexual excitement, its origins murky. He is dimly conscious that it has something to do with the provocation of a woman who does not seem aware of his well, *standing* in the scientific community. (Only last week a woman he had met at a

Wellesley dinner party wrote a note inviting him for dinner and postcoital champagne. When she telephoned she said there was an *aura* about him.) Of course this kind of thing is tiresome.

Nevertheless.

Still.

Has Charade Ryan no awe at all?

Her hands flash, her eyes flash; she springs out of the armchair like a dancer and paces back and forth around his bed.

"Anyway. Aunt Kay—Katherine—whom you have met in Toronto, though you remember nothing whatsoever about her—" It is clear, from the tone of her voice, that this is a particularized item in a more general condemnation. "Aunt Kay is not really my aunt, though she's close to it. She and my mother Bea were half-sisters. Sort of. For a few years anyway. It's complicated, but I'll get to that."

Yes, he thinks. She probably will.

"Anyway, up till now I've thought that Aunt Kay and my mother were either right or wrong about my father, and that eventually, if I was persistent enough, I'd find out which. But after what you said about Heisenberg—I mean, if electrons can exist and not exist at one and the same time—well, maybe the stories about my father and Verity Ashkenazy (the famous Other Woman in the piece), maybe they could be right *and* wrong. Both."

She is beginning, he notes with dismay, to gather up her clothes as she speaks, beginning to get dressed again, though in a rather haphazard and eccentrically disorganized way.

"Maybe," she says, "on odd days, my father is *somewhere* but keeps on vanishing without a trace. And on even days he doesn't exist and never did. Which means that on even days I'm the product of an immaculate conception. Though not, I hasten to reassure you, in the precise Catholic and theological sense. Nothing to do with the sinless germination of the seed of the Virgin Mary in the untainted womb of Saint Ann. And certainly not, I promise you, with any pretensions toward either the messianic or the pure on my part."

"Ah," he says, bemused. "Well. What a relief."

"Oh, quite the contrary I assure you. No. I think it was

another case of microphenomena in uncertain states. I think it was parthenogenesis in the manner of amoebae. They can subdivide themselves just by thinking about it, right?"

Her hand sweeps through a delicate arc, a sort of visual punctuation mark, and he catches hold of her wrist and pulls her toward him. "Why are you getting dressed?" he reproaches.

"Because it's almost daylight," she says, indicating the window.

3. Matter, Antimatter, and the Hologram Girl

"The creation of a hologram," Koenig's colleague, the experimentalist, is saying to a cluster of awestruck undergraduates, "begins with the splitting of a laser beam in two." He is holding court in a corner of the Media Lab, and Koenig stops to listen. "And then," his colleague says, "the beams spread out to caress, as it were, the entire subject—in this case an arrangement of doughnuts, Styrofoam cups, and one hot dog."

Koenig watches with the mildly patronizing disdain of the *theoretical* physicist. There is a certain doggedness to all this, a terrierlike persistence that one has to admire, but when all is said and done, the Media Lab people are little more than brilliant technicians, dealers in nuts and bolts and razzle-dazzle. Experimentalists. It is not that Koenig is an intellectual snob; he quite absolves himself on that score. It is simply that mere electronic hocus-pocus is not particularly interesting, and nor is mere data; and he is not inclined to be swept off his feet by the narrowly empirical until he has a theory that will give it grace and shape.

His colleague is displaying the developed holographic plate in white light now, and the undergraduates gasp as phantasmal coffee cups and doughnuts and a solitary three-dimensional hot dog float in the air. "Is that a dagger I see before me?" someone demands theatrically, lunging at ghostly color. A scattershot of nervous laughter ricochets round the room.

Several young women move closer to their magician-professor and one of them touches his sleeve, possibly believing that energy will leap across the gap or that sorcery is contagious.

"You can do other things. Visual music, for instance. I'll demonstrate." What an exhibitionist, Koenig thinks. His colleague is lapping up attention, fussing with glass plates, lasers, white light. "What I do, essentially, is tape myself playing blues on my sax, run the tape, and then transpose the music into visual equivalents with computer graphics." He has the plate in position now. "It's a sort of collage with photographs, mathematical notations, graphed equivalents of sound, cathode ray tubes, and electronic imagery. I call this one 'Blue Lady.'"

Fanfare. Koenig could swear the room is humming with trumpets, all of them blown by Professor Magician himself. How can the students be taken in? Koenig composes an instant jazz riff of his own, hums it silently, calls it "Cheap Trick."

And then, out of the murky room, out of nowhere, out of the saxophone and the puddle of lasers, steps the Blue Lady, who brushes by them with an ectoplasmic spin.

It is the girl. Charade. Whom Koenig has not seen since she vanished from his bedroom several nights ago.

She twirls like a top, her skirt flaring and rising. From certain angles you can see her thighs, and then as she spins more slowly, languidly, the blue skirt sinks, drifts, floats about her calves and ankles. From everywhere you can see her eyes, which are very very blue, or maybe teal, or maybe blue-green (depending on the lift and dip of the skirt).

Koenig has to lean against a bookcase.

"All done with mirrors," his colleague jokes. "Plus beam splitters and cathode ray tubes and video photography."

In the hallway later, Koenig asks casually, indifferently, "That girl. The hologram girl. She a graduate student?"

His colleague says sourly, "Not your type, Koenig. She'd break your balls."

Tuesdays and Thursdays, the mornings of the large introductory course, Koenig scans the tiers of seats but she does not come. Others come. They knock on his door; they saunter in the lot where he parks. No effort seems to be required; Radcliffe women, MIT women, Wellesley women, faculty and students, murmuring *brilliant,* murmuring *famous,* murmuring *Nobel Prize.* It seems to be an aphrodisiac. He does not remember their names. They come and go and nothing helps.

Nothing helps, because he dreams of the girl Charade. Nothing helps, because in any case the mournful eyes of Rachel, his former wife, are always watching. Nothing helps; but still the women come and go.

"You should be put in a museum, Koenig," his colleague mutters one day in passing. "The compulsive consumer, a macho antique."

Koenig is startled. "Listen to who's talking," he says curtly.

"Not everyone chatted up by the Nobel committee gets to Sweden," his colleague says.

Koenig works late. He is pushing back, mathematically, to that busy stretch of time between the Big Bang and a specific point occurring 10^{-35} of a second later. With present data, he measures the red-shifting of the light from distant galaxies. He works at the borders, at the junction of astrophysics, particle physics, cosmology. What he is obsessed with is cross-fertilization, the braiding of disciplines. What absorbs him is the way the girl seemed to hold words in her hands, and the way she appeared one night (did she not?) in his apartment, and the way she spoke of his wife, Rachel, and the way . . .

More and more he works in the basement of Building 6, rather than in his office or his Cambridge apartment, in case she reappears. He is waiting for her to tap on his door.

Sometimes, on Tuesdays or Thursdays, he thinks he sees her from the edge of his eye as he writes on the chalkboard. But when he turns, it is always someone else altogether, someone bearing no similarity to her at all, except for a braid tossed to one side perhaps, or a few curls across the forehead, or blue-green eyes.

In the murky basement light, beneath coiled ducts, he dallies with the text of a speech that is to be presented at the Science Museum. *Matter,* he writes, *a sense of the solidity of matter, is one of our most persistent illusions. The presence of matter represents nothing more than a disturbance in the field at a given point, the figure in the carpet, as it were.*

"What a sentence," she says. And is still there when he turns.

4. *The Second Night*

When he blinks they are in his apartment again and she is asking, surprised, "Just Koenig? Really? That's your first name too?" And before he has time to answer: "Well, ah, Koenig—yes, it's nice. It suits you."

She hooks her legs over the arm of his chair and watches as he pulls on his pants. "You know," she says, "I haven't decided whether I'm flattered or insulted that you obviously *expected* me to drop by your office again. Eventually."

"Well. I haven't decided whether I'm flattered or insulted that you obviously expected I'd be there."

"No," she says, ruling this out. "Not valid. You're always there."

"All right then. You obviously expected I'd invite you back here."

"You know," she says earnestly, "I feel you seriously misunderstand *why* I . . . It's true of course, that I didn't wander into your office or your class by accident, but I wouldn't want you to misinterpret my reasons. It's not sex."

"Oh." He pauses momentarily between one shirt button and the next.

"Have you ever felt that you were on the lip of a black hole?" she asks him. "And that unless you found something to hang on to in the next few minutes, you'd, as you put it, cross the event horizon?"

After that, everything was irreversible, and absolute annihilation was just a matter of time. So he had explained in Course 8.286.

And has he ever . . . ?

Oh, yes, he has been at the dangerous rims of black holes.

"They eat stars, you said. They eat quasars." As though watching such distant galactic events, she unwinds herself from the chair and stands, looking at nothing, in another of her curious trances. From the window, a faint haze of neon blurs her shape and at the same time gives it a thin radiant outline, a line that shifts and turns misty, so that he has an odd sense of her body as translucent. Her hologram self, he thinks with a slight shock. He can in fact see the blue veins in her breasts, and goes to her and draws the lightest of circles around her nipples with his index finger.

"You're not listening to me," she reproaches.

And then, for a considerable length of time, she can say nothing at all.

She manages, at last, to disengage herself from him without breaking the erotic fog in which they move, but establishing nevertheless a delicate space. She curls up in his armchair again and he watches her from the bed. In a curious way, all this seems to him a mode of sexual contact. It is as though they are still physically coupled.

"No," she says. "It's not sex. It's because of Katherine."

He waits and watches.

"But it's something different again that keeps me," she says. "It's what you *know*. I want to . . . Well, one of my professors at Sydney Uni described me as an academic glutton. He said I was driven by cerebral curiosity and greed, although he found me lamentably deficient in direction and purpose. That's what he said.

"On a reference letter, he wrote that I was 'brilliant but erratic.' Frankly, I thought he could have been more tactful. But my considered response is that *erratic*—in its pristine and original sense—did not have a negative connotation. No, that's comparatively recent, a shift in etymological history. I have nothing against *erratic*, myself.

"*Errare*, to wander, right? And by extension to make mistakes. But that's the human condition, isn't it? Not to mention the best pedagogical method—the meandering mistake-making self. Don't you agree? That's what makes life bearable. I'd say history comes out highly in favor of erratic folk.

"Take Cook, Captain James Cook." She props her elbows on the arm of the chair, rests her chin on her fists, and leans forward—what he thinks of as her earnest and sermonizing pose. He waits for the lecture. "You're almost certainly woefully underinformed about Captain Cook. Americans are. About any heroes and explorers other than their own, as far as I can see. Does the name mean anything?"

"Ah . . ."

"Just as I thought. Well, if Cook had been less erratic, if he hadn't wandered round the Pacific and bumped into the east coast of Australia—this was in 1770—he wouldn't have landed at Botany Bay and planted the flag and claimed the entire east coast of the land mass for King George III. And if it wasn't for that, I wouldn't be here on an Australian passport working for cash in Central Square so that I can hang around and sit in on your course. Curious, isn't it? Shit wages, I might add, but illegal, so I can't complain. In that dive off Albany Street—d'you know it?"

"Funny," she says, watching him watching her. "This reminds me of something in Cook's journal. He got himself trapped inside the reef, you know, the Great Barrier Reef, and strafed the underside of the *Endeavour* so badly that he had to decamp on the North Queensland beaches. Where of course the crew saw Aborigines.

"*Quite naked,* Cook wrote in his journal, which would have made the point, don't you think?

"*Without any manner of clothing whatever,* he added, just a little fascinated, I'd say.

"*Even the women do not so much as cover their privates,* he wrote. Hmm. *They never brought any of their women along with them to the ship,* the old perv went on to complain, *but always left them on the opposite side of the river where we had frequent opportunities of viewing them through our glasses."*

She shakes her head. "What a bunch of voyeurs!

"I can't think," she says archly, "what brought that to my mind. Should I cover my privates?"

"I'd much prefer not." He reaches for her as she moves, with mock threat, to where her clothes are. There is a kind of languid skirmish, arms and legs brushing each other like ribbons, and then she has slithered away from him again, and he is in the armchair, she on the bed.

"Anyway"—she is plumping up the pillows behind her—"from my point of view, of course, it was just as well that Cook was both erratic and possessive, since you people were getting so worked up about flags yourselves. At the same time too. I mean, if the citizens of Boston hadn't done what they did while Cook was on his third and final voyage, hotfooting it to Hawaii to be murdered, then my mother Bea's great-great-great-grandmother, a hardworking thief from Bristol, would presumably have been sent to some plantation in Virginia instead of to Botany Bay.

"And where would that have left me?

"Which says a lot for *erratic,* in my opinion.

"Quite aside from explorers, though, there's all that evidence you keep giving in your lectures: those muon tracks that curl like ferns, and the wandering quark, and all that stupendous power, *explosive* power, nuclear I mean, from the erratic behavior of microphenomena. . . . There's a lot to be said for it, isn't there?"

She sighs. "But academic supervisors, they like straight lines. You keep wasting time, they said to me. Whose time? I asked. Because I am ravenous about their courses. I can't sleep at night for wanting to get through the extra-reading list. So where am I wasting time?

"But Professor Bickerton—I had him for history. Now there was an absorbing course—American Presidential Politics—though it is sometimes the seemingly trivial and idiosyncratic detail that rivets my attention. The Pepys's eye view, as it were. Like this, for example: Eisenhower is making a speech on foreign policy to a packed lecture hall full of students. I can't remember where—somewhere in the Midwest for sure. There's a lot of applause and a few whistles, and question period begins. First question: a girl in a green sweater comes to the microphone. 'Mr. President,' she asks earnestly. 'Could you tell us why your wife wears bangs?'

"Microphenomena again, you see. Why is it, do you think, that the mind veers away from foreign policy and back to the little events? It's an unexpected link, isn't it? Hairstyles and the Marshall Plan. You think I'm just chattering on for the sake of it, but you're wrong. I'm obsessed with the question. I find it overwhelmingly relevant: Why does the mind fasten on the trivial? The inane? On the smallest subatomic particle of the whole?"

Obviously she is not expecting an answer from him. Just as obviously, she expects him to take the questions very seriously.

"At nights," she muses, "when I look up at the black holes— and sometimes they seem to be everywhere, don't you find?— there's this thought about linkages that consoles me. Consider how many hundreds of thousands of them there must be, links which we never manage to trace. Consider the network of 'coincidences' which are simply cause and effect linked by not-yet-perceivable lines, the conjectures not yet refuted, the hypotheses not yet dreamed up. . . . It's mind-boggling.

"Anyway, Professor Bickerton claimed that I had a grab-bag theory of knowledge and a first-class grab-bag mind. First-class, he said. But grab-bag.

"I didn't think that was very nice, but perhaps it's true. I would say that all I have done is gone on collecting a great deal of unsortable material. As yet unsortable. But isn't this good scientific method?

"Professor Bickerton, incidentally, used not to put his clothes on before he lit his pipe. You really must have a very interesting image of yourself, Koenig."

She slides off the bed and sits on the carpet in front of his armchair and reaches up and begins unbuttoning his shirt—yet again—to his considerable pleasure. "Because I have a theory," she says, "that it is during the phase when sexual excitement is winding down that we are our truest selves. My mother Bea would laugh about that right now, if she were here. She used to say to me even when I was very little: 'Charade, you're a different kettle of fish from me. You'll never make your way in the world the same as I have—you like talking too much. You'll drive men crazy. You like talking more than eating and sleeping and I'll bet my last penny, when the time comes, you'll like it more than sex.' "

Having completely unbuttoned his shirt, she climbs onto his lap and curls up with her cheek against his chest.

"I would say that's not entirely true," she murmurs, "but I must admit I find it hard to separate the two.

"Anyway, you obviously have a deep-rooted image of yourself as a *clothed* person, Koenig. Or perhaps it's an astute awareness on your part of what I find irresistible about you. It's true that tweed jackets and chalk-smeared corduroy trousers drive me wild. It all has to do with the absent father, you see, who—if he ever existed and ever engendered me at all—was a university man, according to the recollections of my mother and my aunt Kay, both of whom found him unforgettable, though in different ways. Which brings me back to my hunch."

"What hunch?"

"The one about my father. I told you last time. And I'm elaborating it, now that you've got me reading up on probability theory and indeterminacy and such things."

"Mmm?"

"It sounds a bit crazy"—she shrugs—"but then so does Einstein, and the more I think about it, the more it rings true. So.

"Hypothesis number one: My father, Nicholas Truman, was born in England and shipped to Australia as a boy; he may or may not have returned to England when he disappeared; he may or may not continue to spend his life as a global nomad, writing books, filing stories under a thousand and one different names. That is the particular history, the Particle Theory of my father's life.

"Hypothesis number two: My father was never more than a Platonic conception, an idealized object of adoration, in the minds of various people, most notably my mother Bea and my aunt Kay. He glides forever on the crests of their imaginations. This is the Wave Theory of my father.

"And the same goes for Verity Ashkenazy, his high school sweetheart and university lover, who was intended as my mother; that is to say, he intended that she would be the mother of any children he had. She also existed and didn't exist, in the same incompatible way that the wave theory and the particle theory of energy coexist and were once thought to refute each other.

"Or, to draw an analogy from *my* field of study, are wave/particle paradoxes much the same as what the thirteenth-century thinkers in the Faculty of Arts in Paris would have called an instance of Double Truth, which posits that a concept can be simultaneously true and false—true in the philosophical sense, but false in the theological sense, and vice versa? Of course this theory of the Double Truth resulted in certain excommunications from the Church in 1277, most notably that of Siger of Brabant—though, as you might not know, it was not that the theologians of Paris held the theory to be *untenable*, just downright undesirable. The theologians sniffed Averroës and other heresies, all of which smelled of the loss of power to them.

"Anyway. From either direction, science or metaphysics, it seems a thing *can* be both true and false. So what I want to do, Koenig, is track down the odd-numbered days, the days when my father exists. I'd like to find him in his particular Nicholas shape, as his particle self.

"Koenig," she says, running her lips lightly across his forehead, his closed eyelids, his mouth. "Koenig," she whispers on a low husky note of entreaty. "I've run into dead ends. But surely, I keep thinking to myself, anyone who has a handle on the issues of quarks and black holes, on space that is void of space . . . anyone who can say to me that the selfsame photon is sometimes a particle and sometimes a wave, *depending on the context* . . . well, surely such a person has some answers."

5. Koenig

Some days blackness moves in on him and settles like an internal fog. Almost anything can touch off these moods: a stray comment in a restaurant, a newspaper reference, books displayed in a store. Sometimes it is sufficient to bury himself obsessively in work; at other times Rachel—his former, his first, his only wife—hides inside every equation. Then it may be necessary to draw up someone else's body like a screen, which may or may not help. If the attack is severe, he may have to telephone his daughter in Toronto.

"Is she all right?" he asks. "Should I come up?"

"I don't think that would help," his daughter says guardedly. "She's all right."

"Alison . . ."

"Yes?"

But what is there to say?

"I'd, uh, love to have you come down to Boston for a visit."

"I know, Dad. Perhaps I will one day. Bye."

Sometimes he has to fly up for a day or so: rent a car, drive by, keep tabs on them, reassure himself in some slight way. The invisible guardian, the watcher.

Then back to work; what else is there?

The fracturing of chalk, mid-formula, he has long ago discovered, is a particularly effective way to break out of fog: suggestive of fission, of lunatic Einsteinian energy, of intelligence fizzing and spitting under pressure. Then to turn to the class and smile gently, wearily; to hint at the physical cost of descending from rarefied air to the foothills of explanation. He turns; he smiles. He feels faint.

Because she is there again, the hologram girl, Charade Ryan, high up in the room near the back. He hasn't seen her since that second night when they . . . How long ago was that? How could he have forgotten? After the chasm, the weekend in Toronto, he has not . . .

Her hand is raised.

Yes? he attempts to say. He nods in her direction, but then what is the question? He listens blankly as words buzz like flies. "Perhaps," he says, "if you were to stay behind after the class . . ."

Because she is right about that: talk is what glues one minute to the next. Back in the apartment in Cambridge, Koenig reaches up and feels blindly along the shelf where he keeps words, and hurriedly pulls down multiple sets, double volumes, whole phrases. "Don't leave. Please. I certainly don't want you to leave. I had to go to Toronto and there wasn't time to . . . It certainly wasn't meant to indicate . . ." He relaxes, catching hold of her hand and licking her fingers one by one. "Don't stop talking."

He must have made sense, since she sits in his chair as usual. Though there is no way of knowing for sure, a word being an infinitely unstable element. He deals in hieroglyphs all the time; he knows how they branch unpredictably in the minds of readers, lab technicians, scientific colleagues. And he notices that she is sitting rather formally, sitting forward, ready to get dressed and leave at any time. "Perhaps you should . . ." He is groping for reasons to keep her there, get her talking again. "Perhaps you should elaborate, about your father, you know, be more specific. . . ."

"Well . . ." she says doubtfully.

"You could . . ." he begins, and has to clear his throat.

"Yes, I could tell you a story," she says. "By way of explication. It's something I more or less have to do all the time, for myself. Like marking my position on a map, you understand?"

Oh yes, he understands.

"I'll call it the Tale of Yesterday and Tomorrow," she says. "Because time is definitely something I don't understand and maybe you can explain. Or even ... even if you could just say to me authoritatively: Look, no one understands time. Relativity's made a cocked hat out of time; the very concept's passé. The past isn't done with—it could pop up again tomorrow. The whole thing is up for grabs. Even that would help. If I could have it on the best and latest scientific authority. Just some sort of anchor—no, just a buoy or two would do."

He watches the way she walks around his living room in her unfastened overlarge shirt. He watches the way she touches things, constantly, in passing. She is more agitated than before; she cannot keep still or silent.

He asks himself: How did we get from Building 6 to here? He is still addicted to the habit of assuming temporal chains, to ferreting out cause and effect, even when the route maps go haywire as they usually do.

After the class, there must have been a progression of events between there and here, but it is lost. Very likely it involved frantic calculations about the cleaning lady, since in moments of extremity the mind, which is a faulty and endearing mechanism, always turns to minutiae. (As she, the girl, has commented.) So it is quite possible that before they had even left the classroom (or else later, in his car? or in a cab? or had they taken the subway?) he had asked himself whether or not he had got around to leaving a key for Joanna while he was away in Toronto. And, since he is here with Charade, he must have concluded that yes, he'd contacted her. He must have concluded that since today is Joanna's day to clean, the apartment would look more or less decent.

So here he is again with the girl who is not much older than his daughter, Alison, his daughter who avoids visiting him and whose reproachful eyes follow him constantly but who has left no trail of crayon drawings on his refrigerator door. Those are the work of the children of Joanna, his cleaning lady. He lets her bring the kids—why not?—as long as they come in his absence.

So here he is again with the girl who talks, who talks and talks, who has blue-green eyes, weird hair tamed into a long thick braid, weird name. Charade. And she is more or less young enough to be his daughter. As a matter of fact, he has a son who is only slightly younger than she. His son is a Moonie now, voyaging into the far galaxies of inner space. Lost.

Charade is pacing, pacing, touching the spines of his books on the shelves, touching the moldings of the window frames (he approves of that; she has a taste for sensuous detail; the moldings are old and intricate), trailing her fingers over the large soapstone carving that Rachel bought in Toronto for his birthday years and years ago. (Funny that Charade sensed Rachel's presence after all these years. *Domestic humidity,* she said. He is fairly sure she said that.)

And all the time she is spinning a safety net of talk.

She turns to him suddenly from out of the middle of a sentence. Behind his ribs there is a sensation of pinching and kinking and he tenses, waiting to know what will be expected of him. Apparently, to her, it is both amusing and exasperating that he has dressed again. He has no specific recollection either of taking off his clothes or of putting them back on, but it is most certainly not true that he has an image of himself as a *clothed* person.

He always feels alarmingly exposed.

Even now he shivers and reaches for a robe to put on over his jacket and pants. And she, noting this, pauses. . . .

When she moves back and forth in front of him, he can hear the black nylon whisper of her thighs murmuring one to the other, a come-hither sound, full of solace. But why is she getting dressed? "Don't go." There is something he wants to explain. A stroke must be like this, he feels. First the massive cardiac jolt and then the muscles and nerves simply forgetting their lines; the power of speech going; the ability to walk going; the complicated sequence of picking up a comb and running it through the hair getting lost. On hospital wards, he has seen limp figures in striped pajamas and wheelchairs watch the movement of a nurse's arm with a greedy prurient interest. Now he understands it: not craziness, just a passionate copycat envy. How to begin again? How to recover the knack of swimming smoothly from one minute to the next, to keep on fitting each new day into the puzzle the way everyone else does without thinking. Without thinking. Probably that is the crux of the matter. Talk is glue, and thought is the great and terrible solvent. Everything falls into the well of too much thinking and comes apart at the seams.

Charade pads about like a cat in her stockinged feet.

It is interesting that she has noted the presence of Rachel, of Alison, of his son, *domestic humidity,* though she has mistaken their trails. It is interesting that she has noticed the drawings in the kitchen, the drawings of his housekeeper's children, since, as a matter of fact, he stuck them on the refrigerator door himself. Pulled them out of the wastepaper basket and bought the little magnets (coated-with-vinyl apples, bananas, watermelon slices) at the A&P, and put them there. Joanna, a widow, had laughed and then looked at him sharply. But Charade thinks Joey's green teddy bears invite analysis, and Sara's drawings are ominously neat.

"People like me," he says suddenly, and the insight propels itself explosively from behind some interior dam, "we're like trained monkeys really. Brilliant in limited spheres. But mess up our lines, put a spoke in our wheels, and we don't know what to do."

Charade stops, startled, in front of him.

He notices that a filament of cobweb, drifting down from the ceiling and crusted with motes of dust and light, sways back and forth across her breasts like a pendulum. And then he notices the small black spider, at first invisible against her pantyhose, climbing into view, ascending, ascending, like a mole against her midriff, her chest, her cheek, riding on the heft of some unseen pulley. Of course it means something, but all signs have become to him temporarily unreadable.

"Sorry," Charade says, knotting the tails of her shirt together. "You're afraid you've been saddled with a nut, right?"

No, no, he shakes his head vehemently. God, where do her ideas come from? "It's just that I have no idea what to do," he says. "No idea."

She sighs. "The messiness doesn't touch you scientists, does it? Everything's clean. Everything runs on grooves."

Behind her head, battalions of green teddy bears, drawn in crayon by the son of his cleaning lady, march across his refrigerator door. They all face the same direction; they are all going to the same place, full of green energy that splashes beyond the edges of their limbs. But Joanna's daughter, Sara, keeps all color neatly within its boundaries, and this is ominous.

"I'm sure," Charade is saying, "that people like me, crammed full of literature and history but more or less illiterate in science . . . I'm sure I might as well be mute as far as you're concerned. I'm sure I might as well be speaking Swahili."

"No," he says emphatically. "No, no, absolutely not. Not at all. Keep talking."

"Well," she says, "anyway. It's morning."

"Weren't you going to tell me a story? The Tale of Yesterday and Tomorrow, you said."

"But it's morning. And you have a nine o'clock class."

6. The Tale of Yesterday and Tomorrow

"When the Great Walls were being built," Charade begins, wrapping herself loosely in a sheet and huddling into the armchair in Koenig's bedroom. . . .

"And the walls are everywhere, everywhere," she says. "They run down the middle of subway cars, have you noticed? I'll tell you a tale of this morning's subway:

"You still can't step into the same river twice," says the towheaded boy. He leans against the wall of the car which branches and flowers with graffiti. He must be all of twelve or thirteen years old, and is wedged beneath Charade's left armpit. "For day-to-day in Harvard Square," he says, "Heraclitus is more helpful than Senator Kennedy. Anyway, that's what I'm going to argue. That you still can't step into the same river twice."

"You can't step into the Charles River *once*," his companion answers, "unless you want to pick up an infection. We know where Kennedy stands on Pollution Probe, and that's what counts."

Then a station flashes into view, brakes, sucks out a hundred people, crams another hundred in. The boys in their crested school blazers have disappeared, and in their place is a woman with paper clips dangling from her ears. She nudges Charade and whispers fiercely: "Finally finally finally finally." Charade cannot avoid seeing into the woman's bag, where two dead birds lie rigid in crumpled newsprint. A ritual? Breakfast? The woman is thin as birdbones under seamed skin. "Finally finally finally," she whispers, eyes glittering.

Park Street Station reaches in and whirls her up its funnel to the spinning streets.

"Yes?" Koenig prompts when her silent orbit brings her back through his bedroom.

"Yes what?"

He gestures, mildly agitated, pulling back her words from the air. "Whirls her up its funnel to the spinning streets."

"End of my subway story. She climbed into someone else's tale."

"You sound . . . different."

"Different?"

"Yes. Your voice changes."

"So does yours behind your lectern."

"Yes, but . . ."

"I can't help it. Stories have their own voices; they speak me. You want me to leave after all?"

No, no, he shakes his head vehemently. "Keep talking."

Once upon a time, Charade says, before Copernicus, this city lay still on its pontoons between the Charles River and the Atlantic. Back then, a person could climb out of the subway and step into the same city twice; a person could journey more or less straightforwardly from birth to death, which used to be the last stop on the line; one used to be able to count on that.

Once upon a time, geography was stable. More than that—I

am almost certain—there was once a time when days followed one another in orderly fashion like huge beads on a rope. You pulled your way along, hand over hand. You could stop and look behind you and say: There's the past. You could touch what was beneath your fingers, you could smell it, lick it, taste it. This is today, you could say. And you could reach forward and sense the beads stretching on and on. That is the future, you could say; the things that will arrive tomorrow, that have not yet happened, though they do exist and lie in waiting.

But probably even then—if there was a then—the beads just out of reach curled back to touch the past. Probably time has always been a necklace. Probably it has always been possible to begin the circuit at any point.

And when the Great Walls were being built—in ancient China, in Berlin, in Warsaw and Lodz, in Sydney and Brisbane, in the Punjab, in Fiji, in Toronto and New York and Boston—there were always clusters of law-abiding and curious folk who stood watching the progress of division.

And there was always a lunatic or two to shout: *Beware! Beware!* to the embarrassment of ordinary folks.

On both sides the watchers could see the indestructible present, sweet and straight as a line. Everyman—a chatty fellow—was forever waving to his neighbor across the workers and the rubble. What is this nonsense? he called, and both of them laughed.

Only yesterday, he said in awe to his little son as the wall grew higher, only yesterday we could see the apple tree in our neighbor's yard. His tree was heavy with blossoms; he always gave us a bushel of apples. Remember how you played in the rain barrels under the trees?

The little boy thought he could remember. Into his mind fell a white flock of petals, and the taste of crisp inaccessible apples became a craving on his tongue. He saw a girl in a muslin pinafore whom he chased between the rain barrels. The girl smelled of tree sap and new-mown grass and he pined for her in his dreams.

Daddy, he wept, I want to see her again. I miss her. I want the apple-blossom girl.

What? his father said. What girl? I can't remember a girl. Our neighbor never had any children; it was a constant source of grief to him.

But as his son described her—the hair that fell pale and heavy to her shoulders, her little brown hands, her white pinafore—he recalled how he and his neighbor had always intended a match.

I can remember a time, he said to the grandson on his knee, when your father played in the rain barrels underneath our neighbor's trees on the other side of the wall. I can remember when your father was in love with a beautiful girl who lived on the other side. That was before the wall was built.

I don't believe you, Grandpa, the child said. It's just another one of your stories. There's always been a wall.

Grandfather and father stared at each other.

Out of the mouths of babes, the father laughed. Why don't you admit it, Dad? There's always been a wall.

But . . . the grandfather said, bewildered. You yourself remember the girl.

Ah, that's different, the son said. That was part of my wild and reckless youth when I made dangerous forays beyond the wall. That was how I met the girl. The girl is real.

Of course the girl is real, the grandfather blustered. (He was a stubborn fellow, old and contentious.) Before the wall was built, he said, you used to play with her under the trees. Even God cannot change the past, he stormed.

No one is trying to change the past, his son placated. It's just that your memory is playing tricks. Don't you remember that first time I smuggled her across the wall? How you begged me not to get involved because of the danger?

It's true, the grandfather conceded. There was never a time when the wall was not there. But the girl was real. What became of her?

Who knows? the son sighed. She worried about her own father. She insisted on going back.

I always hoped I'd meet her father, the old man said. I always thought we'd have a lot in common. I used to picture his backyard; I used to imagine how we'd stand and chat if the wall had never been there.

I don't know, the son said. Sometimes I thought he was just an excuse she used. She must have had a father, of course, but I'm not at all sure he lived beyond the wall.

She had a vivid imagination, the old man recalled. And such an unforgettable face. You used to call her the apple-blossom girl.

Yes, the son sighed. I still dream of her.

"Do you see what I mean?" Charade asks.

Of course, for me—she might have said—it's an intense and personal issue, with my father's past and present being such elusive constructions.

But many other examples could be adduced.

In Toronto—not a city that rides high in the Book of the World's Awareness—a certain Zundel snapped his fingers and made the 1940s disappear. He coughed brimstone and a staggering amount of documentation wisped away like smoke from an oven: eyewitness accounts, photographs, newsreels of the bodies going under the bulldozers.

"Of course, you know about this, Koenig," she sighs. "You know all about the trial in Toronto. And in Europe there are academics who solemnly delineate a mass hallucination. There is proof that the Second World War was a hoax.

"And so Verity Ashkenazy and Nicholas Truman," she says, "both were and weren't. That's my honest opinion."

"Perhaps," Koenig says, "if you could start at the beginning."

But Charade sees the approach of morning and falls silent.

7. One Way of Beginning

"Tonight," Koenig says, "if you could begin at the beginning perhaps ..."

But where, Charade wonders, is the beginning? And how does she cut her own story free from the middle of the history of so many others? In a sense, she is the epilogue to several lives.

Well then ...

Here's one beginning, she suggests, in the rainforest, where time comes and goes like a bird.

The birds. To the tag end of trillions of years of decay and growth come the birds: bellbirds, lyrebirds, lorikeets, parakeets. Shadow and rotting sweetnesses lure them. On their wings is such a weight of color that they float dazed on the green air, slowly losing height, drifting down to where Charade sits crushing the mosses and ferns. Oh, she gasps. Oh.

She is five, perhaps six years old, rapt, knees hugged up under her chin. The fallen tree trunk behind her back, given over to creepers, is collapsing softly, and along its jellied spine where a flock of new saplings has a toehold—there is walnut, silky oak, mahogany—the jostling and clamoring for light is constant and silent and deadly earnest. If she sits still long enough, the philodendron will loop itself around her ankles, and kingfishers will nest in her hair.

That is my earliest memory, Charade says.

When I was six or seven, she says, I found a dead man in the rainforest and I kept him as a pet. He was my secret. I suppose he was a swaggie—he might have been someone who had walked from Cairns to Melbourne and was on his way back, or he might have been just a local drunk. He could have been one of my mother's lovers—it's certainly likely. One night when the sky was bloody with the sun (which never went quietly; which was always dragged, kicking, screaming orange and purple, down below the Tropic of Capricorn) . . . on such a night, I suppose, the man drank until he saw lightning, and then he went thundering off to some shack on the side of the Tamborine Mountain. One foot after another, he stepped precisely, he kept his starshot eyes on his shoes, he placed them down gently as eggs on the red clay road, but the rainforest reached out and got him.

It was the lawyer cane probably; those wait-awhiles had their hooks deep in his shirt and trousers when I found him. And his smell had its hooks into me. That was what reeled me in, gasping and fascinated. What I thought I saw, down against the curtained roots of the strangler fig, was a balloon man, slowly inflating. Every day he was bigger. Every day I held a handkerchief over my nose and mouth and watched the ants: the way they embroidered him and covered him with soft brown bunting. Birds spoke to him, and perhaps it was their beaks that punctured his purple balloon-skin.

I heard him sigh.

And then he began to deflate, at first quickly with little shudders and farts, but after that slowly, silkily, peacefully, like a glove as a hand withdraws. Each day he was thinner and flatter. I liked him better then, because his smell had escaped from him, bubbling away between the ferns. When he was clean and white inside his muddy clothes, when he smelled as sweet and yeasty as moss, I put flowers in his eyes. You can be my father, I told him. Jimmy

Armstrong and Michael Donovan and Diane Stolley, they've all got fathers, but we've gone and lost mine.

Do you see how relevant this beginning is? Charade asks. It's a habit that set in early for me, these interminable discussions with profound but inarticulate men.

Or here's another beginning, at school.

Diane Stolley whispers to a circle of girls: *Charade Ryan has a dirty mother. Charade Ryan smells.* And out by the swings there's a chant: *Charade Ryan smells!*

It's true. Tree bark and leaves can be found in my hair, matted in, part of the growth. There is always mud under my fingernails; my bare legs are crisscrossed with scratches, mosquito bites, bruises.

Michael Donovan taunts me: You stink as bad as your mother's snatch.

I guess you'd know, I call back. Your dad looks at it every night. He's always hanging around our place.

"It's astonishing, isn't it," Charade asks, "how early we have that kind of knowledge? At seven and eight, we know how to draw blood quickest and deepest. Maybe later we just lose energy and lapse into kindness by default."

When I was fourteen, she says, and being shipped off to high school in Brisbane, Michael Donovan, without any warning, swung down out of our mango tree and whispered, "Big shot, eh? Bush high school's not good enough."

"I don't want to go," I said (a polite lie, in one sense, and absolute truth in another). "Mr. Bobart says I have to; he arranged it."

"Teacher's pet," sniffed Michael Donovan, but he had his hands behind his back, and he scratched one calf with the other bare foot. "Brought something for you," he said. Two things, in fact. An orchid—everyone knew how much I loved white orchids— and a Penguin book of Australian poetry. He held out his gifts as though they were dead fish caught at the culvert where the road smashed through our shrinking forest.

I was dumbfounded.

Only a month ago he had filled my schoolbag with mud. Michael Donovan himself had no plans whatsoever for high school. Already he was in business with his father, collecting the garbage bins from the school, trucking them to the pig farmers. Already, people said, he'd got a girl in trouble and would have been a father if things hadn't been taken care of down in Brisbane.

I could not imagine him at Wentworth's General Store and Post Office (where the cars came in off the South Coast road) asking for a Penguin poetry book. I knew where the orchid came from; it was a prize bloom, *Tamborine stella,* stolen from the trellis over Mrs. Tierney's front gate. Very likely the Penguin book was stolen too.

"I'm sorry you're gonna go away," he said. And because for once I was struck speechless, because I kept standing there, staring, tasting sexual power for the very first time, he added roughly: "Just don't come back talking with a plum in your mouth. Can't stand sheilas talk that way."

Still not a word would come to me, not one, so I stood on tiptoes and kissed him on the cheek. And then—after he dropped his gifts and grabbed me—on the lips.

But on that other day, back near the beginning of things, back on the day when he said I smelled as bad as my mother's snatch, on that day they had to pull us apart, and I did the most damage. I came away with a chunk of his hair, and with long crimped ribbons of his skin underneath my nails.

Mostly, back then, I was left alone. Not just the boys but the girls, too, steered clear of me. Their mothers warned them against me, in case my kind of family situation was catching, and certainly I preferred the company of my father, the bone man, who grew smaller and smaller in the rainforest. There was nothing I couldn't tell him. I could read aloud to him from any book at all and he never objected.

Books. There's another beginning.

My mum—Bea Ryan, the Slut of the Tamborine Mountain,

Queen Bea, Honey Bea, that Bloody Breeder B.—my mum would stare and shake her head. Never seen anything like it, she would say. There were always brothers and sisters, older and younger, falling all over one another and me. There were always the men, stopping by to have a beer with my mum. It was a small and noisy place, a fibro shack with lizards on the walls, and cracks and holes that were hung with sacs of spiders' eggs. But I would wedge myself into a corner, two sides protected, cross-legged on the floor, a book propped open on my knees, and I wouldn't even deign to acknowledge the company.

How'd you get that one, Honey Bea? the men would laugh. Been fooling around with a cyclo-*pee*-dia, have ya? That accounts for her hair, they would say. (It stuck out in all directions like the pages of a riffled book; it was fair and my mum is dark.) This the little cuckoo in your nest? there was always someone to ask; and that someone always got slapped on the knuckles by Bea. Uh-oh, they would laugh. Cutting close to the bone, is it? Whyn't you ever come clean on this, Bea?

Get out of my house, she would say, and they'd shuffle feet and clink bottles and shake their heads at me. Well, they'd say, wherever she come from, Bea, you got an ugly duckling in that one. You'll never get *her* married off; you'd better learn her to be a nurse. Those girls make good money down in Brisbane. Ask Harry here, he knows. His oldest's a bit broad in the beam for marrying; nice kid, just a bit doughy in the face—right, Harry? But is she pulling in the loot at the Royal Brisbane! Sends her ol' man drinking money—right, Harry?

Every man, says Harry, should have one plain daughter, to look after 'im in 'is old age.

They would drink to that, and forget about me. Not that I minded them, really. Michael Donovan's dad was nearly always there, and Diane Stolley's dad, and Jimmy Armstrong's when he was sober enough. Warmth came off those men, as well as violence. I didn't mind them. That's something I learned from my mum: how to handle men. How not to mind them.

They can't help theirselves, she'd say to me. It's the way they're made, that's all. Can't stand women go on whining about it. You just got to jolly them along, that's all.

Anyway, I didn't notice anybody, I forgot the whole world, as soon as I got my head in a book.

But can I convey, Charade asks, how exotic a book-reading kid was, in that place? Suppose your adolescent son were to take up . . . oh . . . needlepoint, say. A useless thing. An embarrassing thing. A thing almost frightening in its abnormality.

For the teachers, though, I might have been the unicorn itself. I was proof of miracles. I was evidence that doing time in a bush school might even be worthwhile.

Here's another beginning, a significant one, and an ending, too, the painful falling into knowledge, from which there is no going back.

Here is Mr. Murdoch, my Grade Seven teacher.

And here am I: thirteen now and wearing sandals to school (all the girls do, by this age, though the boys still go barefoot and wouldn't be caught dead in shoes, in sissy shoes). I am fanatic about daily showers. I stick flowers—especially orchids—into the fuzz of my hair.

Every morning I get to school early while Mr. Murdoch is alone in the classroom, cleaning the blackboard, writing up the day's lesson plans in a book for the school inspectors. I adore Mr. Murdoch. I am in love with him. When I grow up I'm going to marry him.

"Well, goldilocks." He grins, seeing me. "What did you read last night, as well as under the desk yesterday? Yes, I saw you, sneaking a look at it under your social studies book, you little bluestocking."

I think of this phrase, which he uses often, as a term of endearment. In my fantasies, Mr. Murdoch and I are in a book-lined bedroom in a cozy treehouse at the edge of the rainforest. He lies across the bed reading to me while I dance languidly, sensuously, over by the window, wearing nothing but shimmering blue stockings and garters and a few white orchids here and there. Mr.

Murdoch tries to go on reading, but his eyes are pulled up from the page and over. He pauses; he is mesmerized by my long long legs and blue stockings. Finally he says: "Here. I can't stand it. *You* read."

And so I take the book and I sit in the windowsill and dangle my blue legs into the room and I read. Mr. Murdoch lies on the bed and closes his eyes. "You are a wonderful reader," he sighs. He is in love with me. He wants me to read to him for the term of his natural life.

So each morning when he asks, "Well, you little bluestocking, what did you read last night?" I strive for worthier and more difficult trophies. *"The Last Days of Pompeii,"* I say proudly, "from the Everyman Classics Library." I love the sound of that: *the Classics.* It gives off a fragrance of Latin and Greek and English cathedrals and gentlemen sipping port at Oxford. In the rainforest I have sat and pictured this world in detail. I know it intimately— how everyone speaks the way the Queen does in her Christmas Message, and how everyone drinks nothing but sherry, which they sip ever so slowly like tea that is scalding hot, and how they would never say anything more violent than "Dear me!"—not even during the last last days of Pompeii.

"Dear me!" Mr. Murdoch says. "That second-rate Victorian melodrama. You'll ruin your esthetic taste buds. Well, what did you think of it?"

"It's . . . er . . . I like *historical* things," I say, crushed (I have been dreaming of blind Lydia and her noble sacrifice), "the stuff about Pompeii . . . Did they really have paintings like that on the walls of the villas?" (A brilliant strategy, this.)

"Oh, yes indeed," he says. "Look, I'll show you." And he rummages in his chaotic cupboard for a book. "Must be at home," he says. "Well, I'll bring it around perhaps this evening, shall I? I've got a book of photographs of the excavations."

"And also," I say, dizzy with excitement, "I've been reading *Journals of the Discoverers.* Abel Janszoon Tasman and William Dampier and Captain James Cook and people like that."

"Good heavens!" he says. (He is really impressed; I am almost fainting with pride.) "Where did you manage to get hold of something like that?"

"I found it in the library, in the history section. Can I read you something funny? I copied it out." I fish a scrap of paper out of my pocket. "This is William Dampier," I say.

On the 4th day of January, 1688, we fell in with the Land of New Holland.

The inhabitants of this country are the miserablest People in the world. . . .

Their Eye-lids are always half closed, to keep the flies out of their eyes; they being so troublesome here, that no fanning will keep them from coming to ones Face. . . . So that from their Infancy being thus annoyed with these Insects, they do never open their Eyes, as other People: and therefore they cannot see far.

Mr. Murdoch laughs. "No flies on you, goldilocks."

"Will you bring the Pompeii book tonight?" I prompt, scarcely able to breathe.

"Tonight," he promises. "If I can find it."

He doesn't find it. For weeks and weeks, he doesn't find it. Whenever I think of mentioning it, my throat thickens up. And then, long after I have given up on the visit, one evening when I am coming in late (I try to stay away until the littlest ones have dropped asleep in their bedroom), I am coming in late from one of my usual haunts—the library, the rainforest, the mango tree, I don't remember which—and I see him sitting at our kitchen table across from Mum.

Blood thumps against my eardrums. I spit on my palms and rub my hands together and slick down the flyaway edges of my hair. I spit on my hands again, and rub the sticky dirt-crusted mango sap from my legs. I pelt down to the bottom of the yard where the tree orchids are, and snatch two flowers for my hair.

Grand entrance. In my mind, trumpets.

Here I am, Mr. Murdoch, your little bluestocking, smelling of orchids and books.

Both of them startle, Mr. Murdoch and my mum. My mum the Honey Bea, the Queen Bea of Mount Tamborine.

"Oh Charade," Mum says, jumping up. "I was just saying to

Mr. Murdoch here that I never know where you are. She's probably up a tree somewhere with a book, I said to him. And here you are. Speak of the devil."

"Did you bring the book, Mr. Murdoch?" I come over to the table so that he can see what I have been reading (*Great Expectations*), and so he can see the flower behind my right ear.

"Book?" he asks blankly. He's very busy with priming the hurricane lantern (the power fails a lot on the Tamborine Mountain); he's bending over it, cupping his hand and blowing softly, coaxing, adjusting the wick.

"The Pompeii book," I remind him.

"Oh, good lord," he says. "Pompeii. I forgot all about it. You should have reminded me."

He is still not looking at me. "Is something the matter, Mr. Murdoch?" I run through all the school possibilities, but can think of none concerning me.

"Matter?" He looks at me now, awkward, red in the face. "No, of course not. *Great Expectations,* eh? You've got a real little bookworm here, Mrs. Ryan."

There is something about the tone that makes me feel suddenly as though I'm out of my depth in the river, floundering, the current swirling me in circles.

"Charade," Mum says. "Be a good girl, and just nip down to McGillivray's Pub—the back door, not the front—and tell Mr. McGillivray that Bea needs a little bottle of something for her cold. Tell him to put it on my bill, there's a good girl."

It's a long long way to McGillivray's Pub, and an even longer way back, and when I get back I feel older than the bone man down by the fig tree roots in my own private part of the forest. Through the kitchen window I see them playing cards at the table, and underneath it they are playing feet.

"Sharp as a tack," Mum says. "She doesn't miss a thing. I don't know what I'm going to do with her. I don't know how she's going to make her way in the world—it's a worry."

"She's a regular bluestocking all right," Mr. Murdoch laughs. Judas laughter. "You really should pack her off to school in Brisbane. It's a waste to keep her here. Did you fuck a Circuit Court judge, or what?"

"None of your business," Mum says, smacking him on the back of the hand. It's the kind of slap I've seen Sheba, our tabby, give to tomcats on the prowl. "But if you must know, he was a university man and an Englishman, so there. I've had class in my day." She looks at him through her lashes. "I got a thing for book men," she says.

I go to the bedroom window and call to one of the kids. Kevin, who's three years younger than me.

"Psst! Kevin!" I whisper. "Give this to Mum." And I push the bottle through the window.

By moonlight I make my way into the forest—I don't care if the snakes get me—and I hunch up beside the bone man (I don't visit him much anymore) and that's where I stay all night. In the morning—and here's something new, another beginning, and also an ending—Mum comes looking for me. I can hear the twigs snapping, the swish of branches pushed aside, and so I hide. I run. I know this ground well; it's not difficult to outwit her. I don't want to be intruded on here.

When she gets back I'm sitting at the kitchen table doing homework.

"Charade," she says.

I don't look up.

"Charade," she says. "This is the one and only time you'll catch me explaining the facts of life to you." She takes two chipped and cloudy tumblers from the sink counter, and pours something out of her bottle into each. She pushes one across the table to me, but I ignore it. She clears her throat. "Love," she says, "is one of these women's diseases, like bleeding and babies—you can't do anything about it the first time. You have to have it once really bad, and once it's started, you just have to sweat it out. It's like having the bloody babies. You can kick and scream all you want—it helps to scream—but there aren't any shortcuts. You just got to wait till it ends.

"But here's the difference. The babies keep coming like the men keep coming; that's the way it is. Love's different. You have one bad bout, then you're cured." She drains her tumbler and pours some more. "Cured for life," she says.

"There's one more thing I'll say, Charade, and then you'll never get another word out of me on this subject. You think I don't care. You think I don't know how you feel. Wrong. I know exactly what I'm doing, and why. And I'll tell you why. The one time I had love—a very bad case, a very very very bad case—was your father, Nicholas Truman. Just don't you forget it."

She tosses back her head and drains her tumbler again and then she's off. Off. Careening down the road to McGillivray's like a clipper ship in full angry sail, her hull rocking in the uncertain swell.

I stare at the cracks in the fibro wall. My eyes feel so dry they prickle, a dangerous sign with me. This is what I see: me, dressed in a black bodysuit and bright-blue stockings, sitting nonchalantly in a library in Oxford, reading the Classics. A gentleman, very elegant, with a gold-topped walking cane, approaches.

"What are you reading, my dear?" he asks. "Oh, forgive me. I should introduce myself. I'm Professor Nicholas Truman. I'm a university man." And then he invites me to his house for sherry.

And maybe that is the beginning, Charade says.

8. Fathers

"Fathers," Charade says. "I've given a lot of thought to the subject of fathers."

Fathers, Koenig thinks uneasily. It is not such a simple matter to be a father. A memory comes unbidden: La Guardia Airport, about three years ago, the last time he saw his son.

Koenig was one of the herd coming down the cattle run from the Eastern Airlines Shuttle, buffeted by pinstriped flanks, by tweed flanks, Boston executives, Boston academics, the morning's offload. Koenig's mind was on the conference—in particular, on the paper he was to give—so that when an arm obstructed his path, he simply stopped and blinked at it, disoriented. He observed a hand, a fresh daisy, a printed message from the Reverend Moon; all this before his eyes followed the arm up to the shoulder, the neck, the face. His eyes moved in slow motion, in the ponderous viscous rhythm of a bad dream, instinctively afraid somehow of what he might . . . Was it a mole he recognized? The particular scribble of some vein?

Then: "Oh, for God's sake!" he cried in involuntary disgust, eye to eye with his son, shock to shock.

His son seemed to recover first.

"Dad." The voice quavered: It was part truce flag, part battle standard, part plea. One hand was instinctively thrown up to ward off psychic blows. Koenig was dimly conscious of the other hand . . . what? . . . *hovering,* of flower and tract drifting to the floor, of the hand moving aimlessly, nervously, of its fingers fluttering dove-like (they might have been yearning above an ark) as they looked for somewhere to settle. Then a forlorn note sounded itself (Koenig actually thought, later, that he had heard a bugle, had heard the doleful cadence of the Last Post). He saw the hand falling back, giving up—in a sense, saw it; the movement was monitored in a sluggish region of his mind and was later replayed replayed replayed, always mingled with the mournful bugle replaying the Last Chance, the last chance, replaying the last, the end, replaying replaying replaying. . . .

But the mind is a faulty mechanism, not well synchronized with the affective system.

"Panhandling!" Paternal fury leaped from Koenig's lips well before any knowledge of the word, or any intention, had formed in his mind. "Begging in public. Haven't you any pride at—"

But his son had turned already; his son was running; his son had vanished.

Koenig ran, too, uselessly, into the maelstrom of people. He turned corner after corner after corner. Futile. Gasping for breath, asthmatic, he leaned against a wall and stood there trembling while the crowd lapped at him, knocked, mocked, buffeted. *Jesus,* someone swore, but Koenig couldn't move.

"Are you all right?" a janitor asked.

"Yes," Koenig said, and he went into the men's room and locked himself into a cubicle. He had no idea how long he sat there with his head in his hands. It might have been hours.

At the conference, excuses were made on his behalf for the paper not given.

Fathers, Koenig thinks, and the word bleeds on and on inside him. He watches Charade as though drugged but sees his daughter, Alison: how she either averts her reproachful eyes or is overly bright and . . . and . . . "Brittle," he murmurs.

"Did you say something?" Charade asks.

"No," he says, reaching out to touch her cheek. "Please keep talking. Please talk. You were going to tell me a tale of . . ."

"Ah, yes," Charade says. "Fathers . . .

I've given a lot of thought to the subject of fathers, she says.

They came like flies. In the evenings they gathered like a crust round our kitchen table; they all had cravings for my mum, the Honey Bea. My mum had a way with other kids' fathers.

Ten children, Bea, they would say, and shake their heads. How come you don't take precautions?

I *do* take precautions, she would say. I've taken precautions ten times. I got them and the Old Age Pension, and that's all, for when I'm over the hill.

Fathers were a very hot topic for the children of Bea.

Here's a thunderstorm afternoon and Davey's come home with two black eyes, plum-dark, brilliant as eggplants. "Patrick Burke said I was a bastard. What's a bastard?"

"What we are," Siddie tells him. "All of us."

"Not me," I say. "I'm a bluestocking." The whole world told me so; I thought it was a compliment. Snickety-snack, my thoughts went, pirouetting, making leaps of blue fire. I catch Davey by the hands and dance him round the kitchen table, blue stockings for his blue-black eyes.

"Listen," Mum says. And when she says it like that, you have to freeze. You have to hold yourself so still, you can hear the spiders rubbing their legs against the walls. "I'll tell you what a bastard is," she says. "I'll show you." She is sitting on the front steps, shelling peas into the bowl of her skirt. Thunder growls and farts, but the rain has stopped for a bit, and the puddles are steaming back towards the sun. "Look there," Mum says, pointing to the second step, which is rotting faster than the others, which feels spongy underfoot and gives off that thick yeasty smell that the lizards love. There are three of them, sunning themselves; and in the dampest part of the step, where the hole goes nearly right through, there's a baby wood frog. "Some people gotta chop off a lizard's tail whenever they see one," she says. "Some people got to put salt on a frog's back. No reason. Except the bang they get from watching lizards and frogs go berserk. Some people, because they can't lie in the sun all day, hate the ones who do. That's a bastard. I hope we haven't got any in this family."

Fathers. I used to study them. I keep them pickled in memory.

Diane Stolley's father—an interesting specimen—used to roll around most evenings on the slow way home from work, bringing a six-pack of Four-X, sniffing up honey and sweet time, talking about his wife and daughters.

Diane Stolley's father put a hand inside his pants and scratched. I'll tell you about women, he said. They're an itch. They got this thing drives a man crazy, but he can't let it alone.

Me, he said, I'm a maker of women. Got four daughters, no sons. That tells you something. I'm like Abraham and Isaac and those blokes that got nations started; it takes one strong man and a lot of women. See, you need breeders and cookers and looker-afters to crank things up, and that's what I make. One day I'll be in the schoolbooks next to Henry Parkes and Macarthur and those blokes, one day they'll build me a monument. Billy Stolley: a Father of the State of Queensland.

Yep, he said, I figured that out one day I was driving a truck to Cunnamulla. Down on me luck, I was. Me wife had just gone an' given me another baby girl, third bloody time, ah strike, nine months wasted. So I says to meself: Stone the crows, I'm a doomed man, might as well shoot through. It was cyclone time, see, and there's been flash floods and this rock as big as a house has gone. Clean gone. Jesus, I says to meself, water is stronger than rock. Then this comes ter me right outta the blue—it's a pome: Water is stronger than rock, and cunt lasts longer than cock. Right outta the blue. And so I reckon the man who has daughters is king.

And that's me, said Diane Stolley's father, scratching his balls and reaching under my mum's skirt as she walked to the door with the potato peels. I can appreciate sweet sticky things and I can make them.

Well, King Billy, my mum laughed, slapping his hand in her mother-cat Queen Bea way. Keep your hands to yourself in front of my children, if you please.

And later, over the boiled vegetables and sausage, when I sulked as daughters will sulk: "How can you be so cheap? How can you let a dirty old fool like Diane Stolley's father *touch* you?" she made me sit down on the front steps.

"I'll tell you something, Charade," she said, "that you won't find in any of your books. Every man has a right and an obligation to be a king inside his own mind. Every woman got a right and an obligation to be a queen. And you, Miss High and Mighty, you think you're the book-smart queen of Mount Tamborine. You want us all to bow and scrape. What makes you think you got a right to poke holes in other people's coronations?"

At school, Diane Stolley showed me two things: a tin ring with pink flowers intertwined (won by shooting three cardboard ducks at the Brisbane Show) and the purple welts on her legs—both of them gifts from her dad.

"Your dad is a dead possum's stink," I told her.

"My dad is my dad." She shrugged. "Anyway . . ."

"What?"

"Some nights," she said, looking into the distance, "he sings to us and tells us stories."

"Yeah," I said. Like everyone else, I knew how to draw quick blood. "At nights he tells us stories too. To my mum and me."

She turned away and her fists clenched and unclenched themselves. I owed it to her. In Wentworth's store, her mother turned away from my mum as though she might catch something.

"My dad is my dad," Diane Stolley said again. "At least I got one, Charade."

Michael Donovan's father smelled of slop bins and pigs. When he visited, his smell came before him like an aura. You could *see* that smell: It twisted and turned like lawyer cane; it battened onto the air like a staghorn fern to a tree trunk; he couldn't tear it away from himself, no matter how much he bathed. And he did bathe, in rivers and rock pools and under the waterfall down near the Donovan shack, which had a dunny at the back of the yard but nothing so fancy as a bathtub.

"Don't need hoity-toity when there ain't no woman around," Michael Donovan's father said. His wife, Maureen, died giving birth to Michael.

He was, in his own way, a fastidious man. He would not, for example, take a swig from a passed-around bottle, nor permit schoolteachers (with their chalky hands) to comb his children's hair for nits in the regular fashion. He shaved his sons' heads with a long-bladed razor himself, regularly, so that once a month they looked like prisoners of war. We called him the Slops Man or the Pig Man, but he could speak—after several beers—in a looping musical rage on the subject of kids who put paper and cardboard scraps into the "Food Only" bins.

"I seen a little pig," he said, "cough itself to death because it took a mouthful of paper and plastic mixed in with the bread crusts and mush and soft apple cores. I seen it huffle and puffle and swell up in the face while I reach in an' try to pull back a plastic bag that's half swallowed. I seen it shudder and whimper and turn quiet."

And a hush would fall on all of us children as two beery tears went looking for a path down the crisscrossed leathery cheeks of Michael Donovan's father. Maybe Davey or little Elizabeth would start to cry too. And my mum would take another beer out of the fridge and pour it for Mr. Donovan and pat him on the arm. "You're a soft-hearted bloke, Mick Donovan," she'd say, and she'd smile to herself and he'd smile back and next thing she'd be ordering us off to bed.

But there was another side to Michael Donovan's dad.

Across a thicket of too many beers one evening, he heard a *coo-ee* from out by our mango tree. "Christ!" he said, thumping the table.

My mum, reading well-known signs, said to me: "Charade, go out and see what young Michael wants." My mum was a stepper-in-between. My mum did not like to see child or man—or animal either, for that matter—get hurt.

Well. It was an odd thing, going out there to meet my scourge of the schoolyard under our mango tree. Boys at school have a hard shell around them. They are full of spikes and sharp points. You can't come near them. But under the mango tree at night, Michael Donovan looked small and different, almost naked. Like one of my little brothers in his hand-me-down pajamas, say, when I had to hold his hand and walk him down the dark path to the dunny last thing at night.

Michael Donovan and I stared at each other nervously, like strangers. Like dingos waiting for the fight to start. Around us the air was shrill with crickets. I never thought of Michael Donovan before as someone who might stand out under the stars and pleat eucalypt leaves between his fingers; as a mirror image, in a sense, of myself. Minutes passed. Stars dipped and swayed in the sky; the Southern Cross wheeled above us. And from the kitchen a voice called, "Charade!"

Michael Donovan and I both jumped, and I blurted, "My mum says, what do you want?"

"Gotta see my dad," he said.

"What for?"

He rubbed one leg against the other and looked away, as though the words he needed might be nailed to the broken-down fence. " 'Coz of Brian," he said. Brian was an older brother who worked in Brisbane, where he was, more often than not, in trouble with the police, people said. "Come home this evening and went off in Dad's truck," Michael said. "Smashed it up." He turned to face me and his eyes were big and pale as Cape gooseberries. "I can't get him out from under. He's all bloodied up."

Fear leapt between us, and awe, and some kind of sordid thrill. And suddenly we were both belting across the space to the kitchen steps.

"Mum! Mum! Come quick! It's Brian Donovan killed."

Disaster cuts through beer-fog as a single note, maddening and high, the kind of sound that breaks glass. It careened inside Mr. Donovan's skull, I suppose, and he reached for the fastest relief. He struck and struck and struck. Michael Donovan took the blows on the face and chest and shoulders, yelling, "Dad, Dad, I couldn't stop him. I couldn't help it." A shambling progress was made, a violent blubbering whirlwind of arms and legs, down the steps and into the night where Brian bled.

I stood under the mango tree and listened till the thumping and yelling faded. I knew it would be years and years before Michael Donovan and I would look each other in the eyes again—if ever. Something else I knew too: it was not the blows Michael minded, but the fact that I saw. I thought he might never forgive me for that.

I went down the old track past the banyan trees and silky oaks, swinging down the dangling roots, all the way down to the Curtain Fig and the bone man. The bone man was getting smaller and smaller, and some of his parts were missing, his white geometry in disarray. Pilfering possums, dogs perhaps, other children? He seemed to be disappearing line by bleached line—though he hid quietly under dead leaves and ferns that uncurled themselves like the fingers of a baby.

Are there any good fathers? I asked him.

They come good and bad, he said, and everything in between.

Make me a father, I said. A good one. And tell him to me. And this was the bone man's tale, but it's my tale too. I was always inventing fathers.

Once upon a time, in the Northern Hemisphere, there lived a king who had three sons—well, no, not three sons, because the youngest child was a daughter. And behind the king, crouching at the back of his throne, lived a dream, and the dream had the king in its coils. Sleeping and waking, it had him, until he summoned his counselors to his chambers.

I dream of a land that does not exist, he said. I see deserts, but also small steamy pockets of forest. I see cities that cling to the edges of a dead hot heart as froth clings to the sides of my beer mug. The people who live in this dream have the faces of children. They worship the sun; they do not believe that a world exists beyond their shores; they are full of thoughtless cruelties. As flies rub their legs, these people rub the past from themselves. Interpret this dream for me.

And his counselors said: This is the dream of Terra Australis, O King, which is like unto the dream of El Dorado.

And they read unto him from the scrolls of the sea captains and cartographers:

> But, altho' the remote parts of the southern hemisphere remain undiscovered, we have traces from ancient times, warranted by latter experience, of rich and valuable countries in it. . . . It has been commonly alleged, and perhaps not without good reason, from a consideration of the weight of land to water, that a Continent is wanting on the South of the Equator, to counterpoize the land on the North, and to maintain the equilibrium necessary for the earth's motion. . . .

We read, O King, from *An Account of the Discoveries made in the South Pacifick Ocean,* published here in London in this year of our Lord 1767. This dream, O King, they said, has caused much royal insomnia and the loss of many ships.

And the king said: Send in unto me my three children.

And his counselors answered: This is no voyage and no country for women, young or old, O King. Shall we not send only your two sons?

But the king, being a rare and compassionate father, knew that his sons would take care of themselves. It was when he looked into the future for his daughter that his heart contracted, and so to all three of them he offered a riddle and a prize.

Go forth, he said, and seek the kingdom of my dream, which shall go to the finder. And the solver of my riddle will be provided with ships for the voyage.

Here is the riddle, he said: The country of my dream is beautiful and harsh, a man's country according to my counselors and cartographers and geomancers. A man's country, they insist. A place where women will not be wanted, where it is unlikely that they will survive. When Terra Australis is found, therefore, how shall I people it with women?

And his eldest son answered: O Father, you must send into the dreamland maidens of great beauty and tenderness, whose skills in the making and feathering of nests are legendary. Then the men of that country will learn to desire wives and will protect them.

But his second son answered: O Father, you must cause an itch to fall upon the men of that country, an itch for which the dream of a woman is the only cure.

Then the youngest one, his daughter, spoke. You must ensure that the men of that dreamplace continue to despise and ridicule and underestimate the women, she said. Then the women will learn laughter and independence and they will survive.

And the king was well pleased with his daughter's answer and he commissioned a fleet to sail into the dream in the year of our Lord 1787. And he arranged safe passage on a ship called *Supply* for his youngest child, who stepped ashore on the coast of the dream in January 1788, and who was—so the bone man told me, says Charade—the great-great-great-grandmother of my mum, Bea, the Slut of the Tamborine Rainforest.

9. *Nicholas and Verity*

The lace curtains stir, ballooning softly and subsiding, as though the windows are breathing, and Charade asks drowsily, "Who's responsible?"

"Radiators," Koenig says. "Convection currents."

"No. I meant, who chose lace curtains for your bedroom?"

"Oh." Rachel, in a sense, he supposes. He still chooses things with her ghostly presence in mind. "Ah ... Joanna, I guess. My housekeeper."

Charade sighs. "Was this her side? Her pillow?"

He assumes she is not referring to his housekeeper.

Here I am, Charade thinks, lying within the hollow of another woman's life, just as my mum floated in the cavity left by Verity Ashkenazy.

"Verity stalks me," she says. "She and Nicholas Truman, my father, are always there in the middle distance. Before I was born they walked through the rainforest like mirages, dropping crumbs of delirium, and the Tamborine people licked them up and had visions. That's what Michael Donovan told me. Well, not in so many words, but that was the sense of it, and Michael got it from his brother Brian—the one who was paralyzed from the waist down after he smashed up his father's truck. And Brian had got it on another occasion, before the accident, from their father when they were on the town in Brisbane and his dad was drunk as a bandicoot and talking. But Michael Donovan's dad had an axe to grind, so who knows?"

In the loops of silence between sentences, Koenig hears the whisper of Rachel's pen writing and writing her letters. His daughter's voice reproaches him. His son chants with the Moonies.

"Keep talking," he urges Charade. "What did your father look like?"

"In the mornings he was golden, and glowed like Apollo. At least, that's what I like to think. Since I've never seen him, I'm free to invent and I picture him hovering over Verity like a sort of god of the forest. He kept her safe. He gave her mangoes to suck, and she dreamed of him every night. My mother, Bea, and my aunt Kay dreamed of him too. He was one of those men. . . .

"He was like Krishna, you know? On the banks of the Jumna five hundred milkmaids pined for Krishna, and each believed she was his one and only love. Each could prove in voluptuous detail that the night of the last full moon had been spent in his arms—even though they all knew that Radha could tie him up in the coils of her sari.

"My father, Nicholas Truman, had powers like that."

"You're loony," Koenig says. "You're wonderfully crazy."

"Very likely," Charade admits.

But Koenig wonders: Do I put words into her mouth? She has such a flickering look, and he does have ulterior motives.

"No, no," she says. "If anything, it's the other way round."

"What?" Koenig pivots on one elbow, looking down at her. He is certain, quite certain, that he hasn't spoken aloud. Hasn't even finished a thought.

"First I dream up my man, then I track him down, then he has to hear me through. I was born under the sign of the Darting Tongue when the moon was licking at the Southern Cross. So my mother says. If I stop talking, I'll vanish like camphor."

"Ah," he says lightly, "and then where should I look?"

"Looking," she sighs. "I'm an expert in looking, but not in finding. I've never found my father."

"Who resembled Apollo," he says drily.

"Yes. Though even he was struck dumb by Verity, and I can be specific about her. Well, loosely specific. There's a painting."

"A painting?"

"Michael Donovan's dad did it. That's something, isn't it? A garbage and slops collector, a feeder of pigs, who painted. He used the sides of old tea chests and it was not a habit he admitted to; he kept it a deathly dark secret, I can promise you, but Michael found his hoard at the back of their shack and showed me. There were also crude likenesses of my mother in clotted ochres and greens, a Honey Bea deep in the wattles."

"And Verity," Koenig prompts. "What did she look like?"

"She was tall and pale gold with brown eyes and long, long hair, which she wore hanging loose to the waist. It was black and thick as a tree fern's roots. I'll tell you the tale of Nicholas and Verity that Michael Donovan's dad told to Brian, his older son."

And her voice slid
         over the waterfall
                  at the back of the Donovan shack

and down down down to the *basso* pool at the very bottom of the beer-and-phlegm throat of Michael Donovan's dad,

who says, "There's some women just waiting to be bruised. Don't ask me how or why they got that way, but they give off something, you know? They got big dark eyes, set deep, asking to be made to cry—though they don't, they won't cry, these women. They just get silent. They bruise. That Verity woman—the Ashcan, Bea used to call her—she was one of those."

Mick Donovan could have sworn, so he tells his son, that she had a streak of abo in her, that she stepped out of the Dreamtime, a ghost lubra with her hair black as sin and that golden body begging to be manhandled and eyes that could set a man to howling like a dingo, except she wasn't even born in Australia. She was from somewhere else. "An Eye-tie, maybe," he says. "Some kind of wop. Foreign anyway. I dunno where she was from, but wherever it was she shouldn't have left there. Talked with a plum in her mouth."

He runs his tongue over his lips, licking at the beer mist on his stubble, and his son Brian looks away and winks at a cream-and-molasses barmaid.

"And so did that Nicholas bloke who followed her around, so did he. Talk about plum in the mouth! He musta swallowed a fruit shop, an entire greengrocery," says Mick Donovan with sudden violence. "Bloody Pommy, bloody fraud. His Christly voice come out his mouth wearing corsets and crocheted knickers."

Brian says: "Keep yer shirt on, Dad. The bloke's been gone for donkey's years."

"I only met the blighter once," growls Mick Donovan, "and that was one time too many. He walks into McGillivray's Pub on the 26th of January, 1963, not a day I'm likely to forget, the day Bea Ryan turned twenty-one."

Brian laughs. "Australia Day? Ma Antsy-Pants Ryan born on Oz Day? Pull the other one, Dad."

Mick Donovan swipes his son across the cheek, Brian lurches, knocks over his chair, a bystander thumps Mick hard on the back saying, "Watch it, mate!" and Brian raises his fists at the bystander: "Keep yer bloody hands off my dad."

Mick says: "If I ever hear you talk that way about Bea Ryan again, I'll knock yer socks off."

He drains his glass and calls for two more and gooses the barmaid when she comes.

"I reckon every man jack of us wanted Bea," he says, "and the whole of the Tamborine Mountain was gonna dance at her party that night. I dunno what it was about Bea. She already had a kid by then, Sid Andrews' son, and Sid had buggered off to God knows where. But she still drove us crazier than any six virgins.

"So this party is planned and I have to take Maureen—God rest yer mother's soul. Maureen—and every other sheila on the

Mountain—watches Bea as though Bea is a snake. But twenty-one is twenty-one, and the whole world is gonna drink at this shindig.

"Well, it's January and ninety-six in the shade, and we—the blokes, I mean—are gathering at McGillivray's to wet the whistle before the party starts. We're on the veranda, see, and maybe some of us on the steps, and some others, yeah, I reckon some others are under the trees. There's a sun like a flamin' communion wafer hangin' right against the roof of Wentworth's, 'struth, I thought it'd set his sign on fire, like a bloody spitball of flame it was, just waiting for the half-dark to gobble it. And you can already see the moon standing by, thin as a piece of shell. We're talking women; we're talking horses; we're talking bets. Bill Stolley, the old fool, has just lost his shirt at yesterday's races and is cadging drinks.

"Then this weird thing happens. Seems like every scrub turkey on the mountain hears someone at McGillivray's call its name. Dozens of them, scores of them, maybe hundreds, cackling and scratching, colliding at the veranda rails, dropping feathers and worse in our beer. Holy shit, it was weird. I heard of it happening two or three other occasions, only when the sun and the moon are changing places in that space between Wentworth's roof and the big blue gum outside of McGillivray's."

"Dad," says Brian, "this tale gets taller with every drink."

"And out of the moon," says Mick Donovan, "walking in between the birds like—I dunno, like gods or something—comes these two strangers. Jacky Dobson—he's part aboriginal—he swears he saw them covered with feathers and carrying nets, butterfly nets, bird-catcher nets, people nets. He starts trembling like he's got the DTs. 'Hey, mate,' someone says to him, 'lay off the metho, eh?' And Jacky covers his face with his hands and calls out: 'Watch out for their nets. If their nets come down, you're done for.'

"Those two can hear Jacky, o' course. They stare at him, and then the bloke speaks.

" 'We didn't mean to alarm anybody,' he says in this fancy-pantsy voice. 'We're looking for Bea Ryan. We're friends of Bea's.'

"And pigs can fly, says I. The whole damn pub is cracking up. We can just see Bea sucking on her words to get them all shipshape, plum juice dribbling out of her mouth. We can just see Bea having friends like these.

" 'We've driven up from Brisbane. We have an invitation,' the bloke says in his Pommy voice. He's waving this bit of paper. 'But I'm afraid it's not very specific about directions. Does anyone here know where Bea lives?'

"Someone says: 'Every man and his dog knows where Bea lives. Just follow your own divining rod. Beg pardon, ma'am,' —because the sheila with the big dark eyes has turned to look at him, and we don't use language in front of women. So there's shuffling, like, and a bit o' coughing and spitting, and someone else says: 'She'll be right, mate. She's on her way if you'll hang on a tick. You're *at* the party.'

"But this bloke acts like he don't even know that a voice like his will get him into trouble. 'Perhaps I'll just go out to meet her,' he says, 'if you could point me in the right direction.'

"And someone does, see. Point, I mean. And the bloke whispers somethin' to his sheila, and next thing, pouf! he leaves her there on the veranda, leaning right on the doorway of the bar. I watch him moving down between the sun and the moon in that space between McGillivray's and the blue gum.

"Well, this is weird, you know, and everyone looks at everyone else with his eyebrows touching the top of his bloomin' skull. I mean, the shadow of a sheila on a bar, it's bad luck. It ain't legal; it ain't natural. Unless she's a barmaid—that's different.

"Well, his sheila just shades her eyes and stares after her bloke till he disappears, then she turns and looks at us. She's leaning against the door frame, one foot on the veranda and one in the bar, and then she speaks. It's one o' them plummy voices, but low and sexy, like Marlene Dietrich, you know? And we all suck in our stomachs and take our feet off the veranda rails and watch her.

" 'I wonder,' she says, 'if it would be possible to have a glass of iced pomegranate juice?' "

"Aw, c'mon, Dad," Brian laughs. "Give us a break. *Pomegranate juice.*"

"Swear to God," Mick Donovan says. "Bloody oath. Well. It's like we're all in a dream. It's like everyone's moving in his sleep.

Pomegranate juice? She might as well've asked us for possum milk. Or for that dingo blood that some blokes swear they've seen Jacky Dobson get into, in that cave behind the Springbrook Falls.

"The sun's been swallowed up whole by this, and the moon is on her, on the sheila I mean, and not a man jack of us breathes. Right then, I'll admit it to ya, Brian, even the thought of Bea went clear out of my head, I couldn't think of nothing at all, but I reckon I woulda killed, right then, to know what a pomegranate looks like and find it and milk it and bring it to that long-haired sheila. Turns out she means a grenadilla, but we don't know that till later.

"We're all watching and no one moves.

"Then Jacky Dobson starts in murmuring and chanting and swaying. He's got two fingers out like snake fangs, warding her off, and he's saying: *Watch out for her net, watch out for her net, or we're goners.*

"Maybe it's Jacky that throws her, or maybe just the staring, or maybe we're just all dreaming and the dream turns bad. She puts her hands up in front of her as though she's expecting to be hit, and her eyes get enormous, black as the pit. There's two things I realize I want to do, about equal amounts: One is to have a mouthful of whatever-the-hell-is-pomegranate and to kiss it drip by drip down inside her; and the other is to hurt her, I dunno why. But that's what I say: There's some sheilas born begging for trouble—don't ask me why.

"I know one thing. It feels like I got a live coal fizzing between my legs. It feels like she's pulling me at her on strings—I can't help meself. I got me arms out in front of me, but buggered if I know what I'm going to do when I touch her.

"I figure me hands are an inch from her body—enough to feel the electric shocks coming off it—when she starts shaking. Shaking bad, like an earthquake has her. And she backs away, backwards across the veranda and down the steps and along the path, stumbling backwards, and shaking, and never taking her eyes off all of us, off me in particular. Her eyes have grown bigger than her face; they're like black caves. They're holes to nowhere. Me, I'm paralyzed, standing there like a bloody idiot with my arms stuck out like a scarecrow. Funny thing, she's not noisy, not that sort of hysterical. She's quiet as death, but it feels like sirens are dinging in me ears, and she sure smells crazy to us.

"It's like tasting blood—it does something. We are sniffing at her fear; you can feel us getting madder and madder for having wanted her, a woman like that. Maybe we would've started to chase her, I dunno, if Bea hadn't appeared right then, with the Pommy bloke.

"Bea goes crazy. Like a bloody Tasmanian devil she is. Jesus, I thought she'd have my balls in one bite. Bea is cursing her bloody head off—I'm telling ya, that woman can give a tongue-lashing that'd make a bullocky's hair stand on end.

"But I'm watching the sheila and she is standing there shuddering, rigid, like five hundred volts has zapped her. She turns around towards Bea and the Pommy and gives this little cry that gets stuck in her throat and then she starts to crumple like a tablecloth falling off of a table. The bloke catches her, kinda swallows her up in his arms, kinda combs her hair with his Pommy-pale fingers, and Bea stands there with her hands on her hips and looks daggers at us and pitches in with some brimstone heated up specially for us.

"But what I see, Brian, is the way she is watching the bloke as he strokes the Ashcan woman. That's when I know. I know she wants him bad and I know he's been fingering her. I reckon that is the night young Charade got made in a hurry, which explains that wild little she-tiger what young Michael can't keep his eyes off of. All I know is, I pissed off and went shearing for a year right after that bloody party, and when I come back there's Bea with another nipper.

"They musta gone at it like dogs, I reckon, Bea and that Pom, the fancy shithead, which is the real reason, if you want my opinion, for why Bea is so flaming mad. It's because of the way he's touching that other sheila. Bea's mad as a hornet, except that she turns it on us. 'You bloody dickheads,' she spits at us. 'You bloody uncivilized drongos! I asked them to come, and you better bloody make them welcome.'

"Then the Nicholas bloke looks up at us through the Ashcan woman's hair. 'My apologies, chaps,' he says, in his sick-making

Pommy voice. 'I'm sure no harm was intended. If I explain that . . . well, later, perhaps.'

"And he does 'is explaining later, deep in the bar, men only and everyone blotto. 'When she was six,' he says, 'her parents were dragged off to the camps. She never saw them again. It does things, I'm sure you understand. Allowances have to be made.'

" ' 'Struth!' Billy Stolley says to me. 'I don't know about no camps, but that bloke is a pain in the arse.'

"And I drink to that then, and I drink to that now.

"But I tell ya, Brian, I still have dreams about that woman. About what I might have done if I ever got close enough to touch her. I dunno about those camps, damned if I know what they got to do with anything. But I'm telling ya, son, that woman was strange. Like I say, some sheilas born asking to be bruised.

"And Jacky Dobson was right. She got me, her net come down, and I'm a goner."

10. *Photographs*

Sometimes, Charade says, I think of the droplets of stopped time in photographs, oceans and oceans of it, in all the albums and wallets and drawers and attics of the world. Lies, all lies.

Because the camera falsifies everything, doesn't Koenig agree? There's the picking and choosing, the arbitrary framing, the whole dishonest bag of photographers' tricks, that's for starters; and then there's the self-consciousness of the photographee—even, or maybe especially, in the candid shot.

Do we look like that? she asks him—you know, startled, sheep-ish, *dramatic*—when no one is watching? It's all a sort of untruth, a composed—or discomposed—artifice.

What's interesting about a photograph, she says, is what isn't in the picture. She is looking at his children in their silver filigree frame.

"For instance . . . Is this Sara and Joey?"

"Ah . . . no. That's Alison and Jonathan, when they were little. Sara and Joey are my housekeeper's children."

Charade digests this information. "No second family then?" she asks.

"No."

"You and your second wife never . . . ?"

"There's no second wife."

"Oh," she says, surprised, looking about, as though for ghosts. "It's odd. I've had the feeling . . . They still seem to be around. I somehow thought there was a more recent breakup."

She studies the photograph again. He is afraid of what it might reveal.

"Isn't it ironic," she says, "the way the future isn't shown, even though it's buzzing in front of their eyes?"

She sees the way havoc, which is just beyond the reach of their soft pink fingertips, has been screened out. Alison was leaning toward it; you could see that tomorrow made horrible leering faces in her dreams. But she was being brave about it. This was a photograph of Alison being brave because she was perfectly well aware—poor little stoic—that her parents did not want gargoyles showing up in the family album. You had to look off-camera, to the left of the frame there, to see her fears flapping their batwings.

And could Jonathan, Koenig wonders queasily, see the Reverend Moon waiting in the future with open arms?

"Was it you or their mother," Charade asks, "who told them to look at the camera?"

Koenig says irritably: "I remember that day. At my mother-in-law's house in Toronto. We were happy. It was a good day. All of us were happy."

Charade sets the silver frame back on the dresser.

"Someone took a photograph," she says, "of that party when my mum turned twenty-one." She goes to the window and stares out into the night. "Sometimes the emptiness around the edges of a photograph gets to me," she says. "Winds me a little."

She is still and silent for so long that he feels uneasy. "Shall I pour our brandies now?" he asks, but she does not stir.

He lobs another suggestion into the silence: "Tea?"

He stands behind her and strokes her hair. "It makes me nervous when you're so quiet."

"What?" Charade turns backs to the room. "It must have been a Tuesday," she says, "when my mother worked as a barmaid at McGillivray's. Or else it was a Thursday, when she did the washing for Wentworth's. I was rummaging in the cupboard in her bedroom—looking for a book, actually, one she'd taken from me because I . . . And I found the shoebox. *Stuffed,* absolutely stuffed with photographs, crammed with them, black-and-white, brown-and-cream, no colored ones—they were all from earlier than that. Rotting away, some of them, dog-eared . . . some of them sort of *smashed-looking*—thousands of tiny cracks across the surface. They came spilling out over the floor, whisper whisper, full of secrets . . ."

Shivers went through her. This was backstairs stuff, subversive—she could smell it. She riffled through pictures of women in taffeta skirts and high buttoned boots, generations of babies, bearded men standing beside their drays and looking stern and sad. Then she saw what mattered, a group of people gathered on the steps of McGillivray's, her mother in the middle, young and luminous as twenty-one years; and off to one side, not looking at the camera but at each other, two faces in profile, and right away she knew: her father and the other woman. *Verity Ashkenazy,* she thought. She hid it and read it every day for weeks. She used to stick it down the front of her shirt and climb the mango tree and sit and stare.

Every morning a different history came off it like fog and she took deep breaths, gulping down one past after another.

This was one version.

Cyclone Anna is drumming on the iron roof of the shack and it seems as if half of Mount Tamborine is dissolving and churning and frothing its way down into the Pacific Ocean. Inside the cavern of sound, Bea sleeps. Her lover, Nicholas Truman, sleeps at her side. Their baby, Charade, sleeps between them. Around them the forest drips and slurps and sighs; the rain thunders.

Something screeches—a scrub turkey, or a larger creature, malevolent—and Bea starts awake. At the window she sees the face that is always there. It is pale, pale as a ghost gum, with enormous deep-set dark eyes and long black hair that streams into the rain and the trees. There is no body. Just a head floating on ribbons of lightning and rain.

Bea is not afraid. There is nothing beneath the sun or the moon, nothing that comes on the wings of a cyclone, that can frighten Bea. She pads barefooted to the window and throws open the casement.

"What do you want?" she asks.

Verity says nothing at all, just holds out her pleading arms and makes rain with her eyes, fierce rain that batters through the gullies of Bea's thought.

"You're not getting Nicholas," Bea says. "You were killing him. You were sucking him dry. He was exhausted."

The wind howls through Verity's mouth. The lightning spits. "I have nothing, nothing, nothing," she moans.

"Rubbish!" Bea shouts. "You have every man you meet turning sick with want. You make them dream about you; you want them groveling. *Want, but don't touch!* That's what you tell them. You've got money, you've got brains, you've got this fragile bruised look which I personally find pathetic, which makes me sick, if you want to know the truth, but which seems to drive most people crazy. You've got this goddam gold-embroidered tragic bloody history that you want us all to pay for, pay for, pay for!"

She slams the window shut and climbs back into bed. She props herself on her pillow and watches her baby and her lover, who is tossing in his sleep. At the window Verity is licking her lips and drinking rain.

Nicholas grows paler and paler, colder.

In the morning when Bea wakes he has all but disappeared, all but the hand that is resting between her thighs. Before she can squeeze her legs together it has fallen away. She watches it, pale and slick and blue-veined, slither wetly between the sheets.

She got him, Bea growls on thunderstorm nights. That bitch at the window got him. She swallowed him up.

This was another version:

Cyclone Anna is drumming on the iron roof of the shack and it seems as if half of Mount Tamborine is dissolving and churning and frothing its way down into the Pacific Ocean. Inside the cavern of sound, Nicholas sleeps. His lover, Bea Ryan, the Slut of the Tamborine Rainforest, sleeps at his side. Around them the forest drips and slurps and sighs; the rain thunders.

Nicholas dreams of England, of boarding school, of the richly embroidered past.

In his dream he is walking in the grounds of the grammar school in Eastbourne. Sounds of silverware and afternoon tea chime softly in the air behind; there is a soft smell of libraries and books. And then bam! he is falling down the rabbit hole of his life, falling, falling, falling, and climbing out in a pocket of wet forest on the underside of the world. He is in bed with a woman who is as full of heat as the sun, a warm and slatternly woman, a total stranger.

Bea, he says to himself. Bea. Just Bea. Just be.

Out in the rainforest, from up in the tangle of tree ferns, the will-o'-the-wisp calls again. At first he sees only a piece of phosphorescence, bluish fire licking a tree trunk, a radioactive orchid. Then there is the pale gold face emitting light, and the eyes that are the absence of light (pure pure darkness) and the naked glowing body. Help me, she whispers. Help me. And he goes to meet her with open arms.

She shines against the treetops; the cyclonic rain fizzes and hisses around her; she cannot be reached. He climbs. Steam rises off him. He is mad with desire, wet through. Help me, she says, I can't get free.

What *is* this? he asks, hacking, wrenching, untangling, pulling, cutting. He can't tell her hair from the creepers; there are miles of growth, a rainforest full. It goes back and back to the edge of the forest, the beginning of time. My God, he says, what *is* this?

It's my *past,* she sobs. I can't get free.

She is being pulled away from him by the hair; she gasps with pain. First her golden hips slide away through his arms, then her thighs.

I won't let you go, he vows. I won't.

Already her voice is an echo, fainter than bellbirds: You'll have to come with me, with me, with me.

But what about Bea? he calls. I can't just leave Bea. . . .

You could leave a baby behind, that's fair. That's fair, that's fair, that's fair, the echoes call.

Then Nicholas sees his daughter, the changeling child in the tree ferns, the starling, the glowling, caught in the tangle of creepers.

Yes, he agrees, that's fair.

What kind of charade is this? asks Bea in amazement, staring at the space where Nicholas was, where the baby is.

That is Charade's favorite version of the origin of herself, immaculate confection and changeling extraordinaire, bluestocking, semi-orphan, second brat of the Slut of the Rainforest; but she has others, one for each day of the week, one for matins and one for evensong, one for before exams and one for the long summer holidays that stretch across December and January, one for cyclone weather, one to tell the bone man down by the curtain fig when the sun is hotter than the black stump that is back of beyond in Alice Springs.

And she has Bea's version, which came briefly and abruptly, one day when Charade was in an experimental mood and the suspense was too much for her to handle.

This was what she did. She hid the photograph in amongst the peas in the chipped enamel basin. Bea sat on the front steps with a colander between her spread knees; Charade hid under the veranda, waiting. *Pock, pock:* there was the soft sound of the peas being burst open and stripped, then the muted clatter of green pellets hitting the dish. *Pock, pock, clatter; pock, pock, clatter; pock, pock, clatter.*

Suddenly: silence.

Charade, crouching in cobwebs and dust in the crawl space, held herself perfectly still, her eyes on her mother's face. Ten seconds, twenty seconds. Charade's muscles screamed. Bea stared into the basin of unshelled peas.

There was nothing on Bea's face that Charade could read: not shock, not grief, not anger. Just stillness, like someone waiting for a daydream to lift.

Thirty seconds.

Charade's knees were tucked up under her chin. She thought that she might never be able to unlock her legs; she could feel pain like needles along her calves and behind her knees. She kept her eyes on her mother's face.

"Charade," Bea said. "Come on out of there."

A bluff, Charade told herself, and did not move.

"What is it you want to know?" Bea asked.

Everything, Charade thought. *Everything*.

"A photograph," Bea said, "is no more use than a snakeskin after the snake has crawled out."

"But is it my father and Verity Ashkenazy?" demanded Charade, crawling out from the dust.

"Them two kids?" Bea shrugged. "Yes and no. It doesn't have his smell, her smell; it doesn't tell you anything at all." She began to laugh. She stood up on the steps and held the colander of peas high over her head. "We were all mad," she said. "He was mad, she was mad, Kay was mad, and I was mad. We were all completely bonkers." She laughed again and whirled the colander like a discus and sent it flying across dusty gerberas and hibiscus clumps into the passionfruit vine. The peas trailed it like a dotted green line.

11. On Bea-Particles and the Relativity of Scone Making

"When you disappear," Charade asks Koenig, "where do you go?"

"Oh, here and there," he says vaguely. "Conferences."

"Six nights. You were gone six nights without a word."

He frowns. Hadn't he told her? Perhaps not. When the compulsion strikes, he simply goes. "It was reading week," he says, as though this explained everything.

"You go to Toronto, don't you?"

He doesn't answer.

"You see," she says, "I understand about that. The way you worry about your ex-wife. It's the way Nicholas was about Verity. Do you see your son and daughter too?"

"Not my son," he says, the knife turning inside.

"Sometimes," Charade says dreamily, "I pretend Nicholas does that too. That he, you know, keeps tabs on me. Sometimes I feel absolutely certain that he's walking just behind me and that if I turned suddenly . . . but of course I don't turn, because that wouldn't be fair."

A long silence drifts across them. They fall asleep in each other's arms. Koenig dreams he is at La Guardia Airport and his son is just ahead of him, turning a corner. Koenig quickens his step; he breaks into a run. Charade dreams that someone is about to tap her on the shoulder. They both cry out, waking, reaching for each other.

"Say something," Koenig says urgently. "Tell me another story. Tell me about your mother."

"All right," Charade says. "I was always trying to make her talk about Nicholas and Verity, but I had to trick her. I had to get to them via Aunt Kay. I had to . . .

"Kay and me," Bea says. "We were peas in a pod to start with, and then we were chalk and cheese. Never figured each other out and couldn't do a thing apart. Then one day we just didn't have anything in common. Well, those two came between us—that's what did it. That was the beginning of the end."

"What two?"

Bea is rolling scone dough; her wrists flip and snap. Ritual is important: the forward roll, vehement, involving shoulders; the pause, the lift, the backward arc; and the dough fanning out like a floodplain from the confluence of Bea's thighs and the table.

"What two?" Charade persists.

Bea frowns, pulls in all the dimples and valleys of Bea-flesh for an instant, tightens some knot of muscle-nerve-sinew in the top of her head.

"What two?"

"Your father and that Ashkenazy woman."

"See . . ." Absent-mindedly Charade trails her fingers down Koenig's body. "A moment like that, it felt like D-Day. If I could just make her *say* it. It felt like chipping away at some great . . . some vast mountain of rubble."

Your father and that Ashkenazy woman. Tap, tap: they were inside there somewhere, under the rubble, still faintly alive, still sending out signals, still waiting to be dug out.

"Seems like I spent half my childhood thinking up ways to catch Mum out. I used to keep score; I used to . . . I would ask her about Aunt Kay—it was bait, it was my decoy, because all the stories led back to Nicholas and to Verity Ashkenazy. And so Aunt Kay . . . but how can I explain Aunt Kay?"

"Isn't this where we came in?"

"What?"

Koenig closes his eyes. In the beginning was the hologram, then the girl in his bedroom and . . . "Something about your Aunt Kay—that's where you began. Katherine to me, you said. It seems ages, weeks, since you mentioned her."

"Yes, well." She frowns. "You're the one who's been away."

Something has been evoked that bothers her. She seems to remember a need for caution. She slides away from his arms and huddles in his armchair again.

"Aunt Kay . . ." she says, and he has to wait out another lengthy silence. If he moves when she is in these suspended states, she may take fright and leave. He waits.

"What I'm doing here, you know," she says, "is stalling . . . hanging on to you as though . . . and talking, talking . . . Of course, I'll have to go back eventually—"

"Go back?" He has a sudden queasy fantasy of a green twister sucking her into mathematical blips, and then darkness. Loss swamps him and he half stumbles across the room and draws her against himself, tongue and hands convulsive, geographies interlocking. "Ahh, thank God, you're so . . ." His mouth closes hungrily over hers. Not an abstract flavor, not a hint of the dry burn of mathematics or theory, which are, no question about it, acquired tastes. *Matter,* he thinks with enormous relief. Sweet vulgar heavy Newtonian mass. *Substance.*

"What's wrong? What's the matter?"

"Oh, nothing," he says, relaxing a little, but holding her so that her lips are against the crook of his neck, her cheek on his shoulder. "I just had a silly . . . a fleeting nightmare." He strokes her hair. "It's nothing." The irony of this strikes him and he laughs. "Or rather, it's *not* nothing. Luckily. It's matter."

"Ah," she says. "Matter. One of our most persistent illusions, so you told me. Koenig . . . ?"

"Mmm?"

"These . . . these *nights* . . . We're just, you know it's only . . ."

"Yes, yes." He doesn't want to know what it is.

"Eventually I'll have to go home. I'm just stalling, you know, staving off the . . . The truth is, I can't bear to think I've checked out the last clue and not found him. Nicholas, I mean. My father. That's why in Toronto I was afraid—"

"Afraid in Toronto." He laughs a little, letting her glide out of his arms and hunch up in his chair again. Images come to him: of swept curbs and decorum, of tea and buttery shortbread, of clean subways, safe streets, tacit curfews.

"Aunt Kay . . . Katherine . . . lives outside of Toronto. Sort of nowhere, really, in the middle of woods and on a lake. But she was in Toronto when she saw Nicholas again. Or thought she saw."

"Saw your father?"

"Well, thought she saw . . ." He watches an uneasy laugh pulse up like alpha rays. "With Aunt Kay it's difficult to . . . Now I know what it's like, for her and Mum." Getting uneasy at certain names. Picking a path through memories that might blow up in the face. "I used to watch how Mum . . ."

She used to watch, she watched, she was watching,
    past tense imperfect,
        she was watching the curvature of time.

It's now, Charade, and then; it's only now and then; sing a song of Einstein, a perfect circle full of time. She watches, she does watch, she is watching . . .

Charade watches everything: the way Siddie, her older brother, stiffens at certain birdcalls, the ones that come McGillivray-throated, rising from the lips of the publican's daughter; the way spittle hangs in bright stalactites on the slack chin of Em, sweet Em, the vacant third-born, her younger sister; the way Michael Donovan rubs one bare foot against the other, flylike, when he comes for his dad. But most of all, she studies her mother. What fascinates her is this: There are three strings that can pull her mother's easy body to sudden tautness.

They are making scones together, Charade and Bea, scones that will swell thickly and stickily into the little pinched stomachs of the Bea-lings, that happy-go-lucky multi-fathered Ryan tribe. Bea makes the plain and solid kind of scone: flour and lard, a few raisins, a pinch of soda, a half-cup of milk. Flour dusts her arms, her hair, and hangs above her, shot through with the morning sun. Em, threading buttons to keep the littlest ones amused, laughs with excitement to see the way gold rides through the room on white scone-smoke.

Charade plumps dough into a square for cutting and says carefully: "Are these as good as the scones Aunt Kay's grandma used to make?"

And there it is: a quick tightening of Bea's fingers on the ends of the rolling pin; a ripple that crosses her cheekbones and moves on down through the beads of sweat on her breasts where they rise like oven-ready dough from her shift. It crosses her large and languid thighs and buttocks so that they suck themselves in and shiver slightly—the way horses' flanks do to shake off flies. Charade watches the calf muscles hum like telegraph wires, the toes clench in their worn sandals, the current moving on to the floor, where she sees it dispersing itself in points of light across the cheap linoleum.

"What would you know," grumbles Bea, "about Grandma Llewellyn's scones?"

"You told me." Charade's innocent eyes go wide. "You said they were the best ever made in Australia."

"Well, so they were." Bea crosses herself with a floury hand. Bits of religion cling to Bea here and there like fluff from a patchwork quilt.

"Wrong way, Mum."

"What?"

"You did it wrong. It's this way, see, forehead to belly button, left to right." She ducks from a floury slap. "Why do you always do that when you talk about Aunt Kay's grandma?"

"Because." Bea thumps away at the dough.

"Because why?"

"Because she was grandma to everyone, me included, God rest 'er soul. Nobody that knew her didn't love her."

79

"And you and Kay?"

"Me and Kay, back then, we were like two peas in a pod. Seven years, eight was it? we were sisters in the selfsame house." She sighs and looks into the middle distance. "But Kay," she says, "she was a gallivanter, right from the start. And me, I'm happy stuck in mud. Always gallivanting round, Kay was, round the countryside, round the world. She could be in Timbuktu now. Prob'ly is, for all I know."

"Why'd she gallivant around?"

"I dunno. Started, I reckon, when her family lit out for Brisbane. Nah. Before that, when we were kids in Melbourne. That was before we were sisters; we were just kids who lived near the Ringwood Station. Let's hide on a train, she'd say. Let's go to the Dandenongs. We thought the Dandenongs were the edge of the world. Nah, I'd say, let's play in the paddock and roll in the buttercup patch.

"Back then," Bea laughs, "I was boss. I was older. What I said went." She laughs again. "We were both born the same year, me in January, her in November, but I've always been years and years older."

She wipes the back of a floury arm across her face, breathes deep. "Funny thing, I think about Kay, I always smell grass and the buttercups.

"Melbourne," she says. "I reckon that's mostly what I remember. The railway line and Ringwood Station and the paddock behind our two houses and the buttercup patch." She squeezes her eyes tight shut, concentrates. "And the war and black paint on the windows and no fathers but all those other men, Yanks, hanging round watching the girls, and some of them feeling up the little ones, 'specially me. And then after the war . . .

"I remember the year Kay wasn't there, before they sent for me, after they'd gone to Brisbane. Seems like me dad coughed all year, that whole year, coughed his guts up. This stuff, this *phlegm*, would come up. That's the war, he'd say. I'm getting it out of my system. In the end I had to wash him and all—he hated that—and hold a bottle, you know, for his pee.

"It's funny, can't remember when my mum shot through. Can't even remember my mum. Everyone said she was a bad one, a floozy, I reckon I took after her. I reckon I would've liked her. Well, my dad was a TPI after the war—he didn't last long. Got his TPI badge somewhere; I'll give that to you, Charade, when I'm gone. My dad was one of the Rats of Tobruk, got that badge somewhere too. He was a hero. But his lungs gave out or something. He coughed himself away.

"Kay's mum and dad came down from Brisbane for the funeral and took me back. We weren't any kind of relation but I reckon they felt they ought to, or maybe Kay missed me. And yeah, Grandma Llewellyn, she stayed on in Melbourne. I reckon she would've taken me in but they thought she was too old to cope. With me, I mean. I was what people called a handful." She shrugs. "Or maybe Kay asked them, I don't know.

"But I reckon I got a bit of my mum's blood in my veins, Charade. A bad lot, people said about her, and about me too. So what? I said. I was always going off in the bush with boys, running away. 'Struth, what can you do if it's in your blood? Took them a long time to give up on me, though. They couldn't help themselves when souls were around to be saved—it was an itch they had, the way other blokes go for beer. They were Holy Rollers. Don't get that wrong—they were okay and I reckon I loved them. But all that praying and stuff, it didn't agree with my constitution. I'm not cut out for it, like. You know, there was a magnet inside me or something, and something *pulling*. It was like there was this thing inside me always knew I had to go bush and have men and kids, lots of both. I reckon I've had a good life, Charade.

"But Kay. Blimey. She must've been born on a Sunday, between the first and second hymn; she had Bible-milk in her highchair. Still, I reckon it didn't agree with her either, in the long run, holy-rolling. Maybe that's why she went gallivanting off. I just ran off to the bush, but she ran off to the world and kept on running.

"Praying. I tell you, they were barmy about it. Start of the day, middle of the day, end of the day. You couldn't sit down to eat or get up from the table or set foot in the door or try to leave without somebody telling you to close your eyes for a word of prayer. There were daily mercies, and traveling mercies and eventide mercies. We prayed for them all; we gave thanks for them all, amen. Mind you, back then, even Kay prayed like mad; even I had a go. We were always dragging God round like a swag on our backs; we always had him tagging along. I reckon Him and me hit it off all right; we came to an understanding. Listen, God, I said to him, you give me a bit more rope, I won't say a word about my dad and the war and all that."

Bea crosses herself, wrong way again. "That's for my dad," she says. "He was a Catholic, not the fancy kind—he never went to church. Grandma Llewellyn used to be one, back when, till the Gospel Hall got her and she switched. Just the same, I saw her cross herself once or twice, when she didn't think anyone was watching."

No one, not one, not anyone watched; not one person was watching on a certain perfect day well remembered by Bea—though it must always be kept in mind that the process of recollection is *imperfect* at best—a certain perfect day that slipped on its axis, spun, lurched, skidded to a fault.

"We were maybe thirteen or fourteen," Bea says.

"Funny thing, I always thought Kay knew *nothing*. I always thought I'd have to watch out for her; I couldn't believe how dumb she was. Like men, for instance. I *always* knew what to do about men; I came out of my mother knowing. I reckon my mother slipped me the know-how in her third or fourth month. Before I even started school, old men down by the railroad tracks would give me sixpence for a cuddle. I used to tell Kay. I could make her eyes go round as two-shilling pieces. I liked to shock her. Little old ladies liked Kay in her little smocked dresses; and little old men liked me. I thought Kay'd turn out simple, she was that naïve.

"There was this day. . . .

"See, I could do things with my eyes—sometimes it took longer than others. What I used to do was toss out lines . . . like philodendrons, sort of, like lawyer cane. I used to spin them out of my eyes like a spider does it: I'd make gold-streaked leaves, and white-streaked ones, and just plain dark green, and they'd go sailing out like feelers and wrap themselves wherever I wanted. I used to sit at my desk and just about cover Mr. Carlyle with my vines. He looked like a moon in the rainforest with that pale Pommy face; he never *could* go brown—you know how it is with Pommies, poor blokes. I s'pose, now I come to think of it, it's on account of him I fell for Nicholas later. He was my dry run, you might say.

"He was my scholarship teacher, Mr. Carlyle, and it took me forever to reel him in. Dunno why I wanted to do it so much—I never could stand Poms with their pasty skin and especially the way they talk. But Mr. Carlyle's talk had gone soft at the edges; I reckon it warmed up, got riper, the way a green mango does, you know, if it lies in the grass long enough. Like bananas when the possums have been at them. I mean, you could tell he was a Pom all right, but he was trying—he didn't sound so poncey anymore. You had to feel sorry that the sun didn't like him and never would.

"Maybe it was because he was my Grade Eight teacher, my *last* teacher, because I knew I'd never pass the scholarship. I knew they'd never let Bea Ryan inside a high school, not that I bloody wanted to. And there was this other thing, Charade. University men, teachers and those types, the men who look inside their own heads all the time like they've got bookshelves in there, it scares them, someone like me. See, I was beautiful back then, Charade, no sense pretending I didn't know it. I could make any ditch digger trip over his pick and give a wolf whistle. So that didn't even count, it was that easy. What I liked though, was the way a bloke like Mr. Carlyle would look and look away quick.

"I dunno, I reckon it didn't seem right to him that someone like me looked the way I used to look. It scared him. Like it would, maybe, when the Queen drove around Brisbane waving from that fancy car without a roof; if she'd stuck out her tongue instead of waving; like that. Mr. Carlyle showed me this painting once, in one of his arty books, of this silly bloody woman with no clothes on and fat little boy angels flying round her. Reminds me of you, Bea, he said. He would've felt better if I was pasted down on that page, I reckon, where I was good and safe. Men like that, there's this big ditch you've got to pull them across before they'll touch you. They're dead scared they're gonna fall into something they'll never get out of.

"Well, I dunno, I reckon it's my bad blood, Charade. I loved to pull them across that ditch. It was maybe my favorite thing.

"So maybe that's what it was with Mr. Carlyle.

"Or maybe it was his eyes, cow's eyes, too big for his face. I guess he missed something back there in England; he used to sit at his table and stare out the window and dream about it, while I wound miles of my philodendron leaves round his neck and yanked him in.

"Or maybe—yeah, that's what it was. It was his hands, his fingernails really. I'd never seen a man with fingernails like that. I mean, *clean*. They were like little white pieces of moon; they were the most beautiful fingernails I'd seen. Up till then, I always thought men's fingernails were black; I thought that was their natural color. I used to close my eyes and think about Mr. Carlyle's hands. I used to imagine them trailing down my face and over my breasts. (I had breasts already by Grade Six. The girls weren't allowed to play with me; their mothers figured it was my bad blood coming out. And the men teachers were scared to look.) So I used to spin miles of leaves; I used to spin tree orchids, long trailers of them, and let them settle round Mr. Carlyle's wrists, and I'd pull and pull.

"Finally, one day, I knew I had him. I knew I could start to reel him in. It was one of those hot wet days when everyone is slithering into sleep and Mr. Carlyle is having trouble with his eyes. His lids feel like lead, I can tell, so I give a little yank on my lines. His eyes are practically closed; he's fighting to keep these two slits from locking shut; he's ordering them to march up and down the desks while we scribble away at some fool bloody test or other. And then it happens. I've just got that second when the eye-slits go by me, so I stretch my cat stretch, and I purr and wait. His eyes go by and come back. I can tell when I've got a catch.

"Lunchtime," Bea says dreamily. "Lunchtime comes. . . ."

Bea cat-stretches and gathers up her exercise book and her pens and stuffs them languidly under her desktop. She knows Mr. Carlyle is watching. She rests her chin in her hands and gazes out the window and thinks of the pearl-white shells at the tips of his fingers. If you held his hand up to the light, she thinks, you could see right through the nails. It is half embarrassing, really; so peculiar, so not-like-ordinary-boys, so *unnatural,* that it makes you desperate with excitement to run your tongue over those fingertips.

To see if they are real, to see if they will stay, to see if you will be the same person after you have licked them one by one. It is as though you have stumbled on an angel, pale and shining as butter, sitting quietly on a bench outside the pub. It is a miracle.

All the stragglers have left the room, even poor mad Ethel with her thick bottle glasses, who has wandered back in twice, pawing through the rummage of her desk for a lost orange. Bea stretches and sighs heavily. Mr. Carlyle sits at his desk, watching her. So many green knots, so many tangles of creeper, so many orchids opening themselves to the heat in the room, that Bea wonders if either of them will be able to move.

At first, when he speaks, she thinks it is the ceiling fan beginning to shake its blades—there's a sluggish rattling sound, low and breathy. She raises her heavy lids, a question.

"What are you?" he asks. "A witch?"

A smile begins in the soles of her feet and spreads and rises. She is a witch, a cat, a mote of sunlight. She does not look back as she leaves the room and drifts downstairs and skirts the rim of the soccer field and walks all the way from Wilston School to halfway home where there's an acre of bush and she disappears into uncut scrub.

She knows he will follow and he does—for part of the way. But there's that ditch, the one that gives him nightmares. And it takes one month, two months, school is over, the Christmas holidays are over, before she finally pulls him across the ditch, because it's Finsbury Park, and Kay is still a little girl who is still at Wilston School, who lives inside Grade 8. On a hot February day, Kay is sitting in a mango tree in Finsbury Park with a book, that's how stupid Kay is. And Bea is not thinking about Kay. Bea has hung around the shop where Mr. Carlyle buys his tobacco, she has leaned on the counter and stretched like a cat, and he has followed her out of the shop all the way to Finsbury Park.

What she feels as he lowers himself onto her is what the magnet feels when iron filings approach. Fistfuls of paspalum and wild couch anchor her; her body bucks at the sun; she is crying out.

And then mayhem. A body hurled, someone pummeling, Kay

yelling: "Bea! Bea! Mr. Carlyle, what are you doing? Oh Bea! Mr. Carlyle! Please stop!"

"Jesus!" Bea screams. "You idiot, Kay! You bloody idiot, you flaming bloody retard!"

Kay is huge-eyed and still with shock. She opens her mouth but is mute.

Oh, and Mr. Carlyle! Bea sees his beautiful bouncing pink dick shrivel up and cringe like a worm. She wants to cry; she wants to scream. She starts to laugh. Great gobs of laughter gust up like smoke rings from her lips. "Oh Kay," she splutters. "Oh Kay, you stupid ninny."

A switch flicks within Kay. She turns and walks away with silent dignity, past the lantana clump, past the stringy-barks, and then she runs. Her footfalls reach them like scattershot.

Mr. Carlyle has his head in his hands. Grief is rising from him like a fog. Bea knows its smell and places a hand on his knee. He flinches violently. "Not *Katherine,*" he says, staring at her with horror. "Of all possible people. Not Katherine, our little scholar, our shining light."

"So then," Bea says, squeezing a roll of scone dough in her palms, "I knew Kay had something I didn't understand. I knew she was stupid, and I knew she wasn't, too. Like you, Charade. There's something in you that scares me—I don't know where it comes from. Well, it comes from Nicholas—he had it, too, but it's different in a woman. It's like a man with white fingernails; it's not something I understand."

"Did my father have white fingernails?" Charade asks, breathless.

"Yeah," Bea snaps. "And white fingernails are pretty bloody useless when it comes time to chop wood or feed chooks or make scones." And she slams the oven door shut, the subject closed—though Charade sees she is smiling and biting on her lips. Charade expects her laughter to rise like scone dough.

"You know," Charade tells Koenig. "I've thought and thought, and I don't understand where one life ends and another begins. I don't understand time at all. When I found Aunt Kay (she was lost, you know, for more than twenty years; Mum didn't know where she was), when I found the house outside Toronto and rang her doorbell and she opened it and stared at me that way she has . . . she looked, actually, as though she had gone into shock . . . do you know what I thought?

"Do you know what thought came whole into my head, and almost jumped out of my lips?

"I nearly said: 'Kay, it's just Mr. Carlyle and me, you stupid ninny.'"

12. On Obsession and the Uncertainty Principle

"It's dark," Charade says nervously. "Where are we?" She gropes across runnels of blanket ... not blanket, it seems; something softer, cushiony, something that limits. She feels for his pillow but cannot reach it. "I can't move. I feel cramped. Where are you?"

"Here," Koenig says. "Here. You shouldn't have come—I'm working. But I'm glad you did."

"I can't seem to move." She is fingering a ridge that runs down her left side: a seam? a zipper? the inside edge of a dream? She is feeling for clues, not panicky yet, breathing deeply, in, two, three, and out, two, three. "I can't see a thing. Where are you?"

"Here."

"I can't move." I'm pre-moth, she thinks. Larval. Her arms feel useless as unborn wings. A thought presents itself: This could be a dream of death, or death itself, the last prescient moment. She takes a frantic gulp of air, cries out, thrashes at the sides of her cocoon.

"Shh," he whispers. "Shh. We'll have the janitors rushing in."

"I can't move!"

"Keep still." He gropes for her mouth, puts his hand over it, gently. "I can't find the zipper," he whispers. "Wait. I think— Got it."

The sleeping bag shucks itself off. Charade lifts her arms and holds him. "Where are we?"

"Building 6. My office. You don't remember? I keep the sleeping bag here for all-nighters. I lose track when I'm working on something. I'm glad you found it. Did you get some sleep?"

Charade shakes her head, squeezes her eyes shut and rubs them. "I felt so desolate," she says, remembering, "when you weren't at the apartment." She sees only darkness on darkness, black lines branching like an intricate subway system, spectral capillaries. She cannot remember how she got here.

"I'm glad you managed to get in." Nevertheless he is puzzled.

She says, bemused: "I've never been able to find my way around MIT."

"You certainly startled me," he says.

"You work in the dark?"

"No. I must have dozed off. The janitor must have turned out the light."

"It's odd," Charade says, "but now that my eyes are adjusting, I feel as though we've spent the night here before. But we haven't, have we? Isn't this the first time?"

"You're very forgetful," he says. "You're a bit weird like that. Sometimes you make me wonder whether you even . . . Of course we've done it before; we've often done it. But you startle me every time. I can never figure out how you get in."

"Well . . ." she says, making an effort to remember. "It's so far back, that first time I met you, that I can't quite . . ."

"I know. I've been trying to pin down when that was. I can't remember not knowing you. It was before March break, wasn't it? Before reading week even."

Charade laughs. "Before reading week! I should certainly say so! It was back in the fall term. I came here in the fall. Actually, if we're going to be really precise about this, it was late summer, late August."

That's right, he thinks with a shock. It was before the fall, and classes were just beginning.

Charade huddles against the wall, feels around for the sleeping bag, and pulls it up against her. "It's cold in here."

"Yes," he says. "Well, old buildings. Here, let's . . . we can both fit inside it. . . ." He cocoons them together, snakes the zipper along its tracks, slides a hand between her legs. "Isn't that better?"

Parthenogenesis, no, that wouldn't be the word, he thinks. Is there a word for it?—the ability to fit sexual needs into the cracks of thought and will, without undue hindrance to the obsession in hand.

These seemed to be his stages: intense thought, intense fatigue, then the euphoria, a sort of white-out, the mathematics moving toward the new shore at full speed like a crested wave. Then the girl. That is the point when she appears. Then the sexual frenzy, then breakthrough. That would come next.

Consider Heisenberg. . . .

"I suppose," Charade murmurs into the post-coital calm, "when you think about it, my mother would have had Nicholas and Verity and Kay on her mind while she was giving birth to me, and they would have got into my bloodstream. So it's only natural that I'd think of them whenever . . . well, all the time really, but especially when we make love . . . and it's only natural that history and literature would absorb me from the start, two sides of the same coin, right? If I can sift through all the official fictions of the past carefully enough . . . Sometimes I think the meaning's out there, waiting, like a new star, just waiting for me to focus—"

"Yes," he says, "that's how it is. It's there; I already know the answer I want. I can feel that it's right; I just have to work out the physics and the mathematics of it. . . . I just have to come from the right direction. The solution's millimeters away; I can feel it coming like an orgasm. I feel as though your next shudder will put it in my . . . I think of Rutherford and Bohr—that's the way they worked. That's the way it was for them. I think of Heisenberg when he had his hooks in the skin of an idea."

Charade smiles and holds his hand up to the glimmer seeping in from the window. "White-fingernail people. What were you going to say about Heisenberg?"

"In 1923 in Munich—"

"In 1923?" She frowns and closes her eyes and taps her forehead. "The Uncertainty Principle. Nobel Prize, 1932. Right?"

He raises an eyebrow. "Very good."

"I've been doing my homework. Anyway, history's one of my obsessions."

"Obsession," he says. "That's the *sine qua non*." He laughs. "In 1923, Wien tried to flunk Heisenberg on his doctorate. That was in Munich. Of course, the world is full of academics like Wien, official guardians of the rules. And the Wiens have their ways; they are powerful blockers and delayers and inflicters of damage. Two years later Heisenberg was ill; he was a wreck."

And still the habits of electrons were at him, clawing at him ruthlessly as heartburn. Help, Heisenberg said to his doctor, and was ordered off to an island in the North Sea. Koenig can imagine it: the way Heisenberg paces up and down the beach and thinks. He *thinks*. This is how his breakthrough comes: first the passion, then the hunch, then the computations; spectral lines, frequencies, quantum mechanical series . . . and the famous matrices.

Koenig likes to think of that night when Heisenberg worked without stopping, his theory growing faster than the sunrise. Just a kid, too, twenty-five years old, crying *Lights! lights!* and there was light.

And suddenly Heisenberg is walking out into his own morning, his own shoreline and he's paddling in it—the ripples of it, an entirely new theory—and climbing its rocks. He actually did that. He wrote a letter to Wolfgang Pauli; Koenig knows it by heart: *I was far too excited to sleep, and so, as a new day dawned, I made for the southern tip of the island, where I had been longing to climb a rock jutting out into the sea.*

"Do you see, Charade? He thought of it as a new dawn, and I think of it as flesh that'll swallow me up. One night I'll have it, the complete shape of the question, and here you'll be in my arms."

"Really?" she says drily.

She doesn't like this.

[They kiss], she thinks. She has, sometimes, the sense of watching her life on *his* stage. Or on his monitor. Click, click, she thinks.

Access file, close file. [Curtain falls, is puckered here and there with behind-the-scenes activity, rises again.] Click, click.

"Well," she says, "if obsession is nine tenths of the game, I'll find them. Just as I found Aunt Kay."

It was obsession, she supposes, in the first place, that brought Verity's name swimming up out of newsprint in the *Sydney Morning Herald*.

"Almost two years ago," (Was it?) she says. (Can it be almost two years?) "I was reading for a history exam. Sydney Uni." She closes her eyes. "There's a bowl of soup in front of me, a spoon in my right hand, *Sources of Australian History* in my left. And pages of the *Herald* ... Someone else, one of my roommates, has left pages of the *Herald* strewn around on the table and floor. And then *impact*. Just a filler item in the Personals, which I never read, but it leaped out and smacked me between the eyes. See, I carry it around in my wallet; it's getting hard to read."

She rummages for her handbag in the dark. She finds her wallet, extracts something, smooths it out, a quarter page with hand-torn edges dominated by an advertisement for IXL mango and passionfruit jams. There is a yellow slash of outline (felt marker) at the third item down in the Personals:

> *Would anyone having any information on the whereabouts of Verity Ashkenazy (probably now married; married name unknown, but possibly Truman), who was a student and graduate student at the University of Queensland in the mid 50s and early 60s, please contact K. Sussex, Box 3211, Toronto, Canada.*

"Can you imagine the effect?" Charade asks. "It was like ... like getting a phone call from God."

"I'm not surprised," Koenig says. "Iron filings to a magnet—there are precedents all over the place in science. Coincidences cluster around obsessions; we expect it. Synchronicities, we say."

"There I was," Charade says, "in that ratty student apartment with cockroaches scuffling under the sink...."

She hears the furtive rubbing of one filthy little insect leg against another; she hears the atoms of air colliding; she hears time stop. Her heart is tolling like the frantic bell that rings in peace or war. Giddiness washes her.

She assumes she has experienced a fleeting hallucination and turns her eyes back to her textbook. *Sources of Personal History,* she thinks. Tench's *Complete Account of the Settlement at Port Jackson in New South Wales.* Tench is recalling the anguish of dwindling rations, the passionate hopeless waiting for ships from England.

1790. Here on the summit of the hill, every morning from daylight until the sun sunk, did we sweep the horizon, in hope of seeing a sail. At every fleeting speck which arose from the bosom of the sea, the heart bounded, and the telescope was lifted to the eye. If a ship appeared here, we knew she must be bound to us; for on the shores of this vast ocean (the largest in the world) we were the only community which possessed the art of navigation, and languished for intercourse with civilized society.

To say that we were disappointed and shocked, would very inadequately describe our sensations.

So, Charade thinks. The fleeting speck on the horizon. The false sail. And she looks calmly, sardonically, ruefully back at the *Sydney Morning Herald.*

It is still there.

Would anyone knowing the whereabouts of Verity Ashkenazy . . . please contact K. Sussex . . . Canada

She cannot concentrate, she cannot keep still. She leaves the apartment and walks and walks. She gets on a bus, gets off at Circular Quay, takes the ferry to Manly, takes it back again, and out again, over and over, her eyes on the furling wake, "which was green and white," she says, "and coiled like a scroll."

"A helix," Koenig says.

"Yes, or a helix. But it changes quite abruptly, you know, when the ferry crosses the Heads. And I found myself obsessed with finding the *point* where it changed. You know, when you're coming in from Manly, there must be a line that could be drawn from North Head . . . and then on the way out again, from Circular

Quay, there must be a line from South Head. And between those two lines, the Pacific changes all the rules. You're not really in Sydney Harbour anymore. And for some loony reason I decided if I could find that point of change . . . I must have stayed on the ferry for hours. And then, you know, there was something else . . . suddenly, that space between the Heads, it was inside me. There was this roaring and buffeting and I couldn't stand it, it was deafening, it made me seasick, and I got off at Manly and I ran and ran, and I got on a bus and then off it, and I found myself at Collaroy Beach, and I just walked along the sand till it got dark."

"Like Heisenberg."

"What?" Charade blinks.

"Like Heisenberg on the beach. The breakthrough."

"Breakthrough?" Charade turns the word over, puzzled. "But I was terrified," she says. *"Terrified.* If they were turning out to be real after all . . . what if they were, you know, just ordinary? What if I were to find them and they were nothing special? Just ordinary people. Nothing." She pauses.

She sighs and asks him: "Do you think it's all a fraud? Knowing anything. The possibility of knowing anything."

"Yes," he says. "A useful fraud. In science, first we know, then we prove. It could be brilliant intuition, it could be ego—but it seems to work. Heisenberg and Schrödinger each knew they were right, each knew the other was wrong: wave packets or particles? orbits or matrices? endemic uncertainty? Each forges a proof that proves he's right and the other's wrong. They took the Nobel together in 1933 and had trouble, I suppose, being civil."

"Is it all a joke, then?" Charade asks, appalled. "A century from now they'll be quaint historical examples. There's no such thing as truth, not even in science."

"No," he says, "not a joke. It's all we've got." Our fallible ways of knowing, he thinks, and the enterprise of making maps to link up questions and answers. "They always turn out to be faulty," he says. "Eventually. But they throw up answers after all. And they reshape the questions too."

"Yes," Charade muses. "I think that's true. They knew they

would find a Great South Land for all the wrong reasons. But they found Australia just the same."

"The weird and wonderful routes to truth," he laughs. "The marvelous routes."

"Yes," she says. "Yes. Aunt Kay's for instance. Summoning Nicholas and Verity up from ... And you don't even remember her."

"You keep saying that. I wish you'd tell me what you mean."

"It'll take nights and nights."

"Mmm."

"And how can I ... ? I'll have to go back to the beginning."

Part II

K: The Variorum Edition

Part II

1. In the Beginning

In the beginning, Charade says, when Kay was a child in Melbourne, she was taken Sunday after Sunday to a church where the pastor spoke lightning and thunder. . . .

In the beginning, thundered the pastor, and the child watched the Word skipping and sliding up ladders of sunlight, watched it wink at her from high up in the cave of the church before it slipped through an air vent and escaped. She heard it rumbling about, baying above the trams and trains of Melbourne, that wicked city, and demanding repentance: a barker for God. It called to her: not *Katherine!* but Kay, Kay! it whispered, enticing. She closed her eyes and saw it on the carrousel in the Fitzroy Gardens, going round and round in the eucalypt air, skipping higher and higher until it was with God again.

In the beginning was the Word. And the Word was with God.

It *was* God, said the pastor, *and the same was in the beginning with God.*

The beautiful shimmering Word: round and round and higher and higher it went, in the beginning and world without end, amen.

In the beginning Katherine was surrounded by the Word and by pastors and preachers and grandparents and uncles and aunts and cousins and God and the Powers of Darkness. The air through which she moved was thick was presences, *for we are at all times surrounded,* said the preacher, *by a great cloud of witnesses.* What else, therefore, could she do but walk with them and talk with them and know them all by name and by shape? Even the Noisome Pestilence, whom she thought of as long-legged with a leer and bad teeth and fingernails curling like black smoke. When the Noisome Pestilence passed overhead, there was a roaring in the air and flames fell.

He had passed over Darwin. He had dropped bombs. He flew in Japanese planes.

So thick, so dense with threat was the air, that the windows of the house (it was in Ringwood, on the outskirts of Melbourne) were painted black, for the terrors that stalked about at night battened onto lighted windows. In the mornings, however, as the trains rumbled by the house on their way into Flinders Street Station, the blackened casements were thrown open to the sun and Katherine watched to see who would come riding on the shafts of light. Once a funnel of soot came twisting and dancing in, pointing its toes, lifting its long graceful legs and baring its teeth.

Katherine screamed.

"It's the Noisome Pestilence," she sobbed into her grandmother's bosom.

"We're not afraid of the noisome pestilence," Grandma Llewellyn comforted. "The noisome pestilence can't hurt us." This was because they lived under the shadow of the Almighty. "He shall cover you with His feathers," Grandma Llewellyn said, "and under His wings shalt thou trust."

Katherine looked up into the downy feather-breasted air. It smelled of warmth and pillows and the Velvet soap her grandmother used. A dash of lavender drifted by, a twisting falling feather of fragrance, the smell of sachets kept between clothes in a wardrobe. As it fell it cast a purple haze, the shadow of the Almighty.

Out of the shadow on a mauve day came Katherine's father,

riding home from Point Cook in his RAAF uniform. He's got his wings! the older boy cousins said, excited. Her father came on a dragon that belched sparks and smoke but she had never seen its wings. She hid under the golden-leafed hedge.

"Katherine!" they called, laughing, unable to find her. "Kay, Kay! It's your daddy on his motorbike. Don't you have a big hug for your daddy? Don't you want a ride in the sidecar?"

Katherine watched her mother climb into the motorcycle's side pocket. She watched her father kick at its flank. It snarled; it spat sparks; it roared down the street and under the railway bridge, breathing smoke. The long white aviator scarf around her father's neck ribboned back in the wind like a pennant; the sun touched her mother's copper hair; there were tongues of fire above her mother's head.

"Oh, I want to! I want to!" cried Katherine, crawling out from under the hedge. The sun swallowed her parents up. She shaded her eyes and squinted into the brightness until they flew out of it again. "I want to, I want to," she cried, jumping up and down.

Her father scooped her up and kissed her. "Well now," he teased, "and who might this little girl be?"

"I'm Kay," she said, "and I want to." She wanted to, right up until the moment her father set her down in the motorbike's pocket, until she felt how it trembled and hammered at her bones. She screamed.

Grandma Llewellyn came running. "Really!" she said to her son-in-law. "Terrifying the child like that."

Katherine's father looked sheepish. Through dinner he sat silent, as though all the aunts and cousins left no room at the table for his voice. He played with his fork and made his fingers gallop on the tablecloth, tan-ta-rum tan-ta-rum, and his eyes kept waiting for Katherine's mother to look at him. He whispered something in her mother's ear.

"Why are you whispering?" Katherine clamored, and one of the aunts said in a low voice, "You can have our room for a while," and the other aunts all said: "Shhh! Little donkeys have big ears."

"*I've* got big ears," Kay told her father, climbing onto his lap and pushing back her hair to show. "I can write my name."

She showed him with her new crayons. K, she wrote.

"No," he said, "it's not finished. Like this, see? K-A-Y."

But before she learned A and Y it was time already to go. So there were hugs and kisses and Kay promised to practice with the new crayons and he was gone. She saw his motorcycle disappear under the railway bridge and after that she saw it spread its wings, passing clouds, heading back to Point Cook.

"My father *flies*," she told Bea.

Bea stuck out her tongue. "*My* father was in Egypt," she said. "But your father won't fight. If the Japs get us, it's your father's fault. If the Japs get us, they'll cut off our fingers and kill our dads and rape our mothers."

"What's *rape*?" Kay asked with round eyes.

"Like grate," Bea said. "Like with cheese."

Kay thought of her mother's cream skin being shredded by Japanese graters. Into her sleep that night fell flakes of her mother, a bloody rain, and she woke in terror, crying out.

"Why won't Daddy fight the Japs?" she sobbed.

Her mother and Grandma Llewellyn came running in the dark. They stroked her hair. The *Japanese*, they corrected, are God's children. We are all God's children, they said. And your daddy *is* fighting. It is simply that he cannot kill. It is right to defend your country, but it is wrong to kill. So your daddy looks after the planes and he makes parachutes and things like that.

"I don't want you to play with Bea again," her mother said.

"Oh Bea's all right." Grandma Llewellyn blew out the hurricane lamp and opened the blackened window so that Katherine could see the moon. "You can't shield the child from talk. We are not afraid of what people say, Kay. And we are not afraid of the Japanese. We are not afraid of the terror that walketh by night, nor the destruction that wasteth at noonday. They shall not come nigh us. Because we live under the shadow of the Almighty."

Nevertheless, nevertheless, they prowled about, the great cloud of pestilences, and at nights, when it was necessary to make the long trek through the garden to the outhouse at the back of the yard, Kay looked up in vain for the umbrella of lavender feathers, for the wings of the Almighty. At night the Powers of Darkness stalked unchecked. They were twelve feet tall; she could hear them rustling the leaves, whispering to one another, plotting felonies.

Bea had told her what they did to little girls: they took off all your clothes and tossed you about like a ball, playing Devil's Catch; you could feel their claws in all your softest places; and then they made you drink blood. Bea said it had happened to her.

Katherine would hold tightly to Grandpa Llewellyn's hand, watching the long dark toes of the Terror That Walketh by Night, watching those toes flirt with the edge of the path. She was grateful, then, that her grandfather was taller than the Noisome Pestilence, that he was as safe as the shadow of the Almighty, that he dwelt in the secret place of the Most High. As she sat on the wooden outhouse seat in the darkness, listening to the tinkle of her own water, Grandpa would whistle to keep the presences at bay. "Rock of Ages," he would whistle. Or "Men of Harlech" perhaps. Or "Jesu, Lover of My Soul." And beyond the circle of his breath Kay could hear the night powers gnashing their teeth. Kay, Kay, she could hear them calling.

"They'll never catch me," she told Bea.

"Oh yes they will," Bea said. "They can get through cracks in the house. They'll suck you out one night when nobody's looking."

Bea was older and went to kindergarten already. She lived around the corner, but their two back fences made an L around a paddock of long grass and thistles and buttercups. Every day, when Bea came home from school, they slipped through the fence railings and met in the buttercup patch.

"This is what they do," said Bea, sliding her hand under Katherine's dress and tickling her secret places.

"Don't! Don't!" Katherine shrieked in a pleasurable terror. "They'll never catch me, they'll *never!*"

"Oh, yes, they will," promised Bea.

2. *Sailor, Sailor*

Once upon a Melbourne day, Charade says, after Hiroshima but before all the Yanks had gone home, a man came up to Bea and Kay while they played in the buttercup patch.

"Hi, little girls," he said.

It was a funny word: *hi.* Not a word they had heard before. They said hello, and then they stuffed their fists into their mouths and rolled in the grass and giggled. "Ah've got a present," he said, "for a pretty litty girl." It was a strange way to talk, as though he had fruitcake in his mouth. "M' name's Gene," he said, and they shrieked and bit on their fists to think of a man named Jean. "Ah'm a sailor. And ah've got a present all the way from Tennessee for the prettiest girl in Australia."

"That's Bea," Kay said. Her voice came through between her fingers, mixed in with the bubbles of laughter. "Bea's the prettiest girl in the world. Mr. Bedford said."

"Yes," said Bea. "I am." She had a face that was shaped like an almond. "I've got cow's eyes." She liked to open and close them and feel the lashes brush against her cheek. She liked to pull on the dark curls that grew around her face like tendrils, and let them spring back again. She pulled one across her forehead and stretched it down to her chin. She smiled at the man from behind it.

"Oh," the man said. "Yes, sir. You are definitely the prettiest girl in the world."

"I know. Mr. Bedford said."

Gene picked a buttercup and stuck it behind Bea's ear. "And who might Mr. Bedford be?"

"He's a man at our shop. He gave me a present; he bought me a pineapple iceblock. But it's a secret."

"Aha, but you told it," the man said. "A little girl who can't keep a secret."

"I can so, I can so," Bea chanted. She did a somersault in the buttercups so the man could see the little pink flowers on her panties. The man lay down on his stomach in the grass and took off his white hat. The hat looked like a dog dish. It was the silliest hat they had seen. He set it on Kay's head and she bit her knuckles very hard and nearly choked with nervous mirth.

"Guess ah'm just going to have to give mah present to your cute little friend," he told Bea. " 'Cause ah can't trust a little girl who can't keep a secret."

"I can so, I can so," Bea said, and she pulled the hat off Kay's head and put it on her own.

Kay asked: "Are you in the R-Double-A-F?"

Bea said: "My father was in Egypt, but Kay's father wouldn't fight. He only made parachutes."

Kay said: "Are you in the RAAF too?"

"No, ma'am," he said. "Ah most certainly am not in the RAAF. Ah already told you, ah'm a sailor, a sailor. Ah got me a bee-ootiful battleship for mah home. And ah'm going to take one lucky little girl to see that ship if she can keep a secret." He picked up Kay's foot and unbuckled her sandal and began to play with her toes. "This little piggy went to market," he sang. "And this little piggy ate roast beef." And when he got to the little piggy who ran all the way home, his fingers began skittering up Kay's leg, past her knee, past—

"Don't! Don't!" she shrieked, giggling, and rolling away in the grass. She didn't know whether she liked it or not. She wanted to whisper to Bea: "Is he one of the Powers of Darkness?"

But Bea was turning cartwheels now, and the man was watching her. She cartwheeled in a circle around him and then she sat in the buttercups and unbuckled her sandals and began throwing them into the air and catching them. "Who wants to see a baddle ship, a baddle ship?" she sang. "Mr. Bedford gives better things. But I'm not telling what, 'cause it's a secret."

"On mah ship," Gene told Bea, "you can sit on the big guns, va-voom." He made a circle with a thumb and one finger, and poked another finger through it. Then he put the circle up to one eye. "The windows are round and you can put your face up against them and say howdoody to a fish. But ah guess ah'm gonna take your friend here," and he reached for Kay's foot again. He played the piano on her ankle; he hummed songs up and down her leg. Kay squirmed and giggled and tried to pull away. She thought perhaps she didn't like it. Then she thought perhaps she did. The man sat up and lifted her foot to his mouth and blew between her toes.

"Stop! Stop!" she shrieked. "It tickles." Bea went on playing catch with her sandals, the shoes flying higher and higher. "It tickles, it tickles!" Kay cried.

"Ah've got a present for a tickly little girl," Gene said. "But first you have to tell me your name."

"Katherine," she gasped, twisting and laughing. "It's Katherine Sussex, but I'm Kay. Stop! Stop!"

"Kay," the man sang. "K-K-K-Katy, you're the one that I adore. Oh, Ah love little Katies, Ah do." Bea lay on her back in the buttercups and kicked her legs to keep time with the tossing of her sandals; she pointed her toes, and her dainty feet went up and down, up and down, like birds soaring, plummeting. Gene put Kay's toes in his mouth and sucked them, and waves of something ran right to the tops of her shoulders. He tickled her panties with his finger and she gasped with shock. Sounds came out of her mouth, but she couldn't tell if she was laughing or crying. "Va-voom, va-voom," laughed Gene, catching hold of her feet again. "This little piggy went to market," he said, running his tongue around one toe. "And this little piggy stayed home. And this little piggy flew all the way . . ."

Right then one of Bea's sandals came sailing by and Gene lunged out and caught it. "Aha!" he cried. "Now ah've got you!" Bea squealed and catapulted herself against Gene, and he caught her with his left arm and waved the sandal high above her with his right. They rolled in the grass together. Bea gulped with laughter and kicked and squirmed until Gene knelt in the buttercups and pinned her between his legs. "If you keep still like a good little girl," he said, "maybe you'll be the lucky one to come and see mah battleship."

Kay thought: Bea's the one. It's her he wants to take.

The hammers inside her chest slowed down; she was glad it was Bea. Then again, she would have liked to be the one. Perhaps.

Bea, imperious, commanded: "First you have to put my sandals on."

"Why, ma'am," Gene said. "A pleasure." He sat back on his heels, and pinned Bea's leg between his while he strapped and buckled. She wiggled her toes in the space between his thighs. "Oh, oh," he said. "A regular little witch." He tickled the sole of her foot. "Little witches need to have their bottoms spanked. Guess ah'm just gonna have to take you right on down to mah ship and take you back to Tennessee. We're gonna sail across—"

"Katherine! Bea!" came Grandma Llewellyn's voice. "Where are you?"

Kay and Bea and Gene all jumped as though they had been shot. They sat up still and straight. "Guess ah have to get on back to mah ship," Gene said. He put his fingers over their lips and whispered: "Now ah sure hope you can keep a secret, because if anyone tells about the lollipop ship, the bogeyman comes and eats her up." And then he went jogging away through the buttercups till he came to the lane at the end of Bea's fence.

"Katherine! Katherine!" called Grandma Llewellyn.

Kay and Bea stared at each other.

"Katherine! Bea! Where are you?"

They somersaulted across the buttercups and crawled through

the railings into Kay's backyard and ran up the path to the henhouse. "We're here," they called. "We're here."

And then they said: "Nothing. We weren't doing anything. We were just playing in the paddock."

Grandma Llewellyn went on putting eggs into her basket. "Don't get into any mischief," she said before she went back inside the house.

Kay and Bea looked at each other and then they put their fists in their mouths and rolled in the grass outside the henhouse.

"Jean, Jean! Mah name is Jean!" spluttered Bea, catching hold of Kay's foot.

"Gonna take you to Tennis-y," Kay mimicked.

"Ah'm a sailor, a sailor!"

"Ah'm gonna spank your bottom!"

They shrieked and struggled and tickled until they were exhausted. Then they climbed the plum tree and stared out over the paddock. Sometimes, if they sat very still, a bird came and pecked at a plum. Kay worried at a piece of bark with her fingernail, thinking, thinking. Bea sat hunched on her branch and stroked her ankles.

At length Kay announced soberly: "I didn't like him."

"That's because you're a baby." Bea hooked her knees over the branch and swung upside down, her curls flying. "I told you that's what they do. When Mr. Bedford buys you an iceblock, you'll see."

"Do you like it?" Kay asked.

"Maybe."

"Maybe I do too."

"Not as much as me," Bea said. She moved back and forth like molasses, her fingertips trailing through air. "I always like things more."

Kay tried to decide: what she liked, what she didn't like. It was true, Bea always liked things more. Bea *liked*. What did Kay like? She liked to close her eyes and see things. She saw Bea's hair spreading and spreading; she saw it growing grape leaves that reached out and touched the grass. She saw Bea growing into the buttercup patch; she saw bunches of grapes; she saw stickiness and juice. She saw Jean the Baddle Ship Man: how he walked without seeing, how stickiness pulled him, how Bea's tendrils could wind themselves around him until he wouldn't be able to move.

"I didn't like him," she said decisively.

"I didn't too." Bea shrugged. "But that's what they do. You'll see."

Bea always knew more, so Kay told Bea: "I know what Tennis-y looks like."

"I'm going to go there," Bea said. "Jean's going to take me."

Kay frowned. "I'm going to go there all by myself."

Bea licked her finger and crossed her heart. "I'll go first," she promised.

But Kay closed her eyes and saw that Bea's fingers and toes were sprouting little green pads, that her hair was green, that she was part of the plum tree and the buttercup patch, that she would never get away.

No, she thought. I'll go first. I'll be the one. By myself.

3. Brisbane

Brisbane, Charade begins. . . .

Along the front fence was a leggy colony of poinsettias that had to be cut back and cut back, and down through these each day the arm of the postman would reach. The house was set low against the embankment of road and footpath, and when Kay curled herself under the trees, waiting, she could hear the soft overhead thunder of the postman's coming. She could see the tips of his shoes above her head as he leaned forward, fishing between leaves for the mailbox.

She would climb the oldest and thickest tree and part the splashy red flowers and peer out. "Do you have a letter from Bea?" she would ask wistfully.

There was a year without Bea, and Bea never wrote. Not once. Kay herself wrote to Bea every day.

Today, she would begin, and the news of Grade 3 would follow, in drawings and signs, in the language that lay to hand. The letters always ended the same way. When was Bea coming? Had she asked her father yet? They could both come—there was room on the veranda. Would she please come soon. Love, Kay.

It seemed to Kay that the Shadow of the Almighty, which had covered them all so snugly—like a tucked-down quilt—in Melbourne, did not stretch quite so far as Brisbane. Or perhaps was pulled too thin, full of gaping holes through which harm could reach and twist this way, that way, hissing in your ear: Don't tell, don't tell! If you scream, if you tell, it will just get worse.

There was no Grandma Llewellyn in Brisbane, no Grandpa, no Bea.

Dear Bea, Kay wrote. *Please send me a letter. Love, Kay.*

There *were* letters, other letters, not from Bea; there were many letters, their contents mysterious, but these were given to Kay by her teachers and by her parents. She carried them back and forth, helplessly, knowing that events would whoosh out of the envelopes like sheet lightning. Miss Kennedy would make a slit in Kay's fate with a brass letter opener, purse her lips, shake her head, and send Kay alone to the library while the rest of the class went outside for Maypole dance practice, or perhaps filed off to the nurse for tetanus shots, or perhaps marched to the local theater to see some educational film. All these things were forbidden to Kay.

At lunchtime she was a connoisseur of trees—mango trees, banyan trees, especially Moreton Bay figs, especially broad-leafed dense-leafed trees with low-hanging branches. Kay was an adept of the quick disappearance. She knew the top of each head; she had a God's-eye view. She was privy to many private acts of treachery which flourished like cobbler's pegs and wet-the-beds: she heard what Diana whispered to Leigh about June, and to June about Leigh, and what June and Leigh said about Diana in Diana's absence. She drew certain conclusions about the nature of friendship.

She knew what Patrick and Diana did in the ditch beneath the Moreton Bay fig, how they took turns and giggled; how once Patrick would not give back Diana's underpants, but ran away with them, red in the face with wicked glee. And how Diana, crying, ran home from school. After which, in the course of the afternoon, Diana's mother and the headmaster appeared at the door of the classroom, and Patrick was called away.

A sense of gravity and horrible expectation filled the classroom. The absence of Patrick went spinning and glittering between the desks like fireworks on Guy Fawkes Night, full of dazzle and menace.

Then Patrick returned.

He looked once around the class, defiantly, and tossed his head. Three livid blue lines, roughly parallel, raised themselves across the calf of his right leg. This was a turning point, a notch in the passage of class history. There was always *before* those blue stripes, and *after*. Among the boys, the secret sign was a badge of rank, but the girls were afraid of Patrick; they lay awake at nights in the grip of delicious shivers, thinking about his now purple and yellow-green legs and about Diana's underpants (for somehow the word got around; Diana's mother told June's mother, who told June, who told everyone).

Every morning when Kay, trembling, passed the knot of boys at the school gate, she would glance sideways at the last minute, watching for Patrick's smile. It touched her like something feverish. In dreams she smiled back; in the schoolyard she was afraid to. Once a boy pushed her over, and Patrick helped her up and punched the other boy. In dreams Patrick held at bay packs of dogs as she passed (a bunch of leashes like ribbons in his hand). He intercepted the deadly flight of cricket balls bound for her head. He spread blankets when she fell on the gravel. The shadow that Patrick cast was like the shadow of the Almighty.

They never spoke to each other, she didn't know why.

She did know, since her branch of the mango tree was level with the classroom windows, what Miss Kennedy did during lunch-time: how, after the blackboard was cleaned down, and the copybooks taken from the old wooden press for the afternoon lesson, and the sandwiches eaten, Miss Kennedy would close the door and press her ear against it, as if expecting warning messages from the veranda; how she would return to her desk and remove the gold-tasseled bookmark from the Grade 3 Reader and dangle it down the front of her dress, tassel trailing back and forth, back and forth, like a pendulum. Miss Kennedy would close her eyes and part her lips and her tongue would move like a lizard's.

Kay felt she would run out of storage room for all the puzzling things she knew. Most of her knowledge was of the wrong kind.

She could, for example, rattle through the names of the books of the Bible, from Genesis to Revelation, but could not produce the name of a single horse in the Melbourne Cup. She had never even heard of Phar Lap—"the *legendary* Phar Lap," Miss Kennedy said, incredulous.

On the other hand, she knew that the blue body-paint of Boadicea's warriors was called *woad*, and that King Harold had been felled by an arrow in the eye at the Battle of Hastings.

Miss Kennedy, surprised but grudgingly pleased, asked: "Now just *where* do you pick up these things?"

"In the library," Kay said guiltily. In the library, while the rest of the class engaged in Maypole dancing and sundry other forbidden and licentious acts. "In the picture-book encyclopedia."

Not acceptable, she knew it instantly. She could feel the disapproval like a sudden tropical fog. They would *do* things again, the boys would, if Patrick wasn't with them, and if they caught her alone after school. Don't tell, don't tell, they would taunt. If you tell, we will get you tonight.

She thought of sleep as a trickster to be outwitted. They got her when she fell asleep. They came snarling in packs; their teeth were sharp as knives.

She wished for Bea. Bad dreams would never touch Bea—the very thought was ridiculous. Bea would fling them off the way a terrier shakes off water. Bea had all the right kinds of knowledge. Bea would never be sent to the library, where Kay kept picking up, picking up, haplessly, more useless and dangerous facts. And how could she possibly sort out what it was not permissible to know, and not permissible *not* to know? For instance, for instance, she had gone and *memorized* the page on Phar Lap in the picture-book encyclopedia. She waited and waited and when at last he was mentioned again by Miss Kennedy, her hand shot up. "His greatest win was the 1930 Cup," she said, breathless. "He had thirty-seven wins, the last one in America. And then," she rattled on, "he was murdered by the Americans, but his heart was one and a half times the normal size for a thoroughbred."

There was an eerie silence.

They all looked at her very strangely; she could feel the stares like pins and needles on her skin.

"What would *youuuuu* know?" someone taunted.

Wowser, wowser, wowser! voices said.

"*Youuu've* never been to the races in yer life."

What would you know you know you know? voices chanted later, in the playground. And the circle formed, a kind of dance, a skip, a game. Kay's nerves stood on tiptoe, ready for flight, and she watched. It was what she did best of all, watching; she missed nothing. She waited for the first sign, the direction of the first pleat in the loop around her, the dip toward her, the first shove. She called this the Circle Game. Every night it closed round her like a tourniquet from which she woke gulping for breath, her room blue from lack of air, her nightgown sodden.

Kay wished for Bea. If Bea should appear, *kaboom,* like Jesus walking on the ocean, the storm would seep back into playground chaos, a wave into water.

Kay prayed that Bea would come.

But only the ministers came. Every Monday they blew in, a little coterie of penguins, black and white, and Miss Kennedy called out the religions and the rooms. Methodists to Mr. Clarkson's room, Presbyterians to Miss Waddley's, and so on and so on, the whole school mingling. Kay tried to imagine such good fortune: to be part of an acceptable religion, one that everyone else had heard of, one with a sayable name: Metho, Prezy, C of E, Mick. To be anything but *Others.*

"Others to the library," Miss Kennedy would say.

There were, in the whole school, nineteen of them. *Others.* They looked at one another warily in the library, drawing no comfort, no kinship at all, from shared fate—caged randomly, a small zoo of oddities. Sometimes the code words of their otherness were read aloud by teachers: Mormon; Freethinker; Jehovah's Witness; Jewish; Pentecostal; Atheist.

Others.

They never spoke to one another, but scuttled to the corners of the room, intent on browsing through the stacks, intent on the book in front of the face. There was one girl, a Grade 8 girl—like all Grade 8's as distant as the sun—whom Kay studied with fascination (and with utmost surreptitiousness) in the library on Mondays. The girl had very thick long black hair that shone like glass and hung loose to her waist. She had eyes so large and brown that Kay thought of possums and of cows. And she had stillness; she had the stillness, it seemed to Kay, of a possum when it hears a footfall. Or perhaps of God when he brooded over the waters.

There was a picture of this in the family Bible. God himself was not actually in the picture. He was so still, brooding over the lapping ocean, that even the smoke-thin edges of the clouds were sufficient to screen him. Only His God-ness, a radiance bleeding through, betrayed Him.

The girl in Grade 8 did not mind about the library on Mondays. It was nothing; it fell off her the way water rolls from a bird's wing. She would look up from her book and stare out the window and see something that was not the kindergarten children on the swings and not the gardener. She would watch it for so long (whatever it was) and listen so intently, and hold herself so still, that she would frequently not hear the bell that signaled the end of Religious Instruction.

Once Kay heard the teacher in charge say: "Snap out of it, Verity."

Verity, Kay said to herself, delighted.

Verity of the secrets.

Kay watched; Kay studied; Kay thought. What was the secret of not minding? Of never being frightened? Of letting *Other*-ness slide off like rain from feathers? Perhaps it just happened when you got to Grade 8.

Once upon a Monday, Verity turned from the library window and looked at Kay, looked directly at her, as though she had felt Kay's eyes on her skin. Caught out, unable to lower her gaze to her book, Kay stared back, her breath catching in her throat. Verity, not hostile, not annoyed, watched her gravely. She did not smile. Kay could hear the ticking of the clock, loud as thunder. Then Verity looked away again.

Not till lunchtime did Kay's heart stop flinching and galloping.

Three days later, by happenstance, waiting in line at the tuck shop, she turned around and there was Verity behind her. In a sudden spasm of nervousness, Kay tripped. She stumbled over her own feet and pitched forward, and Verity, reaching out, caught her.

"Are you all right?" she asked—although in fact Kay did not hear the words at all, only the pitch and toss of voice, an orchestral excitement. And she *was* all right, there was no help for it, and Verity let her go, betraying not a flicker of recognition, not the slightest flicker.

But how was it to be expected that a Being in Grade 8 could tell any one Grade 3 child from another?

Mondays. Kay, assiduous watcher, began to wait for Mondays with feverish interest; she became addicted to Mondays. She learned something new. Whenever Verity looked out the window, her right hand was hidden in the pocket that lay demurely flat in the side-seam of her school tunic. Kay, positioning herself at a desk on Verity's right, ascertained that the hand was never absolutely still; it clenched and unclenched itself slowly. Sometimes the fingers splayed themselves out, pressing against the fabric of the tunic like the roots of tree orchids. Sometimes they rippled beneath the cotton, sifting or assessing some object; or objects.

This was surely a fact: the mysterious contents of Verity's pocket were the source of her magic. Kay was obsessed with the hand and with the pocket. She watched so fixedly that the eyes of the teacher-in-charge were drawn in the same direction.

"Verity!" the teacher said—a sharp sudden sound—and all nineteen of the Others jumped. "Verity Ashkenazy! What are you playing with?"

The room went into slow motion; the floor dipped and swayed. Verity turned white and held herself taut, so taut that the air around her cracked. Kay heard it, a painful singing in her ears.

"Verity!" the teacher said again. "I asked you a question. What are you playing with?"

"Nothing, Miss Warren." It was a mere whisper. It was a voice dragged into the room from an immense distance.

"Bring it here, please," Miss Warren said. "Put it on my table. Whatever it is in your pocket."

Something happened. Like the shawling of waves up a beach, a vibration spread across Verity's body, rippling, surfing out from the side-seam of her tunic. Kay, the betrayer, was appalled, she was terrified, to see a crack, a rift, an abyss in Verity's stillness.

"Aha!" Miss Warren said, triumphant. "I *thought* you were up to mischief. On my table, if you please. This instant."

Something happened again. The tide turned. Calmly, almost disdainfully, Verity moved. The room made way for her; the table came to rest at her fingertips. She placed a handful of raisins on it. She held her head high and tossed it slightly and for a fleeting sweeping second looked every one of them in the eye, Miss Warren included. Kay recognized the look: the same one, exactly the same one in Patrick's eyes after he stole Diana's underpants and acquired three stripes on his leg.

But *raisins,* Kay thought with astonishment, baffled. Raisins?

Miss Warren, also baffled, said testily: "No food in the classroom, that's a rule. You will come to the office after school this afternoon."

At which a flicker, a ghost of a smile, crossed Verity's lips, as though this were the most ludicrous, the most hilarious of outcomes, to follow on the revelation of raisins. And then she looked suddenly at Kay, sharply, attentively, and then away.

And Kay, stricken, thought: *She knows. She knows it was me who told.* In a manner of speaking, told.

"And you, Katherine Sussex," Miss Warren snapped. "What are you staring at?"

"Nothing, Miss Warren." Red-faced, Kay dropped her eyes to her book, but the words swam across the page. She wanted to go out and hang herself. She sobbed into her pillow that night. She prayed for Bea to come. All night she tossed and was spiked and battered on dreams, and in the morning she told herself: I dreamed that, about the raisins, about Verity turning white and shivering, about Verity being afraid. Verity is never afraid. I dreamed that, about Verity looking at me. It wasn't me who told, it wasn't me. And Verity is never afraid. She has never ever been afraid.

Furtively, when the next Monday rolled around, she watched for the hand in the pocket, and there it was, the same nervous burrowing . . . as though there had been no reprimand, no brush with a teacher's anger, as though nothing had happened.

Nothing *had* happened, Kay reassured herself.

But then, why did Verity nod at her? Just a small nod. She was almost certain that at the beginning of the class, as they all filed into the library, Verity gave her a slight nod and perhaps a kind of smile, the edge of a smile. And how did she (Kay) know there were raisins in Verity's pocket? Did she know? Because the raisins made no sense. The raisins could not explain the look on Verity's face when she fingered the contents of her pocket so constantly, so restlessly.

She studied Miss Warren. Sometimes Miss Warren glanced in Verity's direction, sometimes her eyes rested on the hand in the pocket. Then they veered away. Verity, Kay thought, makes Miss Warren nervous. Miss Warren doesn't like her, but she's afraid of her. This knowledge flickered across the surface of Kay's skin, pins and needles, tingling, obscurely exciting.

After this—because of this?—Verity appeared one day in the middle of the Circle Game, the real Circle Game, the dreaded playground one, not the one that tightened its coils in sleep. Verity appeared and she walked on water. Kay did not know whether this happened or whether she dreamed it. She has never known. The fall happened—oh, yes, that happened. But did Verity appear? Whenever Kay replayed the last few moments before the shoving and the fall, Verity was nowhere to be seen: neither walking across the pool, nor on the steps.

"And yet, Charade," Kay will one day say, looking back at this moment from the future, "more than thirty years later, I can't shake it. There's this conviction, this ludicrous and irrational certainty, that for a crucial moment she *was* there. Which is crazy, of course, but there you are. I can't shake it."

Back in her childhood, Kay is standing in line on the concrete steps leading up to the swimming pool, her small duffel bag slung over her shoulder, her towel around her neck like a scarf. Three times a week this happens. She is afraid of the compulsory swimming lessons, but then of what is she not afraid? She cheats and does not open her eyes under water as ordered. She knows the deep end is waiting; she does not need the chlorine sting beneath her lashes to remind her. If the water catches her off guard she will be gone, swallowed. . . . The boys will do something; the pool will *drink* her, though if only Bea would come . . .

Then, on the concrete steps, it happens. The circle forms, and

Bea is in Melbourne, and oh, where is Patrick with the stripes on his legs? Where is Patrick-the-sometimes-Protector? Where is the lost shadow of the Almighty? The circle forms. Is it because of Phar Lap or the letters or . . . ? There is always a reason she can never quite grasp. The circle forms; they are pushing; Kay is falling.

Somewhere between the top step and the bottom one, somewhere on the slow golden arc of that voyage which is punctuated by bright visions of shoes and bare feet and flashes of chummy-gold embedded in the chalky pockmarks of the steps, somewhere there, with the bottom step reaching for her but before it folds her in its hard embrace, Verity appears. Verity walks across the surface of the swimming pool at the Wilston State School and meets Kay in the air above the steps. She draws her hand out of her pocket.

"Eat these," she says. The raisins.

Kay eats, the circle vanishes, and someone is dabbing at her bloodied knees. And isn't Patrick there, too, swinging punches? And then there are teachers. And then she is sent home—with a note, of course, from Miss Kennedy.

Kay tears up the note and drops it through a grate in the gutter. She puts spit on her handkerchief and rubs the blood off her legs and arms, though it keeps dribbling down from one knee.

"What happened?" her mother asks, distressed hands to her cheeks.

"I fell," Kay says. Nothing else is translatable, not into the language of parents, and Kay does not try. She says only: "I fell down the steps at the pool."

By night she is running a fever. She speaks of raisins. For days she shudders so uncontrollably that the pastor is sent for, and he presses his hands against her forehead (God's tourniquet, God's Circle Game) and he prays. Raisins, Kay whispers. The pastor is "casting out demons." His prayer is noisy; he is hectoring someone (God? Kay? The powers of darkness?). Kay feels like a paper mouse in the talons of the Almighty. She dreams of Bea; she cries out to Verity.

"No matter how many raisins we give her," her mother says, pressing a hand to her lips, "she keeps on asking for more."

Kay missed one week of school, and also the next.

There was an afterwards, a back-at-school time. Kay was branded now. Like Patrick, she wore stripes, and this gave her a certain kind of status. Once Patrick himself paused in a headlong football rush, seeing her, and made a circle with his thumb and index finger. He winked, and raised the circle high above his shoulder, emphatically, as though it were a medal she had won.

Kay was waiting for Verity's signal. Across Miss Warren's desk they stared at each other, unblinking.

Was it you? Kay's eyes asked. Were you there?

Verity's look went on and on, but Kay could not translate it.

Why are you never afraid? she silently pleaded. What is the secret?

Verity never smiled. Three seconds, four seconds more, her eyes lingered, and then, clear as a bell, Kay heard Verity's voice inside her head: *You already know.* And then Verity looked away.

But I don't know, Kay wanted to shout.

When the bell went, Verity was the first to leave the room. She never spoke to Kay; she never offered raisins. The Christmas holidays blew her right into high school and it was five years before Kay saw her again.

Over Christmas, hidden high in the mango tree, Kay made plans. If Bea doesn't come, she decided, I will run away. I won't go back to school.

But Bea's father died, and Bea came.

There she was, sharing Kay's bedroom, so that Kay would wake suddenly in the middle of a night that seemed noisy with the sound of Bea's breathing, and would clutch at her own chest and think: I made her father die.

Those were the rules of the game. And so, with the utmost diligence, she avoided wishing to see Verity again, lest harm should strike.

4. The Man in the Pandanus Palms

When Bea, my mum Bea, was a child, Charade says, she was impossible. Everybody said so.

"This is the border," she told Kay. Down the middle of their bedroom she made a dotted line of dirty socks. "You can't spread your neatness across."

Bea's side was rank as a forest. Underpants bloomed on doorknobs, stockings fluttered, clothes and bedding ran amok across the floor. There were comic books in geological strata, deep undulating layers of them, and there were other things, stranger things: a MEN AT WORK sign, a railwayman's cap, a schoolroom clock with no hands. "Stolen," Bea announced, patting such possessions with a small contented smile. Under Bea's mattress lurked the deeply and potently forbidden: cigarettes, movie posters, shocking pictures.

Is God waiting to strike her dead? Kay asked herself.

Though Bea would give Him a run for His money.

Once, in church, while Kay's father raised his hands above the bread and wine and closed his eyes and tipped his head back to gaze at heaven, Bea nudged Kay and passed her a Bible. Open it, she mouthed. At the place where the bookmark was, Kay found a postcard. *I fell in love with Surfers,* it said. There were breakers, a curve of white sand, a clump of pandanus palms—the kind that grew in the dunes at Surfers' Paradise and Burleigh Heads. An innocent beach, but high gloss. Glazed lines shimmered and criss-crossed the waves and pandanus spears, and made Kay's eyes water. She looked at Bea, puzzled, and Bea smirked. Tip it, she mouthed, making an up-and-down motion with her open hand and squinting.

Kay tilted the card and looked at it through half-shut eyes. She gasped and closed the Bible quickly. Inside, between the twenty-second and the twenty-third psalms, a man and a woman, stark naked, stood among the pandanus clumps.

Kay's father's voice lifted and fell and circled in prayer, going on and on. Flies crawled their languid way across the pews. Mosquitoes, bloated, glutted with Pentecostal blood, mumbled lazy hymns. Kay stole another look between the psalms. The man and the woman were waiting, their bodies facing her. They were not looking at each other, though their hands were reaching out, touching, playing blindman's bluff. The man was touching the woman's breast and the woman's fingers were touching oh shame oh unbelievable oh act which could not *not* be watched—

"He that eateth and drinketh unworthily," Kay's father said, "eateth and drinketh damnation to himself."

The Bible snapped itself shut, a divine clamshell. Kay waited for its covers to blister; she put her bruised and burning fingers in her mouth. She closed her eyes and felt her heart thumping and saw it as a dirty pulsing little ball that bounced through sewage and mud. She imagined God catching it, in His infinite mercy and patience and sorrow, and dipping it in the Blood of the Lamb and giving it back whiter than snow. Now don't get it dirty again, He said sadly.

She opened her eyes and saw Bea waiting, smiling, angelic in the House of the Lord.

Kay put her hand over her mouth to stifle a gasp that threatened to become subversive, irrepressible, a geyser of laughter. She looked up into the motes of dust, bright and blinding, where they eddied high at the treetop edge of the long slim windows, but God gave no sign, frown or smile.

He can't do a thing with her either, Kay thought. He's the same as everybody else.

About Bea, all grownups shook their heads and smiled. But did Bea care? Did Bea care what anyone thought? She cared, Kay sometimes dared to hope, about what Kay thought.

And Kay, devoted, was prepared to die for Bea. She burned nobly, fervently, for the chance; although she knew how likely it was that Bea, a lightning rod of risk, would be the first to be consumed, going showily, extravagantly, into the Catherine wheel of the future.

It was a kind of miracle that Bea squandered time and attention on Kay, who knew only useless book-ridden things, who so often at school relied on Bea's sharp tongue for protection. (Verity, distant and insubstantial as the angels in heaven, having long ago moved on to high school.)

Yea, though I walk through the valley of the shadow of death, Kay's thumping heart promised, Bea would not let anyone hurt me.

Everybody loved Bea. Everyone said she was impossible.

The first time Kay saw Nicholas, she thought immediately—for some obscure reason—of the man in the pandanus palms.

"Oh!" she said. There were candle flames pricking madly across the plains and hills and valleys—especially the valleys—of her skin.

"I saw him first," Bea said.

Of course it was true. Bea knew the most interesting places; she found them the way a bee finds frangipani trees. "I know a place beside the high school," she said. "You can see things."

Bea was obsessed with the high school, though she herself did not expect ever to go there. "Too dumb," she would shrug, not at all embarrassed. "In *some* ways," she would add, rolling her eyes. Already, while only in the seventh grade (Kay, eleven months younger, trailing behind her in the sixth), Bea earned ten shillings a week working in the shop near the high school; she slipped cigarettes under the counter; she was very familiar with the high school grounds.

It was a new high school on the edge of Brisbane, where the rainforest came down from Mount Glorious in long slender lizards' tongues and licked at the edges of the city. At lunchtime, and late in the afternoon, the high school boys and girls came in pairs and lay down in the long grass that parted and swayed and closed over the seedpods of their bodies.

"But from the trees," Bea said, "you can watch. And I know another place, even better, in Finsbury Park. There's a boy from Churchie who comes there."

"Churchie?"

"It's a high school, you drip, for rich kids. Rich *boys*. Only boys go to Churchie."

Kay followed Bea with awe up into the branches of a mango tree in Finsbury Park. The things Bea knew!

The Churchie boy came alone to Finsbury Park. He hung his hat from a twig by its grosgrain band (of school colors: blue and gray); he tugged at his blue and gray tie so that it lay slackly, a rakish noose, about his neck; he undid the laces of his heavy black shoes and kicked them off; he peeled off his socks. He rolled his trousers (flannel, charcoal-gray) up to the knee. He undid the buttons of his shirt and laced his hands behind his neck and lay back in the grass. The sun glinted off the pale golden down on his chest and gathered itself like a corona on the butter-gold shock of his hair, the beautiful butter-gold hair that fell in curls across his forehead and almost hid his right eye from view.

"Oh," Kay breathed, and felt the pricking and fanning and sighing and burning of the thousand and one tiny flames that lived in the hollows of her body.

Bea's eyes glittered, green flecks on the brown-black; they glitter-darted like dragonfly wings. "His name is Nicholas," she whispered. "He's mine."

And Kay, resisting for the first time in her life, thought: She can have everything else. She can have anything else of mine she wants. I will give her my bottle of mineral sands from Fraser Island, with the blue and purple and pink stripes and loops; I know she wants it. And I will give her my jasmine soap still in its tissue paper and my white stone from the cave on Tibrogargan. I will let her mess up my side of the room and I will do anything she asks, anything else that she asks.

And I will never think about the man in the pandanus palms again—Kay squeezed her eyes shut, blocking out that wicked unforgettable sight—I will never think of him, dear God, dearest God, not ever, I promise, cross my heart and hope to die, if You will just . . .

Nicholas sat up and pulled a paperback book from the hip pocket of his trousers. Bea and Kay held hands and bit their wrists and clung tightly to the branch with their legs, buffeted by shock waves of nervous pleasure.

"He always does that," Bea spluttered. "He reads and reads. And sometimes he plays a recorder."

"A recorder?" The outrageous, the incredible things Bea knew. They had to stuff leaves into their mouths to keep their excitement tied up and out of Nicholas's hearing.

"It's true, it's *true!*" Bea hissed. "Just you wait. He keeps his recorder down inside the front of his pants. It's *true!*"

This was altogether too much and Kay had to hug the branch with both arms and legs to keep from falling out. Squeezing her thighs around the bark, ignoring the scratching, ignoring the sticky sap, locking her ankles together, she bit into the mango bark and closed her eyes and when the pandanus sprang up, grove upon grove beneath her lashes, she only pressed her eyelids tighter and refused to look, not even when Bea swung monkeylike across her branch and tickled her and warned convulsively: "Don't wet your pants. Don't wet your—" Then she whispered urgently, "Look! Look! I *told* you."

Nicholas put down his book and lay back in the grass and there was a recorder in his hands. Kay blinked.

"He keeps it," Bea whispered with wicked gestures, "down inside—"

"I don't believe you."

"That's because you're—"

But Nicholas began to play and they were too lovestruck, too besotted to speak. They were hypnotized. They were ill with desire.

"Oh," Kay moaned. The air was thick with bellbirds, with hymns, with mango music. Choirs of angels swept through the stringybarks.

"Sometimes," Bea whispered, "he pisses in the bushes. I've seen his dick."

Kay put her hands over her ears.

"His name is Nicholas Truman," Bea said. "And after he finishes high school, he's going to go to the university."

"Shhh! He'll hear you. Shhh!" But Kay said it over to herself: *university*. It sounded thrilling, dangerous, an impossible and tantalizing place.

"And when I've finished Grade Eight," Bea whispered fiercely, "I'm gonna work in the shop all day and then he's gonna marry me."

Kay wished it were possible to disbelieve Bea. In a year and a half, she thought, her heart fluttering. In just a year and a half.

"Watch me," Bea whispered, swinging out, slithering, sliding along the slipways of the mango tree and dropping down inside the pandanus grass.

But Kay waited only until she heard the two voices touch each other, matchwood to matchwood. "G'day, Nicholas," she heard. "I'm Bea, from the shop, remember? And Kay—that's my stepsister— she's up there in that tree. She *watches* you." Oh, treachery! There was a quick flare of response, the voices colliding and striking laughter; and then Kay dropped to the ground and ran.

"It isn't fair," she yelled at the wattles. She grabbed a stringybark sapling in passing and yanked it, pulled it over till its tip touched the ground. "It isn't fair," she said, addressing the comment upward. She let the tree spring heavenward like a whip.

Me and Nicholas, Bea said later. Me and Nicholas this; me and Nicholas that. Seventh grade, eighth me-and-Nicholas grade.

"I don't care," Kay told her passionately, savagely pushing beyond the dotted line of socks, picking up underpants, stacking comics. "If he sees your room," she said, "he'll be *sick*."

*   *   *

This is the scene Kay plays and replays.

First the two horses, one blue-black and the other chestnut, are coming out of the rian forest; not the Tamborine Rainforest, where Bea will one day live, but the pocket of forest on Mount Glorious right on the lip of Brisbane. The horses emerge from the hiking paths and stand, muzzle to muzzle, at the edge of the picnic ground. There are riders, of course—that much can be seen; but they are distant. There is no more reason to invest them with significance, or even to wonder idly about them, than there is to pay attention to the man over there at the lookout, the one who is adjusting the telescope, putting in his two-shilling piece, and no doubt seeing everything from Ashgrove to the Pacific in a shining rush.

Bea is not present at this picnic. Bea is absolutely, definitely, absent. Quite often, these days, Bea just isn't around when it's time to leave for a family outing. She has "things to do, that's all."

"Other fish to fry," she tells Kay.

Before the picnic lunch, she is mentioned in prayer by Kay's father. *And Your wayward child Bea, dear Lord, who is precious in Thy sight . . .*

Bea is not present when the horses come out of the forest. Muzzle to muzzle, they crop grass at the edge of the picnic ground. Ten whole minutes, perhaps, Kay watches them idly, not knowing that life is about to change, that time will convulse, turn a somersault, taunt her. In retrospect, it is this calm space (with the horses and riders *there,* in her field of vision) that tantalizes her; that begets an addiction; that has her, on insomniac nights, prodding at ideas of randomness and fate, an eighth-grade philosopher obsessed with the laws of causality.

Is all of it chance? Or none of it?

"Oh, look!" Kay's mother says. "Horses. Let's go over."

Kay lifts her head, curious. Why is it wrong (well, at any rate, still improper, still unsuitable, still of absolute inconsequence at home) to know about Phar Lap, to pause in front of other people's radios and listen for those few frantic Melbourne Cup minutes; but not improper to want to go and see two horses at the edge of a picnic ground? Clues are the stuff of Kay's daily life; gathering data; drawing conclusions. She joins her mother.

Was there a moment . . . ? Could she pinpoint it . . . ? Must there not have been some point, some particular second in East Australian Time, ten hours ahead of the Greenwich Mean, when a certain progression of awareness could have been pinned down, graphed, indicated with tiny black crosses in a mathematics exercise book? And would it read jaggedly, a series of steps? Or would it be an impeccable curve, a flawless flowing from:

1. there are riders;
2. they are wearing jodhpurs and white shirts and bush hats;
3. one seems to be a woman;
4. yes, one is certainly a woman with long black hair;
5. the other is a man who—

And then, considerably before it would have been possible to distinguish either face, what kind of preknowledge is it that reaches out, that robs you of breath, that makes you stumble . . . ? There is a certain space when no record-keeping is possible, the graph of awareness unplottable.

"Hello!" Kay's mother calls. "What beautiful horses. Can we pat them?"

Kay thinks she is going to faint. Pieces of ground slide around her, their motion sickening. Remember Phar Lap? she considers, illogically, calling out, as though this might break her fall.

"Hello!" Nicholas says. The voice strikes her the way God's voice must have struck Moses on the mountain, a divine reverberation. She cannot look. "Hello," he says again, concerned. "Is something the matter with your little girl?"

Little girl, Kay hears and wishes to die. The gap between herself and Bea widens and widens; they are both fourteen; but in the eighth grade, Kay is often mistaken for a ten-year-old; Bea, only eleven months older and already working (she says) for some man in the city, is often taken for a fully grown woman. Seventeen or eighteen at *least.*

"Katherine?" her mother says, startled, looking back. "What is it, Katherine?"

Kay's eyes are watering; she can see nothing but pinwheels of light. "Nothing," she mumbles, rubbing them. "I've got something in my eye."

"The horses won't hurt you," Nicholas says. "You're not frightened, are you? Here, wouldn't you like a ride?" And there is apparently a succession of movements—rather in the manner of a cyclone moving down from the Bundaberg coast—and one of the gods has descended and swept her up and her legs are straddling the shoulders of the chestnut mare and she is looking the other blue-black horse in the eye.

Oh, humiliation. (To be hefted up as though she were a child!)

Oh, bliss.

Nicholas's left arm is lightly around her waist. His right hand, resting in front of her on the red-gold neck of the horse, is looped and ribboned with the reins. She can see each precious knuckle, a press of ivory bone against the tanned skin; she can see the pale down of hairs that begin at the cuff of his shirtsleeve and ride up toward the bases of his fingers; she can see the fishnet, the webbing, the myriad tiny lines of his skin. She has never seen anything so beautiful.

Sea-foam drips from the mouth of the blue-black horse and it whinnies. Nicholas wheels the chestnut mare and laughs, and Kay's mother calls, "Oh, careful, do be careful!"

"Isn't she a pretty little thing?" Nicholas laughs, and musses her hair.

Me, Kay thinks. He means me.

"Isn't she pretty, Verity?" he calls.

It is possible that the blood which is banging against the top of Kay's head and the tips of her fingers will come spurting out like a blast from a firehose, lavishly crimson. She waits for an answer from the rider of the blue-black horse. She knows exactly how that voice should sound.

She dares at last to look, squinting, and shading her eyes.

Verity does not squint. Verity's horse, though it champs and tosses its head, does not move without her permission. Verity is watching Kay with the attentiveness of a collector assessing an object that just might—and yet cannot be, surely?—that just might, conceivably, be so valuable that ... The collector is quiet with excitement, very quiet, waiting to place a bid, not wanting to alert ...

"What's the matter?" Nicholas calls to her gaily. "I won't drop her, you know, Verity. She's quite safe."

Kay has no ordered thoughts at all, though later she concludes that she is certainly not surprised. What could have been more natural? As fish fall back into the sea, as bellbirds keep to the gullies ... What could have kept Nicholas and Verity apart?

Verity asks: "What school do you go to?"

Kay cannot speak, but her mother, embarrassingly helpful, says: "She's at Wilston State. She's in Grade Eight and her teacher thinks she might win the Lily Medal. She wants to go to university."

"Mum!" Kay pleads in soundless anguish, in silent mortification.

Verity says: "I went to Wilston State."

Kay looks at her then. It seems to her that nothing has changed, not the dark eyes, not the grave and level stare, not the hand in the pocket. It might have been yesterday, that day in the Wilston School library. Verity's fingers, their shapes visible against the skin of her riding pants, count and recount hidden objects.

Raisins, Kay thinks.

Verity nods, as though a contract has been agreed to. She does not smile. (Has Verity ever smiled?) She says: "You're Katherine Sussex. I remember."

That is where the movie stops.

Kay could not, no matter how many nights she lay awake, get herself down off the horse, or make Verity explain the years between, or free Nicholas's hand from the reins.

She had, with elaborate and labyrinthine comments, tried to waylay her mother.

"Mum, do you remember that picnic at Mount Glorious?"

"Which picnic?"

"Oh, that time . . . I don't think Bea was there. I think . . . Was there one time when we saw some horses?"

"Horses? We often saw horses. Which time do you mean?"

"Yes, but . . . one time we *talked* to the people on the horses. And . . . and didn't someone give me a ride?"

"Talk?" Her mother sighs. "Strangers were always offering you sweeties or rides or something—it was dangerous; you'd go off at the drop of a hat. We had to keep our eyes peeled. Which time do you mean?"

Kay learned, a year later from her Latin teacher in high school, the word *syllogism*. She loved to roll it on her tongue. *Syllogism*. She saw mind bending backwards, turning somersaults, doing the splits. *Syllogism:* a game of construction and deconstruction.

She wrote on the flyleaf of her Latin primer:

Daydreams seem harmless, but they are dangerous.
I daydreamed that Bea would come to Brisbane.
Therefore Bea's father died.

    Daydreams seem real, but they are just delusions.
    I daydream about Nicholas and Verity.
    Therefore they might not be real.

Daydreams are dangerous and real.
At school I dreamed of someone to protect me.
Therefore I made up Verity and she became real.

    I wanted to see Verity again.
    I wanted Nicholas to touch me.
    Therefore I made them meet.

Kay resorted, finally, to the test of fire. Casually, so very casually, she said to Bea: "Do you remember that boy we used to watch when we were still in Wilston School? That high school boy?"

"Nicholas Truman?" Bea asked.

"Was that his name? The one who used to play a recorder?"

Bea hurled herself onto her bed and shrieked with laughter.

If she hadn't been sent to the library on Mondays, if Bea's father hadn't died, if Nicholas had never lain down beneath a mango tree in Finsbury Park and played his recorder, (if Bea hadn't invented his recorder?), if she hadn't heard that word, that exotic word *university*, first spoken to her, oh irony, by Bea . . . ?

Who would I be, she wonders, if I'd married Merv Watson when I turned eighteen, as asked? After the prayer meeting he'd waylaid her, on an Easter Saturday afternoon, right in front of the church. She was fingering the ragged cedars—was it just a year ago? yes—fingering the cedars and apparently watching the trams rumbling down through the Fortitude Valley and into the city; watching the trams but seeing Bea.

"The beach, naturally, where else?" Bea had said. "With a bunch of friends."

(What friends?)

Katherine pleated fronds of cedar between her fingers and asked herself: Who—apart from Bea—would believe that this is the way I spend Easter?

She saw a wave toss up the bodies of Nicholas and Bea and roll them golden up the Southport sands. She imagined Bea, her wet hair in a stream of laughter, provoking a game, getting herself chased, luring Nicholas away from the group, away away, disappearing between the dunes where pandanus and scrubby ti-trees grew in clumps.

"I believe it's God's will, Kay," Merv Watson said. "Prayer . . . if we seek His guidance . . . morning and evening . . . prayer. Revealed to me, I believe."

"What?" She made an effort to attend. "Sorry. I wasn't listening." And then slammed into an amazing possible future, looked it full in its watery eye. When she caught her shocked breath, her instinct was to say tartly: "God's will? That's the *last* reason I'd marry a man."

"Hubris?" she asks Charade years and years later, different country, different decade. "Did I catch it from Bea? Or else . . . I don't know . . . it takes such energy to rebel against people you love, you have to crank something up. God was grandpa/grandma/

father/mother. I couldn't move. It seemed to start then and got addictive."

"Hubris?" Charade asks.

"What?"

"Did you mean you got addicted to hubris?"

Katherine frowns, poised above several possible landing strips, getting her bearings. "The . . . Where was I? Merv Watson. Not hubris, perhaps, but certainly a taste for rebellion—it seems to date from him. Just wave a flag like *This is God's will* or *These are the rules* and you'll see smoke. You'll smell it. It'll singe my hair."

But Merv Watson. How was she to swim free of the tentacles of prayer and God's will? Constraints: they were everywhere. It is hard, so much harder than fighting dragons, to defend oneself against the innocent; and Merv Watson was an innocent, a hopelessly shy man, though (stiffened by the Holy Spirit) an earnest and fearless preacher on street corners, an expert with carburetors and spark plugs, a garage mechanic and a saint. The soul of goodness, impossibly gentle. Quite, in point of fact, impossible. Oh, help! she telegraphed to Bea, and an answer came, a Bea answer, kindness-coated, of course, but effective; a dishonorable, but oh-so-brilliant cheat.

"Will you marry me, Kay?" Merv Watson asked.

"I'd have to pray about it," she said demurely, trumping his ace. . . .

"Though that gambling metaphor, Charade, didn't come to me then, or even in the university library," Kay says, at a different point on her time-graph. "I knew as little about trumps and card games as I knew about the Melbourne Cup. No, it's only now that it strikes me what a clever little cheat I was. Oh, poor Merv. I'd taken no more notice of him, ever, than if he'd been a hymn-book. . . . But he had to respect God's will."

"And you told him—"

"Oh yes, it seemed kinder. Lied gravely and sweetly through my teeth. Though really . . ." They are pacing up and down the shoreline of a lake somewhere east of Toronto. Katherine picks up a handful of pebbles, starts skipping them one by one. "Really, *was* it lying after all? It couldn't possibly have been the will of . . . Could it? But then, you know, he looked so forlorn. . . ." One of her stones takes seven show-off steps before the water swallows it. She laughs. "He looked so *deflated* that I stood on tiptoe and gave him a quick kiss on the cheek." She skips another stone: five bounces. "I can't explain, I simply can't convey what a wicked thing that was, Charade. In that place, at that time, to that person. He looked so shocked that I did it again. I couldn't help myself. It was cruel, really."

But if she hadn't been cruel?

In the university library in 1961, Katherine Sussex—lucky undergraduate on a Commonwealth Scholarship—closes her eyes and sees herself scrubbing car grease from Merv's shirts, hears several toddlers crying, hears *The Gospel Hour* on the wireless. She opens them again and reaches out instinctively to stroke the spines of the nearest books: Late Roman Empire, history, the wars, the divisions, the turning of the faceted circles, third level below ground in the stacks. She takes a deep breath of the musty air, reassured.

But what saved me? she wonders, amazed, shivering slightly. (*Are you saved?* Merv used to demand of passers-by on the streets of Brisbane. *Are you saved?* he would ask through a megaphone on Friday nights. A beacon fixed at the corner of Adelaide and Albert streets, in front of the Commonwealth Bank, he would call to the lost teeming by: *Brother, sister, are you saved?*) What saved me? Katherine asks herself. Where did it come from, the force that jumped me from Merv Watson's orbit? Was it Bea juice or Verity's raisins? Who was dreaming me? Thinking me out? What quantum-leaped me?

"Oh my God," Bea had shrieked, rolling on their bedroom floor and kicking her feet in the air with glee. "Merv Watson. Oh my God, that's hysterical." Suddenly somber, she sat up, fingers like granny glasses around her eyes. "Well, maybe you should. Yes, I think he's your type. You could pray together for virgin births. You could read the Bible in bed. You could have three kids without fucking."

Katherine pelts the water with stones, a fusillade. "Sometimes, Charade, your bloody know-it-all mother . . ." (Was that where the rift had begun in earnest?) "Your mother and her fantastic claims!" Jets of water spurt up like accusations.

Charade, about to skip a stone, stops. "What do you mean, *her fantastic claims*? What do you mean exactly?"

"Nothing," Katherine says. "Nothing at all really, absolutely nothing. It's just . . . I'm still angry with her." (Is she still angry?) "Sometimes, anyway." (Though at others, she misses Bea so intensely that . . .)

"Get out," she had yelled at Bea, hurling pillows, books, shoes. "Get out of my room and don't come back. You're not my sister. You're not even . . . Get out get out get out."

"Pleasure!" taunted Bea. "B'lieve me, Lady Muck, Lady K, a pleasure. For your info, I got a room at the Duke of Wellington; I been more or less living there for weeks. You could visit, Lady Muck, except I don't serve morning tea."

"The Duke of Wellington!" Katherine was aghast, titillated, enthralled. "I don't believe you."

"I been working there part time for years, you dumb ninny. You and Merv Watson can bring tracts and Gideon Bibles."

"I wouldn't be caught *dead* at the Duke of . . . That's *cheap*. You're cheap, you—you barmaid!" A cushion flew by Bea's head. "You whore!" But Katherine, who knew this word only from the text of a seventeenth-century play by John Ford, pronounced it "wore"—causing Bea to double up in a fresh bout of helpless laughter.

"Oh, you should, you should," she gasped. "You should marry Merv Watson. You should."

"I hate you," Katherine shouted.

"Lady K, Lady K, Lady K," chanted Bea, throwing things into a knapsack, "she doesn't know B from A. She doesn't know prick from pray." She laughed wildly, ducking a shoe. "Lady Muck, Lady Muck, Lady Muck, she doesn't know faith from f—"

Katherine put her hands over her ears.

In the morning she read the message on the wardrobe mirror, whitely scored with a cake of soap.

K: You can visit at the Duke if you want. You have to ask at the bar, they'll show you where. I didn't mean the stuff about Merv, I was joking. B.

"You know, Kay," the pastor said in a kindly voice. "I think you should give our dear brother Merv the most prayerful consideration."

"Katherine," she'd insisted tartly, caught somewhere between guilt and amusement and cold fury. "My name is Katherine, not Kay." But where would she have gone spinning to as Mrs. Kay Watson, K the Unknown, Mrs. Curbside Evangelist, Mrs. Garage Attendant, Bewildered K?

"You know, Kay," the pastor said, unctuously patient, "if we—"

"Katherine."

"Yes. If we close a door in the Lord's face, He'll just come back in through a window. You can dodge all you like, but He'll get you in the end. There's no escaping God's will."

"What about Bea?" she demanded. Free-flying Bea. What pastoral nets could touch her?

"Ah Bea, our lost sheep. Bea least of all. You can be sure God has special plans for Bea."

(—who will give God a run for his money, Katherine thought. Will God go pubbing at the Duke of Wellington, keeping tabs, waiting and watching for his chance?)

"There's no escaping," the pastor said again. "I do not believe it is God's will, this university bee in your bonnet. You are tempting the Holy Spirit; He may have to break you. You can't get away from God's will, Kay."

But Kay has escaped into Katherine, and who will Katherine become while she dodges nets and the network of wills?

Who would I become, she asks herself in the university library, if I were to major in . . . say, history? or one of the sciences? instead of English/French Honors.

She is majoring in English, veering into the Middle Ages, because Verity Ashkenazy is the graduate tutor. She is also majoring in French Literature. The French Department's junior lecturer, a dazzling, a brilliant, a most *European* young man with whom every undergraduate girl is in love, is Nicholas Truman.

"Will he play Proust today, or Villon?" a student in Katherine's section, Richard St. John, asks with archly raised eyebrow.

"Pardon?" she says.

"He plays both roles to the hilt, wouldn't you say? Depending on the day of the week." Richard St. John has published poetry in two university quarterlies, one of them edited in Sydney. He has written a letter to Stephen Spender in England and has had a reply. He has written to W. H. Auden. He knows everything, and sooner or later, it is certain, like all good little Australians, he will be rewarded with Oxford. Katherine believes that he thinks her stupid; she trusts his judgment.

"Villon?" she echoes cautiously.

"Those Churchie boys," Richard St. John says, shaking his head. (He himself went to Brisbane Grammar.) "Dreadful poseurs. Mope, mope, that's the usual, *n'est-ce pas?* Sonnets to the Dark Lady in the English Department, Office 205, pale and wan and lonely proustering, yawn yawn yawn, madeleined out of his mind. Or else it's down at the Duke of Wellington. Roistering. Playing Villon."

The Duke of Wellington. Bea can't speak French but doesn't need to, and is much less confused than Kay. Bea knows what she knows. Bea knows everything she needs to know as she pushes glasses across the counter. Amber foam, like the off-colored wrack on the seashore, braids her wrists, stains the cuffs on her sleeves.

"*La broue,*" Katherine tells her, delivering a final washload left at the house, looking around nervously, severely ill at ease. "Beer broth, it's called in French slang."

"You don't say?" Bea, doing something disturbing with her tongue, blows circles of smoke in Kay's face. "I call it head."

"How can you live here? How can you? Why don't you come home?"

"Come home," mocks Bea. "Where's that?" She blows a corkscrew of smoke that spirals itself around Kay. "What for?"

I miss you, Kay will not say. Who's going to translate the

world for me? she wants to cry. Please, she wants to beg. She says neutrally: "You know I didn't mean it."

"You don't say?" Bea smiles and lets her eyelids droop low and heavy.

Katherine, who knows less and less, breathes the tranquil and musty air of the university library; she reaches up and strokes the dimpled cliff-face of the bookshelves, the fort that protects her, and turns back to her translation.

Wyrd biđ ful aræd!

She translates: *Fate* (the fate of the seafaring wanderer lost in the late eighth century) *is fully fixed.*

Fully fixed? Who fixes fate? Who's the racketeer? Can a bad fate be fixed?

The wanderer stirs up the rime-cold sea with his hands. Katherine scribbles across the tangent routes and circles of her life, a rough draft. She grimaces over the literal translation, feeling for smoothness, reaching for the old mellow lilt of the Noisome Pestilence and the wings of the Almighty in the feathers of whose cadences she trusts. She writes in her notebook: . . . *though, troubled in heart, he rows through the rime-cold sea. How unbending is fate!*

And then, on the scrap paper, adds a question mark: *How unbending is fate?*

To the serried ranks of books, she murmurs sardonically: "How unbending *is* fate?"

Can it be outwitted? Does it lie in wait, gloating, like the will of God?

When Katherine, translation of "The Wanderer" in hand, taps on Verity's office door for her tutorial, there is no answer. Strange. She checks her watch.

Ah, well, there is still so much to be done; how does anyone keep up with all the reading? She hears of students who go to parties, to college banquets, on hikes and trips. When do they study? She decides to sit in the grassy quadrangle, soaking up sun, working on her French. When Verity walks along the cloisters—she will be, surely, coming from the library, where she must have been detained—Katherine will see her. But what makes Katherine glance up from the quad to Verity's office window? What sixth sense?

In any case, Verity is there, standing still as a question in the spotlight of Queensland sun.

Puzzled, Katherine splays her hands open in the warm grass, pushes them into earth, testing for something. Laying her cheek between her hands, she smells not just couch grass and mud, a sweet mix, but chlorine, the school swimming pool, the concrete steps, the musty Mondays in the old school library. *No*, she says, *no*. Meaning: not here, no; that has gone, the old stink of Wilston School. Gone like Kay. I can do what I like with the past; it is easy as plasticene; it only exists now and then.

She is sprawled full length, her *Oxford Book of French Verse* lying open in front of her, the working sheets of a Verlaine translation fluttering, threatening to dart off toward the refectory with a passing cluster of students. Uncertain, Katherine stares up at the window again. Did she pass Verity on the stairs? It's just possible. She has become aware of an alarming tendency within herself to be lost, literally lost, in thought. Concentrating, she folds the rough drafts of Verlaine and closes her book, her eyes on the students: the way they laugh, the way they bump into one another comfortably as they walk, the way their eyes scan the quad, expecting pleasure. What would that be like: ordinariness? the yearned-for unattainable gift of being like everyone else?

Under an archway of the cloisters, she pauses and leans against a column. Golden sandstone: the very words, somehow, speak to her of a new heaven and a new earth, far from the grubby brick church with its steam of worshippers. The golden sandstone is warm and grainy; as comfortable as the lost Shadow of the Almighty. No, not that. As comfortable as the shoulder of Nicholas if she can lean far enough into that horseback memory, that state of bliss, that dream.

Katherine shades her eyes, and yes, Verity is still at her window, seemingly propped there, fixed. Verity, who fixes fate with raisins. (Do Nicholas and Verity still ride together? Did they ever? Where now the horses and riders? And what is Bea doing at this moment? And where is Nicholas? And what now, at the Duke of Wellington?)

Concentrate, Katherine orders herself sarcastically. Can you pass this test? Can you get yourself up the stairs and down the hallway to Room 205; can you slip into the first sentence of a tutorial for which you are running late; can you make it without sliding down a tangent of thought?

She knocks at Verity's door.

No answer.

("Snap out of it, Verity," she hears Miss Warren say in the Wilston School library.)

But is this the same Verity? Katherine considers the lectures and seminars, the crackle of Verity's mind: Verity alert, Verity ascendant, Verity *Scholastica Regina*. No sign has ever been given to Katherine, unless . . . On the first day, when the section list was read aloud, did Katherine imagine a hesitation after her name? She had raised her hand in answer to the roll call, had waited for something. What? Verity's eyes, meeting hers, were neutral.

In the beginning, Katherine thought, we are frightened children. Later, we invent protectors, magic, our whole childhood. It is possible that she looked at me once, accidentally, in the old school library, how many years ago now? Ten years ago. Nothing more than that perhaps, except for a moment with horses at the edge of the rainforest—a mere five years ago, that—a moment, however, that I may have wished into being.

Katherine knocks on the door again, and when there is no answer, opens it slightly, leans inside, and says: "Miss Ashkenazy?" Very shy and formal. Since there is no rebuke, nothing to suggest that she has been brash or intrusive, she sidles in, closes the door quietly behind her, and moves to the familiar chair at the side of the desk. Soft academic noises, these will do the trick, she feels: the scuffle of her briefcase placed beneath the chair, the velvet thud of the books, papers rustled.

Verity is wearing jodhpurs and a white silk blouse and riding boots. Tossed across the armchair by the window are her black academic gown and a riding whip and her briefcase—as though she had finished with teaching obligations for the day (the afternoon tutorial session forgotten?) and was about to drive out to the country where a horse might be stabled. Out beyond Indooroopilly, perhaps; or out through The Gap to Mount Glorious.

Katherine says awkwardly: "I could come back tomorrow."

Verity turns from the window. It seems now as though she has simply been waiting for her student, as though nothing unusual has happened, although, Katherine notes, Verity's eyes seem unnaturally bright and her right hand is deep in the pocket of her jodhpurs.

" 'The Wanderer,' " Verity says calmly enough in her low voice. Her accent is Australian, but espaliered Australian. There is nothing of the scrubby sound of Wilston School to it, no bush or back garden notes. "I'd like you to read it aloud in Anglo-Saxon first. I think we can touch the wayfarer in the sound of that lost tongue more than in the most thorough translation. Don't you agree?"

Yes, Katherine thinks with a prickle of excitement, and a sense that she has always agreed, has always been waiting for this thought to be offered up for her agreement. With only a slight self-consciousness, she pushes out hesitantly into the ancient words, guttural, teutonic, thick with the spume of the cold North Sea. *Oft him anhaga,* she begins. She rows jerkily, and the wide dangerous emptiness of the ocean washes over them.

At *Nis nu cwicra nan . . .* she falters. It seems that a cramp, or some sort of pinching of nerves, has fastened on Verity. Wincing, she has placed a hand on Katherine's wrist, an involuntary act, and then returned the hand to her pocket. Katherine watches the pocket, the way the fingers inside it twist and turn.

As though the reading were a psalm, Verity takes up an antiphonal refrain:

> *"Nis nu cwicra nan*
> *pe ic him modsefan   minne durre*
> *sweotule asecgan."*

Not one is now living to whom the wanderer dares to express himself openly—though Katherine, holding her breath, has a sense of impending revelation.

"It's the anniversary," Verity says in a low voice, "of the last time I saw my parents. May 15, 1943."

Katherine thinks with a slight shock: And I was a few months old, knowing nothing. Safe.

She waits.

"I was at school," Verity says. "We lived outside Le Raincy. I'd just started that year." She goes to the window again and speaks so softly that Katherine has to stand close behind her to hear, and even then she has to strain and at times only the tips of phrases reach her. She has the impression that the words insist on being spoken aloud, that they push up with seismic force through a fault line in the thin crust of Verity's present, but that Verity does not wish the words to be heard. She has, too, a fleeting vision of Verity standing at the curved prow of an ancient boat, a boat without a crew, a boat that has left a ruined city behind it; and it seems to her that Verity sings her lament in the alliterative lines of a language that cannot be translated.

"I was six years old," Verity says. "I can smell the headmaster's tobacco. He has yellow teeth." She is speaking very fast now, very low and fast. "He comes to the kindergarten classroom. *Vérité! Vite, vite! You have to hurry!* The others think I'm in trouble again." She turns slightly toward Katherine, explaining: "I wear the star." She turns away again. "Other children . . . *do* things."

Katherine waits.

"That morning I hid, but Maman gave me a handful of raisins and made me go."

Katherine senses, more than hears, the rest: the headmaster perhaps pushing, perhaps dragging a little girl down the hallway, soldiers in the grounds, the headmaster *hurry* down the back stairs, the tradesmen's entrance . . .

"He pushes me. I can't move. It's so far to the fence and the trees, the pine trees. *Run!* he says. *Run!* So I run."

There is a long long silence. Verity's hand is convulsive in her pocket. At one point she half turns and says distractedly in a flat voice only just barely inflected into a question: "Pine needles?" But Katherine is afraid to answer.

"It's dark and I'm frightened," Verity says. "I rip off my star and walk out from the trees and go home. There's nobody there."

She turns around suddenly and demands of Katherine, astonished: "I was six years old. How did I know to do that, to rip off the star?" Her cheeks are feverish, her eyes glitter, and Katherine does not answer. Verity turns back to the window and looks out at nothing.

The silence goes on and on. "In the convent," Verity says, but never finishes the sentence. *"Je ne parle jamais français,"* she says at another point. *"Jamais, jamais. Je l'ai perdu absolument, une langue morte."* (Is it true? Katherine wonders. Does she never speak French anymore? Or is she never aware when she speaks it?) Verity begins to shiver, at first slightly, hugging herself, and then more and more violently. An ague, Katherine thinks; the lost word is the only one that comes to her. Helpless, she picks up the academic gown and drapes it over Verity's shoulders.

It is as though a curtain has been dropped and raised. New scene. Abruptly the shivering stops.

"There is a certain cultural milieu," Verity says in a clear professorial voice, as if someone has wound her up, or pushed a button, "that the student of Anglo-Saxon must make an effort to enter. For instance, in 781 when Alcuin went from Britain to the court of Charlemagne, the Christianized Anglo-Saxons touched their own past again." She says suddenly, arrested by a thought, "There must have been Jews in Aachen even then"—but it is as though a rogue radio wave, or stray shortwave static, has pushed through her larynx without her knowledge. For a moment she looks at Katherine vaguely, frowning, her head cocked, listening for something. Then she pulls books down from her shelves and resumes her clipped impersonal lecture. "The Anglo-Saxons from Canterbury fanned back into darkest Europe. We have Alcuin's homilies; and Aelfric's, much later." She is looking for something, but can't find it. She sits at her desk again, and indicates the chair for Katherine.

"Well," she says, "anyway, there was a British bishop who was about to baptize a pagan chieftain, somewhere east of Aachen. His own contemporary ancestor, you might say. The chief made profession of faith, but then, on the very brink of the river, one foot in the baptismal water, he paused to ask: 'My ancestors? Will I meet them again in Heaven?'

" 'Ah, no,' the bishop said. 'They cannot enter heaven. They died without Christ.'

"And the pagan chief withdrew his foot from the water. 'Then neither shall I enter heaven,' he said, and not all the threats of hellfire or eternal damnation could sway him. He died heroically, without Christ, believing himself to be damned, rather than set a rift between himself and those he honored.

"That is the tragic sense at the heart of the 'Wanderer' poem," Verity says. "Was the poet Christian or pagan?" Her eyes, this time, require an answer: from student to professor. But Katherine cannot speak. Verity gives a small smile, approving, as though her student has come up with the only proper response. "He was both," she says. "Both." And then, her voice suddenly dropping so low again that Katherine has to strain to hear: "I was brought up Catholic. In a convent. The nuns saved me."

Saved, are you saved? comes a ghostly echo. If ever, Katherine thinks, dizzy, falling into the terrifying well of Verity's eyes, if ever I should see a lost soul, this is she. But *Nicholas,* she thinks. Since it has such power to restore order, to right all wrongs, she blurts it out. "Nicholas," she says.

Verity stares vaguely at the word that floats between them. She frowns a little. The word has a meaning she should know but she cannot remember it. She looks blankly at Katherine.

Katherine knows that the gaps in this story will never be filled out. Not by Verity.

She will never know how long they sat there. It was dark, she thinks, when she found herself on the university bus, alone, riding into the city. She can replay the smell of grass in the quad, the sight of Verity from the cloisters, the sound of Anglo-Saxon intoned, but not the moment of leaving that room.

She thinks she remembers this, however. She thinks she remembers that Verity held out a handful of raisins and that she took one. They both partook and ate.

6. Bee in Her Bonnet

Once upon a time, Charade tells Koenig, Bea made a telephone call from a pub called the Duke of Wellington. . . .

"No," Katherine says. "I won't meet you there. Why don't you come here? Or out to uni?"

"Prude," Bea taunts.

"It's got nothing to do with that. I just feel . . . conspicuous, that's all. I feel alien. I *can't* go there."

"Oh, *conspicuous*." Bea slides into her exaggerated imitation of educated Australian; Pom-talk, she calls it, or uni-talk. "Too la-di-da *alien* for the Duke. What the hell does *alien* mean? Well, uni is too la-di-da for me, Lady K, and I can't come home."

"Why not? Oh come on, Bea, don't be silly. We haven't seen you for months. Mum and Dad aren't—"

"No. You'll see why. The kiosk at the Gardens, then. Two o'clock, I'll be waiting."

And at the Botanical Gardens, Kay does see why, and feels

suddenly faint. She has broken into a run at the sight of Bea's unkempt curls through the latticed arch of the arbor beside the kiosk. Arms outstretched, she has the sense of running toward a missing part of herself. She stops short. She reaches for the kiosk railing and slides onto the bench. "Oh my God, Bea," she whispers.

Bea is pregnant.

(*Down at the Duke of Wellington,* a voice plays itself in Katherine's ear. *Roistering. Playing Villon.*)

The pregnancy is in the early stages, but still, given Bea's flamboyant body and her taste for tight clothes, there can be no mistake.

["How can I explain to you, Charade?" Kay asks, decades later. "That time and that place—it's not possible to . . . How can I convey the impact? If you wore a placard saying AIDS around your neck perhaps, you'd have some equivalent idea."]

"Thought I might shock you," Bea laughs, blowing cigarette smoke between them.

"You don't shock me." Katherine means to seem blasé, but sounds prim. Her lungs are sealed off; black motes dance in front of her eyes. (*Down at the Duke of Wellington he's mine, he's roistering mine, and after I finish Grade Eight we'll be playing Villon.*)

Bea is watching her closely. "Father's nobody you know," she says. And Katherine's breath comes back, stumbling on its way in. She turns away and breathes slowly, counting two three four, calming her jerky pulse. "A farmer from up Tamborine way," Bea says. "He's okay. Got a place up on the mountain, so I'm going."

"Going?" Katherine echoes faintly. Away from the Duke and Villon?

"Oh, stop looking at me like that. And there's no need to tell Mum and Dad," Bea says. She lights a cigarette from the one between her lips, and tosses the butt into lantana bushes. Instinctively Katherine flinches and half moves to pick up the litter. Bea laughs noisily. "Jesus. Hear no evil, see no evil, speak no evil, and always pick up after yourself." But she stubs out the new cigarette on the bench and walks across to the rubbish bin. "There!" She tosses it in. "Got to quit anyway, I guess." She pats her stomach, then asks, looking out over geometric swirls of begonias: "Mum and Dad ever ask about me?"

"You are mentioned every night at family prayer."

"I'll bet."

"They love you, Bea. We all do."

"Yeah, I know." Compulsively she lights another cigarette, sucks greedily, three, four puffs. "Oh hell." She stares at the Camel (no filter) as though it were a parakeet that has somehow alighted and got itself caught in her fingers. She drops it and grinds it with her heel. "Oh for God's sake," she says, "you don't have to look at it like that."

"Like what? I wasn't . . . Sorry, I wasn't even conscious . . ."

"I know you weren't, you ninny." Bea makes a gesture of helplessness with her hands. She picks up the smashed cigarette and sends it on a long slow arc into the bin. "Oh, jeez. What a mess-up, eh?"

"It's kind of exciting," Kay offers awkwardly. "A baby. Getting married."

"Jesus, I'm not getting married. I'm not *that* stupid. Just shacking up, that's all. You can't have a bun in the oven at the Duke. Not proper, is it?" She laughs. "I've been fired."

"Oh Bea." They stare at each other. For a crazy second Kay thinks of Gene the sailorman from Tennessee. "Remember that sailor?" she asks inanely. "In Melbourne. When we were kids."

"What sailor?"

"The Baddle Ship Man . . . Don't you remember? In the buttercup patch?"

"Jesus. The buttercup patch. When me dad was still . . ."

"And a sailor came. He was going to take you to Tennessee."

"Sounds like one of your tall stories. Or one of mine. The stuff I made up, that you believed! God, Kay, I could tell you anything, you were so stupid." Bea laughs. "Oh Jesus, I gotta be getting back to work. I got till the end of the month, and we need the dough."

"Do you have to rush off?" Kay bites her lip, hesitates, then says, "Oh heck, you dreadful woman, I miss the mess in my room," and throws her arms around Bea. "I'll be an aunty," she says. "Just think."

" 'Struth," Bea says gruffly. "Poor little bugger. He'll be shanghaied for Sunday school if he doesn't watch out. He'll have to mind his P's and Q's."

"And his B's and K's."

"And now a word of prayer . . ." Bea flutters angelic eyelids, mimicking familiar rituals.

"For our wayward sister Bea," Kay intones.

"And the child she conceived in sin. Hey, what *is* this? Are you laughing or crying or what?"

"Yes."

"C'mon, Kay, it's no big deal. Just another bee in my bonnet. Jeez, I gotta have a smoke. I'm sorry."

"Bea, as if I care."

"As if you don't, you ninny. So. How's uni then?" She sits beside Kay on the bench.

"Oh Bea, I love it. I have a carrel of my own in the library— well, it's not mine, but no one else uses it, down in the stacks—and I just read all the time."

"Yeah. So I hear."

In one instant all the nerve threads in Kay's body are tugged tight, but something is pushing up up and through her like a geyser. Her voice bleats itself out, as proper and vinegarish as Sunday: "From whom do you hear?"

"From whom do you hear," mimics Bea, exaggerating, sticking her tongue plummily into her cheek. "From who'dja think, you brainy K-storm?" She begins to pace around the octagonal latticed arbor, sucking hard on her cigarette, smoke dragoning out of her nostrils. She says suddenly, offhandedly, passing on dubious information: "Nicholas says you're bloody brilliant."

Kay is stunned into speech. "Nicholas *talks* about me?" She means: Nicholas notices me? Of all the students in his seminar, I am actually more than a name on French assignments? Nicholas actually notices, knows, links me to . . . ? Oh God oh God, does that mean it is so embarrassingly obvious that I . . . ? Does it show when I look at him?

Katherine would like to die quickly and neatly of shame. "Do you mean—?"

"He's got a thing about brains. You and the Ashcan, that prissy sheila. Don't catch *her* getting caught with her pants off."

This coded and convoluted piece of information hits Katherine like a football in the soft hollows of her obsession. She thinks, winded: And your cock-and-bull story about the farmer from Tamborine . . . ?

"Oh for God's sake, stop staring at me like that," Bea says, sending up smoke tornadoes from mouth and nostrils. "It's not his. I know that for certain, worse luck. He was away with the Ashcan woman." Smoke floats in a screen between them. "Uni holidays, *you* should know. Three bloody weeks at the crucial time, so that's that." She makes another circuit of the carved central pole and comes to a halt in front of Kay. "Believe me," she says, jabbing at the air with her cigarette in emphatic punctuation, "when it's his I'm gonna have, I'll tell you."

Katherine might as well be on the Big Dipper at the Brisbane Show, so many waves buffet her, so many peaks/troughs/peaks/troughs giddily passing, so many slivers of hope and anguish. She kneels on the bench and leans over the latticework to face the tangle of lantana, the sweep of lawn, the distance noisy with exotic botanical color. She is afraid she might actually be sick. She feels foolish.

"Kay," Bea says. "Kay . . ." She hooks one arm over the lattice and puts the other roughly around Kay's shoulders. "Look at me, you silly ninny. *Look* at me." But Kay, resisting, brushes her eyes with the back of her hand.

"Oh Kay," Bea sighs. "You can't have *everything*." And when Katherine, startled, turns to face her: "You can't have *everything*, Kay."

Katherine stares at the note that is paper-clipped to her French assignment. It is possible that the entire morning has swum by, she cannot tell; it is possible that if she were to surface from her carrel deep in the stacks, there might be stars above the cloisters and the quad. The note is in red ink from a ballpoint pen, the same ink that has made marginal comments on her assignment and that speaks in a stylish scrawl and clipped Brit accent (Pom-talk) from the lower half of the last page of her essay:

An unequivocal A. Nice work, Katherine—though I'm not sure your evidence is conclusive for the link between Molière, Act I, sc iii, and the incident in Madame de Sévigné's letter. Provocative, nevertheless. And since you've discovered the letters, you might consider doing your next major assignment on them, instead of on the set topic. See me about this.

See me about this. Wouldn't that have been enough? That alone could have sent her into a trance. And then in addition— would you call this afterthought or forethought?—there is the paper-clipped note.

> *Katherine:*
> *We seem to share an obsession with Verity and I thought per-haps you could help me. I'd be interested in knowing what your sharp and perceptive mind brings to bear on the problem. I understand from Bea that you don't care to frequent the usual student joints. The refectory then? A dinner for your insights? Thursday at six. Let me know if that doesn't suit.*
> *Nicholas.*
> *P.S. Trust you'll forgive this unorthodox request.*

Your sharp and perceptive mind, Katherine thinks, dazed. I understand from Bea . . . Your sharp and perceptive mind. Bea says you don't care to frequent . . .

How dare Bea talk about me like that? she fumes; as though I were one of her beers on tap at the Duke.

Then she thinks: Nicholas asks her about me.

Because of Verity, of course. Still. *Your sharp and perceptive mind.* Why does he link me with Verity? Does Bea tell him that? Is it possible that Verity herself . . . that Nicholas and Verity actually discuss . . . ? No. Not possible. Put it down to tattletale Bea.

When Katherine finds herself dreamwalking along Coronation Drive toward the Adelaide Street trams, having got off the university bus a stop too early, it is midafternoon. But is it still Tuesday? Because she knows time can bolt—it has happened to her over and over—while she merely stops to pick a wayside thought. Here's something new, however, the reverse, an Einstein knot: the way time can balk in its tracks, the way the spinning world slows, takes a smoko when heavy business is afoot, buggers off for a day.

How has Katherine arrived on lower George Street, beyond the reach of the tramlines, when she has a tram to catch? She walks past the Duke of Wellington, around the block and past it again. If she does it one more time, Bea might see her, and what are her motives for consulting Bea? On the third circuit she keeps going and gets a tram at the corner of Adelaide and George. How will the time pass until Thursday at six? Will it pass?

The time does pass, *mirabile dictu,* and here they are at a corner table. Beyond the window, allamanda and bougainvillea, brash siblings, clamor at the sun from trumpet throats, and the lawns fall down toward the river where the racing eights come and go in a bright flash of oars.

"Has she ever talked about it?" Nicholas has asked. He means Verity.

And Katherine, silent, has gone on staring out toward the river. I can never speak of that day, she thinks.

"I've pieced fragments together," Nicholas says. "I know her parents. I mean the ones who had her brought out here in '46, the De L'Anneau family, the ones who adopted her. No one knows what happened to hers. The De L'Anneaus have a document: *Believed dead, Auschwitz 1943,* but that's all." He leans over to the next table. "Mustard? No? I find I have to douse refectory food with something.

"Yes," he says. "That's how I met her, through the family, when my father absconded and brought me out with him." He looks out the window, reflective. "I still remember that night, the midnight train to Dover. It seemed like a huge adventure." He laughs. "Younger sons, you know; gambling debts and whatnot. My father, who continues to cut a somewhat shady swath through Sydney these days, thought it was a kindness to his older brother, the seventh earl. I don't know what my mother might have thought. She was left behind with a baby. Anyway, one of the De L'Anneaus married a second cousin of mine at three removes, or some such thing."

Katherine's memory, dizzy, is tossing up random images: Gene the sailorman; the blue stripes on Patrick's legs; Merv Watson with the megaphone in his hands; Nicholas under the mango tree in Finsbury Park. At last, she thinks, the high inaudible notes of his recorder are reaching my ears.

"These days, the De L'Anneaus have a finger in plenty of pies," says Nicholas. "Along with my father. Very hardheaded and pragmatic, people like the De L'Anneaus; well, no more so than your average Catholic aristocrat, I suppose, especially the recently impoverished, especially the ones with Parisian connections, especially the ones who are Jewish if you go back far enough." He surveys the almost empty refectory. "Katherine, my dear, cafeterias are frightfully depressing, don't you think? Next time, anywhere but here. Agreed?"

Next time, Katherine thinks, swallowing hot tea and not trusting herself to speak. *Katherine, my dear.*

"Anyway, I've known her since we were kids. De L'Anneau's her legal name, by the way. I expect she's told you that?" Absent-mindedly he picks up his knife and begins tapping its blade very lightly against Katherine's forearm. He could be doodling on a piece of scrap paper for all the awareness he bestows on this, but the nerves in Katherine's body realign themselves at dizzying velocities. She watches the piece of metal that connects her with Nicholas. "She was Vérité Acier when she came to them," he says. "That's the name the nuns in Le Raincy gave her. She's the one who insisted on Ashkenazy again, as soon as she got here, right from the start." He stops tapping with the knife and leans forward. "My father got that from her parents. Amazing, really, when you think about it: that kind of determination when you're nine years old. Has she talked about this?"

Katherine, eyes on the unfocused allamanda distance, shakes her head slightly.

Nicholas sighs. "Of course she's had the best of medical . . . the best psychiatrists. The De L'Anneaus have been able to see to that"—he gives Katherine the kind of wry smile that assumes complicit knowledge of the business world—"in the wake of recent real estate deals in which my father had a hand. Anyway, we assume that's helped. The psychiatry, I mean. But she'll never speak French; it's a

kind of hysterical muteness." He begins tapping with the knife
again. "And the absurd thing is, you know, she's the reason I
decided to study French—as a callow but lovesick Churchie boy."

Churchie: and Katherine is hurtled back to Finsbury Park when
Churchie was just an exotic word and the golden boy lay in the
grass with his recorder. So constantly accessible in dreams. *Churchie.*
Church of England Grammar School. Katherine's heart sinks; she
withdraws her arm from the tapping knife. The refectory table widens and widens; it is wider far than Finsbury Park. She stares across
unbreachable distances. Private school people, she thinks, are given
something very early on; perhaps it is something they eat, something that tells them they are always right, and even if they are not,
it doesn't matter. State school people are always afraid they are
wrong; they worry about it.

"I thought she might talk to me then. In French." Nicholas
shakes his head, amazed at his own life. "The reasons for doing
what we do!"

Oh yes, Katherine thinks. The amazing reasons.

Her eyes still on the middle distance, on the haze above river
and racing eights, she asks: "Why are you telling me all this?"

"Because I'm afraid. Because she seems to be getting further
and further away."

Katherine, studying his profile (since it is Nicholas who now
stares into the bougainvillea) asks herself: Who fascinates me more,
he or she?

But how does one choose among gods?

"I don't understand," she says awkwardly, nervously, "why
you think that I . . . why I could possibly be of any . . ."

"Nine years old," Nicholas says. "Of course, the weeks in the
forest living by her wits, and then the convent years. All the daily
deceits required and the never knowing when . . . But still, amazing."

"I don't know . . ." Katherine stumbles over words. "I mean,
yes, it is, it is amazing, only it . . ." In another way, she feels, it is
quite unsurprising. "There's something . . ." But can she translate
into words her sense of the rime-cold prow of the boat where Verity
stands? And of the *way* that Verity will always stand, undaunted,
unflinching, the worst already known. Is it possible to express this?

She would need to speak, she thinks, in Anglo-Saxon. "The lighted hall," she begins clumsily, inanely. "Once it's lost . . . I mean . . ." But she gives up and says in another kind of voice altogether: "I don't think you need to be afraid for her."

"Moving further away from all of us," Nicholas says, his barque sailing in other waves. "Other people have noticed. Not I alone."

Not I alone. The private school syntax snags in Katherine's mind. She flinches, scanning backwards for possible errors committed, the grammatical gaucheries of state school speech.

Nicholas leans forward and catches hold of her wrist with a sudden urgency and demands: "In her seminars, do you notice? Is she always coherent?"

"Yes," Katherine says, looking at his fingers on her wrist. "Absolutely lucid. Always." There will be a bruise, she thinks. A permanent bracelet of some kind, a sort of pressure scar.

"Charade," she says, at the shoreline of a much later chapter, "I've thought and thought but I've never accounted for it. From almost any perspective, it's neurosis. Viewed even from the next table in the refectory, it's pathetic. Or just silly. *That poseur* was what someone used to say about Nicholas, another student, a Richard St. John, who teaches at Oxford now.

"Do you know, Charade, just last year I finally spent a day in the library looking for traces of brilliant Nicholas. Not a book, not a single article, going back twenty-five years. What does this mean?

"And yet that day in Toronto last year . . . The mere sight of him . . . I felt as though I'd been shot. Traffic screeching, horns, I could have been killed. And then when he—"

"Wait," Charade says. "Wait, that's a switchback jump. I can't . . . How did we get to Toronto?"

"I thought I'd lose him. I went careening across the street between cars—"

"My father's in Toronto? You found him?"

Katherine blinks. "Nicholas," she says faintly, leaning back against the limestone cliff of her lakeshore. "Even the name, you know, after all these years . . . just saying it."

"He's here in Canada?"

"Here?" Katherine looks about her uncertainly. "Where are we?" she asks, as though a fog has settled around them.

"Kay! Kay!" Charade is pounding with her fists. "Aunt Kay, don't *do* this to me. We're in the refectory with my father, and then suddenly you're—"

"The refectory," Katherine sighs.

In the refectory, Nicholas is asking: "She doesn't . . . drift off? Lapse into silences?"

"Verity? No. Not in lectures or seminars."

"But at other times?"

"Don't . . . ? Don't we all?" Katherine ventures.

"Ah," he says, letting her wrist fall back on the table and rubbing his temples with his fingers. "What lapses. What silences may come."

Katherine says hesitantly, feeling her way: "I think . . . Aren't there necessary silences? Strong ones?" What she is striving to articulate is this: She believes she has the sorcerer's stone in her hands; she believes Verity pulled it from the pocket of her jodhpurs and gave it to her. She believes henceforth she will know what to do at the batwing touch of harm, of fear, of loss. Mute, she holds her cupped hands out toward Nicholas by way of explanation.

"Raisins," she says.

"Raisins?" Nicholas frowns. "What do you mean, raisins?"

"In Verity's pocket. You know the way she is always . . ." Nicholas, quizzical, is looking at her as though she is reading from the wrong page. "You do know," she says, confident in her tiny area of specialization (minor contribution perhaps, an esoteric footnote, but significant), "you do know why she always has raisins in her pocket."

He lifts an eyebrow, bewildered, perhaps even politely amused. "Hmm. Raisins. I've known her a long time but I can't say I've ever . . ." He asks suddenly: "This isn't one of Bea's stories, is it?" He conveys benevolence, affection, the very mildest of discreetly patronizing smiles. "Bea claims you believe anything she—"

Panic. Inner vertigo. Also anger and humiliation fuel Katherine's powers of invention. "I meant it as a figure of speech, actually. *Synecdoche*." She taps astonishing reserves of irony. "Certain things, of course, she *has* discussed with me, especially hunger as both a literal and symbolic issue." A whole prior life for Verity balloons up in Katherine's mind like a dandelion puffball, lodging seeds of event, putting out details, growing yellow as the sun and at least as flamboyant. "But I don't think I should violate her trust." Dizzy now with power, seeing the clouding of his eyes, the quick wince, she turns the knife: "Of course, she's grateful to you, Nicholas. That goes without saying."

Nicholas is in disarray, both his Proust and his Villon hats askew. "Katherine," he says, looking at her differently, "I had no idea you . . ."

And nor did she. It is as though she had discovered a dagger in her hand, or a steel backbone running through the middle of her body. Bemused, she rubs the nape of her neck where it might perhaps protrude. And a part of her frantically signals Miss Warren, dragon lady of the library on Mondays. Is it possible Miss Warren is still living? Daydreaming, perhaps, on the terrace of an Eventide home in Brisbane? And if Katherine were to write her a letter?

> *Dear Miss Warren:*
> *On the occasion of your irritation with Verity Ashkenazy, our Dark Lady of the Others, what did aforesaid defendant place on your table on the Monday of unremembered month inst., A.D. 1951 or thereabouts?*

("Charade," Katherine sighs, kneeling on the limestone shingle and splashing her face with lake water. "I still don't know the answer to that question. Were there raisins, or weren't there?")

Nicholas says: "I knew there was something between you, some connection. I sensed it." He pauses, weighing risks. "I'll tell you something a little odd, Katherine. You could say I became aware . . . You could say I was warned of you in a dream." He makes a graceful gesture of ironic self-deprecation with his hands. "It's, ah, quite exotic in its way. In the dream, Verity and I were riding up near the rainforest somewhere. And then I noticed she had a child in front of her saddle. When I drew alongside"—he gestures again to indicate the illogical nature of dreams—"it wasn't a child. It was you. And I said: What are you doing with one of my students in front of your saddle? And Verity said: She's not your student; she's mine."

He pushes his cup of tea away from him with distaste, and looks around restlessly as though whiskey could be tapped from the air by wishing. "Odd, *n'est-ce pas?* But I must have known, unconsciously, that she had talked to you about me."

Katherine averts her gaze, trusting to the bougainvillea.

"I hope," Nicholas begins. "It's not a question of prying or violating trust; it's just . . . Well, I hope we can talk again." He reaches out and touches the tip of Katherine's finger where it rests on the table. "You're a fascinating little puzzle-piece, aren't you?" He runs his finger lightly the length of hers, crosses the plateau of her hand, explores her forearm. "You're coming on the Arts picnic, I hope? To the Glasshouse Mountains?"

"I don't think—" Katherine says, fighting for breath. "I don't . . . I never go on those things. Too much study. There isn't time. I never—"

"I know you don't. But I hope you'll come on this one. In fact I insist. I want to talk to you again."

"Of course he didn't say that, Charade," Katherine says, tossing pebbles into the water. "Of course that's utter nonsense. But for years that's what I let myself believe. I went on that Arts picnic, that hike up Tibrogargan, with that silly wish as my compass."

7. People Who Climb Glass Houses

"In Toronto," Charade tells Koenig, "the Royal Bank tower is made of glass."

"I know," Koenig says.

Charade is startled. "Oh. Yes, of course you do. I forgot that you . . . I get confused."

He laughs. "*You* get confused!"

"I was confused that day with Aunt Kay."

"In Toronto."

"Yes. In Toronto," she sighs. "It was very confusing. . . ."

"Which is us?" Charade asks, and the mirrored plates clamor back in noisy facets: which is us which is us which is us?

Twenty Katherines laugh; twenty Charades reach uncertainly toward all the Katherines. Mild dizziness swoops at them, and a sense of groping. Toronto passes and repasses like clouds. And the glass tower of the Royal Bank watches impassively.

"I sometimes think," Katherine sighs as taxis thread their way through her hair, "that I owe the reappearance of Nicholas to a random conjunction of Borges and the Royal Bank building. Because it happened here. I saw his reflection first."

Charade shakes her head, a time-swimmer flicking watery daze from her lashes, the race-lanes curling and jumping in the deep shifting pool of her history. "But . . . you've lost me again . . . How did we get to Toronto?"

"You don't remember driving in? And the subway?"

"I mean the twenty-five years in between. From the Glasshouse Mountains to here."

"Yes," Katherine says. The unpredictable pleats in time, the juxtapositions. "It always baffles me," she says. "From 1759 to here, just like that." She snaps her fingers.

Charade blinks. "What?"

"If Cook had sailed farther upriver with Wolfe . . ." Katherine says and trails off. If he'd kept going past Ville de Québec, back in 1759, would these shining obelisks have amazed him any more or less than the ones he saw on the Queensland coast just eleven years later? "If he'd looked round a bend in time?"

Charade puts out a hand—as though to steady herself. Or perhaps trying to catch hold of the reflections that flit through Katherine's mind.

"I know," Katherine sighs. Someone we haven't yet met, she thinks, is waiting for us. "It happens all the time," she says.

"Aunt Kay, *please*," Charade whispers. Her heart is hammering. (Will her father appear on Cook's navigation charts?)

"Are you all right?" Koenig asks in some alarm.

"Sorry," Charade says. "Just the force of that moment coming back, when I thought Nicholas was about to . . . I thought I might fall right through Toronto to Queensland. But it was just, you know, shadows, reflections, the old story. And I'd have to admit" —she trails an index finger down Koenig's chest—"yes, I'd have to admit that the Royal Bank in Toronto, seen from a certain angle at a certain time of day, definitely reminds me of Crookneck. It's the view Nicholas would have had driving up from Brisbane on the day of the picnic. And of course it's the view Cook had from the *Endeavour*."

"I'm making every endeavor," sighs her lover, "but the thread of this story—"

"Cook's *second* voyage. In 1770. I've already told you about it. You know, the Transit of Venus in Tahiti, the landing at Botany Bay, then the long trip up inside the reef, hugging the Queensland coast. In Moreton Bay, the sun hit the basalt and blinded him. From the ship he thought he was seeing glass towers."

"Ah." Koenig reaches for the chair beside the bed and fishes in the pockets of his coat. "Clear as a riddle."

"I'm not making this up," Charade says petulantly. "This is history." She slides off the bed and begins pacing around the room. At the window she pauses, watching him light his pipe, watching the bedroom mirror, where he appears left-handed. Two flames, one in and one not in the mirror, quaver between the booklet of matches and his meerschaum. Absorbed, she watches his right hand, his left hand, dip the twin flames into tobacco. "For us," she says as his mirror-mouth sucks in smoke, "for Queenslanders, the Glass-house Mountains are like . . . well, like Niagara Falls or the Statue of Liberty perhaps. Every Brisbane kid, practically, climbs them; it's a rite of passage. Especially Tibrogargan—you climb it first on a grade school picnic probably, but again and again. We save Beerwah for puberty or later; it's tougher."

Koenig sets his pipe down and reaches for her. "I know it's not logical for a physicist, of all people, but I have this old-fashioned craving for a simple narrative line. Time curves—it can't be helped—but I don't see why plots should." He pulls her onto the bed.

"Plots *do* have to—"

He stops her mouth with a kiss. "Another night," he says, digressing into touch.

And another night, insistent, she argues: "Plots do have to double back on themselves; there's no other way. I've brought you something—it's not a digression. Of course the MIT library was no help at all. I had to get it from Widener and I copied it out from the microfiche. Listen. The log of James Cook, captain of His Majesty's barque *Endeavour,* entry of May 17, 1770, five A.M. Can I read it to you?"

"Mmm," he murmurs, nuzzling her thigh.

Charade's body readjusts itself slightly. *"Some on board were of opinion that there was a river there. . . ."* She glances up over her sheet of paper. "There was. The Brisbane River, which he didn't see."

"The Brisbane River, imagine."

"Beside which river, a couple of centuries later, my mother Bea and my aunt Kay, sitting in the Botanical Gardens—"

"Yes, yes." Timelines, like a tangle of balloon strings, cross-hatch the bed. "But if we could just pin down the Glasshouse Mountains."

She frowns. "I'm trying to do that from Cook's journal, if you wouldn't interrupt. Listen:

> *"This place may always be found by three hills which lie to the northward of it. . . . These hills lie but a little way inland and not far from each other; they are very remarkable on account of their singular form which very much resembles a glass house which occasioned me giving them that name. The northernmost of the three is the highest and the largest.*

"That's Beerwah," she explains, "which I've also climbed. It's a lot tougher than Tibrogargan. The third one is Coonowrin, but we call it Crookneck. I've never climbed Crookneck. It's as sheer as the Royal Bank tower, just a finger of rock."

"Though I'm sure your father, the mythical Nicholas—"

She frowns at that. "Do you want to hear Kay's story or not?"

He raises an eyebrow. "Ah, I'd forgotten which tale we were chasing, but it's hers and not yours. So. Back in the old Einstein-Bohr game, eh? Back in the K box. Are we in Toronto or Queensland?"

"Question," Charade says. "If a woman stands in the middle of Massachusetts Avenue facing MIT, but her memory is so vividly snagged on one particular day of her childhood in the village of Le Raincy that she is unaware . . . that she is *oblivious* to the cars around her and so is hit, run over, killed . . . is she more truly in Boston or in France when she dies?"

"Well put," Koenig says. "The indeterminacy problem in a nutshell."

"Do time and space really exist?" Katherine asks Charade. Or are they, she wonders, like soul and eternity, just clever ideas? Metaphors of explanation. A way of holding things apart in our minds? None of the Charades on the faceted flank of the Royal Bank responds. "Because I stood here last year," Katherine explains, "here on Front Street, Toronto, with the traffic roaring by, and I naturally thought of that hike up Tibrogargan and of Captain Cook's journals; why wouldn't I? And of course I thought of Borges—well, anyone would—the multiplications, the reflections of reflections. And then I saw—"

"Yes," Koenig interrupts, "Memory's holographic—that's pretty well established now. Distributed, not localized. Touch any bioelectric splinter, and the entire thing can stage a replay." He holds her hand up to the light. "Vivid as a hologram," he says, studying her delicate bones and translucent skin. "So there's no certain way of knowing if this is happening now." He draws a question mark, lightly, between her breasts. "Or then," he says.

Charade says archly, "I get better and better in the reruns."

Mmmm, he murmurs as they slide into another intermission.

"As Katherine was saying . . ." he prompts.

"Ah yes. And then as she was saying by the Royal Bank towers . . .

"I saw Nicholas," Katherine says, "and a sort of mad euphoria hit me." She laughs uneasily. "He might have sprung straight from the thought of Borges, but I ran full tilt at the . . ." She watches her twenty heads shaking themselves in disbelief. "I chased his reflection. People must have thought I was crazy." She rubs her eyes with the back of one hand. "Stupid," she says. "Stupid."

"But *was* he . . . ?" Charade ventures, breathless, watching the Royal Bank watching Front Street. "Was my father . . . ?"

"He was wearing, I remember, a white shirt and jeans. I'd never seen him in jeans. And a cloth hat pulled down over his curls. Well, we'd all been advised . . . it's an awfully hot climb. . . . Only his was white, not army surplus like the rest. I remember people were making jokes . . . Nicholas, seventh Earl of Irregular Verbs, stuff like that." Katherine looks about her, vaguely startled as cars brake, as horns rise like Canada geese.

"I think," Charade says urgently, "I think we should find a restaurant and sit down and . . ."

"The strangest sense," Katherine says as a waitress indicates a pine table beneath green-and-white awnings. "I have the strangest sense of *déjà vu.*"

At a pine table beneath a green-and-white awning which has been temporarily erected, the beer is passed from hand to student hand. Katherine abstains. It seems to her, crowded and deafened by the din of talk and laughter, that she is even more conspicuous than when she has stood unwillingly in the Friday-night curbside circle, hemmed in by hymns and megaphones, and listened to Merv Watson lob scripture into the heart of Brisbane. Beyond the rabble of noises, birds call. Only in one sense, she thinks, only in the insignificant corporeal sense, is she present at this rural academic gathering. She pictures herself from a bird's-eye view, a kind of cipher at the edge of the raucous goodwill, not quite understanding the jokes (Bea-talk, and bawdy—she recognizes that) and looking longingly up into the scrub and tree-shadow. If there were a way to cross the open space of brown grass and dust, a way to disappear into those long green tunnels that slope up to the sun . . .

Climbing a mountain is as natural to her as breathing. But it is something to be done alone, or in the company of people one knows very well (Bea, for example), people who will not scratch the great surfaces of peace with unnecessary talk.

From time to time, new cars arrive and a fresh spill of people buffets the picnic grounds; fresh voices and jokes reverberate under the green-and-white awning, oppressing Katherine. She watches for Verity.

Nicholas is already here. Katherine has been aware of this from the moment she arrived, though she can no more look at him than one can look at the sun. Except obliquely. She is aware, certainly, most vividly aware of his white shirt half-unbuttoned. There is some disturbing quality to it, an incongruous note of refinement but also something faintly erotic, set over against all the bright and loud T-shirts, the cotton checks. It is difficult to see Nicholas clearly. Satellites of students, mostly girls, moon about him in a constant cloudy circle.

There is no indication that Nicholas is aware of Katherine's presence, no reason to believe he remembers that he "insisted" she come. Studying him from the edges of her mind, watching him laugh, watching him sip beer from a glass proffered by a girl whose shining body gives off sexual invitation, Katherine wonders: Does he think of Verity at times such as these? Is he watching for her? Does he think of Bea? What categories exist in his mind?

She looks again at the open space between the picnic tables and the treeline at the foot of Tibrogargan. In her mind, she gets up casually and crosses to the trees and disappears up the slope into the scrub. In her mind she rehearses: the shifting of weight, her footsteps on dry leaves, the embrace of shadow. It should be possible. Would anyone notice?

When Verity arrives, it will become simple. They will climb together. Probably.

Casually, sliding the question like an illicit billet-doux underneath the convivial hubbub, Katherine asks a fellow student from Verity's tutorial: "Is ah is Verity here yet?"—knowing the answer, but looking about indifferently as though for something temporarily mislaid. "I don't think I've seen her."

The student raises an eyebrow. "Are you serious?"

"What do you mean?"

ment. She says awkwardly, clearing her throat: "About
. the war, you know."

, bugger that," the girl says irritably. (Margaret? Miriam?
at's it.) "You're not going to trot out that old story about
nts, surely?" Myra sniffs. "Believe me, I've known her for
years. Even if it's true, big deal. Hell, *my* dad's a TPI, left
New Guinea and gets the shivers twice a week. Doesn't
turn you into a bloody—"

ay," someone shouts. "Firewood time. We want dry brush
cones. If everyone brings . . ." And in the general mêlée
ersal that follow, Katherine finds herself—oh, blessed con-
ovement—on the far side of the curtain of scrub and ti-
breathes in the sweet harsh smell of Tibrogargan. She
he picnic falling away from her ankles like molting feathers.
es clatter from her feet and ring like little bells against the
f rock. She listens to them pinging and bouncing, echoing
ar down, a measurement of freedom. Once or twice her
hoes slide suddenly from under her legs, the gravel giving
d she clutches at tufts of spiky brown grass. Along her
, beads of blood appear against white scratch-marks. She
uickly.

ity is wrong not to come, she thinks. No. Not wrong to stay
m the group, but wrong to lock her life up inside a library;
ot to climb the mountain alone, or with Nicholas, or with
ween the sun and the side of a mountain, there is no room
ast; it vanishes. Life is just this. She turns to look out over
b below and flings her arms up toward the sky in an intense
f pleasure. If she were to take a dance step out into space,
eves the air would support her.

s is the way it is for Bea all the time, she thinks. The
lge comes to her like heat through the pores of her skin. In a
izziness—from the sun or the swooping drop to the valley
he turns back to the flank of the mountain. Ahead and
a long stretch of rock, dimpled, hot to the fingers, treeless.
s a ledge and sits and leans back; she can feel the mountain
g like a heart against her spine. She pushes up the sleeves of
se and rolls her jeans up past her knees and turns her face,

"Ashkenazy? She never comes on
a recluse—I thought everyone knew t
you know what I mean." The girl ta
"I've known her from way back. You k
toward Katherine and lowers her voice
beer. "I think she's got Nicholas by tl
even when she's not here—you'll see he
and then. He's all tied up, worse luck.

Katherine thinks: If Bea heard this
the Duke of Wellington and mention,
sort of nonsense one hears around .
popular opinion."

And not by Bea.

The girl persists, holding her bottle
of her lips to indicate the confidential
"She's got some kind of hold on him; t
it. Frankly, she gives me the creeps. Sh
think? And cold as a fish. Frigid, I'm w

Katherine wonders if intensity of
distance between the picnic table and the
count to ten, she thinks, and then I wi
with my hands against the picnic bench
and it will be quite logical to saunter of

"What do you think?" the girl pers

"Ah . . ." Katherine hedges, turnin
her lack of competence in the topic und

"But you must have *some* opinion,
knows you're her protégée."

Katherine's eyebrows buckle with
only . . . It's purely . . ." She is casting
girl's name. Doesn't it start with M? It'
She's someone who is vocal in seminars,
anti-intellectual presence, a sort of devil
Sometimes Katherine has sensed a fizzin;
ity; at other times she has felt the girl i
attention. Katherine herself cannot bear
one who . . . well, who is simply beyo

of asse
Verity .

"O
Myra,
her par
donkey
a leg i
have to

"C
and pi
and dis
fusing
tree. S
climbs,

St
plates
faintly
canvas
way, a
forearn
climbs

V
away f
wrong
me. Be
for the
the scr
spasm
she be

T
knowl
slight
floor—
above
She fir
breath
her bl

eyes closed, to the sun. There will never be words for this, she thinks. It will never need words.

She has a sense of herself as a solar whiteness, without shape, without limits in space or time, pulsing with a kind of exaltation whose only analogue might be the dramatic rush of wind at the rainy edge of a cyclone.

If Verity were to climb the Glasshouses, she thinks, her past would become different. The life of Verity-on-the-mountain would have another history altogether.

But is it *possible* for Verity to climb the Glasshouses?

Might there not, in fact, be planes and spheres and tales that can never intersect?

It strikes Katherine that it might indeed be as impossible for Verity to climb Tibrogargan as for the Wanderer or Beowulf to sail their curved ships up inside the Barrier Reef. Is a sense of the tragic possible along a tropical coast? Can it be maintained? Does it have to be imported from Europe?

Energy—from the sun, or from the heady rush of her ideas—pushes her on and up, over the dimpled rocks. Yes, she thinks, both somber and excited, as though thorny literary problems are solving themselves at last. Verity will always live in Le Raincy; the Wanderer will always sail the North Sea. They can't be translated. But they endure in their original tongues. They *endure*.

Trees overshadow her again, a brown stand of gums fingering the rock. Beneath them the underbrush flourishes, and where a trickle of water drips out from between rocks and collects in a hollow, ferns grow thick and deep. It is possible, Katherine thinks, that no one has stepped into that greenness since the world began. From here, looking back, she can see the striped awning and toy people moving around it, and a row like ants threading its way up into the mountain. Above the tattered leaves there is nothing but sky and King Sun. She feels absolutely insignificant and absolutely omnipotent, immortal even, at one and the same time. Hubris moves through the ferns like a kingfisher; she feels the quick little brush of its wings. She tests her power: standing deep in the pool of curling fronds, she closes her eyes and summons up his white shirt, open over brown skin, his cloth hat, the butter-pale curls. She makes a wish: *Nicholas.*

"Katherine?"

She swallows and opens her eyes, but it is only the girl from her poetry tutorial, Myra—definitely, yes, that is her name—asking: "Why the hell did you take off like that? Whew." Myra wipes her sweating forehead with the cloth hat. "We might as well sit and rest a bit while we wait for the others to catch up." She throws herself down into the ferns, wriggles a little to gain comfort against twigs and ants, and pulls a bottle opener and a Four-X from her knapsack. She seems to fill the entire space beneath the trees; the deep and endless pool of ferns has dwindled to leprous tufts. She flips the top off a bottle and takes a mouthful. "Yech. Warm bloody beer," she says. "Already." Nevertheless she continues to drink, then holds the bottle out toward Katherine, whose mind, in slow motion, considers its response. She shakes her head, changes her mind, accepts it as though in a dream.

Myra raises an eyebrow. "The thing about you," she offers thoughtfully, "is you always just do whatever you decide to do, right? I mean, you don't care what anyone thinks, do you? Like just taking off up the track, back then."

Katherine stares, amazed, the bottle poised on the way to her lips. Logically, she thinks, I could be as wildly blind about her. Myra laces her hands behind her head and leans back into the ferns. "So how do you do it?" she asks comfortably. "What's the secret? You snap your fingers, so to speak, and Ashkenazy waits for your opinion in the tutorial. Or I have to come chasing you up the mountain. Or Nicholas the Dreamboat himself has to keep sneaking looks in your direction."

Katherine has the eerie sensation of having taken a wrong turn in a theater: she has wandered onstage in the middle of a production and now—this is surely an off-kilter dream—both players and audience turn expectantly toward her. But what are her lines?

Myra laughs. "Well, it's certainly not the magic power of your voice, since you're practically mute. Outside of seminars, that is. Is that the secret? Why do I have the feeling that you sent for me?" She claps her hands, sits up, and bends forward from the waist, a mock genie. "What do you want to know?"

Katherine smiles uncertainly and lifts her shoulders slightly to imply: I'm out of my depth. I don't know what you're talking about. There's nothing I want to know. There are definitely, in fact, many things I do not want to know.

"Funny," Myra says, rolling over onto her stomach and propping her chin in her hands, "the way everyone has this compulsion to talk about them all the time, isn't it? I guess it's the waste that drives us all crazy. What does he see in her?—apart from the obvious, I mean. Of course she *is* beautiful, you have to concede that, though it's just her face really, isn't it? None of the other standard attributes that we are all led to believe . . . But it's not as though he's blind to it elsewhere. Let's face it, as one fallen woman to another, you've got to search a long time to find someone who hasn't at least necked with Nicholas. Damned if I know why we let him get away with it." She stretches like a cat, purrs, licks the slow circle of her lips with a tongue indulging in memory. "Well, of course I know why," she sighs. "What I mean is, why do we let *her* do it? Just a twitch on the leash, and whoosh, he's miles away even when you've still got him between your legs in the back of a car. Just what's she got that we haven't?"

For some reason, in the midst of the sensation of inner lurch (the kind of freefall that dreams can open into) Katherine thinks of Gene the Sailor Man at the moment when he turns away to lunge for Bea's sandal.

"There's something manipulative about her," Myra says. "Always has been. I've known her from way back. Same school."

Is it possible, Katherine wonders, to go on and on, day after day, making the discovery that you are even more of a fool than you thought you were yesterday? She asks herself savagely: Does he carve notches on a gatepost somewhere?

"You know how I know?" Myra asks. "The way she had to have teachers eating out of her hand. Every grade, these so-called brilliant essays—about her tragic bloody past, ho hum—but one year the teachers compared, and all the stories were different. It was kind of a joke around All Hallows."

"All Hallows?"

"Yep. Ahead of me, of course, by a good few years, but the stories were still around. And I remember her, sort of. The version that gets me is the parents bombed in the London blitz, and all that jazz. She's no more a Pom than I am, and that accent wouldn't fool—"

"Of course she's not a Pom," Katherine says primly. "She's French and Jewish."

"What?" Myra hugs herself and rolls in the ferns. "French! Oh that's a good one. I hadn't heard that one. And the Jewish kick: well, that started up in Grade Twelve, I believe. Before that she had a vocation. The nuns lapped her up, of course, bless their dear little suffering-loving souls. It's a miracle she didn't break out in stigmata."

Katherine thinks: I have a lunatic on my hands. "Myra," she says patiently. "Think about it. With a name like *Ashkenazy*."

"Exactly. How come her parents used to be just plain Mick and Thelma Delaney, before her father made a killing on the horses? Believe me, Katherine, my dad used to know Mick Delaney, and he reckons—my dad, that is—that her ladyship was born two blocks away from the Banyo railway station. She was baptized a Mick, and her dad used to drive a truck for Tristram's Drinks."

"Myra! How can you say these things?"

"How? Because my dad used to drink with Mick Delaney at the RSL, that's how. They were both at Tobruk, which is the closest Miss High-and-Mighty ever got to France, if you ask me. Hey, here come the slowpokes; they've caught up with us. And Jenny Williamson all over Nicholas still, I see. She thinks she's hit the jackpot, silly fool."

"I suppose, Charade," Katherine muses, "that we merged in with the group and got to the top of Tibrogargan."

Because yes, Katherine remembers how the sweeping view across the Bruce Highway to Bribie Island and the endless Pacific has a bright white flag in one corner: the shirt of Nicholas, open at the neck; the sun on his wheat-pale curls. And she recalls how she pondered the nature of obsession, and the mysterious ways in which we invest objects with power and then wait like vultures for demy-thologizing to set in.

"Though that process is never complete," she tells Charade. "Never. I'm convinced of that now. What still mystifies me is how it comes about that we confer significance in the first place, and then it clings. Totemic objects can never totally lose their power, not for all the demythologizing in the world. Because whenever I think of the Pacific, there's a white sail on it that turns into Nicholas's shirt. And whenever I think of the Glasshouses . . . Which is why, I suppose, by quick train of association, I saw him on the side of the Royal Bank." She frowns and looks uncertainly along Front Street from under the brightly striped awning. "But the curious thing was . . . Well, I'll get back to that later. First things first."

Or last things last. Because it is when the group is dispersing again, as dusk falls on the picnic grounds, that Nicholas, shoving a canvas roll of green and white into the back of a van, reaches out and tugs on Katherine's sleeve. "Want to ride back with me in the van?" he asks.

Katherine has many versions of what happened after this. She would like to think that she politely detached his hand and said something like "Thank you, but I came up in Myra's car and I've already told her . . ." She would like to think she then calmly turned and walked away. She does believe, in all the versions, that she turned a corner that day and began to walk away from her obsession.

But also in all the versions is a certain amount of smoke and mist, and the thudding of her heartbeat, and the clear haunting notes of a recorder. And from somewhere in that time is the knowledge of Nicholas's body, of the star-shaped mole in the hollow of his neck, of his lips on hers, of their legs intertwined—and when could it have been, if not that night? Unless of course it was a few months later, when she was off in North Queensland teaching in a country high school and Nicholas, incredibly, blew into town. Or unless it was the time after that, her twenty-first birthday, when she woke from a dream of him and there he was again on her doorstep.

Yes, that was real. That really happened.

"Happy birthday," he said. "I thought perhaps a trip to the Garden of Eden?" And on that occasion they took the boat out from Cairns to Green Island, where the coral bloomed and where passionfruit lay rotting under the trees. Was that when they finally made love? Because they did. Once. And it would have been, she'd always felt, such a terrible waste of location if the fall hadn't taken place on Green Island. So they slept on the white sand and a snake sunned itself on a rock and she fed Nicholas pomegranates and mangoes and custard apples.

All of which happened, in one sense, only seconds ago: so she knows as she crosses Front Street in Toronto about twenty-three years later and sees a certain reflection and rushes, heedless of cars and pedestrians, full-tilt at the mirrored flank of the Royal Bank.

8. The Tale of Nicholas II

Once upon a time, Charade says, a woman named Katherine ran full-tilt at the side of the Royal Bank on Front Street in Toronto. She thought she saw someone she knew, but the image had bounced from a taxi window to the plate-glass building, and seemed to be walking toward her when in fact it was half a block away and heading in the opposite direction. A doorman at the Royal York Hotel slammed the taxi door shut, changing the freakish angle of reflection, and *pouff!* the image vanished. Katherine, bewildered, stopped within feet of the mirrored towers, rubbing her eyes and looking up and down the sidewalk. She wondered if perhaps she was sleepwalking. She wondered if she had just been jolted out of the kind of nightmare in which one is about to do something unspecified but extremely embarrassing.

On the sidewalk of Front Street she saw wary eyes and snickers and the pressed-together lips of people trying not to smile. They might as well have projected their thoughts onto billboards. *Loony,* she saw in flashing lights.

She thought with a shiver: It's true.

There was probably a medical term for it—manic obsessive? Possibly there were books, articles, treatments, summer camps for the kind of senseless and passionate attachment picked up much too early, back in unimmunized childhood. It was one of those diseases like malaria. It hung around. It skulked, dormant, in the blood, going into remission for years and years, for decades, and then *shazam*, flaring up again like poisoned toadstools after rain.

Something had made her think of Nicholas. (What was it? A headline on a newsstand? The trail of association was lost.) But definitely, yes, first she had thought of him and then there he was. Pathetic. She would have liked to distribute leaflets to the politely smiling bystanders: I'm a married woman, a mother of teenagers, a fulfiller of civic obligations; this derangement is not typical of me.

But it was as though a rip had spread and spread, slick as quicksilver, from the San Andreas fault through the Great Lakes and up the length of Yonge Street. A swift but mercifully brief seizure, she thought, pressing her fingers against the bony rim of her eye sockets. Like an itch, like a rash of poison ivy, the recollection of Nicholas went licking across the surface of her skin, but it would pass. One could read any number of articles about such midlife aberrations, the little kinks and tricky riffs of memory.

And then, at the far end of the block, between the Royal York Hotel and the Whalers' Wharf tavern, she saw him again. His back. He was just turning the corner, about to seep into the city, water into sand. She sprinted, half sobbing, half laughing, heedless of stares.

This had nothing to do with the making of a decision, or with any calculation of the pleasures/costs/complications of seeing him again. There was indeed not so much as a second to consider the oddness of boarding the Royal York's shuttle bus to the airport. She saw Nicholas, in the middle of a fog of soft-sided luggage and suitcase-festooned travelers, climb into the bus. She followed him.

"Sorry, ma'am," the driver said. "Got to get your ticket from the Gray Coach window first."

"Oh where? Where?" she asked, trying not to seem unduly agitated, but in fact breathless, frantic, scanning the bus seats for Nicholas. The aisles were thick with bodies. There was a waving forest of arms craning to stuff luggage into the overhead racks.

"There." The driver pointed, and she sprinted to the ticket window and paid her six dollars and rapped on the now closed doors of the bus until they opened with a pneumatic sigh and then she bounded back up the metal steps.

"Yeah, yeah." The driver grinned. "End of the world if you miss your flight, I know. Six times a day, minimum, I'm offered bribes, threats, and prayers. Trip takes the same thirty minutes, fair weather or foul, ma'am. And the world don't end if you gotta wait for the next flight out."

"Flight?" she echoed, her brow puckered.

She could see Nicholas—the unruly curls across his forehead—halfway back, a window seat.

"I wonder," she found herself saying with appalling brashness to the person beside him, "I wonder if you'd mind . . . ? I'd be most grateful. Oh, thank you."

What did she expect?

Not, certainly, the quizzically amused look of someone who was accustomed to mild outlandishness in women, who took fuss as his due, but who nevertheless was perpetually amazed by the assertive ingenuity of total strangers. There was always a dash of titillation about it, a small shock that aroused him. As for Katherine, awareness of the error she had made was not quite instant—after twenty-three years, one expects some differences—and so it took several seconds for her own incandescence to fade. In those moments something twirled between the two of them, between the man and the woman framed by the vinyl seats and grubby windows of the airport bus: a spindle of misplaced and mistaken sexual excitement.

It cast its own spell.

And then Katherine, beached on the shore of receding euphoria, said faintly: "Oh God." Because he was not Nicholas. Clearly he was not Nicholas. At close range, she could not even call the resemblance striking. (Although, after twenty-three years, would the real Nicholas bear much of a resemblance to the one she remembered?) What she had seen from within the aura of her sudden recollection was a random convergence of details: the general size and shape of his body, the way he walked, the curls. But the curls were not sun-bleached wheat-blond Nicholas-colored at all. They were drab; they were the shade of old and yellowing parchment; they were the colorless color of a once fair-haired boy who is now in his graying middle age.

"Oh God," Katherine said, mortified. "I thought you were someone else." She put her hands to her burning cheeks. "Oh, this is so embarrassing."

"Not at all," he said archly. "Not at all."

"Oh, I don't believe I *followed* you. . . ." She held the ticket stub out between them, for pondering, as an artifact of madness.

"The least I can do," he said, "is offer myself as a substitute."

"Oh, I'm so embarrassed."

"You do that well."

"Pardon?" She looked at him then, took in the meaning of his smile, considered (at roughly the speed of light) several possible courses of action. She considered saying courteously but icily, "I'm afraid you have misinterpreted my behavior," and then getting off the bus. She considered saying nothing at all, simply walking back down the aisle with dignity and . . .

The bus, she realized from the peripheral blur of buildings, was now in motion; she therefore considered, but quickly rejected, telling the driver she had made a mistake, asking him to let her off. It could be assumed that the driver, now negotiating traffic at a dizzying pace on the highway, lived in the constant expectation of new manifestations of lunacy with which to enliven his off-duty hours. "Lady," he would say, possibly gently, possibly rudely, "sit down." He would jab his finger toward the sign which said in two languages: PLEASE DO NOT TALK TO THE DRIVER WHILE BUS IS IN MOTION.

She considered saying with polite and level malice: "I'm afraid I find middle-aged lechery rather pathetic." Or, more savage: "It is not always the case, Nicholas . . ." (*Nicholas?* Had she played this scene before? Had she always wanted to play this scene?) "It is not always the case, sir, that sexual attraction is mutual." And then getting up and moving to another seat.

All these possibilities passed through her mind between one blink and the next. But what she saw in his eyes, what held her, was that spindle of excitement, accidentally, inadvertently, erroneously set in motion. It was spinning like a top. Without thinking, she put out a hand to ward off giddiness, and he seemed to lurch a little too, ever so slightly, so that their bodies came into marginal contact, though their eyes never wavered, both fastened on the thing that buzzed between them. It was mesmerizing, gathering speed, giving off vaporous rings, making *grands jetés* of anticipation. So that it suddenly seemed to her they were in collusion, she and this man (she thought of him as Nicholas II); that they had planned the whole thing from the start: the way he had walked past an open taxi so that his image would bounce onto the Royal Bank, the way he had lured her onto the bus, the way she had so willingly followed. It seemed to her that when she had bought her ticket at the Royal York, she had purchased a brief leave of absence from her life, which was, in its broader patterns, eminently, even tediously, respectable, and certainly devoid of improper excitement. It seemed to her now that she had known all this with absolute clarity in those flurried seconds at the ticket window.

Perhaps he said something. *Do you do this often?* Something like that. Something urbane, thick with innuendo, but not quite patronizing; something that proffered equality of intention and responsibility.

And perhaps she, in the daring language that came to her quite naturally (part of the package deal, part of the ticket), the language that belonged to this sudden timeout from her life, perhaps she said something appropriately ambiguous and arch. *Do you?* she might have lobbed back at him, raising an eyebrow.

Not quite like this, he might have said.

Or it was possible that nothing was said. What did happen (she could be virtually certain about this) was that for the length of the ride to the airport they watched this thing, this kind of economy-class nova that was vibrating and humming between them, giving off heat. Where there was bodily contact—lightly and coincidentally along the thigh, and after some slight jolting of the bus (which happened opposite the Canadian National Exhibition Grounds, or maybe not until the Carling O'Keefe Brewery) also along the forearm—at such points of contact, there was a burning sensation. An exchange of breathing, of the smell and taste of the body opposite, seemed to be taking place.

Katherine supposed that the name for all this dazzle and heat was lust. She did not think it was ordinary lust—though she could hardly claim to be an expert on any of the varieties. Still, passes had been made off and on throughout her respectable married years (colleagues of her husband, one of the doctors at the clinic, her son's gym teacher) and this seemed altogether different. It must have been a case of convergence, she decided; a random confluence of needs and nostalgias, a sort of King Tide of concupiscence.

She thought she asked him, when they found themselves in the hubbub of the international terminal, where he was going, what flight. And she thought he said, rather tersely: "Obviously, for now, nowhere. Back to Boston later." He did something at the Delta Airlines desk, then made a call from a pay telephone, while she waited and watched as if drugged.

It was when he motioned her back through the automatic doors and into the taxi—something about the way he leaned forward and told the driver "Bristol Place Hotel," pointing to it, because the driver was Portuguese, or Mexican possibly, or Guatemalan, or at any rate not in command of much English; and because the hotel was just a step away if one did not mind stepping across tarmacs and superhighways—it was something about the way the curls fell across his forehead and about the quick purposeful negotiations with the driver that made her say to herself: "He *could* be Nicholas."

As though the thought pricked him, he leaned back into the seat and took her hand and ran his tongue across the tips of her fingers. "So who was I supposed to be?" he asked.

A small nervous fledgling of a laugh rose from her lips. "Nicholas," she said, relieved that it came out flat, devoid of meaning. "A boy from the golden years of my youth"—every syllable mocking itself. "Ancient history. What *is* your name, anyway?"

"Nicholas will do nicely. I can fit into that as well as anything."

It is amazing, she thought, how thick with erotic meaning a simple declarative sentence can become when you are in the back of a taxi with your fingers in some stranger's mouth.

"All right," she said. She felt she knew the rules of this game by instinct. The mask, the costume made her brash. She withdrew her hand from between his lips and loosened his tie. "And what's my name?"

"You don't have a name."

Her hand stiffened at the top button of his shirt. "Oh yes I do," she said sharply. Options whirred through her mind again, like symbols on a slot machine. I don't have to go through with this, she thought.

He raised an eyebrow. "Backing out?"

"No," she said evenly, her heart pounding, her voice calm. "But I do have a name. It's Katherine."

She waited, flag planted, daring him to challenge her terms.

"As you wish," he said smoothly. "Katherine."

The sheets at the Bristol Place are stamped, not embroidered, with the hotel's name. Katherine pleated the hem between her fingers as she watched him light his pipe by the window. What could one compare it to, sex with a stranger?

Sex with a stranger, she repeated to herself, as though it were a catechism she might come to believe in time.

It was not unlike finding yourself running full-tilt into the side of a bank: strangely euphoric while it lasted, but afterward . . . not very real; afterward, one felt slightly bewildered and distinctly foolish. And compelled to explain.

She propped herself on one elbow and studied him. He had dressed already. He believes nakedness puts him at a disadvantage, she thought. She sensed suddenly: He always feels naked.

She, surprisingly, felt languidly uninterested in her clothes, though she was covered demurely enough with the sheet. She rather imagined that after sex with a stranger, men (who presumably did this sort of thing all the time; well, not her husband of course; not anyone she knew well, but *men,* men in the broader foreign sense of the term)—she rather supposed they wanted to get away as soon as was decently possible. She did not imagine they dallied for post-coital chats. But Nicholas II showed no sign of haste; he sat on the broad ledge of the windowsill and looked out over Route 407 and the tarmacs and runways and the farthest dreary suburban and exurban reaches of Toronto. He puffed reflectively on his pipe.

He could be Nicholas, she thought again. It was as though she had been given a chance to unravel the great puzzle of her adolescence: here was Nicholas in a petri dish. Freed of need and anguish, she could study him, work him out: a researcher's dream. How was it, why was it, that *afterwards* he was still a stranger who was always walking away? Why would he always be sitting, as it were, in a windowsill with his back to her?

"Are you married?" she asked him.

He turned around, startled, as though she had broken the rules of the game. He seemed to consider not answering.

"Was," he said curtly. "Big mistake." He looked at her, just in case there were unclear boundaries. "Not something I'd do again."

"You left her?"

"In a manner of speaking." He tapped out his pipe, reaching for his jacket, which was thrown across the chair, fishing in the pocket for the pipe-cleaning tool, scraping out that part of his life.

"Any children?" she asked.

He chose to ignore that question.

"I do," she said. "Have children. Three. Two are teenagers, and the other's still in grade school."

He looked at her, startled, then shrugged. "Rough," he said. "Being a single mother." As though he were well acquainted with the phenomenon. (She saw a ghostly trail of sex-hungry single mothers throwing themselves at him on trains, on buses, in the street.)

"Oh, I'm not a single mother," she announced comfortably, propping herself on the pillows and holding the sheet over her breasts. "I'm quite happily married."

"God!" he said, shocked.

For some reason it pleased her enormously that she had the power to disconcert him. "Yes. My husband's an academic. Well, so am I for that matter. My husband looks rather like you. *Quite* like you, actually. In fact, you could probably be mistaken for each other in certain lights. My husband wears corduroys. Smokes a pipe. That sort of thing. What kind of a woman did you think I was?"

"I don't know," he said, embarrassed. "The usual kind, I suppose. Young career star, graduate student maybe, fast track, single or divorced."

"Young!" she said, foolishly pleased. "Graduate student!" *Fast track,* she thought sardonically. She poked at it warily, this exotic view of herself.

"It didn't really matter what kind," he said.

"Ah. All the nameless young women."

"That's right." He came and sat on the bed. He relit his pipe. She thought: He has to be doing something with his hands; and he looked at her as though aberrant behaviors had made them far more intimate than sex. Then he said to the cheap framed reproduction above her head: "There's this crack in my life; I have to keep stuffing it with something. . . . Like the little boy, you know, with his fist in the sea wall." He walked to the window and back again. "Work or sex," he said. "Either will do." Words, explanations, seemed to be caught in his throat; they might choke him. "Today," he said, coughing, "happened to be urgent."

"Yes?" She leaned forward with intense interest. She felt as though she were on the verge of major discovery. "But why, Nicholas? Why?"

"Does the name Zundel mean anything?"

Katherine went spinning, spinning. She held on to the frame of the bed. Now she remembered what had summoned Nicholas from the dormant files of the past. She saw it again, the newspaper stand on the sidewalk in Front Street, outside the Royal Bank:

DID SIX MILLION DIE?

HOLOCAUST A HOAX, ZUNDEL SAYS.

MORE SURVIVORS GIVE TESTIMONY TODAY.

"Naturally, it means something," she said. "The trial, the anti-Semitic crank."

For a moment he looked startled. He looked as though she were privy to disconcerting private data on his life. He shrugged. "I forget everyone knows about it here. In Boston, I have to explain."

Katherine wrapped the sheet loosely around her body and swung her feet to the floor, dragging the bedding like a train. She paced the room. Is coincidence possible? she wondered. "Do we somehow make things happen?" she asked him. "Do you think that's possible? Do we give off radio signals, or what?"

But he had settled into her space on the bed, except that he huddled more, and took one of the pillows in his arms.

"When I was a child," Katherine said, "there was a girl in my school . . . Verity Ashkenazy, her name was. There were all sorts of stories about her. I didn't really figure things out till years and years later. Her parents both disappeared in the Holocaust, but she herself, apparently, was hidden by nuns in a convent. She grew up Catholic, and then after the war—"

"My wife," said the man on the bed, "gave testimony today. My ex-wife. At the Zundel trial."

"I was in awe of her," Katherine said. "She was older than me by several years. She was like . . . how can I explain? People said she was brilliant, but it was something else besides that. . . . She'd been immunized against harm; nothing could touch her. There was something. . . . She gave off something. . . . She fascinated me."

"My wife," said the stranger on the bed, "was part of the group who laid charges." He bent double across the pillow, as though stuffing it into some terrible pain, some gaping hole in his side. "She has nightmares whenever she relives it, nightmares, night terrors . . . you've no idea of the . . ." He put his hands over his ears.

"As a matter of fact," Katherine said, "she changed my life. There was a certain kind of strength she gave me." She looked at something in her cupped hands. "She fascinated everyone. But Nicholas most of all."

"She sobs," said the stranger on the bed. "She writes letters to dead people in France, in Le Raincy—that's where her family lived. Sometimes I think it's heroic and sometimes I think it's perverse." He held the pillow to his face, blocking out the light. "I shouldn't have gone, but I had to be there. You can't leave; you can't abandon someone like that."

"It's all right," Katherine soothed. "It's all right, Nicholas."

"In some ways," he said, "she's a tyrant."

"It's all right," Katherine soothed. "It's all right."

He began nuzzling her, sucking her, biting her impersonally.

Ravenously. She might have been prison rations. Twisting into his need and her own, she unbuttoned his shirt and kissed the hollow of his neck. She kissed the star-shaped mole in the hollow of his neck.

When Katherine woke it was dark, and a stranger lay beside her in bed.

"Oh God," she said, looking at her watch. "Oh my God." Her arm was pinned under the stranger's shoulder.

First the tidal waves of lunacy recede, and then a most ghastly clarity is left in their wake. This is a physical law. She tugged her arm free.

"Wha—?" he mumbled. "What time is it?"

"It's after midnight," she said. "Oh my God. My family will be frantic. I have to make a call."

"Midnight?" he said. "Oh no, I've missed the last flight. Shit. I've got a class first thing in the morning."

"A class?"

"I teach at MIT. I'm a physicist."

"Oh no, not another academic. I seem to be doomed."

"My apologies," he said drily. "I'm sorry, I've forgotten your name."

Her hands, sliding over zippers and buttons, were beginning to tremble with anger. "It's Katherine Sussex," she said tightly.

(Later, surprised, she wondered why her tongue had instinctively reverted to Sussex, why she hadn't given her married name.)

Above the pulling-on of his trousers, he smiled at her. "Thanks for the lovely evening, Katherine." Sardonic, but not insulting. He fastened his belt buckle and then held out his hand. "Koenig," he said. "Actually, I'm the one who should be embarrassed."

They shook hands.

Oh, Nicholas, she incurably and foolishly thought, as the lamplight fell on his curls.

In the taxi, arranging and rehearsing versions and explanations, she saw again the moment at the desk: two strangers paying for several hours' use of a room, a meticulous sharing of costs. She saw the desk clerk's glance in her direction; it was a discreet but unmistakable smirk. She wanted to hit him. Where the smirk touched her, nausea sprang up like a weed. She was feeling queasy. The feeling grew rapidly worse.

"Excuse me." She tapped the taxi driver on the shoulder. "Could you stop for a minute? I think I'm going to be sick."

She had to hang on to the guardrail that ran between the shoulder of the 401 and the hulks, the bland and indifferent hulks of condominium towers.

"It was later that week," she tells Charade, "that I wrote the advertisement for Verity and mailed it to the *Sydney Morning Herald, The Courier Mail, The Age,* well, all the Australian papers. It wasn't because of Nicholas, really. Or only partly. It was the trial, you know, that made him appear. . . . It was the trial that made me want to talk to Verity again."

She shakes her head to clear it of muddle.

"I had quite a few crank letters in response to my ads. Some of them were really nasty. It's frightening."

She sighs. "You think of Verity, you think of people like Zundel, you think of the hate letters, you have to ask yourself . . ." She looks at her hands, as though atrocities might lurk inside them. "You have to ask yourself . . ."

But she cannot formulate the question.

"I'd like to know where Verity is. I'd like to talk to her. Because wherever she is, she has answers."

Part III

The 366th Night and Thereafter

Part III

1. The Kynge's Tale

"Oh," Koenig says. "*That* Katherine." He rolls away from Charade and reaches for his robe and heads for the bathroom. There is a schuss of shower curtain hooks, and the sudden noisy comment of water.

Charade follows, yanks the curtain to one side, and calls over the water: "That Katherine. The one with a name."

She hoists herself onto the vanity cabinet, the Formica cool beneath her buttocks, and leans back against the mirror. She folds her arms, half closes one eye, and takes stock. It is not often that she has a chance to assess him naked. "Aunt Kay thought you were the sort of person who felt more himself in clothes. She's right, isn't she?"

Koenig doesn't hear, or chooses not to.

"Which is curious," she says, "given your continuing reputation as a womanizer. In the dorms, that is. And dating from pre-Me, I'm assuming. I realize I don't exactly leave you much time to—"

He reaches up and turns the shower-head dial to full-blast massage and subjects himself to the battering, though no force is likely to drown out that Toronto day, the trial testimony, the photograph of women and children, including the little girl Rachel (he puts it into clear unassimilable thought: "my ex-wife, Rachel") all of them, in the photograph, abstract as geometry: nothing but lines and angles, their ribs clear as graphed paper. He shuts his eyes and lets the water pound on his lids but the photograph is always there, an arrangement of parallel lines: barbed wire and bones. The photograph grows and grows the way things in nightmares do, it expands infinitely, projected onto the courtroom screen, and from the witness stand his ex-wife's voice says, "There. That's me," as flatly as though she were pointing to a souvenir snapshot taken in front of the Schönbrunn Palace. Everyone looks; the entire packed gallery is watching. There are thousands of people staring at one small naked girl whose hands clasp themselves pathetically in front of her pubic triangle; it is so undefended that all the clothes of the rest of her life won't cover it. And then Rachel looks up into the gallery where he hides behind a pillar and dark glasses and several other bodies. She looks right through him. He is frantic to get out of the courtroom, to stuff his senses with anything, anything: the first second of the universe, the first equation in time, the first woman he sees. . . .

"Do you know," Charade says, cocking her head to one side, "this is the longest stretch of time I've seen you naked? I've never known anyone dress so quickly afterwards."

He is soaping himself the way he does everything else: meticulously, and in graphable patterns. It fascinates her: the way he moves the soap from ankle to thigh in a series of parallel lines. Then, round the genitals and working up to the neck, he follows the behavior patterns of particles within waves: the endless little circles wheeling on, the cogs and rollers and flywheels of perpetual motion going nowhere. Lather is growing luxuriant along his limbs, spreading, foaming, a white fungus, and he turns with a kind of precise delicacy so that the shower water bounces off only the unlathered parts.

"You look like a birdman," she says. "Or a faun or something."

Her comments fall into the well of his absorption; or it could be soapy anger that he sets between them. He is obstinate as a mathematical formula, she thinks; a closed system. A glint comes into her eye. She stretches and slithers; one bare tanned leg, serpentine, follows her pointed toe down the front of the vanity, across the floor, and over the lip of the bathtub, the rest of her undulating after it.

In Koenig's hand, the mathematically minded cake of soap pauses, continues, muddles a pattern of perfect arcs across his chest, pauses. Acrobatic Charade, steadying herself with one hand against the tiled headwall of the tub, fingerpaints (or rather, toe-paints) a wavering line through the foam from sternum to navel to crotch, which she is circling in slow toe-wiggling exploration when the soap slips like a fish from his hand and he grabs her ankle.

"Brat," he says. His tone is not angry, and not playful either. It is almost as though he were speaking of himself; or naming, with considered exactitude, some act of blasphemy. For a second he holds her ankle away from himself, forestalling her, forestalling whatever inevitability he reads in the soapsuds. Then they slither together like wet seals.

Perhaps it is the exhilarating pummeling of the shower; or perhaps it is the way his wet hands move over her—as though she were a woman without a name—that makes Charade toss words into the spray, words that are possibly playful, possibly not. "You know," she says, "in a few more years, you'll be an authentic Dirty Old Man. It's so easy to turn you on, it's a joke."

This gets under the edge of his abstraction. When he flinches, she can feel the scrape along the length of his pride, practically see the pinpricks of blood. Whatever it is that follows—a spasm of shock or of anger—can be measured by the strength with which he hoists her up onto the side of the bathtub. "Is that . . . the name . . . of the game?" he demands, jerkily, rhythmically, coming at her like a jackhammer. "Humiliate the dirty old man?"

"Maybe."

He comes. She comes. The room is full of vapor. He turns off the shower, steps out, pauses. Charade sees his face.

I don't care. I don't care, she tells herself. Nothing reaches him. ("Believe me, Charade," a girl in the MIT dorms has told her sourly. "There's a steady line through his office. The man is an animal.")

She does not believe the girl. She does not want to believe the girl, who may have an axe to grind. When would Koenig have time? But still, she thinks; but still, he could snap his fingers and forget I exist.

Nevertheless she has to turn away. It is true, there is something disturbingly vulnerable about him naked.

With a little flurry of movement, he turns the faucets on again, full blast, steps back into the tub, and stands directly in the line of greatest force. He could be trying to scrape off a layer of skin. When he sees Charade's eyes, he pulls the shower curtain across. Relentless, not even knowing why she does it, she jerks it back again and shuts off the drumming voice of the water.

"All right," he says quietly, resigned, exhausted. "All right," he says, his back against the wall. "What is all this about?" He might be a prisoner in the dock. "Some kind of feminist revenge? A message from Katherine in Toronto?"

"Don't be silly. She doesn't even know I'm here. To her, you're incidental, an illusion, a freakish manifestation of the— Hmm," she says, touching the mole in the hollow of his neck. "I wouldn't call it star-shaped exactly. And I wrote to Mum, you know, to ask her if Nicholas had a star-shaped mole, or any mole for that matter, in the crook of his neck. And she wrote back: *Bloody rubbish. Not a mark, not a blemish. One of Kay's stories again.* So who, I wonder, has the star-shaped mole?"

"Why do I suddenly have the distinct feeling that all the stories were leading up to some kind of attack?" He is toweling himself dry now, first gingerly (the way an invalid pats at his bruises), then with increasing and furious energy.

"How come," Charade demands, "that some people who've given themselves the Gold Star Tragic Experience Award think they have a right to live rottenly ever after? Why do they think they've got some kind of license to treat the rest of the world as shit?"

He holds the towel perfectly still in front of himself, a shield, and stares at her. At last he says, "My daughter sent you." He announces it as fact. Puzzle solved. (He can see his daughter's eyes as he stands and pushes past people's knees, makes it to the aisle, walks from the courtroom with as much tact as he can manage, willing himself not to run.) "Prick him and see if he still bleeds."

"Rubbish. You told Aunt Kay your name was Koenig, and you taught at MIT. If you hand out calling cards, what do you expect? I wanted to see if you really existed. I thought she might have made you up."

"Ah. We're back to Aunt Kay."

"Whose name you didn't even remember."

"I had a lot on my mind," he says irritably. "I barely knew what I was doing that day. It wouldn't have mattered who she was."

"Exactly." She whisks his damp towel out of his hands and holds it between finger and thumb, at arm's length: contaminated material. "It wouldn't have mattered *who* she was. And does that happen to you often?" She drops the towel into the open toilet bowl.

"What did you do that for?" For whole seconds he contemplates the problem, a formal arrangement of porcelain hemisphere (white) and acute-angled towel (plush brown)—an equation whose solution eludes him—and then wearily fishes out the towel and stuffs it into the laundry hamper. But something about the dripping trail of water it leaves across the bathroom floor energizes him. He is certainly angry now. First there is the slam of the toilet seat, which makes Charade jump, then the savage way he opens and shuts the medicine cabinet, dresses, yanks at his belt buckle. She is excited; she is made perversely hopeful; she is aroused by this show of agitation.

"Oh yes," he says, "of course it does. Of course that sort of thing happens all the time." (Thickly now, laying it on in heavy strokes.) "A virgin a night, before you hung around so persistently." (So many available virgins? Careful. This sort of thing betrays his age.) "One undergraduate girl per night," he says savagely. "I had them served up."

"So I hear."

"Oh for God's sake." It is not possible, he is thinking, to translate middle age to youth, or horror to those who have not felt it, or a war to those born after it. "Anyway"—he resigns himself to speaking in a second language, one they can both understand, one stripped of complicated nuance—"anyway, as for the Katherine in Toronto . . . She practically threw herself at me."

"She thought you were Nicholas. She explained that."

"Did she? It so happens that I don't remember. It was the day of the trial. . . ." A procession is winding its way through his head: Zundel and his coterie of hardhats. He stares at the fleshy faces, smug, confidently right, smiling beneath the yellow domes of their helmets. They might be colonists from Uranus, one of the dark cold lifeless planets. He envies them and hates them for their bovine certainties. For them indeed—you can read it in their faces—for them there is no Holocaust; it didn't touch them and therefore it didn't happen. He hates the way they stay calm in court, confident that the riders in subway cars, the readers of tabloid newspapers, the people in the street, the vast and eternal subterranean currents of prejudice, are with them; while the survivors in the witness stand grow shrill in spite of themselves.

Charade says: "According to Rachel Koenig's testimony—I looked it up in the trial records—she didn't come from Le Raincy at all. Her family were Austrian Jews."

He looks at her blankly.

"So why," she asks, "did you tell Aunt Kay it was Le Raincy?"

"What? How could I have told her that? That's your aunt's invention. A lot of it is her invention. That wasn't the way it happened."

"Why would she make up a detail like that? What would be the point?"

"I've never even heard of Le Raincy."

Charade sighs. "Well, I guess this is the end of the trail."

"Meaning what? Why are you getting dressed?"

She raises an eyebrow, tugs at the tail of the shirt he is engaged in buttoning. "Listen to who's talking," she says. "I'm leaving."

"What do you mean, leaving? It's early. It's only eleven o'clock. We haven't had our brandies; you haven't told tonight's—"

"I'm *leaving*."

He knows perfectly well what she means. From the start he has been convinced she would disappear again as mysteriously and suddenly as she appeared. This is a given. He has never believed he has any power to influence the course of events. What image billows up out of the word *leaving*? Answer: the hollow image of his future, a long long tunnel, the infinity corridor, curving back to the first second of unrecorded time, furnished—or overfurnished, by way of compensation for other starkness—with comfortable mathematics. But these are the rules of the game: one always plays as though it were possible to win. And so he says, both hopefully and hopelessly: "But I've bought a jazz record, the one you mentioned, the Wynton Marsalis—and all day at the back of my mind I've been waiting to find out . . . especially now that I find I've *met* her. I mean, how did Katherine end up in Canada? And when? And why?"

"Typical," Charade says, "of the quantitative mind. Seize on the boring and irrelevant facts and don't let go. Of course there are hows and whys for Katherine, but that's another story. Another story altogether, another cycle, another book. It has nothing to do with *my* story. Anyway," she says again, with an extra edge of petulance in her voice, "I'm leaving."

(Because why should he skip right over "leaving"? Why should he react so mildly? It's an affront the way it barely causes a ripple in his evening. Why should it be so easy?—a mere inconvenience for him, before someone else, whose name he will not remember, takes her place.)

Nothing I say, he tells himself forlornly, is going to make any difference. Someone else has written the rules. But he asks, as though he does not already know the answer: "Do you mean *leaving* leaving, or just leaving early?"

"I mean leaving leaving. This is it. I'm off." She has of course no serious intention of leaving if she can help it; she most certainly does not want to leave. But whatever this is, this overwhelming inertia that keeps her from moving on, or from moving back home, whatever it is (and she most certainly does not believe in love, an outmoded, a bourgeois, a prefeminist and colonizing and ludicrous Romantic Idea), whatever it is: why does it have her throwing tantrums and behaving like a fretful child? Passion is an illness, she thinks. Love (hypothesizing for the moment that it exists) is cruel, is hell, is like shedding a layer of skin. Love stinks.

And it is intolerable that he should so take her presence for granted that he has never even asked her what she does with her days, what she lives on, where she disappears to at dawn; is so unpossessive that she might as well not have a name. And so she says with brittle gaiety: "I'm about to shoot through, as we say back in Oz."

"But why?" He gets between her and the bathroom door, shuts it, and leans against it. "Why? I thought this was such a comfortable arrangement."

"For whom?" She is zipping up her jeans. "You think in equations; you dream graphs; you're always off in the far reaches of time and space. Between one night and the next, you don't even know I exist. If I didn't gate-crash your classes now and then, I'd never even have seen you in daylight." (Oh, she has not intended to be so explicit. Oh she has not intended to . . . She is out, now, at the tip of a very long branch. She is losing track of what she means, what she wants. Her Achilles heel is showing. Only fancy footwork can save her now.)

"But why haven't you . . . ?" he says. "You've never indicated . . . I had no idea you . . ."

This is true. He thinks of their encounters as . . . (but does he still? *does* he still think this way?) At any rate, he has in the past thought of their encounters as a kind of supernova occurrence, doomed to fade, an episode in the life of a dying star, but still, for the brief duration, flashy and brilliant. He thinks (or has been in the habit of thinking) of their encounters as a problem equal in subtlety to the problem of the energy density of the universe.

If the energy density exceeds a certain critical value, the universe could be said to be closed. Space would curl back on itself to form a finite volume with no boundary. If the energy density is less than the critical value, space curves—but not back on itself, and the volume is infinite, the universe "open." If the energy density is just equal to the critical density (that is, if $\quad = 1$), the universe is flat. And he does not yet know—no astrophysicist or cosmologist yet knows—if the universe is open or closed or flat; he does not know (as yet) what value   had at the moment of the Big Bang, the moment when the universe was formed; but he does know that the current value of   is somewhere between 0.1 and 2.

As applied to Charade, this theory cannot explain how their encounters fit into any sensible larger pattern. But within the little bubble of space and time where they have found themselves, surely the   value, as it were, is approximately known. Surely they both agree on the pleasure of these nights? He reaches up to take her face in his hands but she pushes them away. "After all this time," he says (reasonable, rational), "you can't just . . ." He makes a gesture of bewilderment. "I can't seem to remember what nights were like before you . . . It's become a habit; it's been months and months."

"Exactly a year," she says. "A year ago tonight as a matter of fact. Not that I expected you to keep track of anniversaries."

"A *year!*"

"Three hundred and sixty-five nights, and a night."

He is stunned. But now her behavior makes sense. Within the scheme of their nights there are rules—the finer points of playing the game—which he has been breaking. "You're right to be angry," he concedes.

"I'm not angry." (Typical, she thinks explosively. Absolutely bloody typical. Apology without guilt or remorse; get off the hook without cost.) "And it has nothing to do with that. Absolutely not. That's a pure coincidence. The thing is, if you recall, I had something particular in mind when I tracked you down." She plugs in the hair dryer and turns it on; she needs a stage and a reason for raising her voice. "I was looking for my father," she says above its electrical buzz.

Theatrical gestures have been planned, he can see that, but bathroom humidity puts a crimp in her sweeping style. She switches off the dryer and reaches for a drawer, but the one she has intended to pull out with a violent tug is stuck. *Shit*, he hears; and other vehement words are muttered while she glances at him sideways, as though expecting, waiting for, provoking, a reprimand. (She is very young, after all, he thinks.) When the drawer gives way, it does so with abandon and she lurches backwards. He watches with amazement the rain of little plastic bottles and jars, creams, lotions, combs, a brush. His drawer, his bathroom. But then, when has he opened that drawer? She scoops everything up off the tiles and crams them all back, a mess; and then fits the drawer on its tracks and slams it shut. She opens it again and takes out her hairbrush. "Of course," she says (and even she can hear her six-year-old's voice, a voice gone beyond any power of stopping itself, the voice of a child who is throwing a tantrum but who teeters, dizzy, on its brink, having misplaced for an awful second the trigger of her rage), "of course, what would you care?"

She brushes, brushes. He can hear the silent count. She could be punishing herself for something, pounding her own head.

Catching sight of his puzzled but fascinated face in the mirror, she summons up a word from the pit of rationalization: "Nicholas," she says. "That was the point of the whole thing. I was looking for Nicholas."

He continues staring, mesmerized, as she drags the brush through her mane, tosses her hair back over her shoulders, bends forward so that it falls like a slow and languid rain to touch the floor, runs the brush through it again and again, an *adagio* movement now, long sweeping strokes that end near her feet, near his feet too, and have the curious effect of seeming to pay homage to something. To what? Not to him, that is certain. Hair, he thinks, is responsible for a great deal of erotic confusion.

She wonders, slightly frantic now: Will nothing goad him to action?

"It's my father I want," she says, deliberately ambiguous, to shock him.

And then, peering out from the curtain of curls: "Oh, don't look so shocked." She straightens up, and her hair flashes in a golden arc above and behind her. "I'm not into incest. But I did want to see what you looked like, since Katherine mistook you for my father. Well, to be honest, first I wanted to find out if you were real. Because it's true, I have to agree with you, I can't tell how much Katherine makes up." She tosses the brush onto the vanity cabinet and scoops the long curls loosely into a topknot. "There's other stuff too. Other reasons. For instance: you cleared out and left your wife and kids. So I thought I'd study you. Maybe figure out why Nicholas left Bea, and why he's never so much as sent me a birthday card. Ever." She is enumerating points on her fingers. "Also, you're a womanizer. And so was Nicholas, at least according to several well-documented views. Three: you're mesmerized by your ex-wife, Rachel, the way Nicholas was by Verity; which isn't quite the same thing, perhaps, but still . . ."

"I see," he says coldly. "A lab experiment."

"More or less. And four"—checking off the ring finger on her left hand with the index finger of the right—"you're about the same age as Nicholas. What year were you born?"

"In 1937."

Even Charade is startled. "See? Same as Nicholas. Isn't that weird?" She sighs. "But what does it prove? Nothing. So I'm heading home."

Is this the moment? he wonders. Is this the time that is inexorably on its way toward them, that nothing can prevent, the final cooling down, the end of the affair? "Home?" he echoes.

"Back to Queensland." If he does nothing definitive now, if he says nothing decisive, she realizes with panic, she will indeed have to leave. "I sort of miss my mum, you know. And Sid and Em and Davey and all the Bea-lings. I even have a hankering to see Michael Donovan again. Finish my history degree instead of dabbling in astrophysics. May I get by?"

"But wait." He does not move from the door. "Wait. You can't do this." He has a sense of the script going wrong. (Of course, all scripts go wrong. They all end this way, but he has a sudden passionate wish to . . . No, no, nothing sudden or passionate. He needs to be rational, analytical. He decides he has been developing in the last few minutes a conviction—call it scientist's intuition—that this . . . this *experiment* has not yet reached critical mass.) "You can't just—"

"Why can't I?"

"Because . . ." He is caught. He is face to face with an answer. He almost says it: *Because I couldn't bear it if you left. Because I think it's possible that I . . .*

He swallows.

"Why can't I?" she repeats.

A second passes.

He swallows again and says: "Because you can't conclude an experiment like that. You can't abandon a problem-set until you've solved it."

She turns away. With an effort she says neutrally, "An experiment."

"The quest for your father. Exorcism, sorting things out, the whole problem-set. You haven't solved it yet."

"It doesn't have a solution."

"Everything has a solution," he says eagerly (his relief is visceral, its origins multiple and obscure), "once you construct a theory elegant enough to eliminate obvious contradictions." We are past the danger point, he thinks. She will stay now. She will start to talk again. "You have to ask the question the right way. You haven't worked at it from enough angles yet. Besides"—he is cajoling her now; in his excitement he leaves the door unguarded and paces the tiny room—"you've got me hooked. It's *my* problem-set now, mine too, and I don't have all the data in. For example"—he waves his arms in the air; he could do with a stick of chalk and a chalkboard—"consider the hypothesis that your mother must certainly know where Nicholas and Verity are. She must have a very good reason for not telling you—that's a significant clue in itself. There has to be more you could tell me about Bea."

"Yes, well, it's funny how I have to do all the talking."

"But . . ." he says, surprised, "in the beginning, I couldn't shut you up."

(And besides, besides, isn't that the way it's supposed to be? He has had—he realizes it now—a vague and surely ridiculous sense that there was something almost preordained about her endless telling of stories. For some reason, he had fallen into the comfortable habit of imagining that it was she who wanted to stop *him* from losing interest.)

He says apologetically: "I've been taking you for granted, but I want you to know . . ." He frowns a little and adds, aggrieved: "But in the beginning, you know, you practically threw yourself at me. You just arrived in the middle of the night at my office. Did I make a pass? Did I seduce you? No. You walk into my life, you rearrange . . ." Now that anxiety about her imminent departure has faded, he begins to feel resentful. "I used to get a lot of my best work done late at night."

"In the beginning," she says, "there was something very odd about the way you walked into *my* story. At the very moment that Aunt Kay was thinking about Nicholas, you walk past the Royal Bank mirrors. . . ."

"What? Just for starters," he says, "we were nowhere near the Royal Bank."

"I might have known you'd deny—"

"The open taxi door was a nice touch. But she was the one in the taxi. When I said *threw herself,* I wasn't kidding. She opened it and leaned out and offered me a ride. But it happened outside the courthouse. The Bristol Place was for real, but she was the one who gave the taxi driver directions."

Charade stares at him. "I don't believe you."

"Tell you what," he cajoles. "If you stay all night, I'll tell you a story. It's my turn, right?"

He *wants* me, she thinks, jubilant, secretly triumphant, turning away in case she cannot keep her smile tamped down, in case it leaks out around the edges of her frown.

Encouraged by the hesitation, he thinks: *We are not yet at terminal density,* and ventures, "I'll put on the Wynton Marsalis record if you'll pour the brandy." And when she turns but still appears to be wavering, he risks stroking her cheek. "If you left, it would be . . ." He is floundering in the slippery language of risk. "I'd miss you," he says, cautious.

For the first time, he finds himself wondering what she does with her days. Our age difference, he thinks. Is it a problem? Would it have any possible bearing on the course of events?

She is not exactly his first—though he shies away from running up a mental tally—she is not exactly his first twenty-four-year-old. He has, suddenly, a petri-dish vision of himself, a view of his life as an Einstein-Bohr thought experiment: What will this man be doing a few years from now? Will he keep bringing younger and younger students, though at less and less frequent intervals, home to his apartment, to this housekeeper-perfect Cambridge apartment, tastefully furnished to please the still-present shadow of his former wife, Rachel? Will he invite the young students, blooming and brilliant, more and more often, but have his invitations ever more rarely accepted? A familiar craving hits him: a desire for the pure and pristine company of an insoluble (and hence endlessly seductive) mathematical problem. He leans toward the clear-cut difficulties of making Einstein apply to anything earlier than 10^{-45} of a second after the Big Bang, of the first simple second of Time. But the curve of Charade's cheek interposes itself, and he puts a record on the stereo.

"So," Charade says. "Tell me a story."

"It embarrasses me," he says, "to talk about myself in the first person, so I'm not going to. I'm going to call this 'The Kynge's Tale' after Chaucer."

Charade swivels on the cushions and raises a skeptical eyebrow. "Oh. You've read Chaucer then?"

"Scientists aren't quite as illiterate . . ." The brandy makes an amber and dignified wave pattern within the snifter; actually, technically, he thinks, a wave *packet,* since the waves are constrained within the sides of the goblet.

"Yes?" Charade prompts.

The first half of his sentence still floats on the surface of the brandy, waiting. "We aren't as illiterate as some students like to think. Liberal arts students."

"You've actually read *The Canterbury Tales.* That's what you're telling me?"

"Well," he hedges, "not cover to cover. But when I was at Princeton—"

"I thought not. There isn't a 'Kynge's Tale.' "

"Oh," he says, crestfallen. "Well, there should be."

"There's a 'Physician's Tale,' which is about as close as you'll get in the fourteenth century to a physicist. Maybe you can use that one."

"I don't need to use someone else's plot." He sniffs the brandy's sharp bouquet with an air of exquisitely offended dignity. "I'm telling you the true story about my encounter with your aunt Kay. Or rather, the brief and torrid Toronto affair of Kynge and Katherine. So I'll stick with 'The Kynge's Tale.' "

"Oh, my," Charade says.

"Once upon a time," he begins, "there was a tormented physicist named Kynge."

"Tormented. *Really!*"

Koenig sets his brandy snifter on the table beside the sofa, walks over to the stereo, turns it down, busies himself with the lighting of his pipe. "Maybe I won't tell the story after all," he says.

"Okay, okay," Charade cajoles. "I'll shut up. But really . . ." She waves her hand around the room to indicate a certain lack of torment in the tasteful appointments of a Cambridge town house. "Plus international scientific prestige, a Nobel Prize brewing, so I hear around MIT (oh, don't look so unsuitably modest), women throwing themselves at you . . . it just strikes me that *tormented* is a little . . ."

"I'll begin somewhere else," he says. "I'll begin at the beginning, or near it. Once upon a time . . ." Here he fiddles for pipe tool, tobacco, matches.

Charade sighs. "A born storyteller you're not."

"Once upon a time," he says, clearing his throat portentously, "a boy named Kynge shone a flashlight on the wall of his bedroom and asked himself: where is the light before it leaves the bulb, and where does it go after it hits the wall? One of his obsessions was born that night. He set out on a search for the birthplace of light."

"Tantara, tantara," sings Charade, making a trumpet with her hands.

"This was in rural Wisconsin," he says sternly. "The boy Kynge came from peasant stock, farming stock, third-generation immigrants, the kind who kept gilt-framed portraits of his great-grandparents over the mantel. Stylized and tiny, in the background of his great-grandparents' portrait, was their neat little Rhine Valley farmhouse. For his third birthday, the young Kynge was given a toy tractor; for his thirteenth, his own set of farm tools. But to no avail. Against all logic and tradition, he fell in love with mathematics and the stars. The high school yearbook summed up his social life with a cartoon: at the graduation ball, he danced with a slide rule, a model of the hydrogen atom, and a map of the galaxy, all of them done up in strapless satin and billowing net skirts."

"Are you asking me to believe," Charade interjects, "that you led a celibate life in high school?"

"My dear child," he says drily, "back in the Dark Ages, when I was in high school, *everyone* led a celibate life. And as for the innocuous dating and necking that went on, yes, as a matter of fact, I was painfully shy in those days. A nerd, as they'd say today. I had a puritan adolescence. I discovered women late in life."

"Ah," Charade says. "That explains it. When do we get to Rachel and the hundreds of women and the torrid Toronto affair?"

"Rachel," he sighs. "It's very difficult for me to talk about Rachel."

There is a long silence, which even Charade does not dare to break. Between his thoughts and her thoughts, the long honeyed notes of the trumpet of Wynton Marsalis slide like suntanned swimmers. Cambridge traffic, muted, thrums from three floors down and a block away on Massachusetts Avenue. A dog barks somewhere. From farther away, sirens. It is a jazz night, syncopated, cool, possibly heading for disturbance.

"I could say this," Koenig ventures at last. "It is impossible to live with someone who is deeply and dangerously unhappy. And it is even harder to leave her."

Another silence. Through the window, Charade watches a neon blinking, one corner of the sky blushing at regular intervals. Something in Harvard Square or by the Common; or perhaps the liquor store on the corner of Massachusetts Avenue. Wynton Marsalis and the sirens knit themselves together, a gifted ensemble.

"And this holds true," Koenig sighs, "no matter how much you love the unhappy person, and no matter how . . . how *impeccable,* I suppose you could say . . . are the reasons for her unhappiness."

Charade has a sudden queasy sensation of weightlessness. What she sees is Bea standing by the window of the ramshackle house in Tamborine; she sees the shutter that falls across Bea's eyes when Verity is mentioned. Charade curls up into the corner of the sofa and buries her face in a cushion because sounds are gurgling up through her throat. She cannot tell if they are sobs or laughter. Nothing but reruns. There are only three channels in the world, she thinks, and they recycle the same old plots.

She looks over the top of her cushion at Koenig, who is staring at the night beyond the window. What's the point? she wonders. I'll never pry him loose from that ghost. Why can't I be as smart as Bea, as clever as my mum, the Slut of the Tamborine Rainforest? *(I reckon I've had a good life, Charade.)* She considers tiptoeing out of the room. He will never notice that she has gone. She believes that there are women who can do that sort of thing: escape from their own plots, intact. She fears that she, alas, is not one of them.

"I'll try," Koenig says, "to tell the beginning and the end of my marriage. I can't speak about the long happy/unhappy middle. And when I say the end . . . well, I mean it loosely and imprecisely. I mean, some point near something that was more or less decisively a kind of ending. I mean, somewhere near the point where I moved out.

"In the beginning," he says. "Or rather, before the beginning, Kynge's roommate at Princeton, who was a liberal arts type, had two tickets to a play. Events intervened. The roommate's girlfriend, for whom ticket number two was intended, was glimpsed necking in the stacks of the library with another, with the roommate's most detested rival. Wretched and bitter and decidedly buffeted by alcoholic weather, the roommate coaxed Kynge (who would much have preferred another night in the physics lab) into keeping him company: for heavy pretheater drinking, for the play, for a posttheater party with the cast, most of whom were the roommate's friends. It had been ascertained that girlfriend and rival (also drama types) were to be on the town in Manhattan for the night. Well-wishers and supporters in the cast gave out the consoling view that the roommate's rival was a jerk, and that comfort would be liberally offered at the postplay party.

"And thus the reclusive and studious and unliterary-minded Kynge found himself sitting fifth row, center aisle, at a drama student production of Christopher Fry's *The Lady's Not for Burning*.

"And thereby hangs a tale.

No curtain, the young Kynge notes uneasily. Nothing to separate stage from audience. He fears something avant-garde and incomprehensible; he thinks longingly of the lab. Beside him, his desperately unhappy roommate Arkwright slumps sideways, a heavy pressure on Kynge's arm. Arkwright's breathing, heavy and slow and fetid, fogs several unoccupied seats. The theater is only half full, not a good sign.

On stage, Kynge notes a large and bulky lectern, possibly part of the scenery, possibly not yet removed from the last mass undergraduate lecture. Dangling against the black backdrop is a frame, obviously plywood, obviously innocent of glass or substantial attachment, apparently meant to indicate a Gothic window. Beside it is a door frame and a door, connecting space with space. Penner, who is having difficulty with the physics course, comes and stands behind the lectern and busies himself with quill and parchment. Sawatsky, whom Koenig recognizes from one of his mathematics courses, stands behind the dangling window frame and sticks his head through it.

Apparently the play has begun, and Koenig fears the worst—and oh God, it is even worse than that. They are speaking poetry. Blank verse. There are metaphors as convoluted as octopi; he can't make head or tail of it. Arkwright begins snoring in a soft purr of whiskey. Koenig lets his thoughts wander to Hubble's observation of the red-shifting of the galaxies, and drowses almost to the end of Act One, when loud offstage noises wake him.

One of the characters, dashingly dressed in boots and cape but a dreadful actor, is ranting: *Of witches she's the one . . .* , after which several onstage exchanges are lost to the noises off, which sound like a locker-room brawl. Even drunken Arkwright stirs in his seat. There are shouts from the rabble, off; then the door, which stands like a foolish obelisk upstage, is pushed open and a girl appears.

When she edges in, and shuts the door behind her, there is a hush: from the noises off, from the stage, from the audience.

Partly, of course, it is a matter of spotlighting and other stage tricks; partly it is a matter of costume: a long black shift and a lustrous velvet cape, darkly green. For Koenig, however, sitting fairly close to the stage, it is the eyes caged within the pallor of the face. Is this acting? he wonders, feeling a spasm of anxiety, leaning forward on his seat to catch her voice.

There is terror in the eyes. When she leans her back against the door and wedges herself into the room, you can tell from her gasping, from her eyes, that she does not expect anything to serve. Willy-nilly, the door will be battered down; she will be dragged off; she will be burned at the stake as a witch.

Will someone say come in? the girl gasps.

And it is all Koenig can do to stay in his seat. There is talk onstage but he does not follow it, though he hears the girl speak of *a sad rumpled idiot-boy who smiled at me,* and knows whom she means. He never does figure out the plot. He knows only from the girl's eyes when the danger is great and when it lessens. He understands, at the final curtain call, that the play's meaning is that she is relatively, ambiguously, temporarily saved. He knows from the girl's eyes, however, that it is not so.

In the hubbub of people leaving, he reads his program. *Rachel Goldmann,* he says to himself.

He has no recollection of getting to the cast party, only of being there and of seeing the girl, still in the plain black smock she wore onstage. She is perched at the end of a makeshift bar. People come up to her, hug her, offer congratulations, buy her drinks. And she chats with them; she smiles. She even laughs once in a while. And yet Koenig cannot shake the feeling that she is still the witch snatched from the stake, that she listens for noises off, that her eyes keep darting to the door, that she is waiting for someone, something, some bearer of harm, to arrive at the party.

He would never have spoken. He would never have had the courage to approach her.

It is Arkwright, the drunken roommate, who throws them together. In a manner of speaking. Arkwright passes out on the carpet, and Rachel Goldmann says she will drive him home. It is natural that Koenig be involved.

Rachel Goldmann drives. At the off-campus attic apartment, she and Koenig drag Arkwright up the stairs. To his certain knowledge, Koenig never says a word the whole trip. He is lost. He is a nervous wreck. He is under her spell.

"Hey," she says at the top of the stairs. "Do you really want to spend the night with this drunk?"

"No," he says.

They go back to her room for a drink (she is sharing a house with six others) and he does not leave.

Did he believe he could change the look in her eyes? Yes, foolishly and naïvely, he did. Was any element of historical guilt, of Lutheran Germanic Wisconsin guilt, involved? Probably. Yes, almost certainly. Does he regret that night? The question, for him, has no meaning. He does not feel there ever was a choice; he does not believe it could ever have been otherwise.

That night red-shifts away from him, farther now than the Milky Way. But its thumbprint is readable as headlines. And when the farthest splinters of the farthest galaxies go spinning far enough into outer cold, they will begin to return, to contract, to arc their elastic way back to the dense core where everything began, is beginning, keeps beginning and beginning again.

"Here endeth," says Koenig, "the first lesson."

2. The Tale of the End of a Marriage and of a Torrid Toronto Affair

Here I am, Charade thinks. Night after night, his place again, nothing ever resolved.

"When," Koenig asks, "does a marriage end?" He is, of course, fully dressed, while she hunches up beneath the sheet, her back against pillows, and watches him. Probably, she suspects, he has forgotten that he is not pacing between a blackboard and tiers of seats. And indeed, he pauses and leans for a moment on the high carved post at the foot of the bed as though it were a lectern. "It's one of those endlessly absorbing conundrums," he says, "like the moral philosophers asking, 'When does a life begin?' Because a marriage has begun to end long before one partner moves out."

Charade conjures up the mournful but haunting face of Rachel Koenig: the translucent pallor, the dark hair, the disconcertingly large eyes. She pictures a delicate scene: two women bowing to each other with wary respect. The older one hands over a torch. Actually, she says, it was hopeless from the start. It began to end, really, almost as soon as it began. It always does, she warns; it always does. The ending is curled up inside the first encounter.

And the younger woman, accepting the trust passed on, lowering her head in deference to a wise sadness (though nevertheless convinced that the race she is about to run will be altogether different) sets out on her leg of the relay. There is some bond between the two women that has nothing to do with the man.

"On the other hand," Koenig says, "a marriage certainly does not end with the final decree of the divorce."

In Charade's vision, the younger woman finishes her lap and lo, here she is back where she began. In the starting blocks her predecessor waits, hand reaching back toward her future. My turn for the torch again, she says. I'll always be around, she promises.

"I think," Koenig muses, "that Heisenberg is relevant here: the wider philosophical implications of his Uncertainty Principle. Because it would be true to say that in a very real sense I was never married to Rachel Goldmann, that she was always inaccessible to me. And it would also be true to say that in another sense I am still married to her and always will be."

Charade thinks of one of his physics lectures: projected onto the white wall at the front of the room is a transparency. *Atomic and subatomic particles as such,* Koenig is explaining, *are merely idealizations, as Bohr has put it. They are useful abstractions. It is meaningless to speak of their existence or their nonexistence. They have tendencies to occur. This slide is of various visual models of the probability patterns of the electron's tendency to be in various regions of the atom.*

She knows he said exactly this, because she wrote it down and memorized it. She memorized it as though it were Greek or a nonsense rhyme. Its meaning tantalizes and eludes her. But what is clear and dazzling and unforgettable are those visual models thrown onto the wall: patterns of light in the shapes of bones, butterflies, concentric circles, Rorschach blobs of illumination, the totemic configurations of a concept that the eye understands but the mind cannot grasp. The eye says: These remind me of the cave paintings of primitive peoples.

Koenig had switched off the projector, and the white wall had stared blandly and blankly back at the students. "The pictures on the wall do not exist," he said. He switched the projector back on: "And they also exist.

"At any given moment," he asked the class, "how would you characterize the existence of those shapes of light on the wall? Could you say, categorically, that they have a material existence? Could you say, categorically, that they do *not* have a material existence?"

In the bedroom of Koenig's apartment, Charade closes her eyes and summons up (with dazzling clarity) the shapes of light which both exist and don't exist, which represent, by their presence (or their absence), diagrams of an electron's tendency to be either here or not here.

"And I subscribe, generally speaking, to the Copenhagen view," Koenig says, leaving the lectern of the bedpost and pacing back and forth from dresser to door. "I think Bohr and Heisenberg won that argument over against Einstein; I think it's past denying. The imprecision of all perception. The observer, by imposing a particular set of questions, also predetermines the answers he will find.

"So the best I can do is tell you a tale of the day that Kynge began to ask himself certain questions, knowing full well that they would lead to a certain kind of answer."

Once upon a time, on a day like any other suburban day, Kynge packed his children into the car and kissed his wife goodbye and pulled out of the driveway of his house in Brookline, Massachusetts.

"Don't forget," his wife said, "to stop at the post office."

Kynge dropped his daughter (four years old) at nursery school, and his son (six years old) at the playground where Grades One through Three were swarming over swings and climbers. At the post office he handed in the card and waited for the registered letter. To and from Toronto, where his wife's mother lived (and where indeed his wife, between the ages of seven and eighteen, had passed the post-European and pre-Princeton years of her life) all postal communication was sent registered, and had to be signed for. His wife's mother trusted no system to work without the taking of extraordinary additional precautions; nor did his wife. The postal clerk returned with a parcel and looked at Kynge strangely. "It's the same parcel," she said, "that your wife returned yesterday as undeliverable. Are you sure you want to take it again?"

Kynge frowned. The parcel was addressed to his wife's father, whom he had never met; who had been presumed dead since 1945.

"Yes," Kynge said, with a brisk confidence he did not feel. "Sorry about the confusion." And instead of driving on to his office, he drove home.

From the moment his car turned into the driveway, he sensed that certain tendencies had suddenly reached intolerable levels. He imposed the first of several significant questions. How long can this go on? he asked himself. He could see that everything was abruptly and unalterably different. He could see, for example, that the hedge of cedars which he had planted on the weekend (the hedge which had been, just a half hour previously, a hopeful row of ten-inch baby-green saplings) was now bushy and overgrown with age, higher than the windows of the house. It was unkempt. It was brown with winterburn and quite unsightly.

Inside the house, his wife, Rachel, was nowhere to be seen— although her immaculate, her fastidious absence was clamorous in the spotless kitchen counters, the dust-free surface of the furniture, the manicured houseplants, the tasteful antiques. The inside of the house was her cocoon. She left it rarely. She curled herself up inside it like sea-slick inside a nautilus shell. For as far back as he could remember, it had been getting more and more difficult to entice her beyond the cedar hedge.

On his third tour of the house, Kynge became slightly frantic and irrational, checking the small and never-used bathroom in the basement, the furnace room, opening the closets. This was against all logic, checking the closets. His wife, having been three years old when the boxcars took her family from one kind of history to another, had both a passionate and an inchoate fear of confined spaces, and a fear of leaving them.

He found her in a section of their bedroom closet. In her half of their wall-to-wall wardrobe. All the clothes and hangers and shelves had been removed, and the closet resembled nothing so much as a carrel in a university library. There was a desk, a lamp, a chair. Head bent over the desk, absorbed in her task, Rachel was writing a letter.

"What are you doing?" Kynge asked.

She flinched, but otherwise remained still. In a low voice (you could not have said its intonation was fearful, nor could you have said it was without fear), in a voice which intimated that an interminable wait was now at last over, a voice that almost seemed to express relief, she said: "I am writing letters."

"To whom?" he asked.

"To a lot of people," she said. "To Aunt Grethe, and to Frau Sachs, and to Malka—she used to play hunt-the-beetle with me—and to—"

"Rachel," he said. "Rachel, all those people . . ."

But what was the point of saying that all those people were dead?

"Yes?" she said. She raised her eyes and looked at him then, looked at him with the eyes of an animal in a trap, the eyes of someone waiting to be carried off, to be arrested, to be mugged, to be stabbed, to be raped, to be committed to an asylum, to be burned at the stake. She was waiting for the end that had always been coming toward her.

"Rachel," he implored, as though she could be cajoled into seeing herself from where he stood. "This is insane."

"Is it?" she asked.

"You have to forget," he said. "You have to put it behind you and forget. They are gone, those people, and nothing will—"

"For me," she said, "they are not gone."

And he knew only too well, of course, that time curves, that clocks in motion slow down, that a human heartbeat orbiting space runs more slowly and therefore returns younger than its twin on earth, that particles accelerated to the speed of light increase their life spans by seven times, that time is nothing more than a very imprecise word.

Nevertheless he sat on the bed with his head in his hands and asked her: "Rachel, how long can this go on?"

When he looked up she was calmly writing again, sitting there at her desk in the closet, dressed in the plain black smock that she had worn in the long-ago play.

There was nothing he could do, so he left. He drove to his office. He threw himself into his work, his classes, his discussions with students. He worked late, and although he could not remember exactly why it had become essential to work long and obsessively that night, although the morning had dwindled to a sort of bruised ache just below the level of consciousness (the way a forgotten dental appointment can keep one anxious and uneasy), he succeeded in putting off until after midnight the return to his domestic life. He knew, as soon as he pulled into the driveway, just how intolerable that life had become. He knew by the sound of crying, by the way his little children sobbed and whimpered, by the way they cowered from him and followed him with their wide accusing eyes.

About some things, looking back, Kynge is uncertain. Did he forget to pick up the children from school? Was he at fault? Is his memory scrupulously accurate? He is willing to concede that Rachel may not have been wearing the black shift on that day. It is, in fact, almost certain that she was not. He will also acknowledge that the day the letter-writing came out of the closet, as it were, the day it first manifested itself in this extreme form, was a day when some other severe disturbance had occurred to trigger it: perhaps it was the time their little boy was hit by a car and rushed to hospital; or it may have been the time that the local synagogue was fire-bombed. It is even possible that there was only one day in all the years of their marriage when she actually hid in the closet and wrote. As time goes by, he is less and less certain about the desk and about whether there was more than one letter.

But other facts are beyond dispute: the sense of a chasm opening, that was a fact. And a fact needs logical causes—which he has tried, with varying ways and scripts and successes, to provide. It is certain that as he fell, as he went free-falling through this chasm of nothing, as he clutched at its sides, shifting gears in the Toyota and pulling back out of the driveway, a cry escaped him. *Out of the depths had he cried unto* . . . And the cry was picked up.

On radio signals, on needy antennae, along nerve ends, in eye-to-eye contact, his cry kept being picked up. At the office one of his students was waiting, a flawless young woman, a woman unmarked by history, a woman whose understanding of the situation was instant and compassionate and total. And he did what any man *in extremis* would do. It is certain that this student, or another, or yet another, was later waiting in a restaurant in Harvard Square, and in a hotel room in New York, and at a conference in Miami. Sometimes, when he gave papers at international colloquia, she, they, one of the sympathetic young women, showed up in Zurich, in Paris, even in Moscow. It is certain that she once leaned out of a taxi and beckoned, right in front of the courthouse in Toronto, and when he got in she said to the driver: Bristol Place Hotel, near the airport. She had no face and no name. She came and went and left him hungry.

And furthermore, it is beyond dispute that when he had left his house that morning, the morning of the dead letters in the closet, his children had worn the untroubled eyes of happy innocence. His son (six years old) had been dreaming of a Little League game, and his daughter (four years old) had been cuddling her teddy bear and singing a nursery rhyme to herself. But when he returned that midnight, they were frightened, they did not understand, they accused him, they turned against him. His son, suddenly tall as a beanstalk, announced that he was not going to college, that he wanted no part in the academic rat race, given what it had done to his parents' marriage. His son said he was going out west to build log cabins and live on the land. His daughter was tearful. "Daddy," she sobbed, "how could you do this?" How could he? she asked her brother, who gave her a daisy, who gave out daisies and leaflets at La Guardia Airport.

What is certain is that whenever he looked at Rachel, she was sitting in the closet in her black shift, writing letters to all the people she had lost.

"How long can this go on?" he asked himself, knowing both the answers.

Charade sighs and runs an index finger lightly up and down his chest. "Yes," she says. "I see."

The lace curtains in the bedroom, long ago chosen because Rachel would have approved, lift and fall as silently as mist; and the curved shells, the Cluny lace shells—embroidered in pure and heavy cotton—offer themselves in undulations, sink under their own weight, billow forward again. Charade keeps her eyes on the ruck of French knots that gleam like the eyes of molluscs. "After you moved out," she says diffidently, "and Rachel, ah, moved back to Toronto . . . When you go there from time to time—to Toronto I mean, for weekends . . . actually, you've done it at least five times since I've known you. . . ." But she decides not to pursue the question she is looking for, and instead says: "The Zundel trial. It's difficult to see how, if she'd become agoraphobic . . ."

Koenig frowns. "It comes and goes, her bouts of it. And the trial, bearing witness—it was essential for her, essential." He stares at the curtains, leans out of bed to feel them. He seems to expect the nubby texture to speak clues to his fingers. "Still, the agoraphobia. It's possible," he concedes, "that some aspects loom larger in my mind than . . . than they would, for example, in the mind of my son or my daughter."

He contemplates the possibility of other presents and futures. "I don't know," he sighs. "It might have been different. If I'd imposed different questions. It's like theoretical physics. First the hunch, then the conviction, then the theory. Eventually some experimentalist, in a lab somewhere, finds the data to back you up."

Charade contemplates the mole on her lover's neck; the mole that is not star-shaped, not really, though if she squints a little it does seem to grow points. She touches it lightly, the mole that never marked the skin of Nicholas back in his Queensland mountain-climbing days, though now it does. At least in the mind of Aunt Kay. And it is difficult, now, for Charade to blink a twin mole away from her father's neck. Could she say categorically that a star-shaped mole played no part in a fleeting erotic encounter at the foot of the Glasshouse Mountains and on Green Island? Could she categorically say it's her father she's searching for? Or is it someone or something else? And what? And why?

"The same holds when it's the other way round," Koenig says. "You can't trust experimental evidence, you can't accept it, until you have a theory that explains it. And one of the things that stands out is the way Rachel used to work fertilizer in around the cedars. She wanted them to hide the house." This piece of evidence is extraordinarily convincing to him. Extraordinarily pleasing. He re-laxes. "After she went back to Toronto to live," he can now concede, "she wasn't as bad. When I saw her just before the trial . . . she was doing very well, I thought."

"I understand," Charade says, "about the blur. Painful things, repression . . . all that." She clears her throat discreetly. "I mean, all the nameless comfort, and so on. But still, Katherine did have a name, and you did remember . . . well, eventually you did. And you claimed . . . you said some fairly startling things about the Royal Bank and the taxi . . . well, you know. I do think I'm entitled to something just a little more specific."

"Yes," Koenig says. The curtain, which he has been pleating between his fingers, floats back against its window. "All right," he says. He hooks his hands behind his head. "Well, there's really not very much to tell. She was sitting in the gallery at the trial. Your aunt, I mean. Katherine. She was as obsessed with my former wife as I was. That's why I noticed her. There was something so intense, so . . . I don't know. It was the way she was staring at Rachel.

"You know how it is," he asks, "if someone behind you is staring at your back? How you somehow sense it, and turn? Well, she was watching the dock, and I was watching her profile, and then she turned and saw me.

"That's all I can remember, really. She looked as though she'd seen a ghost."

Charade thinks back to the first moment in Koenig's office, the first time she sat in on his class. Do these cataclysms—beneclysms? —mean everything or nothing? Do they speak of entanglement forever after? Or have they no significance at all? And if they are just visual or glandular spasms, why this lodging like burrs in the memory?

"I think," Koenig says, "there might have been some kind of blue flash. I think if you'd asked around, other people might have seen that too. It seems to me that there was a crackling sound." The kind sparklers make, he thinks. That was the way the connection leaped across the room, a licking flickering thing. "And after a while—I've no idea, really, how long—we both stood up and left. Like sleepwalkers."

Charade ponders the meaning of the wound that opens and closes faster than the shutter of a Leica. Charade, whose generation does not believe in love; Charade, who despises the possessive, the exclusive, and the very concept of jealousy (outmoded as dinosaurs, the Books of Hours, clipper ships, handwritten business letters, ice chests, flappers, hippies, marriage), asks herself: Am I tormented by one obsessive fuck? Is it Rachel, or Aunt Katherine, or all the nameless students behind these little daggers?

The daggers sneak between one thought and the next; the daggers are ridiculous; the daggers are embarrassing. Charade does not, strictly speaking, believe they exist. The daggers hurt.

"I'm sure she was the one who hailed the taxi," Koenig says. "I'm sure of that. Because I remember how she got in first and leaned out and held the door open.

"It's interesting," he says, "how she didn't want to tell you she'd gone to the Zundel trial. We couldn't stop talking about it. I'm not sure who was more obsessed, her or me. I know I couldn't shut her up. That was why I missed the last flight back." He makes an effort to be done with that night and says lightly: "I'm doomed to go to bed with talkers."

We inherit plots, Charade thinks. That's the explanation. There are only two or three in the world, five or six at the most. We inherit them and ride them like treadmills.

"When we weren't talking," Koenig says, "it was pretty torrid—I do remember that." He covers his eyes with his hands. "But I can't remember anything much. Anyway," he says, "she must have been the one who decided on the Bristol Place, because I couldn't remember its name."

3. A Tale of Hobnobbing with Doms

Charade reaches behind the heavy coiled radiator in the hall-way and feels for the envelope that should be taped to the wall. Yes, it is there. Can this be interpreted as commitment of a sort? Or has he always done this, done it for all the nameless visitors? She removes the key and lets herself into the apartment and waits.

All day she has been promising herself that she would not come. Sitting in a dive in Central Square, the one where she works as a dishwasher, barmaid, jill of all trades (illegal, no papers, below-the-minimum-wage cash payments, afternoon and early evening shifts), she stared into a mug of beer and told herself: There comes a point. Et cetera.

"Listen, kid, ya been great." That was Joe Parisi, her boss, eager employer of illegal labor, no race or creed refused, an equal opportunity exploiter. "It's just getting too hot, is all. Too many Salvadorans, makes it rough all round. Immigration creeps wherever you look, sniffing everything down to the ice cubes."

"Yeah, I know," she said. "It's okay, Joe. I've been thinking of—"

"And that's not all. There's other fuckers poking round too, God knows who and I don't plan to find out."

"Joe," she said, "it's okay. I've been thinking of heading on home anyway."

"Well, great. Beer's on the house," he said. "Lissen, I got a friend is a lawyer. Let me know, huh? A kid like you, straight, clean, no complications"—he holds her arm up to the light as though it were a bolt of cloth, as though he were quality-control foreman on color—"ya know what I mean? Shouldn't be no trouble at all to go legal."

She considers that: a student visa, a legal life in the dorms where she camps. (Not that she's the only one moving from room to room: a black market service, covering for absentees, filling cracks, keeping parents happy; *dormies,* they call them.) But then again, she tells herself: There comes a point.

So she sat at Joe's counter, finishing the drink that was on the house, and wrote to Bea.

Dead ends in all directions, she wrote. *Just as you promised, Mum. And another thing you told me a long time ago, about love, that women's disease. Have one bad bout and then you're cured, that's what you told me. So I'm coming home for the cure. Don't worry, no baby. See you soon. Love, Charade.*

She walked past the Central Square post office and mailed her letter; then she told herself: I'll hang around the dorm tonight, pack my things, spread the word that I'm leaving. I'll say goodbyes. Or maybe I'll take the INBOUND subway to Boston and browse the bookshops one last time. Maybe I'll have a final splurge on re-maindered books.

Yes, that's what I'll do, she tells herself as she drops her token into the slot on the OUTBOUND side of the tracks and, preoccupied, stares down the smoky tunnel and waits for the train to come snaking its way out from the city. Or else, she thinks, I'll spend the night holed up in the Humanities Library, nowhere near Building 6 or Physics. I'll start working my way out of science and back into history. Yes, definitely, she decides, as her body from sheer habit walks itself onto the car bound for Harvard Square, takes the escalator up to the street, walks through the Yard, past Mem Hall, into the region of elegant old Cambridge houses gone condo or turned into apartments. Faculty Row. It is as though she were being dreamed.

Enough is enough, she says to herself as she feels for the key and listens for the sound of Koenig's car.

Koenig, as he pours two brandies, comments on the importance of meandering discussion as a prelude to breakthrough. He waves a hand, summoning up analogies: like stretching exercises, he suggests, to the long-distance runner who will break a record. If she sifts enough family anecdote, the answer that lies waiting to reveal itself will surface. He talks and talks. Consider Heisenberg, he says, on the eve of the matrices thing, a mathematical breakthrough. . . . Koenig cannot stop talking. He is weak with relief, but dares not say he is glad she came for fear of raising the issue of departures. Whenever he pauses, a sense of endings rises through the silent cracks between words.

I must be out of my mind, she thinks. You can't pry anyone loose from an obsession. He belongs to Rachel and his guilt and always will, the way I belong to loss and absence. We all go round in circles; we're doomed.

What can she say of the effect that is produced by his hand and wrist as he gives her the brandy? It is just a hand, after all: veins cross the back of it like small bunches of string; light catches a few hairs beneath each knuckle and at the wrist. It is just a hand. The fact that certain regions of her body respond extravagantly; that she wants to put the hand against her cheek, her breast, her belly; that she wants to taste it and stroke it: all this is just one more convoluted, arcane, and ludicrous game.

As for me, Charade thinks, I'm bailing out.

". . . and Bea," Koenig is saying. "She has to have answers—it stands to reason. It is Bea you should be talking about."

"Bea's difficult," Charade says. "It's hardest with someone who's too close. Bea's a patchwork. I'd have to cobble her together from other people's talk, Michael Donovan's mostly, who got it from his dad. And from Babs, who used to be a barmaid at the

Duke. I tracked her down. But Bea's difficult. I'd be very unreliable on Bea. We'll have to skip her."

But she will tell him what happened in England.

Koenig raised his eyebrows in surprise. "England? What has England . . . ?"

"I told you, early on, when you never paid attention to me. It was England I went to first, before Toronto."

Koenig's relief is so visceral he can taste it in the brandy. She is talking again; she is wound up; she is off and away.

"It was Aunt Kay's advertisement that started this whole wild-goose chase. The ad for Verity, you remember what I . . . ? Right. But I didn't write to Aunt Kay—I'm not sure why."

Koenig watches how she clasps and unclasps her hands.

"Well, I suppose I know why." The hands are clenched, keeping boundaries clear. "Mum and Aunt Kay . . . there was a final rift, I guess." When the knuckles uncramp, Koenig notes, and come to rest against the dimple in her chin, at these moments she has the air of a child at prayer. "It was round about the time I was born," she says, and the knuckles turn white again. "I seem to have been . . . It appears there were multiple explosions." She laughs briefly. "Yours truly," she says, with a self-deprecating flourish of her hand, "was the *efficient cause* as the philosophers would say. And when the fragments settled, pouff! Nicholas and Verity had vanished. And Aunt Kay and my mum have never spoken to each other since."

In a burst of nervous energy, she pulls a football jersey over her head. (Football jersey? Whose football jersey? With whom does she stay in the dorms? An uneasiness settles on Koenig's mind. What does she do with her days? But he is too nervous, or too superstitious, to ask.) The jersey is much too large and hangs almost to her knees.

"I wish you wouldn't do that," he says.

"Do what?"

"Perch on the windowsill like that. It's not safe."

"What you have to understand," she says, "is the way that ad affected me. In black-and-white in the *Sydney Morning Herald*. It was like . . . God might as well have spoken in thunder. I thought:

My God, they're *real*! They're real people, those two; they're not just legends. It was like a . . . I don't know. A conversion. Suddenly nothing else was as important. I had to know everything."

Sometimes, because of the slightly matted mass of curls, Koenig cannot see her face at all. "Mum was upset." Her voice comes muffled through the curtain of hair. "Let sleeping dogs lie—that's all she said."

Charade snaps her fingers. "But I was obsessed." She taps her forehead gently against the windowpane: idiot, dreamer, naïve fool, she implies. "I'm still obsessed," she says. "What I am is an editor of my own past. I collect versions of my prehistory, arrange them, rearrange them, and then tell them to you."

"Aha"—he risks joking—"if you hadn't met me, you would have had to invent me."

She misses that one, and describes at a breakneck pace how she combed the records at the University of Queensland. Musty boxes are invoked with vivid gestures, piles of them, mountains of them, crammed in storage rooms off the registrar's office, personnel and employment records smelling of the Second World War and the fifties. He half closes his eyes, watching the ballet of her talk, the fizz, the animation, her garrulous hands. He is waiting for the blaze, the *grand jeté,* and here it is: the moment when she found some terse and impersonal entries under those fabulous, those mythical, those perfectly real and ordinary names, Nicholas Truman and Verity Ashkenazy. They had both resigned, within days of each other, at the end of the academic year of 1963.

"Which," Charade tells Koenig sarcastically, "falls at the end of the calendar year, not in May, Australia being in the southern hemisphere. I was born," she says, with a carefully timed theatrical leap down from the sill, "that October. And they resigned in early December. And over here," she says as she settles in the armchair and hugs her knees, "JFK was shot in November, which came, believe it or not, to have a bearing on my first month of life.

"What is curious," Charade says, "is that there are plenty of people still teaching at U of Q who were there when Nicholas and Verity were. And not one of them knows where they went or why.

Or so they claim. Now that strikes me as more than passing strange."

And then there was Nicholas's father, Charade's grandfather, the younger brother of the seventh Earl of Something, who was supposed to be a real estate swashbuckler in Sydney.

There were tales, Charade says, in every pub from Bondi to Parramatta, but they all petered out into haze. No one knew what had happened to the flamboyant Pom. According to one version, he'd been so drunk at a yacht-board party one night that he'd fallen overboard and drowned in Sydney Harbour within sight of the Cremorne ferry dock. According to another, there had been shady deals, too many quick speculative turnovers of waterfront property, and he'd left the country posthaste, just an inch ahead of the law.

The only thing, she says, the only clue that struck her as grazing against possible truth instead of legend, was dropped by an old-timer at The Rigged Ship, a pub on Circular Quay.

"Alfred, his name was," the old-timer said. "We used to call him Alfred the Great. He had a kid, a smart little bugger, young Nicky." Charade felt pins and needles run along the full length of her arms. "Chip off the old block, young Nick was. Always reckoned that kid would get himself in and out of trouble as many times as his old man did. Should have placed bets on it.

"He came in here, Alfred the Great did, he came in here one day and drank five whiskeys neat.

" ' *'Struth!'* I says to him. 'You trying to croak?'

" 'Jesus, Jesus,' he says. 'It's Nick. Gotta ship him back to England fast.'

"Had to bugger off fast himself then, he said. Perth, I reckon he said. Or Borneo, was it? Somewhere like that, some bloody place at the edge of the world."

And then? And then? Charade asked.

But the old-timer cadged another beer and drifted on to grievances against horses and jockeys, certain winners who had let him down.

And apart from that, Charade says, there was just that one afternoon in the staff club at the University of Queensland. . . . For the umpteenth time, she'd gently removed the hand of a professor from her thigh, and this time, from deep in the fog of his third beer (and an unrelated bitterness over an article rejected for publication), he'd taken offense.

"A bit up yourself, aren't you?" he'd demanded. "Like your father, the bloody Pom. There's always someone to watch out for you lot, isn't there?"

"How do you mean?" she'd asked quickly, alertly. "In what way, watch out?"

"Always someone to pull strings. Keep things out of the papers."

"What things?"

"What things indeed." He had smirked, bending close, and Charade sensed a sharp appetite for nastiness. Instinctively she leaned away a little and something ugly showed in his eyes. For a second she thought he was going to strike her, but he stood and bowed sarcastically and said with soft menace, "What things indeed."

Turning to go, he swayed slightly. A barstool rocked, paused, crashed over. "What things indeed," he murmured, leaving.

"I was frightened then," Charade tells Koenig. "I knew I was tracking down an answer I wouldn't want to know." (*Let sleeping dogs lie, Charade.*) "But obsessions . . ." She gestures helplessly. "Anyway, I reckon that whatever happened was hushed up quick and clean, and the records were laundered."

And what was the sum total of the evidence in Verity's file? Almost nothing. Reason for resignation: *personal.* Forwarding address: left blank.

And this was what she found on her father. Reason for resignation: *Offered position in UK.* Forwarding address: c/o *Alicia and Penelope Truman, 36 St Ann's Mews, Twickenham. London. U.K.*

"They're his aunts," Bea told her. "His father's sisters. You're not going to get anything out of them, from what I heard. There's another sister, married, and she's worse. Let sleeping dogs lie, Charade. I had a good time with your father—what more do you want?"

In Koenig's bedroom, Charade muses on that. *"There was good sport at my making,"* she says. The football jersey bounces lightly at her thighs. "That's something. That's definitely something. I don't know why it isn't enough."

"Why did he go back?" she'd asked Bea.

And Bea told her: "A certain kind of Pom always does."

"They left together, right?" Charade asked. "They got married before they left. Or else in England. They must have, right?"

Bea had gone on shelling peas, and the peas drummed into a chipped enamel bowl like hail.

"I was mad that she didn't answer," Charade confesses, pleating the football jersey, rubbing one bare foot against the other like a fly. "I tried to goad her."

Here is Charade in a tumbledown house in Tamborine, with a cacophony of voices, the sounds of younger half-siblings, in the air. "I guess I have more half-brothers and sisters in England, hey, Mum?" She sticks her tongue in her cheek and says in a plummy Brit voice: "My little brother, my half-brother Julian, is going up to Oxford next year." She laughs. "What do you think, Mum?"

And Bea says quietly, "I got no opinions on that," and goes on shelling peas.

The in-between, Charade says, is tedious; the letters sent to the Misses Alicia and Penelope Truman and not answered, the saving up and getting there—all that's another story, and a boring one, not worth telling. But the being there is worth a short tale.

Once upon a time, Charade says, a young woman with the improbable name of Enigma, a young woman armed only with her Australian accent and a foolish quantity of hope, went tapping on the door of her history. There was a brass knocker beneath leaded glass inserts, a profusion of wisteria at the lintel, and lavender, hollyhocks, and roses in all directions. The house was in Twickenham. When the door opened, she smelled the Edwardian era.

"Oh, my *dear*," said Miss Alicia Truman with a rustle of violets.

Her sister Penelope put a hand to her throat, where the points of a lace collar quivered.

"We shall have to enter her," Alicia said, circling her slowly. "Yes, her name will definitely have to be inscribed. She has Alfred's eyes. Another branch, another twig."

"When will it end?" asked Miss Penelope. Her breast rose and fell beneath the purest wool cloth, cloth so woollen and so pure that a phrase (from Thackeray? from Carlyle? from Burke?) lodged itself in Enigma's mind: *woollen stuff*. She wanted to touch it, to know the intimate and whimsical kiss of hackles. She half reached out with a questing hand.

Penelope, incredulous, clasped her arms across her breast and stroked her woollen stuff herself—an involuntary gesture—in search of comfort. From the napped surface of her sleeves rose sweet and musty and calming thoughts of Harrods, though her visitor caught a whiff of camphor.

Alicia patted her sister's arm. "The sherry, my dear," she whispered. She made her eyes go very bright. "I think it's absolutely dashing to have a young . . . a young *connection* from Australia. We've met some *lovely* Australians, haven't we, Penny? Remember that ball before the war?"

Miss Penelope offered sherry (Bristol Cream) in Waterford crystal, and turned back to the decanter and the sideboard. At the nape of her neck, the collar of Valenciennes lace betrayed not so much as a pucker, not a wrinkle, while she poured a quick glass and gulped it down. It was delicately done. She refilled her glass. "Lovely," she confirmed, though a small furrow between her eyebrows bore witness to a struggle in summoning up Australian names. "And you mustn't think," she murmured on a swell of graciousness, eighty-proof strong, "that anyone would dream of blaming you for where you were born."

"Nor for the circumstances," Miss Alicia hastened to add.

"Every family has its Alfred," Miss Penelope sagely observed.

Oh, Alfred, they sighed, smiling at each other and settling onto the Queen Anne settee. What a naughty boy he was. What scrapes he used to get into. Remember the country weekend in Buckinghamshire? Oh dear, they laughed. Oh dear. And their laughter was like music boxes being opened.

"Australia was the best place for him, really," Alicia said. "Some very fine families have sown their wild oats in Australia. Though Father was furious at first."

"It was the suddenness, you know." Miss Penelope shook her

head. "And the waste. Such a splendid marriage, vis-à-vis society I mean. Thrown away, simply thrown away." She flicked her frail little right hand over her shoulder, once, twice, three times, to illustrate reckless abandon. "And taking little Nicholas with him."

"His poor dear wife," Alicia sighed.

"He was besotted with that boy from the start. The actress's child, wasn't he?" Penelope shook her head in fond dismay. "Oh, Nicholas, Nicholas, what a little madcap he was. Bad blood will out, I'm afraid."

"Sarah—Alfred's wife, you know—was a saint about Nicholas, an absolute saint," Alicia said. "Alfred was so . . . impetuous, so stubborn about things like that. Insisting on grammar school and riding lessons and having Nicholas always in the house. *Living* here, I mean. Just as though he hadn't been born"—here Alicia rolled her eyes slightly upward to show what a woman of the world she was—"on the wrong side of the sheets, so to speak. Sarah was a *saint* about all that."

"She looked very well in black," Penelope mused, the impeccable gowns of the impeccably abandoned Sarah in her sartorially educated mind's eye. "She was very fortunate in that sense." Penelope again stroked her own woollen stuff, which had talismanic powers, and cast down her eyes. "But in other respects . . ."

"Though once we came to realize . . ." Miss Alicia, conspiratorial, leaned forward on the settee and lowered her voice. "He was such a naughty boy about liaisons. One could never know *who* might make trouble. It was a gallant thing, as it turned out, a gallant thing—even Sarah had to agree. I mean," she said, with a thrill of horror in her voice, "imagine if he'd been *here* when the scandal broke."

"Of course"—Penelope smiled fondly, indulgently—"he has made it most awfully difficult to keep the tree up to date. The unofficial side, I mean, the ah . . . But the records, *complete* records, must still be maintained."

"Oh, dear, yes," Alicia said. "Branches and twigs, branches and twigs, you have no idea."

"The tree?" Enigma blankly inquired.

"*Two* South Africans!" Alicia gleamed, leaning into the fabulous labyrinth of family history like the winged lady on her Rolls-Royce.

". . . that we know of," Penelope said. She touched the points of her collar.

"Another branch," Alicia explained. "Before Alfred sacrificed himself . . . oh, yes, well before he left for Australia . . ." She dropped her voice to the whisper favored for daring pronouncements. "He was only fourteen the first time. Right in the house with a scullery maid. Father was stunned." She fortified herself with sherry. "Oh yes, from well before his marriage, but it didn't stop there, the bad boy. Even during the marriage I'm afraid there were . . ." She paused delicately, searching for a word.

"Love children," Penelope said.

"Oh yes. We don't even know how many. And now each of those . . ."

"It's a kind of epidemic," Penelope said, discreetly reaching for the decanter.

"One of them, we understand"—and Alicia leaned forward, her eyes glittering, a hand to her palpitating heart—"in fact the first one, the scullery maid's son, went to India with the Fifty-eighth Highlanders in '46 and *stayed on*." Her eyes invited Enigma to consider possible battalions of Anglo-Indian cousins.

Enigma smiled and said politely, "My father, Nicholas. He came back here in 1963?"

Isn't it adorable, they smiled to each other, the way she *talks*? Such a quaint, such a wittily outré accent, the Australian one. Oh, and as for Nicholas, they smiled, settling comfortably back into anecdote shared and worn smooth as a pebble. A chip off the old block, we're afraid. A regular scamp.

"One of his, it's the little Canadian one I believe?"—Alicia raised her eyebrows at Penelope, who nodded in confirmation—"she's only fourteen or fifteen, a very sweet child. She's at Thornhill Academy for Girls. She comes to visit once or twice a year and plays her clarinet for us. Your half-sister, dear. Isn't that quaint?"

"My father . . ." Enigma's voice faltered just a little. "Then he didn't marry the woman who . . . ? What happened to the woman who came here with him from Australia?"

Both the Misses Truman leaned forward slightly on their cushions, fluttering, giving off a soft whirr of interest. Enigma thought of hummingbirds around a syrup feeder in a garden trellis, the way they marked time in air. What woman? asked the bright waiting eyes of her father's aunts.

Enigma said carefully: "I have reason to believe that when he arrived back in England, he was either married to, or traveling with, a woman named Verity Ashkenazy."

A little gasp of shock escaped from the tastefully arranged lives of the Misses Truman, and trembled through their silver-gray curls. *Ashkenazy,* they murmured. Or rather, their lips silently shaped themselves around the word. "Your *mother?*" they breathed as one, and Enigma saw herself catalogued with the Anglo-Indian cousins: exotic, racy, not so much disreputable as endearingly, nonthreateningly, deliciously dangerous.

"No," she said. "Nicholas, ah, left my mother, in a manner of speaking, for Verity. At least, I think so."

They patted their knees with the air of having sewn up a complicated matter (though not without a smidgen of regret, not without wistfulness for the risqué road not traveled) and ran index fingers along the trim creases of side seams and pleats. To the best of their knowledge, they confessed, there had been no woman with him that time, though perhaps dear Sarah . . . He hadn't realized, you know, that she wasn't his mother. Oh dear, such a shock it had been for poor Sarah when he turned up like that without warning. They smiled; it was typical Nicholas behavior—oh, dreadful dreadful really, but only to be expected, and rather lovable in its own outrageous way. And they did find it charming to have this Australian connection. It made the tree so interesting, so far-reaching, a kind of King Oak of the genealogical forest.

Enigma cleared her throat and put her Waterford goblet on the side table and gathered up all her courage. "And where is my father now?"

Oh, my dear, they smiled, turning up their hands (it was like Queen's Birthday doves released from cages in Buckingham Palace). Oh, my dear. With the most elegant, the most sinuous of movements, they shrugged their shoulders. Who could say? they wondered. Who could even hazard a guess at the name he was writing under now?

"Footloose, incorrigibly footloose," Alicia said. "When I pick up *The Times*, I ask myself: Could this be from his pen? Or this? With absolutely no way of knowing, of course. No way at all."

"India, Africa, Uruguay." Penelope shook her head in wonder. "Sefton claims—you'll be meeting Sefton shortly—Sefton claims there are books and books by your father." A born storyteller, a writer for newspapers, even a novelist, so people said. At any rate, a compulsive liar. "Sefton says there's a tragedy behind it, that he can't stop running. But really, you know, I don't think we need a theory like that. I think it's simply . . . well, son of an actress, gypsy blood, that sort of thing."

"Though you must admit, Penny, it's perfectly Alfred, too. It's really very very Alfred. He used to drive Father mad with his stories."

"The position," Enigma said. "He came back to take up a teaching position. Which university was it, could you tell me?"

Dear me, they said, reproachful, mildly offended. They could be quite quite certain that Nicholas had never been one of those. Swashbuckling perhaps, a bit of a rover, a dilettante, a literary man in the sense of Dr. Johnson or Oliver Goldsmith or even Laurence Sterne, that naughty trifler; a literary man who roamed the world and wrote amusing pieces under a pseudonym. But he had never been one of those scruffy university people.

"One could say, I suppose," Penelope mused, "that Marlow is scruffy."

"Marlow's kind of scruffiness," Alicia said firmly, "is different. But there have never been, I am pleased to say, any academics in our family."

"Well," Enigma said, standing and smoothing down her skirt, "perhaps I'd better be going then."

But, my dear! they protested. You simply can't leave yet. We haven't had dinner. And we've planned a little surprise for you. Your cousins, your second cousins have been invited, our sister Isolde's children. In a sense, they explained, strictly speaking, they belong to your father's generation—they're his cousins, at least; but

Isolde was much the youngest, and her two are not much older than you are. They're *dying* to meet you; they'd never forgive us if . . . And you *will* be surprised, oh, won't she? We're not such old fogies as you think. And besides, they said, Marlow and Sefton, they're in the same kind of, ah, the same *demimonde* as Nicholas. *Artistic.* Bohemian connections. Why, it's probably no time at all since they last saw him.

And so, of course, Enigma was seduced, and she dallied, and "Oh!" Penelope clapped her hands with delight. "I can hear them now."

"I'll have dinner served," Alicia said.

"Personally," Marlow announced, a forkful of roast pumpkin poised meditatively between the dinner plate and her mouth, "I can say that everything I do, every artistic statement I make—and I'm speaking particularly of my more recent work, especially the experimental feature films that Sefton and I have worked on in the last five years—every cinematic declaration is done for the sisters."

Enigma, working her way through Brussels sprouts that had been boiled rather longer than was necessary, waited for clarification.

"Not that many of them thank me for it," Marlow said.

Sefton, seated on the same side of the dinner table as Enigma, swiveled sideways. He watched Enigma with inordinate interest, and translated for his sister. "Marlow is years ahead of her time. She's a genius."

Yes, it's true, acknowledged the lowered eyelids, the slightly twitching eyelids of Marlow, who was absorbed in mashing her pumpkin with her fork.

Enigma studied her second cousin, the genius, who was gaunt and hollow-cheeked, a little carelessly malnourished, perhaps, in a style that Enigma suspected was thought of as "interesting." Marlow's abundant hair, of no particular color, was pinned up very loosely in a topknot. Strands fell about her neck and face, not unbecoming. She wore a man's shirt and a man's pants, both baggy, bleached to a wan absence of color, purchased from an exclusive survival-clothing mail-order catalogue (the labels were stitched to the outsides of the pockets). Aggressive Bohemian, Enigma would have called the style. Every few minutes Marlow reached down inside her shirt and scratched. Her feet, which were bare inside handmade sandals, seemed clamorous; look! they demanded: my toenails are ragged and filthy. And I don't give a fuck, they seemed to say (unless you fail to be shocked).

Alicia said brightly: "We saw a lovely Australian film, didn't we, Penny? All those dear little schoolgirls on a rock somewhere. It was terribly sad."

"I cried and cried," Penelope admitted.

"Oh, *really.*" Sefton put a hand to his brow. (He was dressed in Expensive Bohemian, leathers and velvets.) "Such schmaltz, my dear aunts, you can't be serious. Appallingly portentous stuff. We find Beresford, Peter Weir, and those chaps rather . . . infantile, I think is the appropriate word."

"Absolutely *dreary,*" Marlow said. "Dreary," she repeated, stifling a yawn. "All that bourgeois symbolist crap." She reached down her shirt and mopped at something with a damask napkin. "Of course, one can't expect post-colonials to do *radical* work. White post-colonials, that is. They're too busy proving themselves to Mummy Empire." Sefton emitted a single trumpet note of laughter. Marlow contemplated Enigma as though trying to determine how much translating down she should do. "Sefton and I," she said, having made an assessment, "are very involved in Third World artistic endeavors."

Penelope patted Marlow's hand, much as though she were a difficult spoiled child. "Sefton and Marlow were in Australia last year," she said. "For a film festival. They were showing one of Marlow's films, the one she made in Australia."

"Ah, yes?" Enigma inquired politely. "Which was that?"

Sefton said: "*Fuchsia, labia, and other antipodean flora.* Highly satirical on the Americanization of your cities." He appeared to be memorizing the surface of Enigma's skin. Embarrassed, she met his eyes for a moment, but to no avail. He was impervious.

"And on your impossibly primitive men, and the plight of your women," Marlow said. "We took an avant-garde approach, of course."

"Not widely understood in Australia." Sefton shook his head

in incredulous memory. "You would scarcely credit some of the questions the press asked Marlow in Sydney."

"Absolutely *dreary*," Marlow said.

"But then," Sefton sighed, "what can you expect in a country that has fish knives?"

They both found this killingly funny.

"Our hostess," Marlow said, speaking exclusively to her aunts in the manner of an adult discussing unintelligible adult matters over the head of a precocious child, "our hostess in Rushcutters Bay, an unbelievably *vulgar* woman, *dreadfully* nouveau riche, insisted on serving a fresh fish course absolutely *every* night." Marlow pulled down her bottom lip and pinched her nose and mimicked a heavily nasal Australian accent. "*Catch of the day,* she would say. We thought we would *die*."

(I *won*der, Enigma asked herself, if they *think* in italics.)

"With fish knives!" howled Sefton, dabbing at his eyes with a linen serviette. "Oh dear, it was priceless."

(The tableware theory of moral value, Enigma noted. One of the more profound offshoots of Late English philosophy and Third World artistic involvement.)

"But our little Enigma," smiled Sefton, leaning archly against her side and rubbing an affectionate second-cousinly hand from thigh to armpit, "wouldn't dream of using fish knives. She has *far* too much good taste."

"Do you use fish knives?" asked Marlow.

Enigma thought of the trestle table in Bea's kitchen at the edge of the rainforest: the press of grubby little bodies, the laughter, the tussle for the insufficient number of mismatched and battered knives and forks. "No," she said. "In point of fact, we don't use fish knives."

"You see." Sefton raised a Waterford goblet, triumphant. "Blood and good taste will out!" He slid the back of a hand skillfully up the inside of Enigma's sweater and pressed her breast. "Any time you're ready to leave," he offered, "I'll drive you home."

"Thank you." Enigma smiled. "But there's really no need. I can take a cab."

"What a shame," Sefton said. "I had so much chatter to pass on from Nicholas."

Beneath the tablecloth, Enigma pressed her hands tightly together.

"How absolutely dreary," Marlow said. "Personally, I think the Electra complex was one of Freud's more luridly silly theories. I can't think of a more boring topic than fathers."

"Perhaps," Enigma said, "if you're sure it isn't out of your way, Sefton?"

And in the car he said, well it wasn't the kind of thing he could prattle on about while changing gears, but if she would come in for a drink . . . and if you'd just, he said, outlining particular tastes, bite the nipples, just so . . . a little harder perhaps, and push your index finger . . . ah, in there . . . gently now. He was fastidious. About sex, she should know, he was something of a connoisseur of the more unusual . . .

Oh Nicholas, yes.

Well, a bit wet in some ways, Sefton was sorry to say. They'd shared a flat for a while and that's how he knew. Nicholas had nightmares and babbled on about things in his sleep. Oh, this and that, and something that happened in Australia. Sefton never could make any sense of it. And then, in his cups you know, where he often was, Nicholas was a compulsive talker, a storyteller—only it was the same story over and over again, a thousand versions. A thousand pseudonyms, too: the same story under different names, set in different countries. First in magazines, then in books. A compulsive neurasthenic type. Sefton curled his lip with distaste. Bit of a Lord Jim, he was. Saw himself as a tragic hero, had to be always on the move, have a woman in bed by night, talk or write stories all day to keep the black dogs at bay. She could count herself fortunate, Sefton said, that he'd removed himself from the family in a decent and honorable way.

Now, if she could bite his nipples again, a little harder . . . ah, lovely, lovely.

Dear Mum, Charade wrote.

A dead end, as you promised. Except you have to think the best of anyone who escaped from all that. They're enough to make an undertaker laugh. So why am I sitting in The Red Lion getting drunk and feeling depressed?

And Bea wrote back: *What did I tell you? That's what comes of hobnobbing with Poms.*

"Bea," Koenig says. "It's Bea I want to hear more about."

Charade warns: "I won't be at all reliable."

"Ah, well. Who is?"

Charade closes her eyes in concentration and knocks lightly on her forehead with one fist. "Open sesame," she says.

"I didn't necessarily mean immediately." Koenig sets his brandy down. "Another night," he murmurs as he slides a hand along her thigh.

Part IV

The B Text

Part IV

1. Rainforest, Scrub Turkeys, and the Bowerbird Solution

Scrub turkeys made her think of her dad: all that cocker-doodle-doo for a start; the bright red faces and crests (too much booze in her dad's case, his veins rubbling like cracked bricks); and their silly in-and-out necks (*Say that again, mate, and I'll knock yer block off*). But mainly it was that weird fussing around the nest mounds, gobble gobble, scratch scratch, checking on the eggs that were cooking away while their frumpy little hens buggered off (just as her mum had done) leaving their chicks behind them.

For an hour at a time she could watch.

When Siddie and Charade and Em were still babies, ages two, thirteen months and three months, before the other seven had been thought of, before she had even realized Em was not quite right, not quite all there, Bea would wake on the spike of the first cry. Blackness was so black then, night was so night, that objects had a blue edge. All the edges touched. She felt her way along the blue lines; there was no need for light. She would feed her nestlings—the sweet little scamps—and settle them back to sleep.

It was quiet—before the sun, before the birdcalls, no sound but the deadly funnelweb spiders inspecting traplines. (They hung in ghostly cones, whitish, in the lantana outside her window, and Bea had that kind of hearing. She heard the placing of eyelash legs on the web-threads.) Otherwise: outside the window, a thick pelt of hush, predawn, even the cicadas tuckered out. And inside, nothing but the soft snuffle of babies.

Something held Bea; something about the eggshell heads and the frail bleat of their concave pulses. It made her catch her breath and place herself between the cots and the funnelwebs. She would memorize each scribble of blue veins, the nautilus-shell ears, the slow ballet of fingers and the way they moved as spiders move when stepping across damaged webs.

Bea loved the messy world of babies, the slow-turning sloppy-sweet days. She loved all viscous things: dribble, semen, milk oozing from her breasts, mucous ferns under logs, fungi, slick spittle from the scrub turkeys fussing at their mounds. And here they were. First light, first rainforest noises: the gobbledegook of those finicky fathers scratching outside her window.

She tucked mosquito nets, safety nets, around each cot.

Bare feet on the cool linoleum, she would pad across the kitchen, boil a bit of tank water in the dented kettle, and steep some tea in her tin mug—she drank it strong and black, but with two spoonfuls of sugar—and then she would slip outside. Ah, the bright dense world. Sometimes laughter left her mouth like a bird, astonishing her. It was all hereness, nowness. In the rainforest, nothing was *then*. Her back against the casuarina, ferns at her feet, she watched the turkeys peck sunrise out of the scrub.

Here was dad, cock of the walk, dad the builder: scratching at the ground, paddling, spittling, making nest-paste out of mud and leaves, out of twigs, out of garbage, out of vegetable peels, piling it up, pew! what a smell, what a compost heap, what a beaut oven for eggs. And here was mum, the little slut, shaking her ass feathers, letting whoever wants watch her while she spreads her twiggy lizard-skin thighs, plop plop plop, mails her eggs into the slot, and takes off. Gobble gobble gobble, look what I did, flutter flutter, a little dance step, chook-step, two-step, aren't I—one, two, three—a clever chick?

Not that Dad cared.

"Your mum was a good-time girl. A bit of a ratbag." That was what he'd say when she came looking for him outside the pub. He'd be stinking of booze. "Bea, luvvy," he'd say. "Come here." He'd hoist her up on his shoulders (sometimes slipping, sometimes dropping her, depending how many he'd had) and make an announcement. "Here she is, cobbers. Here's the present what Shirl the Ratbag left behind. This is me Honey Bea, the apple of me eye." And his mates and cobbers and Blue Moon regulars and other assorted drunks would give a wobbly cheer: hip hip hooray for little Bea.

She liked that, being up on his shoulders, men below and all around clamoring to chuck her in the ankle, blow her kisses, put a sixpence in her hand.

But if it was a Sunday afternoon and he was giving her a ride on his bike round the Ringwood Lake, his comments were different. Kinder. (She learned that early: men were one way when other blokes were around; another way when they weren't.) Bea would be curled up on the bar of his bicycle, side saddle, inside the cave made by his chest and his arms and the handlebars. "Yer mother was what she was—she had an itch," he'd say tranquilly, rambling on. "I don't hold it against her. I sez to her, Bugger off if you want to, Shirl. I'm not stopping yer. But the moppet is mine. No bloody way yer taking her." And he'd lower his head and nuzzle Bea's curls as he pedaled.

"Dad," she'd giggle. "Dad, watch out, we'll have a smash."

In his fashion, till he couldn't get out of bed anymore, he was a good father. When he was coughing up his guts, when she had to hold the milk bottle for him so he could piss in it in bed, he'd get tears in his eyes. "Ah, 'struth, Bea," he'd say. "This ain't something a nipper should 'ave to do." He'd go on and on about the shack up the Condamine then, the one he was going to build for the two of them, get a few sheep, have Bea grow up somewhere clean. "I mean clean, bush clean, not just no-dirt clean." The coughing would get him. He'd spit and slobber and sob a bit. "Honey Bea, promise me something. Marry some bloke who'll get ya out to the bush. A farm or a shack, I don't care—just go bush. Promise me that."

"Yeah, okay, Dad," she'd say. "Yeah, I promise." She was eight at the time, not yet the sister of Kay, who'd gone gallivanting off to Brisbane, brainy Kay who read books but knew bugger-all about nothing. She could imagine Kay's eyes if Kay could see her now, holding a bottle round her dad's dick. She missed Kay; she missed having Kay listen with round eyes; she missed holding court.

He died at home, her dad. A week earlier she'd said: "Dad, I'm gonna get a doctor." Not that she had the faintest idea how to do that, but she reckoned Grandma Llewellyn would know.

He sat up like a bolt of lightning had hit him. "You do that," he roared (cough cough, spitting in a wad of sheet), "and I'll tan yer hide. I didn't get away from the Japs to die in a bloody hospital. No bloody doctor's gonna get his bloody hands on me."

"Dad," she said, because Father McEachern had come calling, "what about Father Bob?"

"And no bloody priest either," he cough-coughed. Though a day later he told her: "You can get Father What's-'is-name, but not a minute before I tell ya."

No, he said, in ten different and colorful ways. Not today. And not tomorrow either.

On the third day, seven A.M., she made him his toast and poured his glass of milk (*health piss,* he called it) and went to his room. His mouth and eyes were open and there was a lot of muck on his pillow, blood and phlegm and black stuff and the kind of smell the worst pubs gave off. The sheets stank.

What she did: she climbed on the bed and curled up the way she used to on his bike and put her face against his chest. She sobbed and sobbed at the top of her lungs. The only time ever. Not even Kay knew, not Father What's-'is-name. She never told anyone, not a soul; there wasn't a being alive who could . . .

Not true. She'd told Nicholas one night. God knew where in the world that secret was holing up. Somewhere safe, that was certain, though he'd tell it and tell it and tell it, put it into different shapes and colors till he wouldn't know which was which himself and no one would believe a bloody word. If you had to tell a secret, tell a tale-teller. What a talker, what a golden liar.

And maybe, yes, perhaps she'd let something slip to Charade

once, when Charade was pestering her for history again. The only way you could get that child off your back was to give her another pellet of the past; then she'd hive off up the mango tree or somewhere and play with it for hours. That child could talk black into blue, but who ever believed a word she said?

And Nicholas. How many versions had he given her about him and that pastry-pale woman, that Ashcan sheila? How many lies about him and Kay? What about the time he arrives on her doorstep, breezes in for his bit of cuddling and smoodging and the rest of it, and then when he's leaving, abracadabra, pulls this snake out of his pocket, this pink coral thing for round her neck.

"What's all this about?" she'd asked him. "What would I want with la-di-da stuff like this?"

"From Green Island, Bea," he'd told her. "The Barrier Reef." And as he waved goodbye from his car: "Kay and I both thought it would suit you."

And then Kay tells her the Green Island story. For Kay's bloody twenty-first, she bloody gets Nicholas. It can still make Bea spit. Yeah, but *what* did Kay get exactly? She still didn't know for sure if they'd ever. Let alone the others, but she didn't give a hoot about them. She didn't even care that much about the Ashcan—that was different; that was weird. It was Kay she couldn't bear to imagine . . . Ah, 'struth, forget all that. Let it go.

(God, she missed Kay sometimes. Sometimes she missed her so bad—the rotten sneaky book-smart Nicholas-chasing ninny—that she could smell their old bedroom, the books, the socks, the cheap perfume Bea herself had swiped from Woolworth's, could smell the whole caboodle in the very middle of lawyer cane and staghorns and monsteras and rotting logs. Oh Jesus, Mary, and Joseph.)

Oh Jesus, Mary, and Joseph, she sobbed and sobbed against her dad's stinking shirt until all the sobbing was used up, and then she splashed her face with water in the kitchen and climbed through the back fence and crossed the paddock and the buttercup patch and went and got Grandma Llewellyn.

And now it was scrub turkey time, and the sun was leaking into the Tamborine Rainforest. Well, Dad, I kept my promise. I got some bloke to give me a house out bush. Not much I can say about

Sid but I can say this: He had a bit of land and a shack and he left it behind. Didn't wait for Siddie to be born, even. Just shot through. He went shearing, I reckon, which was in his blood at least three generations deep, *all among the wool, boys, all among the wool, he shore at Burrabogie and he shore at Toganmain.* I lost a few of me blokes that way: they all dreamed that they shore in a shearing shed, and it was a fucking womanless dream of matey joy. What the hell. I had to work in the bar at McGillivray's while I was big as a blimp with Siddie, and ever since for that matter, not that I'm complaining. I've got by, along with a bit of cleaning and washing at Wentworth's, that kinda thing. And McGillivray's been good to me. He's true blue, that bloke. (Funny thing, we went at it a few times back when. He still carries a torch, maybe—well, sometimes I think that, catching a look—but not one of the Bea-lings is his.) Anyway, Siddie's dad was a decent bloke, leaving me the shack, but he wasn't the scrub turkey kind. Who is? Except you, Dad.

Bea sipped her first tea of the morning and watched the turkey-time show. Here was the fusser. First he stuck his head down his own little homemade volcano—the way nobody alive can ever stop themselves gawking down a mail slot just to see if their letter has made it, just in case the law of gravity got changed. Here was red-faced daddy scrub turkey, whose floozy had just feathered off (*Good riddance, Shirl!*), checking to see that her eggs were inside his personal oven. (And where else could they have got to?) Then up went the red crest; out went the breast feathers; cocker-doodle-doo, I got three eggs on the slow bake in here. Blowing his own gobble-gobble trumpet, the showoff, the silly galah.

He was the hatcher, the worrier. What Bea loved was the way he set his head to one side, laid his cheek on the walls of the nest mound, testing, testing. Sometimes he took fright: oh shit, oh 'struth, *blimey,* mate! Temperature not quite right, too hot, too cold; walls not thick enough; the hearts of his tiny not-yet-chicks ticking in some pattern that alarmed him. At any rate, his turkey stethoscope gave Red Alert. (And over there, three trees away, not giving a damn, is his floozy. Shimmying her downy ass and scratching for worms.)

Not your ordinary dad, the scrub turkey. Fair dinkum neurotic, he was, the way he'd rush about dabbing on earth and leaves and vegetable scraps, keeping oven temperatures right on the button. Day after day, year in year out, Bea watched him, silly bugger. She turned around, and there were Siddie and Charade in school. Not Em; Em never went to school; Em's father was that drifter, the Norwegian, the one got beat up that night at McGillivray's. She'd taken him home, dragged him practically, McGillivray helping; put iodine on his cuts and he'd stayed a month. Took off again. None of her men were scrub turkey fathers.

Bea finished her mug of tea and turned around and there were four, five, six more children in the shack. Seven children, eight children, nine children, ten. Not all of them hers, people said. Some of them were cuckoos in the nest. (Gossip gossip, buzz along the bush telegraph lines, very proper Brisbane girls, ssh, whisper, got themselves into trouble, hush, hush.)

Bea said: It don't matter to me how they got here. Every last one of them's mine.

They all went by the name of Ryan.

Charade was the one who worried her. "Mum," she'd say, "why'd you tell people Trev and Liz are yours? I remember how Trev came: you went to Brisbane to see a man about a dog, you said, and the next day there he was. He was one year old already; he was *walking*, Mum. And we just got Liz last year when those people came in their snooty car. Don't tell me not, because I stayed awake that night and hid behind the couch and listened."

"You got some objection to having Trev as a brother?" Bea asked.

"It's not *that*—" Charade began.

"You got some objection to Liz?"

"No, but Mum—"

"Trev and Liz are my kids, same as you. Don't you ever let me hear you say different."

"But Mum, what about Siddie? Which way did you get him? What about me, Mum?"

"Here's the goods about you, Charade." But something would happen to her: frown, smiles, tightenings and untightenings chasing themselves across her face. She couldn't say the name. She couldn't be the one to start it. Charade had to wind her up.

"Was Nicholas my dad, Mum? Was he truly and ruly?"

"Yes, he was. Quit pestering me, Charade."

"Tell me about him, Mum."

"Nothing to tell. He wasn't a Tamborine bloke. He was a university man; he had books coming out of his ears, just like you. You sure didn't come in a car, if that's what you want to know."

Ten were noisy; ten sometimes crowded Bea out of the shack, especially Charade, who had to know everything, another golden talker, a chip off the old taletelling Nicholas-block. Bea had to get away sometimes, had to slip down past the casuarina, past the curtain fig, walking deeper, deeper, to where the rainforest swallowed you down in one green gulp. It could do precisely that if it wanted. Once she took hold of a loop of monstera vine and it moved. Aghh, she screamed, and not a sound came out of her mouth. Eye to glassy eye, she and a python took stock. She watched it swallow, watched the undulation slide along its slimy throat. Goodbye world, she thought. But it spelled something out with its neck, skywriting, and slithered off.

She took slow deep breaths. She walked on. Here the light could barely get through; it was murky as night and pew! Oh God, oh pew, a stinkhorn. She held her nose and looked behind a fallen tree that was soft as foam rubber. Just as she thought: bloody Maiden Veil fungus.

That's me, she thought, watching how the flies came, how they drooled, how they couldn't stop coming, landing on the lace, crawling up to the stinkhorn cap. Weird things, Maiden Veils, pretty and demure as a bride, with a smell like rotting meat. What she saw: three white pricks, as fat and long (ten inches) as even Bea could wish pricks to be, jutting out of the squishy log, pushing themselves up a crinoline skirt, a bridal skirt, a skirt of white lace that fell around them like ballerina's tulle. Flies (dupes, go-betweens) crawled up the skirt to the helmet, the tip of the cock, the stinkhorn cap, getting spores on their sticky little feet.

That's me, Bea thought. Always got flies up me skirt: favorite fungus of the forest, the Queen Bea of Tamborine Mountain.

Would she ever lure Nicholas back?

Yeah, one day, she sometimes reckoned. But over there, outside the edge of the rainforest, beyond Beenleigh, beyond Brisbane even, beyond both the Stradbroke Islands, where the rest of the world went wheeling: who could say where he was? Or whether . . .

Ah, 'struth, in other ways she could never shake him off. Some days she didn't think he'd get rid of her too easy either. Maybe he reached for her in his sleep; maybe she hung around him like a charm he couldn't get undone. What she could never figure out was *why*. It wasn't the Pom talk—he was the only Pom that she ever could stand—and she'd had lovers who were just as good. It couldn't be that. What he was, was the boy with the recorder, the boy who was under a curse. *Circe*. That was his word.

"Bea," he'd moan, coming to her straight from that Ashcan sheila. "She's getting further and further away. I can't touch her. Literally. She won't let me. We're both of us under a curse." Bea would cradle him in her arms and between her legs; he'd suck her breasts. "I can never make her happy," he'd sigh. "And I can never get away. She's like Circe." She'd stroke the soft skin inside his thighs. Time would stop; they'd slither in and out of the slick saucer of each other. "Ah Bea," he'd sigh. "Bea." He'd kitten-lick her, purring to himself. "You can shut down thought."

She'd stiffen; she couldn't help it. I got thoughts, she would want to say, green snakes sliding through her brain. But thought was something he got somewhere else: from the Ashcan sheila, from Kay.

"Your little sister's quite something," he said once. "A king-fisher mind."

Hiss, hiss, went all the green snakes, forked tongues flicking. And Bea saw *thoughts*, Kay's thoughts, darting blue as birds, sweet as bloody wild orchids, putting out branches, tendrils, spinning lawyer-cane hooks, reeling him in.

Did it work? In the world they had gallivanted off to, the world beyond Stradbroke Island, had Kay's kingfisher thoughts swooped off with him? Was he telling her the tales of once upon a rainforest night . . . ?"

She turned around and here was Charade back from Sydney, Charade the student, the university woman, up from Sydney with a torn bit of newspaper that she waved like a flag. *Sydney Morning Herald*, no less.

Would anyone knowing the whereabouts of Verity Ashkenazy, et cetera, et cetera, a post office box, please, in Toronto, where the hell was Toronto? In Canada, Mum.

Okay, Canada then. Bloody Kay, like a bad penny, could have counted on that, she supposed. So that's where she buggered off to. But was it good news or bad? Mr. and Mrs. Nicholas-Kay of Toronto, but if he was there with her . . . *Verity Ashkenazy, possibly married, married name unknown but possibly Truman.*

So he wasn't there with her.

Kay was fishing for Nicholas—that was what it meant. Though maybe not. Kay always had a thing about the Ashcan; she thought the Ashcan knew everything there was to know. Fat chance. That iceberg, that frigid snob, that manipulating bitch, that Circe.

Look: there was Nicholas. She always reckoned he'd come back as a bowerbird, black as Old Nick himself, the stud of the rain forest, just his type, holding court in his bower. Bea stopped to watch. Bea held herself still as moss. Between the twin towers of twigs, all that peacockery, all that showoff stuff, the bowerbird (male) stepped this way, that way, a mating dance. What a poseur. (That was a Nicholas word. He'd said it about some bloke who was keen on Kay, some university bloke. She had to ask Kay what it meant. And Kay said: "*Nicholas* is a poseur." That was after the Glasshouse Mountains trip. Kay was mad; Kay was icy as a Melbourne swim. About what, about what? So Bea knew that something had happened.)

See what I have built, the bowerbird said in his dance steps. Look at all my brocade: he liked blue and green; he pointed his left claw, his right claw; he dipped his long beak. Bea saw flowers, bits of paper, bits of glass, a piece from her own ripped blue floral dress, *that bloody thief!* taken from her clothesline last week. It was like a blooming modern painting, his bowerbird bower, blobs of color all over the shop. Will you walk into my bower, little henchick? Will you climb my twiggy towers, see my etchings, let me ruffle your feathers, kiss your downy ass, let me tell you another tall tale? *Oh oh oh totus floreo,* another Nicholas song, another bit of bowerbird junk, what a wonderful bowerbird am I. Will you, won't you, will you, won't you, will you walk into my bower? Will you, won't you let me add your little birdy heart like a charm to the hundreds on my chain?

Bloody Nicholas.

And just look at those stupid bowerbird hens lining up: into the bower, out again, a bloody production line. Stuff it.

And then off they went, all the stuffed little, lonely little hens, to build the *real* nest, lay the eggs, hatch them, feed them, and grow them, without a skerrick of help from His Highness, the Lord of the Bower. This was the Bowerbird Solution, the answer to the Scrub Turkey Mum.

Oh, stuff it. That's the way it is: cop the sleepy smug look in that little hen's eye. She's not complaining.

Is Bea complaining?

No. Yes. No. As long as Kay hasn't got her kingfisher claws . . .

Bea turns around and there's a letter from Charade, two letters—one from England, one from Toronto—well, whadaya know? Kay's just as much in the dark as Bea is. Bloody Green Island again. Star-shaped mole! Pull the other one, Kay.

God, she misses Kay.

She misses nosy Charade.

And where is Nicholas building bowers, holding court, telling tales?

2. *Goodna*

This was the pattern: first Bea had to get someone (Joe McGillivray usually; sometimes Mick Donovan) to give her a ride down the mountain to Beenleigh. There was a Golden Fleece petrol station with a restaurant, very fancy: printed menus, proper beer glasses, bread and butter knives, paper serviettes pleated into waterlilies beside your plate. It was right on the Pacific Highway, and that was where the Brisbane bus came in. Flashing arrows promised: ANYTHING YOU WANT WHILE YOU WAIT! QUEENSLAND BEER ON TAP. YATALA PIES, SIX KINDS, BEST MEAT PIES IN AUSTRALIA!

"A bit pricey," Bea sniffed, scanning the menu.

"Ah, c'mon, Bea. Once a month." Joe McGillivray, publican, was keen to make a splash. "Pie's on me." It was Joe's special joke, each time, to ask the waitress about the serviettes. "What's this then? Frilly toilet paper?"

The Halfway House they called it, meaning halfway to Surfers' Paradise, halfway to those beaches clogged with johnnies from Melbourne and Sydney and God knew where else these days, Japan, America, you heard all kinds of gobbledegook. Once in a blue moon she and Joe would drive down with the kids in his battered Holden. Horrible. Not the surf, naturally, and not the miles of white sand, which were as good as ever—a blooming miracle, those beaches, and always would be, world without end. But the place was thick as Vegemite with bodies. Not to mention the bloody arcades! *Aw Mum, c'mon Mum, please please, some more candyfloss, Siddie's got some, c'mon Mum.* And then getting the stragglers out of the shops and across to the beach and basting them so they wouldn't burn to a crisp in the sun and then once they got in, the little buggers, you couldn't drag them back out of the water. *Aw Mum, just one more time, Liz has had lots longer than me, just one more go in the surf, Davey's still in, how come I gotta? Aw Mum, c'mon Mum, please?* And every time you turned around, you tripped over someone's thighs, someone's buttocks, someone wearing nothing more than two bits of colored string; you could hardly see the sand for bare flesh. "Funny," she'd say to Joe, "I reckon I've lost me knack for people. I been living on the mountain too long." Yeah, Joe would say. Him too. The few regulars in his pub were his limit. Otherwise, give him possums and wombats any day.

"So what's brewin', Bea?" they'd ask at the Halfway House. "Got itchy feet? Gotta blow the cobwebs away? Gotta whoop it up in Brisbane once a month?"

"Yeah, yeah." She'd smile. "Babs'll be waiting for me. Gonna kick up our heels."

"Like back in their old Duke of Wellington days. You notice how she don't let me come along?" Joe raised bushy eyebrows. "I gotta put her on the bus and bugger off. Just what do they get up to? That's what I'd like to know."

"Wouldn't you just."

"Gotta send young Charade along to keep an eye." Joe winked. "A kid in tow, they can't get up to too much, know what I mean? Keeps them outta trouble."

Once a month Bea did this. Sometimes she took Charade with her, sometimes not.

But what did she and Babs do when the bus got into Brisbane— which, depending on traffic, took an hour or more from Beenleigh?

Just how did they kick up their heels? Answer: those Duke of Wellington sheilas, those movers and shakers, they went and sat in the Botanical Gardens like any two lace-and-lavender ladies from the Eventide Homes. Sometimes they sat in the kiosk; more often they found a bench somewhere with a lot of bamboo and papyrus around, somewhere private, somewhere where you could watch more ducks than drunks or metho drinkers. While Charade, who was seven, eight, nine, climbed trees or floated boats in the pond, they sipped tea (or maybe beer) in paper cups; they smoked and swapped stories until it was time for the Ipswich bus. They'd check their watches, and Charade was twelve and curled up in a tree fork somewhere with a book. They'd get scones and jam and cream at the kiosk, and where was thirteen-year-old Charade? Down by the bandstand talking to boys, likely as not, and they'd have to drag her away because it was time for the Ipswich bus.

The bloody Ipswich bus.

Bea (and Charade, if Charade was there, but at the age of fourteen she put her foot down; she'd go to Brisbane all right, but you couldn't get her on the Ipswich bus), but back when, Bea and Charade would make the trip out, not quite all the way to Ipswich (but still, another hour in the bloody bus), get the visiting over and done with (*God!* Babs would say, *you gotta be off your rocker, visiting a place like that!*), and get the bus back into Brisbane. Babs would meet them again at the terminal, they'd drive out to Babs's flat in West End, and that was it. Some whoopee.

Maybe they'd have a church hall spree on the way to Babs's flat, pick over the secondhand clothing for the kids (Babs had four; she had a bit of trouble making ends meet). They'd stop in at the church in West End, the big one on Vulture Street where Babs went on Sunday nights every once in a while. Well, you know, she said, it was the music mostly, for when she felt down—and when didn't she?—and also they always helped you out in a crunch, like if you ran a bit short on food before the end of the month.

"You ever go to church these days, Bea?"

"You gotta be kidding," Bea would say. "Too many people still praying for me soul. I can't give in."

"You send the kids to Sunday School, but."

"Yeah, well." Bea grinned. Shrugged. Looked sheepish.

Then the two of them, Bea Ryan and Babs McGinnis, ex-barmaids at the Duke, ex-George Street beauties, would discuss the news of the world, the significant and shattering events of history, the trends, the Great Depressions, the boom times. Remember McGinley? Babs would say. The one who used to come in after the sugar cutting gave out, back from Cairns regular as clockwork? Remember Ross Andrews? Jesus, Florrie Sears—remember her?—she always had the hots for him. Remember that bloke with the tattoo on his you-know-where? I wonder what happened to him. I tell you who I saw last week, you'll never guess, Pete Kennedy, remember him? The one with the crooked prick; it had a bend in the middle— old S-bend Kennedy. What a scream, what a riot, remember? Remember the night . . . ? Remember, remember, a litany old as the hills, telling off men like beads.

"And what about Nicholas?" Babs might ask. "What about Charade's dad? You ever see him these days?"

"Ssh." Bea would frown, looking over at Charade. "Little donkeys have big ears."

"Okay, okay, the Big N. You still carry a torch for him?"

"No comment," Bea would say. "Scratch that one."

Oh men, they'd laugh, throwing up their hands. *Men!*

"Still, I got what I wanted," Bea mused. "I got me kids."

Babs screwed up her face. "I wouldn't say no to something better. Wouldn't kill me. I could do with a man around the house."

"I dunno," Bea said. "I dunno. I reckon I've had a good life."

Come morning, Bea and Charade got the bus back to Beenleigh. Till the next time. Once a month, regular as moonrise, Bea left her Bea-lings and turned her back on the rainforest and went to see if Brisbane was still where she'd left it. "Siddie can handle things for a night," she'd say. "A regular scrub turkey father, that kid. More reliable than Charade, I'm telling you. Never can tell when she'll bugger off with her head in a book. The world could fall in, and she'd have her head in a book."

"Bea," Babs would say as it got close to time for the Ipswich bus. "Let it go. You don't have to do this. I reckon there's a rule that we don't have to do stuff like that. No one has to. It's bloody well morbid."

"No way I'm going. You can't make me," said Charade, once she turned fourteen. "I'm staying right here with Aunt Babs. I've got a book. I've got exams to study for."

"She's fine here, Bea. Let her stay. If you ask me, you're crazy to go yourself."

"Yeah, well." Bea would shrug. "I dunno. I reckon I gotta. If it was you, Babs . . ."

"If it's ever me," Babs said firmly, "I wouldn't want anyone I know to see me. I'm telling ya, Bea. If it's ever me (Jesus Christ, touch wood!), I don't want you bringing me flowers. Ah *'struth.*" She'd light another cigarette. "You never know when enough's enough—that's your problem, Bea. You never did." She'd inhale and hold it long enough to wreck her lungs. "Was Jimmy the Bookie still in, last time you were there?"

"Yeah, yeah," Bea sighed. "Still taking bets on the side. He'll be rolling in it, if he ever gets out."

"What about Maeve?"

"Not last time. She's in and out. She gets dried out and goes home for a while. Then she hits it again, and goes round exposing herself and they chuck her back in."

"Jesus." Babs shuddered. "We didn't do so bad with our lives, Bea. Touch wood. I'd never want to end up there. I'd rather die."

"Yeah, well."

"What about Sleeping Beauty?"

"Same as always," Bea said. "Reckon I'll have another beer before I go."

It was easier that way. Easier if she'd had just enough to make her *shambly* (a nice word that, Siddie's word)—though Bea would have to swipe a handful of mint leaves from some garden on the way to the bus stop. She'd have to chew them or they'd never let her past the front desk.

"Here we are," the bus driver would say, letting Bea and Charade off at Goodna. "Sooner you than me, luv. I wouldn't touch that place with a forty-foot pole. Not if you paid me."

What did Charade remember of the trips to Beenleigh and Brisbane and Goodna?

She remembered Babs. A high-voltage woman—that was how Charade thought of her in later years. She was someone who vibrated, who gave off the kind of steady hum that turned heads, that burned up anyone who came too close, that left Babs's own nerves in a constantly inflamed and smoking state. When Babs lit one of her cigarettes from the stub of the last, her fingers trembled. When she laughed, Charade believed she could see blue flame. There was a glow about Babs that few people could resist for the short run. In the long run, the charred men reeled from her house.

When Babs McGinnis and Bea Ryan walked down Queen Street to wait for the Ipswich bus, Charade saw people fall like dominoes in their wake. Not just men. People turned; people crossed the street to see them better; people looped around in their tracks and followed.

Babs McGinnis talked with her hands. She made manual lightning. And then Bea would laugh, and the laugh of Bea Ryan was something to haunt people's dreams: a throaty laugh, so sexy and infectious that children joined in; women felt edgy but couldn't stop themselves from smiling; men thought feverishly of ways to meet her—they racked their brains for something witty to say to her; they considered a mad sprint, a collision, anything to touch her. And Babs laughed with her hands, made her hands flutter like birds, whoosh, whoosh, how her fingers went off like sparklers, and Brisbane held its breath and stopped to watch.

On the bus, after Babs hugged her goodbye, Charade warily inspected herself for scorch marks.

And what could Charade say about Goodna, that place of lost souls? She remembered grayness, endless variations of grayness: in the grounds, where even the flowers seemed defeated; in the reception room, where gray officials asked gray questions; in the corridors, where gray ghosts passed up and down, seeing nothing.

Close to Bea, however—and Charade stayed very close indeed and held her mother's hand—close to Bea there was a bubble of light and color.

Bea would stop in the common room, where a woman wrapped in a gray housecoat stared at nothing. She might have been a goblin—no, a troll—folded up into one corner of a couch. From her crossed arms and clenched hands, knuckles and elbows protruded like little white arrowheads, and her hair writhed spiky and snakelike about her face. Charade shivered. Charade thought of someone dipped in a rubbish pit. She bit her lip and tried not to look at the woman's legs, but they pulled her eyes and she stared with horrified fascination. Was it real skin? It was shiny, wrinkled as used tissue paper, the shinbones pushing so close against it that they seemed about to cut their own way out. The woman wore grubby socks, short ones with the cuffs rolled over, and a pair of men's slippers a couple of sizes too large. The socks gave her a clownish look, a grotesque circus look: World's Oldest Little Girl. Perhaps the most awful touch was a satin ribbon tied to a lock of her hair, a dirty pink satin ribbon, its ends trailing across her forehead.

"Maeve!" Bea called, and the bubble of light fell across the woman's face. "Maeve darling." And Bea would laugh and bend over and hug her.

Something happened then.

There was a thing Charade had seen at school, a thing her teacher had done to show the way plants breathed. First a jam jar was placed on the windowsill and filled with water, then red dye was added, then a lily was placed in the jar. Now the miracle: Michael Donovan took bets on how many minutes as the lily sipped up color through its stem, blushed along the cheek of its creamy petal, bled along its flutes and curves, became a striped lily, then a strawberry one, then a blood-red bougainvillea lily.

This happened to Maeve. "Bea," she sobbed. And color began to move through her. "Oh Bea, oh Bea, where did my ribbons go?" And the color moved past her socks, past her knees, over the bony elbows, up to her cheeks. "I hid my sequins, Bea," she laughed. "They can't find my sequins, they can't take them away." She gurgled. She began to do little bowerbird dance steps in her floppy slippers. Her excitement spilled into tears and giggles, into strange behavior.

Charade, fascinated, watched the housecoat open and close, open and close. She saw tattered lace drawers.

"There, there, Maeve." Bea was motherly, calming, a gentle buttoner-upper, a re-tier of pink ribbons. "Let's just sit."

On the gray couch in the colorless room, Bea and Maeve sat in their bubble of light, and Maeve put her head on Bea's shoulder, and sometimes Bea sang. Sometimes it was "Lily Marlene." Sometimes it was the lullaby she'd used for Charade, for Siddie, for all of them, the same song that drifted out to the mango trees on the side of the Tamborine Mountain.

Charade would think with amazement: Mum loves Maeve. Mum really loves her.

Did Bea love the Sleeping Beauty? Charade couldn't decide. When the bubble of light that moved with Bea fell across the Sleeping Beauty, nothing happened.

"Is she blind?" Charade asked.

"No," Bea said. "She's looking at something we can't see. It gets in her way."

"What's her name?"

"Her name's Sleeping Beauty."

"No, but her real name, Mum."

"That's what the nurses call her."

"Why hasn't she got any hair, Mum?"

"The nurses shave it off. If they don't, she pulls it out. She hurts herself."

The Sleeping Beauty sat in a rocking chair by the window, her back straight as a ramrod, her possum eyes black and glittering and fixed on something only she could see. Her skin was as white as that of a china cup. There was something breaktaking about her shorn head. It was as though the bones themselves were . . . what? Charade fumbled through words and decided: *proud.* She had proud bones. All of them: the high cheekbones, the forehead, the gaunt sockets, that carefully held spine. Her feet were tucked under the long gray skirt, and you could never see her hands; she kept them tucked somewhere too. But the head! It made Charade think of African sculptures in art books in the school library. An African or Egyptian queen, but white as milk.

This was what Bea did: she stood behind the rocking chair and stroked the down on Sleeping Beauty's bony head. (Charade had seen her do that with Trev, with Liz, with all the babies, stroking head-fuzz with a fingertip while she rocked them to sleep.) Bea would push the rocking chair and hum. At the first movement of the chair, Sleeping Beauty's feet would shoot out, rigid, and Bea would softly rock, softly rock, humming sounds without words, and the feet would relax, would disappear back under the folds of the skirt. That was the only sign the Sleeping Beauty ever gave.

Did she like being rocked and sung to? There was no way of knowing.

When Bea was done, she would kiss the top of the downy head. "Say goodbye, Charade," she would murmur.

And Charade, with a thrill of dread and awe, would stand on tiptoe beside the rocker and place a kiss on that high cold cheek.

Charade remembered how Maeve would follow them down the corridor, giggling: "They can't find my sequins, Bea. I hid them good." And she remembered the man whose breath smelled like a public toilet who called after them: "Put your shirt on Ulysses. Last race at Doomben, can't lose."

All the way back to Brisbane, Bea stared out the window of the bus.

"Mum, Mum," Charade would pester. "What did Maeve do, Mum, before she went to Goodna?" But she had to poke Bea, and pull at her sleeve, as though Sleeping Beauty's disease were catching. "Mum? What did Maeve do?"

"She's a dancer," Bea murmured, heavy-lidded. "At The Black Cat, on Elizabeth Street. Leave me be, Charade. Stop pestering."

"How long ago, Mum? She's old as old can be—she must be a hundred. How long ago did she dance?" Charade tugged and tugged at Bea's sleeve.

"She's still a dancer," Bea said, slurring her words, tapping her forehead. "She's still Black Cat Maeve."

"Mum, how come you're so sleepy?" Charade jiggled in the bus seat, strangely excited, strangely frightened. "What about the Sleeping Beauty, Mum? What did she used to be?"

But Bea stared at the Darra Cement Works, flickering by.

"Christ," she said to Babs every time, the second she got off the bus. "Christ, I could do with a drink."

3. Jacaranda Time

A letter came.

On the very day the jacarandas dropped their first purple, Bea showed it to Babs, and Babs sneezed.

"It's the jacarandas," she complained, her eyes streaming. "They do it to me every time."

They were sitting in the Gardens, a ruckus of duck-feeding nearby, and three purple trumpets drifted down onto six-week-old Charade. The blossoms stirred, twirled, slumped like tired ballerinas, drifted off into the grass. Bea touched wood. For good measure she crossed herself, rather haphazardly and clumsily and, in fact, inaccurately; but it was a leftover habit from her dad, who had died in jacaranda time. (Not that he knew, not in Melbourne. Nevertheless almost the first thing she remembered, one of her earliest memories of Brisbane, was jacarandas molting all over the place and Kay's eyes widening with shock. With gratifying shock.

There was blood and black stuff on his pillow, Bea said. *It was still dribbling out.*

(*Oh Bea!* Kay whispered, a white hand over the trembling O of her mouth.)

There was something Bea acknowledged to herself, though not in words, and not even in the clear-cut shape of thought. It was something registered in the flow of quiet and disquiet in her body; it was to do with the kinds of expectation that keep a life on its cogs: the din of cicadas at night, cyclones in January, men hovering, men buggering off, milk in her breasts. And for Kay to be Kay.

Bea's hands clenched themselves around two tufts of grass and yanked. At the tearing sound, at the sudden sharp smell of earth, she let her forehead butt against the ground. *Bugger Kay!* But her fingers relaxed and she smiled in spite of herself. Bugger Kay.

Babs sneezed again, and another small cyclone of flowers came down. Bloody hell, she grumbled, batting at them with a straw hat, taking swipes, swatting the air, lunging into space.

"Ahh! careful!" Bea had entered that phase where the world was either me-and-the-babies or *not* me-and-the-babies, and where everything that was *not* me-and-the-babies was fraught with possible harm. She fussed. She bent over Charade, fanning off the December heat—not that anything helped. Down in the grass, however, if she burrowed down where the sprinklers had been, it was soft and cool; well, cooler; and now she was sorry she'd left Siddie in Tamborine. She touched wood again, thinking of Julie, the Wentworths' thirteen-year-old daughter and the local child-minder. Whatever is going to happen, happens; that's the sensible thing to believe. But still. Sometimes, when beer glasses and counters were being washed at McGillivray's, there'd be a splintering sound; things could slip through Julie's hands. She should have brought Siddie with her. She shouldn't have brought Charade. She shouldn't have come.

Ah, stuff it. Take the bull by the horns was her dad's advice. Dig in your heels. So. She picked up one of the jacaranda trumpets and put it in Charade's hand. The fingers closed around the flower and around her own finger like tiny grappling hooks. *God,* she thought, feeling faint, dizzy, as the great wave came swooping up, something inside pleating itself into surf, a swoon warning.

Did you ever get used to it?

Wanting to *eat* them, wanting to *die* for them, wanting to wrap them up in silk and tuck them somewhere inside your own body to keep them from harm?

She put her face down close, panic kicking at her, till she felt Charade's wisp of breath on her cheek.

"Don't," Babs advised. "She'll get a rash. The jacaranda, I mean—get it off her." She sneezed again. "I can't read this, my eyes are too puffy."

"It's from Kay," Bea said. "Came two weeks ago."

"Jeez," Babs sniffled. "Kay." She sneezed again. "She makes me nervous. Eggheads always do. She as churchly as ever?"

"I dunno." Bea had never seen the university. No one spoke English there, or not English you could understand, and when Kay had begged, *Oh c'mon, Bea, please, I want to show it to you,* Bea had refused. I'll tell you one thing, she had said to Kay. You ever start talking to me with a plum in your mouth like those stuck-up uni sheilas, you can kiss my arse. And Kay, reverting to the ways of the buttercup patch, had stuck out her tongue and wiggled her fingers from her ears. *Me?* she'd said. *You gotta be joking, Bea.*

"I dunno," Bea sighed. "She's different." Not churchly, not such a ninny anymore. "Not stuck-up different. But different." And perhaps what Bea meant was that Kay wasn't keeping to the rules, not playing the proper role of Kay, not gasping with awe, not putting shocked hand to mouth.

"Haven't seen her since before you left the Duke, when you were big as a bus with Siddie," Babs said. "Where's she been?"

"Teaching up north. Near Cairns. She's home for Christmas."

"Yeah?" Babs dabbed at her eyes. "You gonna see her?"

"Yeah."

"She know about Charade?"

"Not yet." Bea rolled over onto her back and looked up through purple at the sky. "Me and Kay," she said. "I reckon we both wanted the same thing for our twenty-first. I reckon both of us got it."

"Listen, Bea, I gotta get away from these bloody jacarandas." Babs couldn't stop sneezing. "So wha'dja both get?"

"Dumb question."

Babs peered at Bea through watery eyes, frowning. "You mean Nicholas?"

"Yeah."

"Serves you both bloody well right then."

Twenty-one. Almost a year ago now, and Mick Donovan is hanging over her kitchen table; there's a bellbird outside the window; shrike thrush get their noisy tuppence-worth in; summer hangs heavy; the mountain is wet and green. The 26th of January, 1963, Australia Day, and the twenty-first birthday of Bea Ryan. Over the babbling of Siddie—fenced in on the veranda with cushions and tea chests—she is listening for every truck, every car, every sound of tires on the dirt road.

"Listen, Bea," Mick Donovan is saying. "Say the word and I'll walk out on Maureen tomorrow. Swear to God. Don't matter a bit to me about little Siddie." He goes to the veranda to prove a point, hoists the baby onto his shoulders. "Bonzer nipper," he says, flexing fatherhood muscles, showing them off. "I'll take him on any day." Meaning: provided you are part of the deal.

"Listen," he says. "Ya can't work as a barmaid all your life. It's not right." He is offering, in shorthand, the security of runaway husband and pig farmer.

Bea hears a crunch of tires from beyond the mango trees, outside McGillivray's, and goes still.

" 'Struth," Mick Donovan says, on the prongs of exasperation and desire. "You listening to me, Bea Ryan? Who you waiting for?"

"No one. Just some people coming up for my party. Brisbane people."

"A bloke?" he growls.

"*Jesus.*" It annoys her, anyone keeping tabs. "You think I'm the kind who only knows blokes? I got a whole busload of women coming, fr'all you know. My best friend, Babs, from the Duke of Wellington for starters. And my sister Kay for another." (Liar, liar. Bea bites her lip. She has always had a king-sized scorn for liars, yellowbellies, people with gravelrash chests, the ones who chicken out. She can take her licks.) "Yeah," she says, hands on her hips, feet apart. "Could be a bloke. So what?"

Is it her fault that Kay is off in North Queensland teaching, getting rich, meeting fancy schoolteacher blokes? Is it her fault if Babs can't come? (Of course Babs couldn't—a new baby, a new man; it would have been a waste of time to invite her.) A certain kind of smile—though she tries to hide it—quirks up the corners of Bea's mouth.

Mick Donovan scowls and shuffles.

(At McGillivray's, bets are being made.)

"What I'm telling ya, Bea . . . say the word, and it's done. I'll stick around, starting tonight."

But her eyes are out there where the bougainvillea is. She might be a dragonfly, transfixed, hearing the footsteps of spider legs on the funnelweb. A car door slams. Is it . . . ?

Ignition. Tires again. Someone driving away.

Bea's body goes slack. Not yet then, but he'll come; she knows the kind of bait he can't resist. She has written a letter. She imagines how he will read it, smile at it, preserve it, and how it will be, say, like finding a horse that can sing, but not just any old singing horse, a *Bach*ing horse. She laughs. It had taken him half of one afternoon at the Duke to explain that joke, but he had thought it worth the trouble; and it is this, perhaps, this lunatic exotic intellectual tenderness that holds her. Anyway, he will have to come to deliver his witty lines; he's addicted to her pleasure in them. She knows this; he doesn't know she knows. He will spin long strings of sound that will please her as much as—and make no more sense than—noisy pitta birds fossicking through leaves.

"Bloody hell," Mick Donovan fumes. "Wake up, Australia. What I'm tellin' ya . . . and I'm deadly serious, Bea . . ." A crinkled vein ticks at his temple. "Maureen's *expecting* again. You don't seem to— Which means I'm damned to hell, but it don't make a bloody . . ." He is painting broad peacock-blue strokes; he is sloshing color all over the mountain; he is painting the lurid edge of risk. "Bloody hell, Bea, I got young Brian's eight years old and me wife's *expecting*, and here I'm offerin' ya—"

Mildly startled, Bea turns from the window. "What?" she asks. "Sorry, Mick, I wasn't listening. Wha'dja say?"

When she looks at him like that, he can never say a bloody word. The breath sticks in his throat. He crosses the veranda and spits into the hibiscus and ferns. "You gonna dance with me tonight, or what?" he demands, abashed, confused. He lifts a hand toward her and drops it again. The stakes are too high. No sense scaring her—you never can tell with a woman like Bea; you can't predict how she'll . . . She might slam her door shut in your face for another month.

He backs off.

"Oh Mick," she laughs, grabbing him by the hands, laughing, giving off sparks. She dances him round her kitchen table. "Mick me darlin', me darlin', me darlin'," she sings. "Whatever ya want, Mickey, luv. Course I'll dance with you tonight—what a stupid question."

He is practically blinded. She's a blooming skyrocket when she winds herself up. "Jesus, Bea," he laughs, wrestling with her, biting at her shoulder. "You bloody witch." He grapples her to the floor.

"Mick Donovan!" Mock outrage. Rolling deftly out from under. She smooths down her skirt and touches her hands to her hair like a prissy church lady up from Brisbane on a picnic. "When I got guests arriving any minute!" she says.

"Bloody hell," Mick Donovan fumes. He has to rearrange himself as he staggers down her steps. "Just wait till I get ya dancing, Bea, that's all I promise. I got something I been keeping for your twenty-first." He stops at the bottom step and gives her the look. "I'll be waiting for ya, Bea." Stressing each word, pelvis butting the air. "See ya, then." She is leaning over her veranda railing now, arms crossed beneath her breasts, teasing him, daring him to get rash, her eyes on his crotch. "Bloody witch," he murmurs, helpless. Nodding, nodding. (Aren't they agreeing to something?) "I'll be waiting at McGillivray's," he says.

Bea is savage with excitement, ruthless. "Mick darlin'," she says, licking her lips. "You're a bloody animal, you know that?" She blows him a kiss.

She is quite quite mad with happiness. It amazes her, really, that she doesn't set fire to the railing. She can feel her own heat. She could lift the mountain if she wanted to; she could make birds fly backwards. Anyone who comes close is done for, she knows it. *My turf this time, Nicholas. You'll never be able to leave.* Her eyes gleam like a cat's.

"Bloody hell." Mick Donovan grins, gearing up for the chase. He whistles all the way to the pub.

When it happens, late in the afternoon, just on twilight, Bea is worn out with straining for the sounds of tires all day and doesn't hear his car at all. There's just a footstep on the veranda and she looks up and he's there. In the doorway.

God, she thinks, going weak. Who can explain this? It never makes a skerrick of sense. She has to hang on to the kitchen table, though this has become extraordinarily difficult, since her hands like the rest of her are water now—no, not water, something slick and slow: honey that's been warming in the sun.

"Bea," he says. "What a delight. Diana the huntress cornered, the nymph in the woods. I received the most irresistible epistolary enticement in the post last week. Your orthography is a connoisseur's delight."

"Christ, Nicholas, you bloody Pom." (She is laughing the way Siddie laughs, in gurgles, in rising bubbles. Is she making any sense at all?) "Why don'cha speak English? When are ya gonna learn to talk like a normal bloke?"

"Alas, alas," he sighs, sardonic hand over his heart. "Ever the outsider. I've missed you, Bea."

"Bloody liar."

The kitchen table is between them (and possibly history, language, the past, the future, incurable obsessions, the religion of hopeless hope). It's no use resisting; it's pointless. Is it *his* eyes? (They are very very blue.) Is it hers? (There are green flecks, green as a cat's, in Bea's brown eyes.) Some force that no one understands has all their nerve ends jangling. They bend across the table like two magnets.

Bea has a sensation of falling, of going backwards through her life, very slowly, helpless as a mouse in a parachute's talons. It seems to her that this is the slowest love she has ever made, that everything is happening under water, that she has molasses arms, molasses legs. Odd, the things you remember, the silly details that lodge themselves somewhere. He is lying on her bed (when did she let go of the kitchen table? how did they get into her bedroom?); he is golden as butter, not leathery like other men, not real. He is as smooth to touch as a silkie in a dream. She has her hands on his shoulders, her knees tucked into the dimples on the outsides of his thighs. She is coming slowly down, very slowly, as slow as mother-of-pearl shell falling through water. It takes years. She is watching his cock disappear. What she notices, the last thing she sees before they lock into a fit, are the two creases, the V at the borders of his fuzz: they are a different kind of whiteness, creamy, two frail milky lines that pierce her as the pulse on Siddie's head pierces her.

Who can remember anything at all about the commotion itself? But those two creases, that creamy V, can swim up from wherever it is that memory lurks and she will have to catch hold of something, will have to press the back of her hand against her lips.

(Jesus, Bea thinks, nearly twenty-five years later. What sense does this make?)

All this takes a very long time, so long that it is possible the party is over without her, the guests all gone home. (Though next week Mick Donovan, in a drunken fury, will say: *Christ, you must have gone at it like dogs, you fucking overheated bitch.*) In Bea's bedroom, the clock runs slow. After years and years and years, when the fit has subsided and there is nothing she can do to stop the lock from unlocking itself, when his cock leaves her with a quiet little slurp of goodbye, with a sucking sigh, when they are lying very wet and very exhausted, Nicholas says: "We could live like this, Bea."

Over them, like a dome, is their own post-thunderstorm weather of damp peace. Nicholas gestures into it. "We could—I don't know—farm silky oak and walnut and ash. Breed orchids. I could read Proust and write poetry. You could spin cloth of gold."

The crazy Pommy, the silly galah.

"In the Bea-loud glade," he says, and she watches as his voice builds a life, watches a Nicholas-and-Bea world take shape: minarets, caravans, banners of silk. He claps his hands and the Slave of the Ring appears. Deck the Queen Bea with jasmine and honey, he commands. Cover her with cinnamon and cloves. Loony Nicholas, the golden talker with tales on his breath.

And then.

"Bea," he says, leaning on his elbows, kissing her on the lips. "We'd better go. I left Verity at that pub down the road. You don't mind, do you?"

You don't mind, do you? Her mind grapples with a translation of those words in the vacuum where the eye of the storm is passing, and then hailstones large and sudden as boulders come pelting down; a cyclone is ripping an illusion to shreds.

"I had the dickens of a time convincing her to come," he says. "You know what she's like. You have to help me, Bea. She's getting worse." He buries his face in her breasts. "Help her, Bea. I want you to save her."

The details of shock are no clearer than those of euphoria. Buttons are buttoned; limbs move; smiles get fastened into place. Who expects it to make sense? Who was there when the morning stars sang together? Who watched when the sea was hemmed with sand?

"Sometimes, Bea," he is saying, "I wonder if you yourself realize. I wouldn't want to make extravagant metaphysical claims, but you do have . . . *something*. A touch. You could hardly not be aware of it, could you? Best not analyzed, I suppose you would say?"

What the bloody hell is he talking about? She is watching for the spaces between words (those treacherous rocks), feeling her way. That is where she must swim. Take it slowly; move this foot, then this one; grope with hands turned clumsy as flippers. Ah, and the chill, the black water. She cannot remember a January that has been so cold.

Do they cross the veranda, collect Siddie, go down the steps? Apparently. And at McGillivray's there is something going on: there is one hell of a hubbub, a general commotion, a bunch of yobbos making catcalls and jokes. Bea can smell the same sort of ghastly thing you smell when a lamb is snagged on barbed wire and dingoes are gathering.

God Almighty.

She runs blindly, but for some reason the sense of barbed wire is so strong that she runs with her hands in front of her face. She could as easily abandon her dad in his stink and his sodden sheets as watch this. She doesn't remember much: the stumbling up the steps, shouting, a certain amount of cuffing ears, lashing around with her tongue, letting them have it. Then (she thinks) there was a long embarrassed silence, the men sheepish, Verity shaking like a sick dog, Bea herself drained and shaking (the bloody infectious shivers going the rounds like the wind through shivery-grass), and Nicholas . . . ah well, let that go.

Over his shoulder Bea and Verity are eye to eye. Endlessly, endlessly Bea has replayed that look; or rather, Bea has never disengaged herself from that moment whose meaning will forever tantalize her: there is the image of barbed wire and a creature snagged; that translation is always present. There is another thing, a black black black thing, but where does it come from? From Verity's eyes? Or from Bea's thoughts? It is the black gleam of an ace trumped.

Someone lurches and drops a glass.

" '*Struth*," Bea says, her eyes flashing. "Ya bloody pack of dingoes. Can't ya bloody behave yerselves with me guests at me own bloody party?"

Aw shucks, Bea, nobody meant . . .

"Well," she says, climbing onto the bar and holding high a glass of beer, flinging up her arm so that foam flecks fall like confetti. "It's me twenty-first birthday, dammit. Who's gonna dance?"

Twenty-one. Kay's twenty-first, November 1963. Of course Bea remembered it. She had Mick Donovan drive her down to Beenleigh in his truck; she bought a card that had pink satin balloons on it, real satin, very fancy, with cushiony stuff glued under the satin so that you could press a finger into each balloon. She mailed it off to North Queensland, where Kay was teaching.

And Kay wrote back. *You will never believe who showed up at my door on my birthday. I have trouble believing it myself. It was*

*an absolute fluke, but he's been a Visiting Tutor this year. They
have to visit all the external students. We never know when they're
going to drop in. He's been a couple of times, actually. The first
time was nearly a year ago (just after your twenty-first.) He told me
he'd been to your party. But this time was an incredible fluke—it
was just sheer good luck. He hadn't even known it was my birthday. We went to Green Island again.*

Anyway, see you in December. Lots to tell.

Hah, Bea thought. I'll bet.

And what took place in the kiosk of the Botanical Gardens, at the
foot of George Street in Brisbane, on a steamy December day in
1963, just one hour after Bea had shown Kay's letter to Babs, just
six weeks after the birth of Charade, and just two weeks from the
assassination of John F. Kennedy—an event which seemed to hold
some relevance for Kay and none whatsoever for Bea?

According to Babs McGinnis, who knows as much as anyone
(which is not much) about that meeting, it was briefer than either of
the parties intended.

("But Babs is something of a problem," Charade tells Koenig.
"In the long run, nothing she says is reliable. If there was something
Mum didn't want me to know, Babs would back her up. I have to
take her with a grain of salt. And getting anything from Aunt
Kay—other than JFK talk—was like trying to get blood from a
stone.")

So: Babs McGinnis, not under sworn oath, maintained that Bea
had planned to go straight from the rendezvous at the Gardens to
the 6 P.M. Beenleigh bus; and that instead she had appeared, just a
little after 3 P.M. and with Charade in her arms, at Babs's West
End flat.

"Didn't she turn up?" Babs asked, surprised.

"Yeah," Bea said. "She turned up."

"What happened?"

"Nothing," Bea said. "Can you drive me back in for the six
o'clock bus?"

"Sure. You want a drink? Beer? Wha'dja talk about?"

"About the bloody American President getting his bloody head shot off," Bea snapped.

Bea is at the kiosk first. She sits on one of the benches and leans back against the lattice, with Charade in her arms, in such a way that she can watch the path winding in from the George Street gates. She wants a few moments to accustom herself to the sight of Kay again before she hears whatever Kay has to tell.

It is as she feared. There is a radiance to Kay, and so Bea knows. She can feel a pain beginning behind her forehead and opening downward and through her like a rift valley. Verity is one thing. This is another.

"Bea!" Kay calls. "Oh Bea." Running, laughing, hugging, dangerous happiness slopping in all directions so that people turn and feel a pang of envy—you can see it in their eyes. "Oh my God, a baby, another one? You never even told me! Oh, how gorgeous . . . He or she? Oh, she's adorable. What's her name?"

"Charade," Bea says, waiting (that's what this is, all right, a bloody charade), waiting, swaying, poised, watchful, ready to snake away or strike.

"Charade?" Kay's eyebrows go up; she laughs. "Charade as in . . . ?" There's a second's awkward pause, a feeling for context. "I like it, Bea. It's got class." Kay is not full of awe, or shock, or anything but her own excitement. "Bea," she says, "I can't wait to tell you. I've won a scholarship. I'm going to America—can you believe it? *America.*"

These meaningless words eddy past Bea like yesterday's tram tickets. City flotsam.

"*America!*" Kay says again. "And at such a time, an assassination. It's like being catapulted from the outer suburbs of history to the core of . . . of . . . I don't know . . . My God, Bea, it's like . . ."
—Kay is shredding bougainvillea leaves with a fingernail; Bea is waiting for the real reason for all this frazzle—"it's like having your whole life suddenly *translated.* . . . Who will I become, over there? There'll be, there would have to be, it stands to reason, a sort of quantum difference. Unpredictable changes. I mean, it's inconceiv-

able here, isn't it? Can you imagine a Prime Minister shot?" She sits down momentarily beside Bea, bounces up again. "Well, can you, Bea?"

"What?"

"Shot. Can you?"

"Yes," Bea says.

"What? You can? Are you serious? How can you think something like that?"

"Like what? What the bloody hell are you going on about?"

"About President Kennedy, about the assassination. Oh *Bea*." Kay gestures with good-natured exasperation. "I'm leaving the first week in January," she says. "I'll go straight into—listen to this—the winter semester. That's what they call it."

Bea shifts position and adjusts Charade in her lap.

"Actually," Kay says—she cannot keep still—"it was Nicholas's idea." Bea leans forward slightly, listening for the undercurrent. "He encouraged me to apply. As a matter of fact—"

Bea strikes.

"Yes," she says. "He told me."

Kay lurches. (The thought does not come to Bea in the shape of that particular word, but that is her judgment.) Kay puts the back of her hand against her mouth. Bea, waiting, counts seven full seconds before more words make a rush on the silence. "Bea . . . ?" Kay stumbles. "Is Charade . . . ? Is Charade . . . ?"

"Yes," Bea says.

"That's one of my versions," Charade says. Koenig is stroking her hair. All night they have lain naked together; she is still in his arms. "But it doesn't quite work. There are too many gaps."

"It's all right," he murmurs. "We learn to live with whatever we have to live with." He brushes her cheek with his lips. "After a fashion."

"I used to lie awake at nights," Charade says, "inventing the event. I was *there*, that's what's weird. Somewhere"—she knocks on her forehead with her fist—"there must be neurons and synapses that store it."

"Yes," he says. "And others whose job it is to screen it."

She leans on one elbow to look down at him. "You think I *do*, in some sense, know what happened?"

"I think it's possible."

"God," she says, digesting this. She burrows back down into his arms, the wiry pelt on his chest against her cheek. "The thing is, my mum and Kay, you can feel the connection still—God, you can *feel* it. So why, for nearly twenty-five years, haven't they . . . ? *Why?*"

"There's no theory elegant enough to answer that," Koenig says. "Maybe after particle physics, after the *Theory of Everything* is cut and dried . . ."

"And Nicholas, my father, my *father*. Not so much as a sign. Why doesn't he . . . ? *Why?*" She pummels the pillow with her fists.

"Ah," Koenig sighs. "That's easier to understand."

"When will he come?"

"Perhaps he has. Perhaps he's watching all the time."

"Well," she says, "I make him watch. My Nicholas, I mean, the one I've made. I make him watch me all the time."

The one you've made, Koenig thinks, can be calculated to strike terror in the other's heart. Who can compete with his own mythology? He strokes Charade's belly, the tuft of hair, the soft flesh between her thighs, not to arouse either of them, they are too sated for that; but to indicate protection, sustenance, solace. On her skin he draws a frail blueprint of hope.

"I have another version," Charade says. "You see, there's Green Island to think about. And this version came to me entire, in a split-second, the day I rang Aunt Kay's doorbell in the house beside the lake outside Toronto. It was the way she looked at me, the shock in her eyes. I look like Nicholas, I know that. Mum says it; Babs says it; Michael Donovan's dad has said it. And that would be enough, I suppose, to explain . . . But I don't know, I just had the feeling there was something else, something more, in that look.

"So here's my second version."

* * *

Kay was first at the kiosk in the Brisbane Gardens, and when Bea arrived it was Bea who had to lean against the lattice in shock.

"Well, wha'dya you know?" she said. "Jesus, Mary, and Joseph, who'd have thought? You been home?"

"How could I?" Kay asked. "They think I'm not arriving back until next week." Kay sank onto the bench and faced her. "Bea?" It was a desperate and convoluted plea.

"What?"

"It's Mum and Dad—you know what this would ... So I can't ..."

"Christ," Bea said.

"Bea, it would break their hearts. They'd die of shock."

"Yeah," Bea said drily. "That's for sure. You'll be the subject of a few prayer meetings, that's also for sure. How'dja get away with it?"

"I taught till a few weeks before the end; then I had to resign. They're the rules. So I don't have a job anymore. Not here. I applied for one overseas—I saw an ad for teachers. I leave next month. Bea ... ?"

"What?"

"I can't just give her away."

Bea said nothing.

"So ... so *would* you, Bea?"

"Would I what?" They stared at each other and Bea turned white. "Bloody hell," she said, and had to sit down. "Bloody hell, Kay, you've got a nerve." She lit a cigarette and asked harshly. "Boy or girl?"

"A girl. I've called her Charade."

"You seen him since?" Bea wanted to know.

"Once. On my twenty-first. I told you."

"So he's seen her. What the hell did he say?"

"He said it wasn't the first time, and he was sorry."

"Jesus," Bea said. "Bloody Nicholas."

Kay's eyes were still asking: *Bea, will you?*

"Bloody hell," Bea swore. "As well hung for a sheep as a lamb, right? Our wayward sister Bea, and who'll think twice? All right then, I will, but *Jesus,* Kay."

And after that, how could they ever speak to each other again?

"I don't know," Charade says, "I don't know. It came and went, that version, in a second. Like a bird flying in one window and out another. It doesn't quite add up either. I mean, they'd never have let Kay keep teaching that long, not back in those days."

But why did so much happen in late 1963, when Nicholas and Verity vanished from sight? And what was the translation of that look in Katherine's eyes? "And why . . . ?" Charade begins.

"Hush," Koenig murmurs, his lips in her hair. "It doesn't matter any more."

The last streetlamp blinks off.

"Look," he says. "Now you can see the constellation of Taurus. And if we had a telescope, the Crab Nebula would wink its neutron eye."

But Charade is asleep in his arms.

Part V

Truth, Physics, and Other Questions

Somewhere someone is traveling furiously toward you,
At incredible speed, traveling day and night,
Through blizzards and desert heat, across torrents,
                  through narrow passes.
But will he know where to find you,
Recognise you when he sees you,
Give you the thing he has for you?

Hardly anything grows here,
Yet the granaries are bursting with meal,
The sacks of meal piled to the rafters.
The streams run with sweetness, fattening fish;
Birds darken the sky. Is it enough
That the dish of milk is set out at night,
That we think of him sometimes,
Sometimes and always, with mixed feelings?

"At North Farm"
John Ashbery

Part V

1. The Crab Nebula Dream

*One of the most spectacular events ever seen by humankind
was recorded by Chinese astronomers on July 4 A.D. 1054. A
supernova explosion, caused by a dying star, left behind its
remnants and formed the famous Crab Nebula. The Crab is an
expanding cloud resembling a Fourth of July starburst. . . .*

*But it was not until the twentieth century that astronomers
discovered a neutron star spinning rapidly at its center.*

*The spinning star has an enormous magnetic field and sprays
matter like a hose or a lighthouse as it turns.*

—NEIL MCALEER: THE MIND-BOGGLING UNIVERSE

Down the long corridor of Charade's sleep someone kept coming, the footfalls never getting closer. She could almost see who it
was, but not quite, because the corridor twisted and turned—which
was odd, since clearly it was MIT's Infinity Corridor, which runs
straight as a die from Massachusetts Avenue to the Crab Nebula.

When she turned the corner into Building 6 (Physics), she was aware of subtle changes. For one thing, the sign: THE UNCERTAINTY CORRIDOR IS CLOSED UNTIL FURTHER NOTICE. WE REGRET ANY INCONVENIENCE. For another, the corridor itself was no longer a corridor, not really; more a tunnel carved out of rock. She reached out, striations regular as ribs. It's The Cut, she thought with surprise. I'm in Sydney. I'm down in The Rocks near Circular Quay. There was also the scrubby reassuring texture of Koenig's chest hair and of Tamborine underbrush, both of them neatly planted on Arbor Day by order of the City of Cambridge and the children of Boston.

She ran toward the footsteps which kept coming and coming, fainter, louder, never farther off than now. Was this pointless? Echoes bounced like neutrinos. When she called, hallooing, the rubble of her voice was everywhere, all directions at once. Wait for me, wait for me, wait. Unevenness in the rock floor caused her to trip and skid so that for whole downward stretches she was in fact falling, turning as she fell, head-over-heels cartwheel style, a pulsar, a fragment from the Crab Nebula blast. She had no idea The Cut was so endless, that they were still extending it, and in the same old way too, that was plain. She could hear the convict chains and the chink of chisel and mallet. Tap tap, tap tap, tap tap. She ran and ran.

She passed the Harbour Bridge and the North Shore beaches and the Hawkesbury River; she crossed the border into Queensland, keeping up a steady jogging pace, Coolangatta and Surfers Paradise on her right. Always the tunnel curved ahead, always the footsteps, always she had to stay alert for trains, running between the tracks, flattening herself against the wall when the subway cars rushed by. Brisbane loomed ahead; there was never any mistaking the smell of that city, the way it came at you in a familiar wave of frangipani and jasmine and a yellow splash of allamanda flowers. She passed the Botanical Gardens and the kiosk and made straight for the center of town, for that section where the underground concourse fans away from the Harvard Square trains and curves into a loop. That was where the supernova stopped, that pulsing spinning blinding splinter of star, the Crab Nebula junk. That was where the buses came in.

She waited, along with Harvard students, Radcliffe students, the bag ladies, the underground drifters and huddlers. It seemed a long time. Somewhere behind a pillar the footsteps marked time (though when she looked, there was a cunning scuffle, a red-shift). At last, shuddering, the bus arrived, the bus for Goodna, and she put two quarters in the slot and climbed on board. Where the star stopped and pointed, she got off.

Goodna was no different, the same gray smell, the gray halls down which the footsteps were coming faintly toward her. She followed, though they never got any closer. She saw Maeve, who opened her housecoat by way of greeting, she saw Jimmy the Bookie, she stopped at the door of Sleeping Beauty's room, where Crab Nebula spilled its light.

The footsteps kept coming and coming.

Sleeping Beauty was in her rocking chair by the window, her shaven head splendid and frightening as Circe. Charade stood in the doorway and watched, and the chair, all by itself, began to rock. Very slightly, very softly, creaking just a little, certainly not enough to blot out the sound of the footsteps, faint though they were.

In profile, the head was not unlike Nefertiti's. Or like that of a prisoner of war. It turned, and in the slow arc of its turning, Charade felt the coming of a heavy answer. She felt it like the leaden drag of menstrual blood, she felt panic, she wanted to run but couldn't move. Very slowly the head turned, very slowly, somewhat stiffly, a little awkwardly, testing a mechanism of movement long out of use. But the eyes, which had been vacant for so many years, were now focused and pulsar-bright.

"You came," Sleeping Beauty said. Her lips did not move, but the words were nevertheless so clear that Charade could feel their sharp edges. The words spun and glittered like pieces of star. Fragments, hundreds of fragments came to meet them, a reverse explosion. They piled themselves up around Charade—Charade of the leaden legs, the cast-iron body—Charade, who was frantic to flee but could not move, who was deafened by a voice and by footsteps.

Sleeping Beauty tilted her head slightly to one side.

"Is he coming?" she asked. It seemed that the air, by arrange-

ments of waves, made the sounds. Or perhaps she willed them on Charade. Her lips never moved. "Is it he?"

Words spoke themselves through Charade's lips. "He is coming, but not getting closer."

Sleeping Beauty's eyes lost luster as water runs out of a sink, as a star crosses the lip of a black hole. Suddenly. Absolutely. She looked at Charade without looking, and Charade, feeling the high kick of panic again, strained against her own leaden weight in a ponderous effort to back out of the room. Too late, the event horizon crossed. The hands of Sleeping Beauty, which had never been seen, removed themselves from the gray folds of skirt.

Entreaty? A warding off? Defense?

Without volition and in fact against her will, Charade took a step, and as she did so the outstretched arms, although they were blind and rigid, swung like compass needles in her direction. She took another step, then another, a millstone walk. Now the bald head and its downy stubble were at eye level, inches away. *Say goodbye, Charade*. Charade's fingers hovered, tentative, then stroked, the way Bea used to stroke. And at the instant of contact, knowledge came. Crab Nebula exploded. Sleeping Beauty opened her hands and they were full of raisins. Charade took one and woke with a cry.

2. *Wave Mechanics*

What is transported along the wave is the disturbance caus-
ing the wave phenomenon, but not any material particle.

In the apartment off Harvard Square, dread beats like a heart,
each beat deafening as chaos. Charade is curled inside the tent made
by Koenig's arms and his chest and the bed, in the crook of his
heart, and would like to stay there. Her own dread pulls at her, her
own fate, which is as common and as horrible, as incomprehensible,
as that of any other sleeper in Boston, as ordinary as black dribble
in the mouths of the dying.

"Koenig," she murmurs. "Oh Koenig."

It is a kind of prayer, and even saying the name gives momen-
tary comfort. She buries her lips in the coils of his chest hair, that
matted and graying bulwark.

He does not wake.

"Oh Koenig," she whispers again.

She would like him to open his eyes and dissuade her. She

would like him to snap his fingers and discount the dream. She wishes the dream would vanish, the way dreams do, into some black crack of absolute non-recall.

But Koenig sleeps.

As she slides away, his arms stir and make a reflexive effort to hold her, then go slack. *No,* he moans. But a restive nerve claims him. His muscles twitch and relax. He rolls over to face the wall.

Charade tiptoes to the kitchen and switches on the dim appliance light over the stove. In the demimonde of shadows and thick silence and mute domestic things, she sees signs and portents, fantastic messages, a code of horrors: tongs, red-hot coils, knives, graters, grinders, slop bucket, plug hole, freezer. The telephone huddles like a black listener between the fridge and a row of green-and-white canisters. She shivers. She dials zero.

"Directory Assistance, please," she says. "For overseas calls. Australia."

Convoluted explanations are required. Country code and the area code for Queensland, she has those; but the number she needs is for a pub, McGillivray's, in Mount Tamborine. Yes, yes, of course it is the name of a village as well—surely the operator knows that. Isn't she in Brisbane? No? San Francisco, using onscreen data? How confusing. There is, says San Francisco, no onscreen listing for Mount Tamborine. Ah. Well then, Charade supposes it must come under Beenleigh, which she has to spell for the computer. There is a blip blip blip, the computer thinking, connections being made, a long beep, and then a new synthetically generated voice takes over. *The number you need requires an additional rural routing code of static static static ... This is a recording ... If you need further assistance static static white noisssssssse.*

Charade begins again. On the third attempt she gets a number and writes it on the memo pad beside the phone.

She tries to remember the time difference, and eventually concludes: It will be tomorrow afternoon there. Late afternoon already. If Mum is on afternoon shift, she will answer the phone in the bar. She dials the number.

"G'day," says a broad Australian voice, male. "McGillivray's. What can I do yer for?"

"Joe?" Charade's heart is hammering in her chest.

"Half a mo'. I'll get 'im for yer."

"No, wait! Who's speaking?"

"Davey Ryan here. Who'dja want?"

"*Davey!*" My God, Davey! In her absence, his voice has crossed the cusp. He's become a man.

"Who's speaking?" Davey sounds puzzled, having heard the long-distance pips. "Where're ya calling from?" She's not an Aussie, that's for sure, whoever she is.

"Davey! It's me. Charade." She is half laughing, half sobbing with longing.

"Who?"

"Charade. Me. Your *sister*, you silly drip."

"Bloody hell!" he says. "Charade! I don't believe it. You sound like a bloody Yank. Where the hell are you?"

"I'm in America. In Boston."

"Christ Almighty," he says.

"Davey, I have to talk to Mum. It's urgent."

"Jesus," he says, tense, concerned. "What's happened?"

"No, no, nothing's wrong, not that kind of urgent. I'm fine. I just want to talk to her."

"She got a letter from you," Davey says. "Weeks ago. She's been flashing it all over the mountain. Says you're coming home."

"Yeah." In that instant, Charade realizes it's true. "Yeah, I am. Davey, can you go and get Mum? I'll call back in a half hour."

Davey roars with laughter. "You been gone too long, kid. Even the mountain's changed. You know what Mum went and did?" He pauses dramatically. "Wait for it," he crows. "She got the phone put in. Because of you, I think, to tell you the truth. She's been awfully jumpy since you went."

"Yeah, well. Give us the number then."

"Mum? It's Charade."

"Hello?"

"It's me, Mum. Charade. I'm calling from America. I called McGillivray's and Davey gave me your number. How are you, Mum?"

"Charade!" Bea wonders, if she lives to be a hundred, will she ever outgrow this inner lurch, this sense of her children as unbelievably fragile and perpetually prone to harm, this wish to cradle them in her nest mound, to cover them with her wings and keep them safe. She presses her lips together and leans against the wall of her kitchen. Through the window she sees a crow at the mangoes again.

"Mum? Can you hear me?"

"Yeah." The telephone is still a foreign object to Bea. How can you feed into it the things you might want to say? "I can hear. You sound different." She concentrates on the mangoes. Must get Trev and Liz to climb the tree this arvo, pick the rest before the crows get the whole bloody lot. She'll get Liz to help with the mango chutney. "You finished gallivanting yet? The little'uns have been asking. They miss you, I reckon."

"Yeah, me too. I'm coming home, Mum. Mum"—Charade takes a deep breath and holds it—"do you still go to Goodna?"

"Wha'dya think?"

"And they're all"—she is twisting the cord around her fingers—"they're all still there? Jimmy the Bookie? Maeve?"

"Jimmy's died. Dear old Maeve's in and out, in and out."

Charade can hardly breathe now. There is a terrible constriction in her chest. "And Sleeping Beauty, Mum? Is she still there?"

"Yeah. Still there. Same as ever."

"Mum, I have to ask you something."

"I reckoned you would, sooner or later, Charade."

"Is she Verity, Mum?"

Bea sighs. "Yeah. She's Verity."

"Mum . . ." Charade's hand is trembling. Her back against the kitchen wall, she slides to the floor and sits huddled. "Is Verity my mother?"

Through the window, Bea watches the crows, how they peck and peck, how they worry at the mango till it falls. Then they leave it to rot. They leave it for another perfect piece of fruit. They start again.

"Charade," she sighs. "Why can't you let things be? Why can't you let sleeping dogs lie? Why do you want to know everything? You think *knowing* is so great?"

"I don't know why, Mum. No, I don't think it's so great, but I have to know, I just have to, that's all. She is, isn't she?"

"Yeah, she is."

"What happened?"

"It's not pretty, Charade."

"Was it me? She went mad because of me?"

"Don't ask stupid questions. No one can answer stuff like that." That part of it, in fact, Bea understands: she remembers the helplessness, how she used to feel ill with anxiety, how there were frantic and lunatic things she might have done to keep any one of her babies from harm. So she understands, in a manner of speaking, given everything else. "She tried to drown you, Charade. They took her away, and Nicholas brought you to me."

"Oh God," Charade whispers. "Oh God." She is blind, she cannot breathe, something burns across the surface of her skin. She rocks herself on the floor of Koenig's kitchen. Where is all this salt water coming from?

Bea is talking. Bea watches the mangoes fall. "Listen to me, Charade. There's things that happen, and there's things that *matter*. And me and Nicholas . . . as far as I'm concerned, me and Nicholas made you right here, in this house, on the day I turned twenty-one." *'Struth,* she thinks. And the thoughts that have never taken shape before push, shove, fizz their way out, a geyser of astonished outrage. Me, someone *looks* at me and I get pregnant, so *how? why?* Bea sighs. "Verity's your mother. But me and Nicholas made you, that's the truth."

"I know that, Mum." Yes, I do, Charade thinks. I do know that. "Mum, did Nicholas leave her? Is that why?"

"No, that's not why. He wouldnt've . . . Well, anyway I reckon he wouldnt've. Ah 'struth, who knows? Nicholas is Nicholas. But she . . ." Bea sighs. Another mango falls. The crows leave. There is a crimson flash of rosella parrots. "She always expected him to leave. She expected everyone to leave. She always expected to be alone."

"I didn't find him, Mum."

"Yeah. Well."

In the eternity that ticks away between them, Charade hears

the whole Pacific on the line: the long shush of white noise and waves, the static, the shuffle and ping and collision of disturbed molecules of air.

"Mum," she laughs nervously, "this is an awfully expensive silence."

"Yeah," Bea says, watching scrub turkeys scratch at their nest mounds. Somewhere in the rainforest a bowerbird preens and she sees his dance, his shimmer, in her mind's eye. There are things, she thinks, that a person can't forgive himself for. He'll have to keep running from them forever, he daren't look back. That's the way things are. "Yeah well. Don't be too harsh, Charade."

"Do you think he'll ever . . . ?"

"Who knows? Charade, remember the tree orchids on the mango? There's one just out. I can see it from here. Funny, when you were little, you always had to have one of those flowers in your hair."

Charade is dizzy with homesickness. "I'm coming home, Mum. God, I miss you all."

"Yeah, me too." A female scrub turkey shakes her feathers outside the kitchen window, a kookaburra laughs, Bea taps her foot to keep time. "I'll spread the word, Charade. Reckon we'll have a party."

"Yeah. That's beaut, Mum. See ya soon, then."

"Hang on, I gotta— Charade? Listen, there's no need to tell Kay about, you know . . . She sort of . . . She always wanted to . . . The thing is, Verity was, I dunno, bloody magic for her. No sense spoiling that."

"Mum, I think she knows. I think she knew when she saw me."

"Yeah. Could be. You've got Verity's eyes, not the color, but the shape or something. Sometimes I see her looking out, scares the hell out of me too, Charade."

So maybe now Kay will forgive Bea at last. Now that she knows. And Bea, who has let that little cruelty go glittering on through the years, is Bea willing to . . . ?

Bloody Kay, though. All these years wondering if she and Nicholas . . . star-shaped mole indeed! Through the kitchen door, Bea can see the bed where still and always . . . She sees the hollows of his thighs, those milk-white creases where her body swallows his cock, his eyes, oh God his blue blue eyes—and in the bleating hollow of his neck, the brown mole in the shape of . . .

Bea frowns. *Was* there a mole? Was there ever a boy with a recorder? Bloody Kay, bloody bloody Kay, bloody bloody bloody—

"Mum? Are you still there, Mum? Do you want me to give you Aunt Kay's number?"

There is sweat on Bea's upper lip. When she rubs the back of her hand across it, it shakes a little. "What?" she says vaguely. "Kay?" There are two whole seconds of silence. "I don't know, Charade. Let sleeping dogs lie, I've always said." She can see the crows at the mangoes again, they can never leave well enough alone. Somewhere a bowerbird keeps up the same old dance. "Yeah," she sighs. "Give me Kay's bloody number."

Charade sits on the floor, seeing nothing, till first light comes through the Venetian blinds. Then she tiptoes into the bedroom where Koenig is still sprawled in sleep, one arm flung up across his face like a child. How beautiful he is, she thinks. She stands and looks at him.

Losses, losses, losses.

Will he miss her?

Perhaps, she thinks, he will miss me enough to write.

(*'Struth, who knows?* Bea asks. *Nicholas is Nicholas.*)

And Koenig is Koenig, Charade thinks with a terrible pang.

Before she can change her mind, she kisses him on the forehead and on the small mole (not star-shaped) in the crook of his neck and gathers up her things and leaves.

And with that, as Scheherazade said to King Shahryah when the thousand-and-first night had come, *she vanished like camphor.*

3. Probability Theory

What we observe is not nature itself, but nature exposed to our method of questioning.

—WERNER HEISENBERG: Physics and Philosophy

Details assault him. In his sheets there is a hollow, a very slight concavity, which is as permanent as the scar on his ankle—a thing his body keeps as a souvenir of a five-year-old's fall from sharp rocks. Some of his sweaters smell of tropical flowers. There is a towel he has—once he had to fish it out of his toilet—that he has washed and disinfected but never uses; although he keeps it hanging in his bathroom and will sometimes lean against it, hugging it, as it were—a foolish ritual and one that embarrasses him deeply.

His research continues to absorb him, and rumors circulate that he is being considered for a Nobel Prize. He is working obsessively on several theories. One of these is his theory of magnetic monopoles, whose elusive traces are a knotty issue, an *inelegance,* in the grand unified theories. No experimental evidence has yet surfaced to prove the existence of the magnetic monopole, though he has conclusively established, mathematically and theoretically, that its mass is about 10^{16} times as heavy as the proton.

Another theory whose ramifications he elaborates is that he invented Charade in order to explore, absolve, assuage his desertion of Rachel; in order to poultice the great gaping wound where his absent children are; in order to still the earthquakes and nightmares set off by the Zundel trial.

Experimental evidence certainly exists to suggest Charade is *hologram* rather than *substance,* though relativity theory shows that mass has nothing to do with substance, but is a form of energy. It has been amply demonstrated that when two particles collide with high energies (in an accelerator, say; or in Building 6; or in an apartment off Harvard Square), the two particles break into subatomic fragments, but those fragments are not smaller than the original particles.

The most revolutionary aspect of his "inflationary" theory of the origins of the universe, he reasons, is the notion that all the matter and energy in the observable universe may have emerged from almost nothing. He is tempted to go one step further and to theorize that the entire universe evolved from literally nothing.

Another theory is that it was not he who invented Charade, but that he is being slept, or dreamed, and that she invented him. There is a certain elegance to this theory. It contains her need to articulate her search for some perfect object of adoration, perhaps her father, perhaps not. It contains her need, in the light of the tragedy of her mother, Verity Ashkenazy, to ask incessant and unanswerable questions about the nature of pyschic damage, about the role of victim, about blame and responsibility.

Originally, also, this theory accommodated his niggling doubts about her father's name. Saint Nick? Old Nick? But on this score he took a scientific and quantitative approach. To satisfy his compulsive and pedantic itch, he paid a graduate student to comb through old volumes of *Index to Social Sciences and Humanities,* and to check various European indexes, especially French ones. The student came up with two items. Both were references to papers on the trickster figure in medieval French *fabliaux*, presented (though neither paper was ever published) by Nicholas Truman, for whom no institutional affiliation was given. One paper had been presented at a conference at Lyons in 1965; the other at a Learned Societies Conference at Queen's University in Kingston, Canada, in 1973.

He ponders Bohr and Heisenberg and the Copenhagen interpretation of interpretation: that what is observed is preselected—*imposed,* perhaps—by the observer. He considers Heisenberg's warnings on the imprecision of all perception, and is consequently wary about leaping to unwarranted conclusions based on the recent and slight evidence of the unpublished papers.

Nevertheless he has formulated a revised and tentative theory whose elegance appeals to him. His theory is that Charade does indeed exist and that he is in fact in love with her. (He is old enough to find the term *love* appropriate, or at least approximate, for the confusion of pleasure and emptiness and want that swamps him when he thinks of her.) This theory assumes a considerable degree of symmetry between their two life stories, but then that is hardly a matter of surprise to a physicist.

There is a somewhat alarming hypothetical correlative, which is that he could contact her and that she might (that is, if of course she still thinks of him with any sort of fondness, or indeed if she still thinks of him at all), that she might be persuaded to . . . ?

This hypothesis contains so many risks that he fears, like Dirac taking fright at his own mathematics on negative energy states, he may pull back from the edge of discovery.

He has days, however, of rash and preliminary courage.

In the basement of Building 6 one day, he waylaid his colleague from the Media Lab.

"You still doing anything with holograms?" he asked casually. And had to clamber over marathons of his colleague's moody predictions, his monologues, his obsessions; had to be dragged off to the Wiesner Building to watch laser displays, Jupiter simulations, and then . . . suddenly, there was Charade, insubstantial and absolutely real, twirling like a tree ornament through a corner of the Media Lab.

"How . . . ?" he asked, swallowing, his throat going dry. "How'd you do that?"

"From a photograph," his colleague said. "Elementary stuff. I've lost interest in it."

"Yes, I see. But the, ah, girl looks faintly familiar. She a student?"

"Hmm?" His colleague frowned. "Can't remember now. Used to hang around the dorms, *a dormie*. Can't remember who she was. Not your type, Koenig. You can be sure of that."

Koenig keeps a crumpled scrap of memo paper attached to his fridge door with a magnet. It is next to the crayon drawings done by his cleaning lady's son and daughter when they were little, a long time ago, actually he was someone else then, though it often seems yesterday. There are two telephone numbers on the scrap of paper and he knows, having verified this from the long-distance operator, that the area codes are for a rural town in Queensland, Australia.

One day he is going to place a call.

Actually, quite often, almost every night in fact, he lifts the receiver and begins to dial the numbers. But then he thinks of Heisenberg and the indeterminacy question, and wishes to keep the ending open.